Let Them Look West
Marty Phillips

LET THEM LOOK

by

MARTY PHILLIPS

JACKALOPE HILL

An imprint of Antelope Hill Publishing

Cover art by Owen Cyclops:
owencyclops.com

Edited by Taylor Young
Formatted by Margaret Bauer

The author can be contacted at:
MartyPhillips@protonmail.com

Antelope Hill Publishing
antelopehillpublishing.com

Paperback ISBN-13: 978-1-956887-32-7
Hardcover ISBN-13: 978-1-953730-78-7
EPUB ISBN-13: 978-1-953730-83-1

Author's Note

What you are about to read is a fantasy story in the technical sense. Realism is sacrificed at times in service of a dream. As is the case with nearly all real dreams, including the one that follows, fantasy as the absolute victory of one's desires is made impossible by the limitations of one's gullibility within the dream state. This story is not in the service of a happy dream, nor is it a nightmare. It is perhaps most accurate to call it a mundane fantasy. This book is dedicated to my family and the friends who have helped in proof-reading, editing, or simply offering encouragement in the process. It is especially written for my brother. You believed in me from the beginning, and for that I will always be grateful.

Marty Phillips

CONTENTS

PART I

Tabernacles in a Strange Land

The thought of flying out to the middle of nowhere filled Rob Coen with apprehension. The sickly sensation had consumed him for weeks. He was even more distressed by the fact that his own actions had created the entire situation. He could trace the domino path of cause and effect straight back to a few seemingly inconsequential actions. He could do this because he had sat at length more than a few times and traced the history.

The first domino had tilted in the lunchroom at *The Times* where he worked as a journalist near the bottom of the pecking order in the politics department. He had been writing mostly local and some minor national campaign reporting for a few years, but his was not a household name, even in the world of journalism. Rob was a step above the interns and rookie reporters, and that was just about the extent of his influence. He had learned over the years to find the delicate balance between the dangers of too much ambition and too little. Rob was reasonably comfortable inhabiting the reliable yet unremarkable middle ground.

On the day in question, the interns and younger writers milled about or sat over sandwiches wrapped in glittering, transparent plastic, Styrofoam and paper cups of cheap, acrid coffee, boxes and cartons of tepid and quasi-organic ostensible food hunted in corner markets, gathered from bustling bodegas, or maybe even cobbled together hastily in the cramped kitchenettes of their shared living spaces.

It was a typical scene. Carter Owens, the only of the editors who deigned to eat in the lunchroom, haunted his back corner at a small table by the sink and worked his way through the daily crossword, glancing up occasionally and surreptitiously through his anachronistically out of fashion wire rimmed glasses over his coffee mug after taking a sip. His presence was uncommon but not unusual, and the happenstance of it on that specific day formed the final wavering impact of the first domino into the second. In retrospect, his involvement and appearance seemed more foreboding and anomalous in the way only recollective imagination can revise visions of the past. His perfectly white hair and cropped beard now gave off an unnatural impression.

The writers began to discuss a recurring and mundane hypothetical about who would be their ideal interview subject. The answers were all predictable: rising star progressive politicians, technology visionaries, household name musicians. Rob found the question idiotic and the answers painfully but expectedly unimaginative. Normally in such a situation he would sit back and drink his coffee and eat his turkey sandwich as all the mind-numbing chatter formed a distant hum in the back of his head. On that morning for some reason he decided to give his own input once there was an auditory space wide enough to fit in a few words. It was not in character with his typical adherence to carefully maintained obscurity. Rob had tortured himself in the many nights since, lying awake and analyzing his motives for opening his mouth. He had come to the conclusion that there was no motive, that it was a paradoxical accident of probability and incomprehensible external forces.

"My dream interview would be with someone the media tends to view as hostile. Interviewing somebody with positive momentum in the journalistic world is boring." He did not realize how insulting the comment sounded until it was out in the open.

The room went quiet for a few seconds before one of the more assertive young politicos asked, "Ok, so then who *would* you interview?"

Rob let out the first name he could think of that fit his description, "Governor James Alexander." He knew that the phonetic sequence comprising the name was enough stimulus to elicit immediate disdain from his colleagues. A burst of scoffs and mild protestations sounded around the room.

"He's a crank," someone replied after the initial reaction died down.

"What's the point of that?" a younger fresh-faced intern asked. "Interviewing people like James Alexander just grants them legitimacy."

To everyone's surprise, Carter Owens spoke from his corner of the room. His voice was startling by its very presence and clear but quiet. Every head turned in silent curiosity. "James Alexander already has legitimacy. To say that is not an ethical judgment. It's basic reality." The intern blushed at the admonishment. Owens then turned to Rob. "Why don't you pitch the interview to Margaret?"

"I hadn't seriously considered it," Rob deflected. "It was just a hypothetical."

Owens did not say anything more. He only gave one last scrutinizing glance before returning to his crossword puzzle.

At the time, Rob thought little of the conversation in the lunchroom. A few days later Margaret Hunter, the politics editor, called him to her office. Since she was his superior, it was a common request and nothing to set off his alarm bells. He was entirely unprepared for what came a few seconds after he settled into a reddish-brown leather chair facing her expansive glass desk.

"Rob, I heard about your idea to interview Governor Alexander, and I think it's good. It's unexpected honestly, but good."

"Really?" he asked. It was all he could manage in the sudden confusion. He felt very warm and cold at the same time. He stared at her slightly creased, fifty-something features for a hint of a cruel joke in the words. Nothing. He plunged inward to his murky resting place beneath the surface of his externally sensory faculties to reconnoiter. Had Owens told her? Of course. He was the only possibility. But why? What boomerang of cosmic injustice existed beyond Rob's understanding? He surfaced to get some context from what Margaret was saying.

"He has been out of the public eye for a bit, and that fact could present an opportunity. If we want to reintroduce the world to James Alexander, then it must be appropriately dramatic. He is such a polarizing figure. I think an in-person interview could really blow the doors off."

"Wait, you want me to go to Wyoming?" he asked, trying to mask the incredulity.

She smiled encouragingly. It was not a feeling she could project effectively. "I know you have reservations, Rob, but this is a huge opportunity. Something about the notion really struck the editor-in-chief."

"The editor-in-chief?"

"He has an eye for these things. This is your big break. If I were you, I would just jump in with both feet."

"I understand," he murmured quietly. A "big break" was the

sort of thing he had been trying to avoid. He tried to smile but was unsure what actual expression resulted. Rob understood that he would not have a career for much longer if he tried to refuse the assignment.

He called the governor's office that same afternoon to make an initial inquiry. Between rings, he hoped into the void of silence on the other end of the line that an in-person interview was out of the question. "I see, yes, the governor is a busy man," he could see himself saying. The woman he spoke to on the other end was very friendly and extremely accommodating. By the end of the conversation, he had a three day visit in his calendar and a stone resting in the bottom of his belly.

Rob spent many hours of the days leading up to the trip in Margaret's office listening to her advice, taking notes, and nodding along with a serious look etched on his face. He became painfully aware that this was as much a risk for her as it was for him. She had arranged some company money for him to go.

The journalists more attuned to the universe's underlying cruel irony shot him little savagely sly looks and made ominous comments during the time before he left. The less attuned made jealous jabs about his all-expenses-paid trip and how it would practically be a vacation. "You'll be able to get out of the city," they said. "Man, what I would do for a few days of peace and quiet," they said.

He packed for a three day stay with a sensation of complete dread. On the ride he hailed to the airport, his legs felt numb. He floated through security and along the terminal like a disembodied phantom. As the plane taxied on the runway, his stomach lurched in exaggerated imitation of every sudden movement and mechanical clunk of the aircraft. The ascendant roar of the takeoff was lost to the white noise of his brooding mind. He stared longingly at the emergency exits and wondered if he aimed his jump perfectly, could he send himself directly into the engine's turbine and mist out in a vaporized and combusted cloud into the thin air behind them. He smirked at the thought.

The governor of Wyoming was not the kind of person he had imagined ever interviewing, despite his hypothetical assertion in the lunchroom. James Alexander won his election in a tumultuous time and had taken advantage of a wave of reactionary revivalism across America's Heartland and the Middle West. He had declared that he had "no interest in whoring the state out for a dollar." In one of his more well-known speeches he declared that "the term GDP stands for goddamned pointless." He had said that there was no use making people rich if their souls gave out in the meantime. He declared that man was meant for greatness and not to be enslaved by "trade and toil and money and oil." These would have been fine sentiments if he was not a religious nut.

Within the first year of his first term, he held a special vote on whether the state should build a next wonder of the world and dedicate it to the risen and resurrected Son of God. The vote passed. James Alexander decided to call the monument Mount Calvary.

The luminaries of national politics and culture reacted to the developments in Wyoming first with shock, then knowing nods and finally open derision. One commentator famously called the proposed monument, "a big pile of dirt to serve as a burial mound for the passing of a fanatical specter soon to be put to rest in this nation." A more sympathetic journalist wrote in reply:

> *There is an energy to Alexander's revolutionary politics, his plans for the monument and transformation of the state of Wyoming. Yet I cannot help but sense a desperation, as though some integral part of what was once America is slipping through his fingers and he seeks perhaps tragically to grasp at it before it is gone entirely. Everyone knows the identity of this passing ghost, but they cannot articulate it completely. They touch parts of that desperate thing it is but cannot fathom its entire being. Is it the civic traditions of a Christian people? Is it the dream of a waning European diaspora? Is it the flickering remnant of that dying thing a certain kind of American called "The West"? It is all of those things yet none fully, and everyone knows the extent of its meaning deep down.*

As a matter of consensus—the consensus of late-night television hosts, celebrities, finance commentators, and cultural critics—this passing was laughable and welcome, and they partook in the clownish lampooning of a funeral procession.

Mount Calvary remained in the national spotlight as it ran into a skeptical state legislature. During the stalling period, private donors in the state began their own funding drive to break ground. Before a year had passed, the construction fund enjoyed generous attention from all the old, forgotten and obsolete lost causes around the country. It became a point of pride for a certain kind of citizen to pinch pennies and put in what they could. Millions of dollars poured in from those who wanted to see the monument made if only to stand as a relic in defiance of the elite national, political, and commentary class. The mocking and gawking by the critics in the media likely made the project more viable than Alexander's own efforts. Eventually the massive influx of contributions and interest convinced most state legislators and they fell in line.

The monument had officially opened for visitors after two years of construction and enjoyed a massive pilgrimage of curious onlookers, true believers, and naysayers. It was a man-made mountain built atop an existing rise of earth. A spiral shaped pathway two miles long led up to the summit, and visitors traveled it up passing by murals of the Stations of the Cross along the way. A second shorter path led back down beside artistic tributes to the Resurrection and early Church.

Rob had read about all of this and the governor's life in the days leading up to his departure. The son of a Dakota oil worker, James Alexander had no interest in politics or religion for most of his early life. He worked in agriculture in his youth, as a mechanic, and eventually put himself through school to begin work in finance. He tried his luck at this for several years and made a comfortable living for himself in New York City. In his mid-thirties, Alexander had an awakening of some sort and left his career in the city for local politics in his home state: first as treasurer of a county and then mayor of a modest town of over ten thousand. That was when the transfigured James Alexander fully appeared. His gubernatorial run as an independent candidate against the sitting Republican was the surprise of the political season. He organized his political base in the churches, speaking as a guest in every congregation he could find, no matter how small. The pastors liked him because his antics brought people in the doors who would never attend a Sunday service otherwise.

Rob Coen figured it was a smart play. He could not fault the strategy from a tactical perspective. Hot potluck meals, some good speaking from a charismatic man, and an opportunity to feel for a little while like you were a part of something, had been the winning combination of local and state politics for about as long as it had existed.

The incumbent governor hit back, of course, framing Alexander as a radical and a hypocrite. National pieces condemning Alexander's cold-hearted and ruthless moves in the world of finance broke in the major papers of record. Nobody seemed to care. Alexander addressed the bad press in his stump speeches with the reply that "God can transform even the most ardent sinner into a loyal disciple. I will never deny the iniquity of my former life! When I belonged to the devil, I wanted to be his best soldier. The same holds true now, but now I'm working for the man on the white horse."

The people of the state, by and large, loved it. There was no ambiguity in James Alexander. Unlike the other politicians, he never hedged or adjusted depending on who was his audience. He famously went on a hostile evening talk show and took his licks from the host with a placid grin. The host asked him, "How are things going in the nineteenth century these days?" The audience broke into thunderous laughter. Alexander replied without missing a beat, "Well, we don't have television or stand-up comedians, so I'd say we'll probably make it just fine." He was the internet sensation the people loved to hate, but he had also discovered a weary undercurrent searching for a secret love.

Rob flipped down the tray table and opened his laptop. He minimized the research tabs on his browser and opened the document of potential interview questions. To say that he wanted to trap the governor into saying something controversial would be too explicit. Controversial statements would come from the man to be sure. Alexander was a bigot after all. He was, however, a clever bigot. Rob's goal was to guide the conversation toward a climax of some kind. He had not yet decided on what the crescendo of the overall movement would be. He found religious talk boring but was willing to suffer it to get at some deep-seated and yet unrevealed idiosyncrasy of Alexander's identity.

The governor was not married and had no children. There could be something in that. It seemed a contradiction that a religious fundamentalist of his kind had no family. Following such an avenue could be tricky. Rob did not want to come across as overly ruthless in his inquiry. Surgically extracting some hidden hypocrisy with too much zeal may backfire, although he doubted the readers of *The Times* would bat an eye. The two of them would probably spend most of the conversation talking past one another.

A feeling of emptiness surged into the journalist as he stared at the screen with slowly unfocusing pupils. What was the point of this? The plane would land and he would go to meet the man and they would speak different languages and the readers of *The Times* would taste the blood in the printed lines and smile knowingly to themselves, and nothing would change. Rob would return to writing his politics in the city pieces and Alexander would return to ruling his theocracy. The sun would rise and set, and everyone would move on unchanged.

With a deep sigh he rested his head back in the seat and closed his eyes. He focused on the slowly morphing darkness behind his eyelids and tried to clear his thoughts entirely. With luck, a good idea would come to him before he landed. He daydreamed into a sudden oblivion.

The next thing he knew, he was waking in the cold breeze of the air vent blasting down from above and the sharp voice of the flight attendant declaring that the plane was making the final approach to Jackson. Hours had been wasted. A feeling of indignation overcame him but slowly gave way to slightly apprehensive resignation. Rob stared down at the small city below nestled in a smooth spot beneath the towering Teton Mountains.

The plane landed without much jostling on the runway of the tiny airport, and after a moment of muted stillness, the passengers began filing out. Rob sat at his window seat, bleary-eyed and groggy from the unexpected sleep, and retrieved his carry-on bag from the overhead bin only after the plane was nearly empty. The stewardess smiled and thanked him as he stepped over the small gap from the plane to the boarding passageway into the terminal. The airport was quite small but inviting in a frontier sort of way. A rich, amber-colored timber comprising the support columns and ceiling of the interior gave an alien, rustic feeling right out of the gate. He had to finalize his rental vehicle and sleeping accommodations before anything else.

Rob followed the signs for the car rental desk, but as he passed through the arrival gate into the main portion of the airport, a voice stopped him.

"Mr. Coen? Is that you, Mr. Coen?"

Rob stopped in his tracks and turned slowly toward the voice, rather startled that anyone in this place would know who he was on sight.

A thin man in gray slacks and a sage-colored button-down

shirt approached him while holding out a slightly shaking outstretched hand. He looked to be in his late fifties with a tanned and creased, clean-shaven face and bristly, well-groomed dark hair with upwardly creeping gray areas at the sides.

"Yes." Rob confirmed a little hesitantly. This was an unexpected development.

"Mr. Coen, I'm Jordan Banks." He paused as Rob took his hand and shook it. Banks wore a distracted smile as he thought of what he was trying to say. "Well I guess you could say that I am your concierge service for your time here."

Rob let the hand go and furrowed his brow as politely as possible. "*The Times* is paying for my rental car and hotel, so I shouldn't be needing anything right now."

"Nonsense," Mr. Banks replied. "You are a visitor in this state and a friend of the governor, so we will show you hospitality."

A ripple of abrasive annoyance coursed through the journalist. This was a twofold affront: the politeness of the request combined with the insistence formed a grating assumption that he would accept the offered hospitality. "It is not a good policy to accept gifts and favors from an interview subject," Coen stated firmly. "It raises the question of bias or favoritism."

Mr. Banks laughed through his nose. "Mr. Alexander reads *The Times*. He's not worried about people thinking a ride and free board means he's suddenly your favorite politician. A thousand free rides and a thousand free beds wouldn't make up for half of the editorials." The older man's wry grin remained on his face as he turned and began to walk toward the exit. He waved for Rob to follow with one arm held high over the shoulder.

Rob was paralyzed. "Let me call my editor." He slipped his phone out of his laptop bag. Banks merely nodded in an understanding way and took a few steps back to wait patiently at a polite distance. The call went straight to voicemail. Margaret must be in some sort of editor's meeting. He kept the phone held up to his ear to give himself a moment of consideration. What would happen, exactly, if he went along with whatever Governor Alexander had planned? He wanted his own hotel room and car, but snubbing the man right away might carry its own set of complications. He lowered the phone.

"What exactly is the plan you're proposing?" he asked Banks.

Banks perked up and returned to conversational distance. "Governor Alexander is staying at Camp Hope currently. He thought it would make sense for you to stay in the lodge there for both your convenience."

"I told his assistant over the phone that I would have my own accommodations," Rob explained.

Banks smiled and reached one hand back over his head to rub the skin on the back of his neck in a bashful gesture. "When I told the governor a few days ago that this was the week you were coming, he was pretty insistent you get the full Wyoming treatment. He said that if you are going to write about him and the place, then it makes more sense to experience it as much as possible."

"And if I stick to my plan?" Rob asked.

"You're welcome to stay here in town if you like," Banks replied with a shrug. "Honestly, you'll get much better access at the camp. You'll have your own room and free run of the place."

Rob gave his phone one last glance in the hope that maybe his editor had sent him a text message in reply. Nothing. "Ok," he relented. "We will do this Alexander's way."

The older man smiled. "That's good to hear. You'll have your privacy and space to work. Camp Hope is not very busy this time of year." He turned and began to move toward the exits. "You don't have any luggage, do you?"

"Just my carry on." Rob concluded that this was an obvious power play by the governor, a clear attempt to put him in an unfamiliar situation, one where he was not in control. He would not let Alexander have the upper hand. After the fog of his unintended sleep began to wear off, he drew on a newfound resolve.

The air was cool outside, and the massive sky hung over everything in an immense pale blue canopy. Rob slowly turned a circle as they walked into the parking lot and stopped as he noticed the immense Teton Mountains jutting up to the west over the top of the terminal building. The scale of them was jarring to his urban sensibilities. They seemed to sit back broodingly over the open plain below and stare down with unassailable condescension. Banks had reached the vehicle, an old, cream-colored Lincoln Town Car in pristine condition. He opened the trunk, and Rob dropped his carry-on bag into the yawning mouth.

"Feel free to sit in the back or the front. I don't mind," Banks commented after closing the lid and crossing over to the driver's side door. Once the car was unlocked, Rob slid onto the tan leather of the front passenger seat.

"Coffee? Food? Anywhere you want me stop on the way?" the older man asked helpfully.

"How far is it to the camp?" Rob asked.

"About a half an hour's drive."

As part of his famed Wyoming Plan, Governor Alexander had constructed camps all over the state in the past few years. They were complexes of lodges and cabins with barracks to house state workers and depots to store the equipment for projects they undertook. Rob had read a bit on them in preparation for the trip. State residents could stay in them at no cost for an allotted number of days in the year, and they attracted paying tourists from all over, especially those who had come to see Mount Calvary or partake in the guided hunting, fishing, or hiking available in the surrounding areas. Alexander had often referred to it as "Frontier Mobilization." About a year prior, an old-school nature reporter had profiled them over the course of a few months and wrote a long-form narrative entitled: "Tabernacles in a Strange Land." It missed the Pulitzer by one half of a split hair.

"You never said if you wanted coffee or anything," Banks reminded him.

"Coffee is fine," Rob stated, making some notes in his notebook about the looming foreboding of the mountains, the buildings they drove by, and the general appearance of the city and inhabitants. Banks insisted on driving through the downtown area. It was a mix of Western frontier architecture and a modern stereotyped approximation with timber overhangs and facades on the storefronts. Unsurprisingly it had the feel of a resort town: small and wealthy and primarily designed with tourism in mind.

After stopping at a drive-thru coffee shop, they began the journey in earnest. Banks drove slowly and cautiously with deliberate, exaggerated movements, as though he was, with every motion, trying to prove that he was the most reliable person for the job.

Rob clicked his pen for a minute and watched the scenery some more before delving into the task at hand. "Jordan or Mr. Banks? Which is it?"

"Jordan is fine," he clarified, smiling serenely at the road.

"You mind going on the record for me, Jordan? While we drive? I'd like to get some background for my article. You lived here long?"

The older man's head bobbed up and down while his eyes remained locked straight ahead. "I have lived here all my life for the most part, moved a state over for work once or twice, but that's it."

"How long have you known the governor?" Rob wanted to keep the questions coming quickly. He found that this method elicited the most honest answers. Conversation let people get too comfortable, which led them to hedge and embellish. Sometimes if they got too comfortable then they would let something slip which they hadn't intended, but Rob did not have the time for that method. Maybe he would with the governor, but that would take more than a half hour window of conversation.

"I've known the governor since before he was elected but not long before. I worked for him on his first campaign." Jordan replied.

"Were you his driver then too?" Rob asked.

Jordan chuckled hoarsely. "Yes, as a matter of fact I was, among other things: scheduling with churches and other groups who wanted to host a campaign event, organizing his schedule, fielding calls. I did this and that. He has a secretary now, so he doesn't need me for much, apart from driving when he doesn't feel like it."

"So, you still work for him?"

The older man's brow furrowed as he stared at the road. "People don't really work for Mr. Alexander. It's more like we work with him toward and for something else."

Rob could barely keep from making a noise to indicate his disturbance at the cliché. He had found himself a true believer. "And what is that thing you're all working toward? God?"

The corners of Banks' eyes creased with countless, tiny fissures, and his lips pulled back over his teeth in a self-conscious and childish smile, as though he were fourteen years old and caught playing with the old toys from the attic which he was too old for now. "We would like to believe that's the case, as anyone would. Maybe it is the case. We must believe that. The governor certainly does, and that's good enough for most people. It's the process that matters the most. He always says that 'there is victory in the striving.' One cannot make the kingdom of God on earth. I think once he used a mathematical term, said that Wyoming ought to be an asymptote infinitely approaching God. Not particularly sure what it means, but I liked the sound of it."

"Would you say that things have improved in the state under Governor Alexander? Tangibly, that is." Rob knew the answer before he had even asked the question. He had seen the popularity polls.

Banks nodded slowly. "Yes, it's a completely different place. There is a new energy. Lots of people would call us flyover country—" he faltered for a moment, perhaps realizing that his passenger was exactly the sort of person who would say such a thing. "But it certainly doesn't feel that way. We are a destination of a sort now. You should see the flocks of people who come to Mount Calvary. People come from Europe, China, Mexico, South America, all over. It has brought new life. It's not all good, obviously. Not everyone likes the way the governor does business or has his same vision for how things should be."

Rob figured Banks was talking about the state university, although it was ancient history at this point. Back when the governor first came into office, there was a major outcry from much of the administration and some of the student body that his backward ways would be damaging to their ability to educate and would reduce the number of out-of-state applicants. The president of the university had made a public statement presenting a document signed by dozens of administration and faculty members. They had argued that the governor's regressive policies did not offer a healthy climate for higher education, that universities were the avant-garde of society, and that any laws the legislature passed under his auspices would cause damage to their recruiting abilities or their chance to be competitive. The governor responded by scolding, "I have seen the subsidies that this state gives to the college, and I would say the word 'competitive' hasn't been in your otherwise expansive vocabulary for a long time."

Protests followed, and then the rest of the nation took notice. Reporters and out-of-state demonstrators flocked to the college. The most vocal professors and faculty became social media celebrities overnight. People changed the pictures of their online profiles in solidarity. A firestorm raged for days. The university administration canceled classes as things became unmanageable. The governor held a press conference in which he simply and solemnly stated that he would give the president of the college two days to return things to normal and resume classes or he would request the state legislature hold an emergency session to pull all funding from the school. "They want me to call in the state police for all this commotion. I'm not going to do it. They want a show. They won't get a show. You either do your jobs or I will pull your funding and you will die on the vine."

The president of the college would not have it. He got the mayor on his side. The mayor was already skittish about the troubles at the school endangering the economy and safety of his city. He had not been a supporter of the governor during the campaign, and this gave him another opportunity to voice his displeasure with the, as he called it, "strong-arming tactics of a tyrant."

Two days passed and business had not resumed at the college. The state legislature agreed to meet for the emergency session at the beginning of the next month. The day after the deadline, classes resumed. Administrators realized that the governor was showing no sign of backing down. Two days after the deadline, Governor Alexander arrived at the college to meet with the president. Alexander informed him that the board of supervisors, two of whom he had appointed himself, had met and decided to dismiss him. Then Alexander met with the mayor. By the end of the week, nobody in the national press was talking about the school. The board of supervisors chose a new president who proceeded to clean house, firing any administrators who showed any allegiance to the former leadership. It was at that point that everyone knew how the governor intended to run the state.

"I think he had the idea of the monument planned long before he became governor," Jordan Banks offered, interrupting Coen's brief period of musing. "I think he even mentioned the idea to me during the campaign. He used to talk about how people used to build monuments all the time, and that it used to be a mark of pride for a people, a cause for inspiration."

"Well, he's still the governor, so that wasn't his end goal," Rob mused aloud.

"His goal is to make the people an army of God," Banks commented seriously. He swallowed with finality afterward.

"Has he said this himself?" Rob asked, his pen hovering over the notepad.

"No, not at all." A sudden nervousness and self-awareness came over the older man. "If you write that down, then make sure to clarify that I said it." The driver's neck had flushed red.

"Well is it true?" Rob asked, purposefully leaving the request unanswered.

Banks cleared his throat. "Symbolically, maybe, and I'm just talking about my own opinion." At this point one hand had come off the steering wheel and closed in on itself with the thumb and forefinger outstretched and touching at the very end. The point where the two nails met tapped deliberately on the steering wheel like a bird adamantly pecking to accentuate each new qualification absolving the governor from any of this opinion. "It's just what I've observed. His style is quite military: the camps, the reorganization of the state workforce into corps, his emphasis on discipline. That's all I mean."

"And that has helped the state?" Rob asked.

"It has. We had three of the top ten fastest growing communities in the nation last year. Lots of people are moving here. I figure that must mean he's doing something right."

"What about the increase in hate crimes against LGBT individuals?" Coen asked, making use of some of his earlier research. "What is the governor doing about that?"

Banks' brow furrowed again. "I don't speak for the governor. Besides, I'm not entirely sure what statistics you're talking about."

It seemed that he had hit on a sensitive subject, and Rob made note of it. "There were a few articles about it earlier in the year. I'll just ask the governor about it when I meet him."

"I'm sure he'll know more about it than me," Banks replied.

They drove south toward a town called Hoback on US Highway 191. Rob could see signs for Camp Hope as they neared. The Snake River ran along to their left most of the way. Just after they crossed over a bridge, so that it ran on their right, Banks turned the wheel and the Town Car peeled off the highway onto an asphalt drive. The narrow road curved smoothly away toward the foot of the mountains. They passed under an imposing wooden archway with the name of the camp painted in bright white letters. The large piece of timber constituted a relief, carved with the state's landmarks, signs, and symbols. The wooden forms were large enough that he could make some out from the passenger seat. Smooth plains and trees surrounded the landmarks with mountains watching over them all from the back. Rob saw Devil's Tower, Old Faithful, and a large looming hill with three crosses at the summit, which he could only assume was Mount Calvary. It had already been amalgamated into the identity of the state, along with the other notable locales. The narrow asphalt road meandered on a slight upward grade into the shade of massive trees.

"What sorts of trees are these?" Coen asked his driver, breaking the silence that had descended over the last few minutes of the drive.

Banks, by his bodily movements and facial response to the question, appeared all too eager to embark on a topic that would not result in his replies being printed in a news article. "Mostly pine with some Douglas fir and spruce."

Soon, buildings came into view between the trunks of the trees. They hid in clusters, camouflaged somewhat due to their naked timber walls. The car rolled past groups of small cabins and stables, sheds and barns with tin roofs, piles of gravel and bark dust, and cords of firewood. Everything they passed had the oddly contradictory combination of rustic construction and minimalistic frontier architecture alongside the brand new: shiny State Corps pickup trucks and Jeeps, rows of tractors and heavy equipment. On a rise above it all, nestled against the steep craggy edge of a bluff, stood a large lodge building surrounded by a huge wrap-around porch around the base and a matching balcony above. The massive logs which made up the exterior walls glistened slightly with the rich, reddish golden-brown of finished wood, and the railings and frames were made of black wrought iron. A steeply peaked, gray, metal roof, likely made in such a way to easily shed the snow, gave the building an appearance harmonious with the sharp, triangular forms of the trees and distant mountains.

Rob turned from the scenery outside the car to glance at his chauffeur. "So, this is a base of operations for state workers? Does the governor live here?"

Banks cleared his throat. "Yes and no. The camps operate as living quarters, storage, and motor pools for the State Corps. They rotate from place to place as needed for new restoration and renovation projects. The governor does the same. He doesn't live here all year. Usually in the late summer and fall, when tourism starts to die down in Jackson, he stays here for a while. Typically, he resides at Camp Resolute, which is much closer to Mount Calvary. I think he likes to be close enough to see it, but that could just be my own attribution. It is, after all, his pet project."

"But he is here now?" Rob asked.

Banks nodded. "You can speak to him in the morning I'm sure.

He will be in meetings all evening though. Until then you will have time to get settled and get to know the place a little. Governor Alexander has someone tasked with showing you around and answering any questions you may have about Camp Hope, so you shouldn't want for diversion or information today."

Banks pulled the car into a parking space in a side lot to the right of the immense lodge building. He engaged the parking brake and exited the vehicle with some stiffness and a grunt. Rob clambered out also, stretching his limbs after all the sitting he had been doing that morning. He met Banks by the trunk to retrieve his carry-on.

A light dusting of brown pine needles blanketed the asphalt of the small lot where they had stopped. Banks gestured toward the large porch which wrapped around the bottom of the structure. "Unless you prefer bunking in one of the barracks with the corpsmen, the governor would be happy for you to stay in the lodge where the rooms are a bit more accommodating. They are usually reserved for state officials, representatives visiting on business, paying visitors and such. As a guest of Mr. Alexander you are entitled to all the privileges that come with that status. You should be quite comfortable."

You should be comfortable. Rob was beginning to tire of these presumptions. He should find none of this surprising, however, after accepting the invitation to stay at Camp Hope at the governor's behest. While following Banks to the front door of the lodge, he was reminded of the potential gravity of his decision to comply. Why had he so easily allowed this man to persuade him to come along? He could be relaxing in his own hotel room in Jackson at this very moment instead of walking into unknown circumstances at the governor's mercy. This could be a form of manipulation to put him on his back foot. What would his editor say? His neck burned at the thought, and his carry-on bag increased in weight and pulled more heavily on his arm and shoulder. He nearly stumbled on the planks of the steps up to the porch, and he was acutely aware of every movement and potential misstep.

Banks gave him a curious glance over his shoulder upon hearing the clattering noise. "Watch your step, Mr. Coen," he commented almost playfully.

Rob had noted that as they entered Camp Hope, Jordan Banks' mood became lighter and brighter. They passed through heavy wooden doors into a massive entryway. The vaulted ceiling was probably thirty feet above them, and a giant chandelier made of antlers hung down from it. The walls and ceiling were made up of bronze-colored wooden paneling. The floor was smooth slate stone covered in some kind of semi-glossy protective enamel. Directly ahead on the far side of the room two stairways made of timber rested on either side of a second large doorway. They both led up to a balcony which ran around the upper reaches of the entry room, and he could see two doors into other areas of the second floor on the far wall above. The interior of the lodge had a musty, earthy smell, and the air was slightly too cold to be considered cozy.

"Let's get you a room upstairs," Banks uttered the words while crossing the room to a large, wooden, writing desk in the far left corner of the room. He passed to the other side and rifled in the drawers for a moment before extracting a sizeable book from inside. Banks retrieved a compact case from the pocket of his slacks and opened it over the desk. He gingerly removed a small set of reading glasses and put them on before flopping the leather-bound book open and leafing through the pages.

"Do you want things quiet or bright?" he asked, glancing up with an index finger pushed against the page so that the lowest segment of the digit jutted outward from the rest due to the pressure. His eyebrows were raised and knotted in the middle slightly and eyes squinted, no doubt holding the same strained formation used when he struggled through the spectacles to make out the small letters on the paper.

"What do you mean?" Rob asked a little apprehensively.

"We have two rooms open right now. One is closer to the back of the lodge, so it is quieter, but you won't get as much light through the window, since it's closer to the mountain. The other one's closer to the front. There's more light in the morning, but the crew get up early and there will be a lot of hustle and bustle and equipment noise."

"I'll take the front. I can sleep through anything," Rob commented.

Banks made some notes in the ledger before returning it to the desk and then placed the glasses in the case and returned the case to his pocket. "Well, let's get you situated." He crossed the room to the farther stairway, which was on the right. Coen followed him, his footfalls joining in the chorus of rhythmic thudding impacts on the timber. The noise was so cutting in the calm of the entry room that it seemed as though the two of them deliberately struck the wood with some other purpose. Rob felt suddenly paranoid about the sound and in the next instant wondered why he had. He was lost drifting in the void outside the self of seconds before, wondering if he had split off into another version of reality. Banks glanced around the open expanse of the room as they ascended. Such useless coilings of thought strangulation were no doubt far from burdening his mind. Rob felt a faltering ambush of envy at the simplicity of his companion and then let it fall away.

They turned left at the top of the stairs and entered a door which was situated midway between the two flights and stepped into a long, carpeted corridor running crossways fifty or so feet to either side. Rob followed his guide to the right, and they reached a ninety degree turn to the left where the hallway ran approximately another hundred feet. Doors lined either side of the corridor at roughly the same interval as the rooms in a hotel.

Banks stopped at the second one on the right side and pushed the door open. "This is you right here," he explained. "I'll let you get settled and—oh shoot!" He patted his hip and breast pockets with open palms. "I forgot to get the key to your room. Ask me later and I'll get it for you. My office is the door at the end of the hall. I'll probably be there most of the evening. Once you have everything in order head down to the front again. Justine will give you a tour of the place."

"The governor is here though, right?" Rob asked as Banks turned to head down the hallway to his office.

"Yes," Banks answered, smiling with a touch of bewilderment. "You'll see him in the morning. He's very busy right now, but he made a point to carve some time out for you. He really is very pleased that you've come out. He likes to talk to people who are interested in his work." He was trying to reassure his guest and had clearly noted that Rob had asked a similar question earlier.

Banks left him standing in the doorway of the empty room. Finally he was alone. Rob entered his quarters and closed the door behind him. The space was modest, not as cramped as he had expected, although rather sparse in amenities. To his left against the middle of the wall rested a double-sized bed with a roughly carved, wooden headboard and frame. A rather homey looking quilt lay draped over the spread. A nightstand of the same simple, wooden construction sat next to the head with a lamp, alarm clock, and book of some kind resting on top. Pale light beamed in from a wide window directly across from him, and heavy, green curtains hung so that they covered the outer edges. There was no television facing the foot of the bed like in most hotels, merely a cabinet with a box of tissues on one edge and a mirror on the wall above. A table and two chairs sat beneath the window, and beside them, along the wall from the cabinet, he spied a door into what was presumably the bathroom. The floor was hardwood-like but a number of thick rugs covered most of the surface. They bore simple geometric patterns of earthy hues. Rob stepped over to the bed where he set his carry-on and laptop bags and then continued to the window where he pulled the curtains back the rest of the way to see what was below his room.

All he observed outside were trees and the parking lot where Banks had left the town car. Two men in work clothes passed by after a moment, and a slight breeze stirred the pine needles sprinkled on the surface of the asphalt in small swirling eddies. Aside from those few bits of movement and the blankness of the gray sky, he saw nothing of interest and decided to go meet this person who would be giving him a tour. He turned the lock before he left and hoped that Banks would indeed be available to give him his key before too long.

Rob traced the path back around the corner and out the door into the entry room where he noticed now what he could not have seen before: a set of metal letters above the doors they had entered a few minutes earlier. They were constructed of black cast-iron, reading: *"Nunc Semper Liberi Sumus."* He could recognize it as Latin but had no inkling of what it said. He stood gazing at them with an unfocused stare, feeling a bit bewildered. A slight motion below drew his attention. A young woman was standing beneath the balcony and peering up at him with a curious expression. She had been so quiet and still that he had entirely missed her until that moment.

Once it was clear that he had seen her, she asked, "Rob Coen, I take it?" He nodded, and she motioned for him to come down while resuming her introduction, "I'm Justine. I'm going to show you around the place."

To say that Justine was not the sort of person Rob had expected to give him a tour of the camp would not be accurate, since he had possessed no definite expectations. If, however, expectations had existed, then he was quite sure she would not have been part of them.

The first reason he was certain of this was because she was young and good looking, two qualities he had seen no evidence of existing in Alexander's Wyoming thus far. Additionally, at least where he came from, this place was most often associated with backward, stiff, and patriarchal fundamentalism. It did not follow that youthful, attractive young people were not capable of existing in such a place, but they were certainly not the first types that came to mind.

Justine was conventionally attractive, with pale skin, large, dark eyes, and straight brown hair which reached a few inches below her shoulders. She had a smooth, broad, and somewhat pronounced forehead. It was almost moon-like and gave her face proportions which narrowed sharply from the top down to her small chin. This gave her a more childish appearance than was warranted by her age, which he would put somewhere between nineteen and twenty-one.

"Yes, Rob Coen, thank you," he replied while beginning to descend the stairs. As he drew nearer, he could make out that she wore simple, practical work clothes: denim pants that were slightly more form fitting than one would expect, scuffed, brown work boots, and a light-brown canvas work jacket over a checkered red flannel shirt. There was something oddly familiar about her features that he could not quite place, and, as he drew near enough to reach out and shake her small and very warm hand, the feeling of recognition did not depart, so that he was nearly certain he had seen her before.

As she turned to lead him toward the door, Rob pulled his notepad from the inner pocket of his jacket so that she could see it. "You don't mind if I write things down as we talk, do you? That this is all on the record?"

Justine shrugged carelessly, as though the notepad were a stick or a rock. "Sounds good to me. Which room did they give you?" She turned and led him toward the door.

"Uh. Not sure the number. Right hallway and second door on the right."

"That side is better," she commented. "Banks' office is in that hallway. If you need anything, he's usually in there watching old DVDs from the first campaign."

They had passed through the door and onto the wraparound porch at this point. Rob was struck by one specific detail of her comment. "Old DVDs from the campaign?"

Justine glanced back over her shoulder while stepping down onto the walk leading away from the lodge. "Recordings from the campaign events, rallies, church meetings, and all that sort of thing. Banks filmed almost everything on the campaign when Governor Alexander was running for his first term, and now he goes back and watches them all the time. I'm sure he wouldn't mind if you wanted to take a look at it. It's just a bunch of old stump speeches and that kind of thing."

Assuming that her description was accurate he was intensely interested. An undiscovered cache of videos from the primordial and volatile early days of Governor Alexander's political career could be worth any discomfort he had to endure on this misadventure. Better yet, it could provide evidence to Margaret that deviating from the plan to stay in Jackson had paid off. An odd thought struck him. Of course, this young woman must know that the old recordings would interest him journalistically, so why mention them? Was she trying to help him? A worming sensation of suspicion invaded his brief moment of enthusiasm. He could not account for it, aside from attributing it to his journalistic tendency toward paranoia. He would have to ignore such feelings if he wanted to squeeze every opportunity from this venture. If Rob was going to be trapped at this camp and at the mercy of the governor's people, then he would make the most of it, play along, and be a good sport. People loved that experiential, narrative, long-form journalistic style of the writer living alongside the subject. He began to convince himself that not going to his own hotel had been a calculated move, that he may have suspected deep down the journalistic opportunities he could discover by staying here. After all, if he believed it, then his editors might also.

Justine was leading him along a gravel path which crossed over the asphalt drive he and Banks had traveled on the way up. He sped up so that he walked side by side with her and got back to work. "So you work here at Camp Hope? Do you work directly for the governor?"

"I work here when I'm not in school, since my parents live in Jackson."

"College?"

"Yeah, college."

"What are you studying?"

"I'm probably going to go into state work. I started early. I was in the youth volunteer corps in high school, the Hospitaller division."

Something shifted in the dark inner region of Rob's mind, like the languid and unconscious flopping of a sleeping man's arm as he rolls over in slumber. He experienced symptoms of realization without the full manifestation. "Hospitaller? The name is familiar, but you'll have to jog my memory." Rob always erred on the side of ignorance. The desire to avoid looking uninformed was the enemy of complete interrogation.

"For the most part, addiction treatment and rehabilitation," she said simply.

Then Rob remembered. The governor had run partly on a

strong anti-drug platform. He had described the existence of addiction, particularly opioid, as a scourge upon the people of the nation. Unlike some, who framed the issue in warlike language, he had described it as a disease, and with any disease, sometimes extreme measures were required to heal the body. He went so far as to say that if someone was an addict living on the streets, then they would be scooped up and made clean and sober whether they wanted it or not.

Now that one had exploded across the headlines. National pundits opined that Alexander would pass sweeping and mandatory drug testing, that he would shred Fourth Amendment rights, that there would be roving squads of jackbooted stormtroopers rounding up anyone even under suspicion of being a drug user. Like any of the media firestorms, Alexander fed off it. He shouted from the stump that the commentariat in Washington wanted people drugged into a helpless stupor. He argued that they wanted people to have just enough freedom to choose an indolent life of numbed feelings, stunted sensations, and blind consumption.

After he won, and Alexander announced a partnership with the state legislature to form the Hospitallers and led a successful push to increase state mandatory minimums for possession and distribution for all opioid and amphetamine substances, the chorus decrying him a tyrant rose again. He had proven the pundits right.

There was, however, one difference in his plan from the prophecies of the intellectuals. Steep prison sentences could be avoided completely. A junkie in possession of a large amount of illegal drugs could go without spending a day behind bars on the condition that he submitted himself to the care of the Hospitallers. The program was described as part rehab and part boot camp. There had been some journalism on the topic, but not enough to give Rob an impression on the inner workings or effectiveness of the program.

This would likely be one of few opportunities to learn more, so he decided to pester Justine about it for a while. "I've only heard cursory information about the Hospitallers. I'd like to know more if you don't mind explaining."

She shrugged. "I was young and just a volunteer, so I didn't do too much that was involved with the more sensitive operations of the corps. I mostly helped with supply inventories and grunt work.

The largest focus when I was there was relocating the homeless. By that point a lot of the problems with drugs were under control."

"Is it true that they took people by force?" Rob asked, noting that she gave him a quick sidelong glance when he asked the question. "I only heard things secondhand," he qualified.

She slipped her hands into the pockets of her canvas work jacket and took a short breath before responding. "Taken by force." She repeated and let the words hang momentarily. "That's how somebody with the heart of a big city would say it. The primary goal was always relocating the homeless and assisting the police with drug rehabilitation for criminals. Virtually everyone picks the Hospitallers over prison."

"Some choice," Rob commented under his breath, but she heard him.

"If you really want to make the argument that living fix to fix as a junkie and begging or stealing your way to the next high is a way of living that is worth being able to choose, then you won't find much agreement around here. Someone who is choosing misery needs help to learn better choosing. Making some argument that getting people out of that cycle, whether they want it or not at the time, is somehow stepping on their freedom doesn't do a whole lot to make people better off. Ask any of them after they're clean if they wish their freedom to choose misery had been preserved. You won't get many people expressing regret."

Rob wrote it all down word for word. If he had thought Banks was a true believer, then this girl was the high priestess of Governor Alexander and God's kingdom of the state of Wyoming. Of course they would set him up with a real zealot. Whether carefully orchestrated or not, the readers of *The Times* were going to eat this up. It was like touring North Korea with the great leader's chief propaganda officer. Even as he thought it, Rob could not help feeling a twinge of guilt at his own cynicism. She was earnest, and he must be careful not to let his prejudices color his work too much.

They had reached a cluster of large buildings which were unlike the cabins and lodge in that they had aluminum siding and a clearly utilitarian appearance. Justine stopped by a door on the side of the nearest one and turned to face him. Her expression was serene and not marked with any evidence that he had bothered her with his comment or that her forceful reply had changed her mood from its prior placidity.

"This is the stable," she explained. "Do you like horses?"

"I'm not familiar with them," Rob responded, a little uncomfortable with where this was going. He was not overly fond of animals. He found their unpredictable behavior and habits infuriating. "I'm sure I'll like them," he added, so as not to sound like he dreaded the prospect of interacting with them.

She opened the door and they passed through a narrow walkway between two walls of wooden slats until they entered a large aisle running down the center of the building. The dirt floor was coated in powdery dust, and Rob could smell the rough tinge of straw. His nose began to itch. The hay fever would be running wild now.

His ears picked up the muffled, syncopated beat of the absent-minded stamping of the animals all around them. They were hidden from sight but not hearing. Justine arrived at one door and slid it open slowly with a whirring sound so that they stood face to face with a large, brown horse, which, upon seeing them, pulled its nose back toward its chest in an odd mixture of what appeared to be fierce determination and a balking sort of nervousness. It then punctuated the movement by flicking its black tail.

"This is my horse," Justine explained. "His name is Babieca." She began running the palms of her pale hands down from the forehead to the nose of the animal repeatedly to soothe him.

"What are the horses used for?" Rob asked, standing awkwardly a few feet back, holding back a sneeze and willing the tickling sensation to leave his nose with every shred of his mental capacity.

She continued stroking the horse's nose while replying. "It's much easier to get around on many of the mountain trails here on horseback. Some of the foresters and rangers use them for transportation and as pack animals. The cattlemen use them all the time as well. I mostly just ride Babieca for fun, though. I guess it's just one of the perks I get around here." She rubbed her hands along the horse's neck on either side and added in a babying tone, "compared to the others he is *very* spoiled."

Something seemed odd about her comment regarding getting perks, as though she had some special status here that he should know. The mounting pressure in Rob's sinuses added to the annoyance caused by the seemingly innocuous statement. He felt as though there was some big secret that was being kept from him.

Justine turned and smiled. "You can pet his nose. He's very friendly."

Rob raised his hand and felt the animal shift slightly as his skin made contact with the short, coarse hair along the bridge of the nose. He was overcome by a sudden wave of discomfort with the realization of where he was. He, a man in his early thirties, alone with a girl of maybe twenty years. As he gave Justine a surreptitious sidelong glance the discomfort became more pronounced as he was reminded of how attractive she was in that way which was hard to explain. The paleness of her smooth, wide forehead and the darkness of her hair made a stark contrast that seemed almost unreal in sharpness. He had noticed that when she was not making an effort to smile, her mouth rested in a severe expression. She seemed aged beyond her years: jaded yet idealistic at the same time. It was a bizarre combination of disparate forces: alluring, cold, naive, perceptive, confident, aloof, convicted. She stopped patting Babieca's neck and left him alone in the stall with the horse. Rob rested his hand on the nose and stared with an unfocused gaze into the glassy and nearly black eye. The thick lid drooped at intervals as the creature dozed in the calm following the initial stimulus of their entry into the quiet stall.

"Why did they put me with her for the afternoon?" he asked in a whisper, as though the animal could understand or held some hidden knowledge in the area under the sunken spots beside its ears. Was it to make him uncomfortable, or to disarm him? How carefully had these circumstances been crafted to control what he would write about the governor and his kingdom?

Justine returned to the stall. "Put your hand out like this," she instructed and held out a small hand with fingers spread so they were bent slightly back. He mimicked the motion with his own hand. "Closer to his mouth," she said. He moved his hand closer to the horse's nose. She then set a small, slightly withered carrot onto his palm. Babieca stirred, smelled the carrot with deliberate blasts of breath, and moved his muzzle over to the object of interest. Large rubbery lips began closing on the carrot and pulling at it bit by bit. The hot, moist air of the animal's breath poured warmly onto Rob's skin as the lips worked and searched for purchase while sending jolts of terror down his spine at the prospect of the horse unintentionally biting him. With a sharp crunch and then a muffled, wet, grinding noise the morsel was gone.

"Have you ever been this close to a horse before?" Justine asked.

"No," he admitted honestly. "I grew up in the city."

"Most people are scared or at least nervous. You could be a natural. I can show you how to ride one of the older mares if you want."

Rob let out a short, dry laugh. "That is not going to happen, but I appreciate the offer."

"Well, then I can show you the workshops if you like," she offered.

"That sounds good."

She gave the horse one final pat on the neck and moved around Rob to the stall door. He turned and followed.

After leaving the stable they walked further down from the lodge toward a large collection of long barn-like buildings. They went by large heaps of gravel, bark dust, and rock which he had seen previously from the passenger seat of Banks' car.

"Is this all for public works projects?" he asked.

"Some, yes. Renewal and restoration isn't exclusively for parks and public roads. The engineering corps builds housing for the homeless and even does renovations on homes owned by the poor or those damaged by natural disasters."

"How is that sustained? How does the corps support so many government workers?" Rob wondered aloud. "How does the state afford so much labor?"

"The state corps are not lucrative careers," Justine explained. "They were never meant to be. Everyone who joins is aware that they are going into civil service. You're guaranteed room and board, hot meals, and a small stipend, and that's it."

"It doesn't seem like it would be easy to motivate people to take a deal like that," he commented skeptically.

"The motivations aren't the same here as places where everyone does things just for money. Sure, there's some of that. You have to pay the bills, but the state has been energized by the governor. People think about it like a project, something they are part of and want to work for. Many people came here from all over just to be a part of it."

She was talking about the influxes of people who had immigrated to Wyoming after the governor began enacting his new policies. He had made it clear that he wanted anyone who was interested to flock there. It was basically a nationwide recruiting drive. He guaranteed a place to live to anyone who wanted to move. It was a plan based on the Amish barn raising. If anyone wanted to move to the state but could not afford it, the state corps of engineers would build them a simple cabin residence on state land. The presumption was that new residents would be invested in the community from the start.

"So this is all because of the governor?" he asked. "You think he is the only one who could have done it?"

"He woke a lot of people up from living just to live. A lot of people around the country don't have much to live for except buying stuff and going to work—if they even have a job. I think there is a strong desire to be part of something tangible."

"You don't think American nationalism is good enough?" he asked, half sarcastically.

"It's not present enough." Justine replied. "Where is it? At football games? Public service announcements? It's like a god that doesn't even know you or even care to. It's basically a joke." She paused, becoming a little self-conscious. "What I mean is that what it means to be an American has changed so much that it's basically meaningless."

"Well, it means being free: liberal democracy and all that," he offered.

"Free to do what? Earlier you tried to tell me that freedom to be a junkie is a good thing. Freedom isn't anything. It's an absence of purpose. Some people can live productive, decent, moral lives in that framework but not many."

Rob shrugged. "Yes, but why does that matter? One of the points of liberal democracy is that a person can be as involved or uninvolved as they like. Apathy about some collective existence is the right of any citizen."

"And how is that working out?" she asked defiantly. "How does the quality of life seem to be in the drug addicted, fragmented, selfish, atomized, modern America?"

"People are fine. The advent of social media and demographic shifts, automation, they all create structural discomfort in the short run. Societies eventually settle into a new paradigm."

Justine smirked. It wasn't malicious but there was something in the expression which cut at him. "For caring so much about the individual and their freedom to make choices, you sure switched to clinical and collective language pretty fast when it came to the downside. Besides, if it's all so good in the rest of the country, then why did so many people want to come here? The governor never offered wealth or promised success, just a place to belong and a common purpose. You don't become the fastest growing state three years in a row because you offer something nobody wants or needs."

"You don't become the whitest state offering something everybody wants or needs," Rob murmured, a little more resentfully than he had intended.

Justine smiled: "Only someone with the heart of a big city," and she left it at that.

Their walking had slowed during the verbal skirmish and Rob had fallen a few steps behind while making some notes in his notebook. He decided to lay off the incendiary insinuations. "So it would be accurate to say that you're a big fan of the governor then?"

"Sure," she replied. "He's great."

"You know him personally?"

She glanced at him quizzically. "Of course. I worked as one of his assistants last summer. I went all over the place with him to meetings and groundbreaking ceremonies and all that kind of thing."

Something was building up inside of Rob Coen, a mounting pressure of frustration and confusion, a blood-blinded fury that he had kept under wraps thus far in his attempts to be cordial and a diligent journalist. It had been veiled in a cloud of sickly resignation and foot-dragging discontent. Now it was electrified, no longer inert. First the interception at the airport, which he thought he had gotten over, and then being at the mercy of the governor's schedule with only a vague promise that they would speak in the morning, and now this young woman—a girl still really—with her cryptic closeness to Governor Alexander and her way of speaking which was a bluntly honest charade.

He may be at their mercy but he was not at their whim. He stopped and let her keep on walking toward the clatter of the workshops until she turned slightly, noticed his positioning, and stopped in the middle of the gravel path. Her wide, white forehead, small nose and large eyes, the whole thing heart-shaped and placid, was still so familiar for some reason.

His voice was a little sharper and harsher than he had intended, but he was still a few hours ahead from the flight and starting to get tired. This, combined with his building sensation which had not stopped, made him more careless than he would have been otherwise.

"What is this exactly? Who are you? I'm getting a little tired of the runaround." He took note of the obvious annoyance in his own voice and paused to adjust. "I appreciate the hospitality, but you have to understand if I'm a little defensive, a little suspicious. I just came here to interview the governor." He halted abruptly there because he was unsure of what else to say or any other way to express his deep disturbance.

She looked perplexed, and the bit of her which was still childlike passed across her features for the briefest instant in a mix of embarrassment and indignation. "You mean Banks didn't tell you who I was?" As she asked, the placidity returned with perhaps the slightest hints of mischief and imperiousness.

"No," Rob answered, almost visibly shrugging with his tone.

"Oh, well, the governor is my uncle," she explained simply.

Rob was dumbstruck for a moment before it all began to fall into place and make perfect sense. He almost laughed aloud at the sudden change in his understanding of the circumstances. He even felt a little embarrassed. "No, Banks did not tell me. Forgive me for my annoyance."

"It's fine," she responded, a little coolly. "You should be grateful that I agreed to babysit you for my uncle today. You could be stuck with Banks all day and be having to listen to his boring stories about the glory days. Who knows though? You're a journalist. You would probably like that."

Rob, diplomatically, did not agree or disagree. She turned to resume their progress to the workshops, and he fell in line. The possibilities for lines of inquiry with Justine had just multiplied greatly, and his head buzzed with activity as he tried them out in branching hypotheticals.

They reached the rows of long, metal-sided buildings, and the noise of power tools, motors, and voices were such that he had to shout his questions, "So you obviously knew the governor when he was just your uncle and not into politics. What was he like back then?"

She shook her head as they walked past open bays with equipment under repair, implements he could not recognize under showers of sparks, and the otherworldly shrieking of air tools cutting in through the ambient din at moments. "I didn't really know him back before he was in politics. Sure, when I was a little kid he visited sometimes, but I don't really remember that. He was in finance and worked back East for a while, and we never saw him during those years. It wasn't until he quit that and moved back that I really knew him at all."

"And he's related how exactly?" Rob asked, trying to stay close to her so that he could pick up every word over the noise.

"He's my mom's younger brother," she explained. "They had a brother a few years older than her too, but he died."

"You mind if I ask how?"

"Heroin. That's one reason why he was so big on drug reform and started the Hospitallers. He didn't want anyone else to lose someone like he did. I think he felt guilty because he was off in the city when it happened too."

The narrative was locking into place in Rob's head. "Let me guess. He wasn't very close with his brother?" he asked.

Justine turned and gave him a pointed glance. "That would be accurate."

"Do you know if he was interested in politics at all when he was younger? Did your mom ever mention that it was a long-term goal of his?"

Justine shrugged. "She doesn't talk about it much. She says he was always restless, that he used to be scared of time passing when he was a kid. He would come and ask to sleep in her bed when he was six or seven because he said he could feel time rushing by and couldn't stop it. She told me he was always good at history in school and was quiet and bookish but polite. She's got a few anecdotes like that, but she's never said he was in student government or anything."

Rob was slightly taken aback by the detail she had offered into Governor Alexander's childhood. It was very personal. He was suspicious of the candid statements, of course. One must take nothing at face value, especially when it seemed like a fortunate bit of information simply dropped at his feet.

They had passed by the workshops, and the noise began to die out behind them. The path they followed wound through a screen of pine trees, which he recognized from visiting relatives in New Jersey. He was familiar with their characteristic straight trunks and sparse branches reaching out into green, bristly tufts. On the other side, they reached another collection of smaller structures that had the appearance of barracks in an old, nineteenth-century, frontier fort. Justine explained that they were the bunkhouses for the workers.

"I had to stay in bunks kind of like these when I was with the Hospitallers," she explained. "It can be pretty uncomfortable, but you get used to it. I will always be glad that I spent time in the State Corps. It teaches you a great deal about giving up comfort and working hard. I don't think most people understand that."

She was good. Rob had to give her that. He could certainly see why Governor Alexander would use his niece as the preferred emissary to the reporter from the big city. Despite his clinical approach and desire to view her analytically, she seemed very genuine and even a bit disarming at moments. When the time came to meet the governor, he would have to be sure to take him on his own merits and nothing more.

After meandering between the bunkhouses for a few minutes, as Justine explained the strict rules for cleanliness, hygiene, and morning assembly, and after Rob asked how such things were enforced, she explained that the corps were segmented into divisions with overseers who passed down discipline according to the state workers code of conduct.

"I can show you around the lodge a bit more if you like," Justine offered.

Rob agreed, and they followed a path which led up past the parking lot where the immaculately maintained Town Car rested in the spot Banks had parked it. Justine was just about to cross the asphalt drive to the front of the lodge when two, shiny, black sedans pulled up between them and the wraparound porch before gliding to a stop a few dozen yards away, nose to tail. The front passenger doors on each opened along with the rear, right door on the car in the back.

Three men emerged. The one who stepped out of the front of the forward car was older and casually dressed: khaki pants, a light blue button-down shirt, and a fuchsia-colored sweater vest. He was balding and had just a strip of gray hair running along the back of his dome-like head down to his sideburns, along with a slightly darker gray moustache. The two other men who stepped out of the rear car wore dark fitted suits. One appeared younger and was blond. The other looked older and had dark features. Their hair and attire were attended to perfectly down to ironed pocket squares. They could be models for all Rob could tell, and they had that big shot, city lawyer aura about them, that electromagnetic field that pulls in money and repels legal scrutiny with extreme force. He could practically smell it.

The older man in the sweater vest brightened upon seeing the governor's niece. "Hey, Justine. Is the big man ready to see us?"

"I've been out, but he was in the conference room when I left. I'm sure he's still there and will be late into the night. Besides, he's always ready for you."

The suited men crossed to the trunk of their sedan and began pulling out briefcases and two pieces of rolling luggage.

Rob leaned over to Justine and asked quietly, "Any idea who they are?"

"No idea specifically. They're here on legal business with my uncle though."

The three men finished with their luggage and made their way up to the porch, craning their necks to murmur to one another conspiratorially. The older man had not even appeared to notice Rob who was standing only a few feet from Justine.

She continued her explanation, "The older guy is Arthur Walden. He's retired now." She put a strange emphasis on the word 'retired' as though it was a cover for another word and Rob should have some inkling of what it really meant. "He was my uncle's lawyer after the first campaign and during his first term. He's probably the closest person to him and most trusted as far as advice goes."

"Do you know what all this is about?" Rob asked. "The meeting and lawyers and all the legal business?"

"No," she stated simply and then added with a smile, "And even if I did, I wouldn't tell you."

He smirked. "Hey I have to ask. It's my job."

Walden and the city lawyers clattered up the steps and then through the big wooden doors into the lodge. The drivers pulled the two sedans into the side lot. Justine peered at the front of the lodge as though she could see through the walls and see the governor sitting alone and waiting for the new arrivals.

"You seem worried," Rob commented, trying not to sound like a disingenuous manipulator. He had no reason to care, aside from the expected, utilitarian, journalistic ones. She knew that of course, and he caught a glimpse of a slight flush on her neck, along with a pulling at the connective cords visible through the skin.

She turned and gave him a subtly defiant look. "You know, Walden is going to do a number on you. He did not like the idea of you coming here, and he despises journalists."

He had embarrassed her with the too personal observation and now he was paying the price.

"I'll keep that in mind," he managed.

Justine was all business now. "If you would like to get situated in your room, then you have free reign of the place. Dinner is served from five to seven. Banks will be able to get you a visitor's pass. Did you have any more questions?"

He didn't mention that she had offered to show him around the lodge. "No, thanks. Will you be around?"

She shook her head. "I live in Jackson with my parents. I'll be back day after tomorrow."

"Thanks for showing me around the place. It really was nice meeting you," he said, feeling suddenly very empty. He had not expected to meet someone like her in this place, and now, since she was leaving, his circumstances would revert back to the mundane expectations to which he had resigned himself for days up until his arrival. He stuck out a hand and she shook it very formally. He made note again of her very warm and slightly dry skin as she gave him a characteristic grim but earnest smile. He then followed the path of the lawyers up and to the front door of the lodge. He gave one, final glance back and just barely spied the back of Justine's head bobbing as she walked downhill toward the lower outlying buildings of Camp Hope. He made a mental note to adjust his approach if they crossed paths again.

Once inside, Rob took the stairs up to the second floor, turned right then left through the hallway and passed by his room on his way to the end of the hall. The door to Jordan Banks' office rested slightly ajar. He opened it fully with a slight creak. Banks sat behind his desk with his reading glasses on and glancing through a packet of paperwork. The room was dim with only the golden glow of a desk lamp pouring over the wooden surface and the older man's hands. When he heard the noise indicating a visitor, he peered over the rims at Rob. His face was strangely shaded in the darkness above the lamp's illumination.

"Ah, Mr. Coen," he exclaimed and leaned forward and tapped a finger at the foremost right corner of the desk to indicate a small object. "Your room key as promised."

"Thank you," Rob replied, taking the key. "Justine said something about a visitor's pass?"

"Yes." Banks nodded and removed his own set of keys from a

belt clip and opened one of the drawers, hunching over so that his back showed as a shifting mound above the far edge of the desk. "This," he said, holding up a laminated card with an attached lanyard along with his room key, "will get you meals and access at state parks and monuments if you should choose to visit any over the next few days."

"Thanks again." Rob turned nearly all the way to the door before remembering something else. "Justine mentioned that you have an old collection of recordings from the campaign. She also said that you would probably be open to letting me go through them."

Banks held up his index finger to indicate that he had remembered also, rose from his seat with a grunt, and crossed the room to a set of folding, wooden, closet doors. He pulled them open to reveal an old CRT television on a rolling stand and rested his hand on a plastic bin on the shelf below the screen. "These are all the DVDs. Feel free to come in and look through them when I'm not around. I just ask that you not take any of the disks out of the office, since these are the only copies. I've told myself that I need to archive them all, but every time I take them out, I just end up watching them some more." He paused and gave a pensive, rueful smile at the floor between them. "Honestly I'm the only person who has had any interest in watching them all these years. It's a little sad, I guess, retracing the past. I had a sort of dream to put it all together into a documentary or something, but I never got around to it. Somebody would probably pay good money for all of it to produce their own movie, but I could never do that. I couldn't trust anyone else to tell the story right. They would cut it all up and splice it into something ugly, I'm sure. You know? Just take out all the bits that could be made to look unflattering. Maybe someday I will do it though."

"It's not a bad idea." Rob admitted. "I'll probably take a look tomorrow or the next day." He paused long enough to indicate an intent to end the interaction. "I'm going to go get settled."

"You get along with Justine?" Banks asked before Rob could make it entirely out into the hall.

"Yes," he asserted. "She is very articulate for her age, very professional."

"She is wise beyond her years," the older man mused wistfully, "and smart too. The governor knows it. He likes to keep her around. I think he has plans for her. She will be a formidable ally to James. Sometimes I think they're more alike than she is her mother. The governor's sister, that is. I do think she has a great future."

"Yes, she does." Rob agreed.

He used the break in the conversation to give a nod of finality and slip out into the corridor with a hasty "Thanks again."

If Banks had gotten enough leeway to change the subject, then there was no telling how long he would have been stuck in the awkward dance of swiveling between polite nodding and whirling toward the door. Rob unlocked the door to his room and stood in the dimness after closing it behind him. It was late afternoon at this point and the shadow of the mountains above the lodge had darkened his window. The geometric patterns of the rugs covering the hardwood floor seemed to jump out at him as he stood in a moment of aimless contemplation. After a few seconds he shook himself free of the spell, and although he was tired, he did not rest. He opened his carry-on at the foot of the bed and laid out some toiletries before running the water in the shower. The bathroom was small: a simple sink on a tiny cabinet, toilet, and an upright shower which was maybe three feet by three feet. The water oscillated wildly between boiling heat and tepid mediocrity. He chose not to be boiled alive.

After showering, he turned on a small, electric heater he had discovered below the window and sat at the table wrapped in a towel to go through his notes. He was under prepared, which was not customary. The squandered time on the flight over had not helped. He had the FBI stats with highlighted hate crime data, cost numbers for Mount Calvary, estimates of tourism income, demographic shifts in the last five years, an intriguingly woeful statistic on college application numbers from students in the state, gross domestic product, and the list went on. None of it was inspiring. None of it indicated one hard-hitting question he could formulate. Luckily, he had gotten some ideas from his talks with Banks and Justine. He wanted to know more about the Hospitallers and discipline in the state corps. He also had the insight of the anecdote from James Alexander's childhood, the fear of the passage of time, and the later one of the brother dead from heroin.

He found an open wireless network and began to do some cursory digging on the Hospitallers. There was an explosion of opinion pieces clustered around the initial announcement in regards to the Fourth Amendment implications and habeas corpus. He smirked at a title from his own publication opining on how the Department of Homeland Security should designate them a terrorist organization. Another gem read: "The Case for Removing Wyoming from the Union." He bookmarked it out of curiosity. Finding data on the success of the group proved difficult. There were estimates on successful rehabilitation but no hard numbers. Since the Hospitallers were not a law enforcement group, there was no rigid documentation. As far as police numbers went, drug related arrests were down significantly over the past few years, but that could just be due to the initial crackdown after the governor was first elected.

CHAPTER

3

After an hour he realized that dinner was being served, and he did not want to miss it, since he had no way of knowing whether he would have a chance to get food anywhere else. He changed from the towel into another set of casual clothes. Through his tiredness, the dislocation of his current setting and his mulling over potential questions to ask, he barely even experienced or remembered the walk down through the dim hallways to the entry of the mess hall.

The room was immense and reached up two floors in height to the peak of the roof. Three large antler chandeliers, like the one in the entryway but larger, hung down and bathed the room in warm light. Large, gray, stone tiles covered the floor, and two, massive hearths burned on either side of the hall to his right and left. A few dozen people sat in clusters at sizeable and circular wooden tables. They looked to be mostly workers in the corps: young men with beards, a few older, some women and all wearing work clothes or simple casual attire of mostly denim and flannel. Another group milled around a wide counter at the far end of the room where staff served food.

A feeling of great uneasiness came over Rob upon realizing that he knew nobody in the room. It reminded him of the middle school years and transferring from one pack of hungry-eyed and unkind miniature people to another with the unknowing stares that seemed to swallow him up. "Pupil's pupils" was what always echoed in his adolescent brain, a punishing and juvenile play on words which had been his own inside joke with himself as were all those years and his current recollections of them as well.

He crossed the room to the counter in the overly self-conscious nonchalance which could not be avoided. It was the same one he had used in new schools when he was young. The movement and his awareness of it was one of those existential meta-observations

40

he had learned to ignore after it first reared its head to avoid falling into an infinite, coiling thought strangulation. He made note of menus in little, clear, plastic stands on the counter and leaned in to take a look. Roast beef, chicken pot pie, some kind of vegetarian stir-fry, pork chops, and a collection of typical sides which all sounded very mundane and utilitarian. The lack of ethnic dishes was a relief, since he didn't want to imagine what nightmarish and vague approximations would appear in their place.

A stout, middle-aged woman with a red face and graying, brunette hair gave him a raised eyebrow from behind the counter. He tugged on the lanyard to show his visitor's pass.

"You know what you want?" she asked—not unkindly, but businesslike and as though she did not have any time to wait around on the kind of people who had trouble making up their minds.

He obliged her prejudice. "I'll have the roast beef and mixed greens, thanks."

She gave him a card with the number 56 printed in bold, black lettering and scribbled on a pad before stepping away.

He retreated away from the hubbub to an empty table where he could wait undisturbed. While stealing glances at the hall and the people around him, every detail became apparent. Many bowed their heads slightly to pray before eating their meal. It was so alien to him yet so fitting, given the setting, that he did not know what to make of the sudden confusion that stirred in his chest. He did not resent the motion, but it did not aid in dispelling the feeling of dislocation which had been relatively constant. It had departed when he talked to Justine though, and he wondered whether she bent her head and prayed before she ate her meals. He considered Banks' comments that the governor had plans for her and whether or not she knew of any such potential plans or had her own goals separate from them. He hoped that he had not offended her too greatly with his halfway sincere observation that had ended their interaction so abruptly.

"You're the reporter, huh?"

A deep voice cut in suddenly, and a jolt of terror ran down Rob's spine. He had been found out. The solace was broken. He turned toward the sound just in time to see a large hand shooting in like a rocket. He raised his own to intercept and shake it just in time. He had no idea what would have happened had he been a second slower.

The voice belonged to Arthur Walden, the retired lawyer and confidante to the governor. He was standing over Rob and looking thicker and more imposing than he had appeared on first sight. While certainly retirement age, there was a youthful and vigorous aura around Walden which was not apparent until this moment, and he demonstrated it clearly with the crushing force of the handshake. Walden helped himself to the seat to Rob's left with a harrumphing in his throat and pulled it a little closer to the table. The distance between them was uncomfortable but not unbearable.

"I saw you over with Justine when I showed up. Sorry I didn't introduce myself then, but we were in a hurry. I'm Arthur." His tone was self-assured and cadence deliberate but somehow also meandering, which belied his directness. He did not give Rob enough time to acknowledge his statement. "What made you want to interview the governor, Mr. Coen?"

The use of his name without Rob providing it and this cutting straight to the point could only mean that this man was suspicious of his intentions. Rob began to feel a little hot under the collar, and it had little to do with the two, roaring hearths.

"I pitched the idea at a lunch meeting," Rob explained, almost breaking out in nervous laughter at the characterization which, while technically true, was certainly not the aim of his fateful comments in the lunchroom at *The Times* a few weeks prior. "My editor liked the idea. They wanted to send me out, so here I am."

Walden made no reply for a moment. He did not even make any motion indicating he had heard. He just sat and stared unblinkingly at the journalist for a while. Finally he worked his mouth in consideration a few times, so that his moustache formed a steep arch above his upper lip, and then responded. "You see, I was against this. I told the governor that he shouldn't be spending his time going on the record with the big city papers, since every time it's a damned assassination attempt. You people are like a dog that's been trained to bite or fight or something and you never lose that need to bite. Never. You aren't hateful, really, not in any complex ideological sense. It's just what you were trained to do. It's in your DNA. If you don't make a constant effort to stop yourself, then next thing you know you're biting somebody who you may not even dislike personally. I told the governor he could get the nicest, sweetest reporter right out of college and it won't make any damn difference, that whatever you put in you get poison out the other side."

Rob wasn't even offended by the man's tsunami of blunt invective. He was a little in awe. "So this is on the record then?" he managed after a moment.

"Sure it is. I can give you a transcript if you want." He reached up and patted the breast pocket of his shirt behind the sweater vest. "You don't think I'm recording this conversation?"

"Of course," Rob said dryly, not quite sure if Walden was stringing him along.

The older man continued, "And that's the best possible scenario, that you're exactly what you say, which is just a journalist from the city. Don't think for a second that I don't know how some certain elements operate."

At the word "elements" he leaned in uncomfortably close so that Rob thought he could feel the warm air of his hoarse whisper.

"You lost me," Rob stated, rallying from his initial bewilderment.

"They have come before and in different forms," Walden declared with one eyebrow raised. "They are never what they say, and you're never quite sure what they really are. Sometimes it's the journalist looking for a story, the businessman looking for inroads into the state, or the celebrity trying to meet up and make some buzz for themselves at one of the monuments or meet the governor himself. There is no one form every time."

Rob was not sure if Walden was entirely sane. He seemed to think they had a common understanding, but the journalist was completely baffled. He leaned in toward the retired lawyer. "Are you talking about demonic forces or something?" It was a blind stab.

Walden snorted. "In a way, but I was never one of the religious types who usually get along with the governor. No, my boy. I am talking about something far worse than demonic powers. What I mean, if I must spell it out, is a federal agent."

Rob laughed. "You think I'm FBI or something?"

Walden scratched his moustache and chin compulsively with a large, meaty hand. "He laughs." The older man hissed back in a whisper. "What makes you so sure that you aren't a fed?"

"Well I think I would know."

"That's where you're wrong." An index finger jabbed at Rob to punctuate the statement. "Just because they don't pay your paycheck or give you clandestine orders in a parking garage doesn't mean you aren't doing exactly what they want you to do. And hell, if they can get the same thing for free, then why not?"

"Don't you think that's a little...well, paranoid?" Rob asked.

Walden snorted. "I suppose if you're so naive, then that's some evidence that you're a journalist and nothing more."

Rob continued to smile stupidly. He was still unsure whether this was a bit or Walden believed every word. He was starting to believe the latter. Either way the man was not done.

"What's more valuable? A fed who knows what he's up to or one who isn't even aware of it? If it walks like a duck and talks like a duck then it's a goddamned duck. A rose by any other name, that sort of thing. Think about it: a big city journalist comes out to visit us. Why? Information. Your story is your intelligence. To what end? We both know that deep down you don't like the governor. How could you?" Walden's tone shifted to one of understanding, commiseration even, so that Rob almost thought the man would pat his knees reassuringly at any moment. "Look at who you are and where you come from. Look at who you write for and who pays your paychecks. So whether you fully intend to or not, you will come here and obtain information, talk to his people and see his operations, and then present it with the intent to frustrate his goals or damage his reputation. You tell me that you are not a federal agent? Free work for them as far as I see it."

"What makes you so sure that I want to hurt the governor? Just because I write for *The Times*?" Rob asked, irritated now that it was perfectly clear the retired lawyer was in earnest.

Walden scoffed and folded his arms atop his belly. "You can't be serious," he stated bluntly. "Your publication compared Governor Alexander to Francisco Franco after his last gubernatorial victory. You have been writing for them for two years. You have no pull yet. Their voice is your voice. Besides, judging by that Marxist den you inhabited for six years, I can reach some conclusions."

Walden had done his research and was at least familiar with Rob's education and job history. Rob was not overly shocked, but he still felt a sickly pang of ominous dread in his stomach.

Walden resumed, "There is always a larger structure in the great permutation of the modern machine. If the federal overmind is able to commandeer the national morality, then there is no limit to the number of agents under their control. Collections of human minds are just another form of real estate. They staked their claim on yours early."

Perhaps Walden was not crazy. It made a kind of sense in a paranoid way, although Rob almost expected the retired lawyer to bring up black helicopters at any moment. In fact something about the characterization of the "federal overmind" and its hijacking of the "national morality" sounded familiar. Rob decided that directness was the best course with this individual.

"Justine said something about American Nationalism being meaningless anymore, that it isn't enough. That, along with your hatred of the feds, makes me wonder if all the op-eds about secession are all that histrionic after all." Rob paused and met Walden's glittering gemstone eyes which sparkled at him from the caverns beneath his big bluff of a bald forehead. "Of course the governor has denied any insinuations disguised as questions that come from the press, but surely you know that New York City and Los Angeles, in their heart of hearts, would be glad for you to go. It seems like you aren't opposed to the notion." He was going to give as good as he got from this character. "Hell, with all the lawyers roaming around and secret meetings going on here you would almost suspect some unexpected precipitation at Fort Sumter tomorrow."

Walden gave a wry grin, shifted in his chair and let out a chuckle of begrudging respect at the statement. At least that is what Rob hoped it indicated.

"My contempt for the federal architecture is very real. I may not find it distasteful for its godlessness as Alexander and many others do, but I have my reasons. Say what you will about Alexander, he knows how to use the law. They may call him a tyrant in your coastal city-states, but he is not a lawless one. He follows the Constitution. He knows precedent. The feds want any excuse to intervene, so any loose and idiotic independence talk is coming from them, not Alexander.

"So then why all the lawyers? What is it all about?" Rob asked.

Walden grinned mischievously. "Is that how you journalists work now? You just throw yourselves against a wall over and over trying to break through?"

"When dealing with a wall, sometimes," Rob murmured.

Walden unfolded his arms to scratch at the side of his head and then returned them to the former arrangement. He raised his chin so that he peered down at Rob through slitted eyes. "Imagine that you are following a path through the deep woods. You cannot stray from the path or you will be lost. Somewhere in the dark entanglements of the forest is a beast far more powerful than you, a creature so immense that it would devour you with little effort in an open confrontation. If the monster surprised you, then there would be no chance of survival. You do not know when or where, but somewhere along the path it will attack. You know some things about the beast: what it eats, generally how it stalks its prey, but no more. How must you survive?" Walden ended his question with one eyebrow slightly raised cryptically.

"Why do I have to follow the path?" Rob asked trying to mask his irritation. He did not like hypotheticals, especially the kind which seemed to rely on arbitrary constraints.

Walden shrugged. "Because the path is the only sure way to where you need to go."

"And how do I know the beast will come for me?"

"Because it is the nature of the beast. It comes for everyone who goes on the path."

Rob shook his head. "I don't know. Is there an answer for how to survive?"

"There could be. Is there a way out of the riddle? I am not certain."

"Then what's the point of the hypothetical?"

"It is a small window through the wall you are throwing yourself into with these questions." Walden stated grimly, his chin down now and his thick body hunched forward over the meaty hands which clasped between column-like legs that strained at the material of his slacks.

Surely the federal government is the beast, Rob mused. The real question is where the path is leading. Do they intend to draw the beast into an ambush? He filed the questions into the back of his mind for later.

The middle-aged woman from behind the counter arrived with a large platter and set it in front of Rob. Walden raised his head at the sudden stimuli, like a dog roused suddenly from its dozing on the living room floor. She took the card with the number 56 printed on it and turned to leave.

"Table service? What is this?" Walden demanded in mock outrage. "I always have to get up and walk to the counter when you call my number!"

"Like he would hear me while he's stuck here listening to you go on and on," she shot back.

"Whoo," the retired lawyer breathed out in a low tone as though physically wounded. He had a sudden realization and swiveled in his seat toward the woman and clutched after her with his hands. "Diane, wait!"

She stopped and turned around.

"Diane, the ribs from yesterday. Are there any left?" Walden asked breathlessly.

"God almighty!" she exclaimed with an exaggerated rolling of her eyes and marched emphatically back to the counter.

"Diane, please! On a plate if there are any left!"

She did not turn back again. Walden swiveled back around to Rob and smiled like a wicked schoolboy. "She'll bring 'em."

"I have some more questions if you're willing to stick around for a few minutes." Rob commented.

"You aren't even going to touch your food?" Walden asked, sounding almost offended.

"I don't want to eat in front of you," Rob admitted.

"There are dogs," the older man explained, "Who will not eat unless they are alone."

"I just don't want to be rude," Rob retorted dryly, fully aware that Walden was trying to draw parallels with his former canine characterization to get a rise out of him. He was hungry though, and the food looked better than he had expected. The beef was not overdone and sat steaming in a savory smelling pool of its own juice. The fresh greens had a rich, healthy hue and were not wilted. He could make out what appeared to be spinach, endive, and dandelion.

Walden was peering at him while he made the inspection. "By all means dig in. Don't hold back on my account."

"Before I start, let me give you something to chew on so that you're not just watching me," Rob replied. "How did you meet the governor and end up being his lawyer? Justine told me you are one of his closest advisors. There has to be a story there." He opened the napkin bundle of silverware Diane had left on the table and took out the knife and fork. He cut the corner off of one of the hefty slices of meat. Walden had not responded, but Rob skewered the piece with his fork and raised it to his mouth anyway. The juicy morsel exploded a salty, bloody tang onto his tongue. It gave satisfactorily between his teeth. Hints of rosemary and thyme imbued the meat and rolled subtly across his tongue in waves.

"Better than you thought, huh?" Walden asked with a satisfied smirk.

"Very, very good," Rob admitted.

"Wyoming beef, fresh," the retired lawyer explained. "Alexander pushed the beef big-time. He used to say that when the settlers first came here there were thousands of bison with no antibiotics or automation to maintain them. All they needed was the land. You would not believe the amount of beef we ship out of the state. Every bit of it is as good as what's on your plate."

Rob swallowed and nodded. "So, what about you and the governor?"

Walden worked his mouth and made his moustache do the inchworm act again. His eyes clenched slightly, and his brow wrinkled as he traveled under the dim shadows of the past. He began slowly and deliberately. "James Alexander and I did not start out as allies. This may come as a surprise to you, but I worked for his opponent, the incumbent Republican Governor George Collins. I was one of a few lawyers who worked for him on occasion. I got the most work because I got the best results. When Alexander made it clear that he was going to run as an independent and actually made a mark in the first polls, Collins put me to work on Alexander to smell out anything that could be used to nip him in the bud."

The greens were as good as they looked, and some kind of light vinaigrette coated the leaves. Rob glanced up from his food and nodded on occasion so that Walden would know that he had not lost interest. The motions were likely unnecessary, since Walden seemed to be on a roll.

"Of course I started by looking into his dealings from when he was in finance: who he knew, what he traded, your basic checks for insider dealings. He was close with some guys who got nailed for some pump and dump rigged IPOs, but there was never any clear link that he was involved or knew anything about it. Collins sent me all the way to New York to chat up his old pals, posing as a potential investor from flyover country. They had some stories: gentlemen's clubs, rip-roaring nights out on the town, the typical coldness when inflicting financial wounds on the competition, but nothing outside the milder sins committed by any man mired in the world of money. I brought everything I had back to the governor, and he sent it out to the national papers to writers who were friends of friends. A few of them wrote for *The Times*, but that was before your time. None of it was solid, none of it was enough to do real damage, but it got people murmuring for a little while."

Rob was surprised by none of it. Only the naive or uninitiated would find journalists working as mercenaries for political parties as hired assassins shocking or unexpected. He had never done it himself. He was too small a fish for such work, although he had seen whom the editors met frequently and whom they invited to the monthly dinner parties. There was a constellation of connected dots to be sure. After swallowing another bite of beef he gave Walden a nod and coaxed him on, since the older man had trailed off and seemed to be silently lost in a memory. "I remember some of those stories from when I was in college. Lots of innuendo. They weren't going to win any awards with that material. They did raise questions though."

"They did," Walden agreed with arched brows above still faraway eyes. "Collins was not really all that worried about his position at that point, and the race was not in the national eye yet. There was not enough money around to pay for any deeper digging. Alexander had no notable endorsements except for a few religious organizations. He had no relationship with any of the oil companies or livestock firms. There are few resources for an independent candidate. So Collins left off and coasted. I went on vacation. I had been down in Florida for a few weeks when I got a call on the golf course that they needed me to come home and get back on Alexander. I had completely unplugged while enjoying the warm weather. During that time Alexander had become a national phenomenon. I had no idea. I don't think I had turned on the television once the whole time I was there. Apparently one of his stump speeches became some kind of internet phenomenon. All the late-night hosts were vivisecting the crazy zealot running for governor in Wyoming. His poll numbers were still climbing.

"Collins was smarter than most. He knew that there was no such thing as bad press, so none of it was a welcome development. His mistake was agreeing to debate, hoping he could head Alexander off and slow the momentum by presenting himself as the stable and sane candidate. It backfired. People all over the country streamed the debate online. The Democrat didn't have a prayer anyway, so he just meekly presented his ideas. Collins went after Alexander though, but the madman turned it back on him dialed up to ten. The poll after the debate had them neck and neck. The race took on a life of its own. It was no longer a gubernatorial election in a state with a population smaller than some cities. It became a testing ground for a new politics which fought for the soul of a people. It sounds cliché now, I'm sure."

Walden smirked and leaned back in his chair before crossing his legs with a grunt. "My vacation had no end date, but those new developments cut it short. Soon I was back in New York retracing my steps. I was instructed to go after anything that could contain a germ of iniquity: ex-girlfriends, gay bars near where he used to live, his old landlords, any place at all he frequented back in his finance days. Nothing was off limits." He gave Rob a sidelong glance and then turned his attention toward the counter at the end of the mess hall and let out a booming exclamation. "Praise be! I knew that you would come through for me!"

Rob turned to find the source of the man's sudden elation. Diane was approaching with a plate of ribs and a mix of mock resentment and slight embarrassment on her face. After she set down the plate, he grasped her hand in his. "Thank you, kind woman!" he exclaimed dramatically as she wrenched her hand free and retreated, mumbling under her breath about how she was a fool to be suckered by a self-serving old man. Walden didn't seem to notice any of it. He sat smiling down at the ribs. His movements became quicker and more energetic. Every change in direction of his darting hands and arms was a kitten's playful ambush on an inanimate object. The sight of the meat augmented his already youthful vigor. He lifted one curved rib between two thick fingers and his moustache arced up as though it were a living part of a moronic sea creature, some urchin recoiling from physical stimuli to protect itself from harm. After a few audible bites into the meat, Walden was back into his recollections, punctuating them at times by the loud sucking of the grease and sauce from his thumbs. If Rob had not been so engaged in the details recounted to him, then he probably would have attacked the man out of disgusted outrage at the sound.

"You see, the pressure was starting to grow on Collins, and he had new resources due to the urgency. He was always good friends with the boys at UBI Energy. He had always ensured that the state cultivated a friendly climate for UBI when it came to access, drilling, pipelines, you name it. They had no such promises from Alexander, and why should they? They had not even talked to him at that point. James Alexander was supposed to be a non-factor in the election."

Walden gnawed at the first bone for a moment before tossing it aside for another which he used to gesture occasionally.

"When my second dive into the history of James Alexander started, I was still technically working for Governor Collins, but I was also working for UBI. I did nothing for them directly to get paid. I never set foot in their offices, but they paid me as a consultant while I did my digging. It was another layer of motivation you could say. It was also how they could get around contributing directly to the campaign financially."

This was turning out to be quite the impromptu interview. Rob had finished his food and sat back in his chair scrawling down every last detail he could manage.

"At that point I had the resources to chase down any leads no matter how minor. There were a few trails I had left untraveled the first time around because they had not seemed worth it. One was a rumor from a landlord that Alexander had assaulted a woman. It had seemed thin at the time. I hadn't found any corroboration, but I decided to give it a go."

"Tracy Robinet." Rob cut in with a tone of realization.

"Precisely." Walden confirmed, jabbing the bone at Rob.

It was no feat of insight that the name had popped into Rob's head. It had been all over the papers. Many had presumed that it would be the scandal that would finally end the insurgent candidacy of James Alexander. It almost had. How Walden had gone from would-be author of Alexander's destruction to his most trusted confidante was beyond a capacity to forgive that Rob Coen could understand. Perhaps the relationship had been due to some admiration on either man's part. Maybe Alexander respected Walden's investigatory capabilities. Perhaps Walden admired Alexander's ability to weather the pressure that followed. Most likely both had contributed.

"Clearly you already know the story," Walden said.

"I'd like to hear it from your side," Rob replied, not wanting to miss any chance at fresh details.

The second bone clattered on the plate, and Walden took up another, but the retired lawyer did nothing but gesture with it. He seemed just as engrossed in telling the story as Rob was in listening. "There was a reason why nobody in Alexander's firm ever mentioned anything about the incident. Tracy Robinet was one of his coworkers. I went out drinking with some of his finance buddies one night and held back. I let them get a little sauced before floating the question by in a way that they only knew I had heard a rumor and was curious. They were still a little cagey even after four or five cocktails. All they really knew was that something had happened between Robinet and Alexander before he abruptly quit and moved back to Wyoming. They had heard that he had attacked her. Now I knew that I had a potential goldmine. Thing was that Robinet no longer worked at the firm either. She had moved back to Ohio to be near her parents a few years earlier. It wasn't hard for me to track down a number and approximate residence. I just needed a reason to approach her. I agonized over that one for a little while." Walden finally took a bite of the rib and gave an evil grin. He chewed for a moment and swallowed. "I have done some unsavory things in my day. I am a man of the law, yes, but when you get in the dirt sometimes you have to just jump in headfirst." He trailed off, taking another bite and chewing methodically.

Rob was unsure whether he should say something to break the sudden spell or let the older man come around in his own time. He decided to wait so as not to spook him. Walden was clearly not proud of whatever he had done next, and Rob did not want to tip the delicate balance away from disclosure. Once Walden started speaking again, Rob breathed an inaudible sigh of relief.

"See, what I did was go through the parents." He smiled again, but a little shamefully, or as close to that emotion as someone like Walden could manage. It was a little off-putting. "I figured if she had gone years without saying anything about it, then she probably didn't hold whatever had happened against him. With parents though, it's different. I figured if she had ever told them, which was unlikely, then she had probably glossed over bits or kept whatever happened vague. People usually do that sort of thing either out of embarrassment or just not to cause a fuss. I guessed right. I cold called her father and was straight with him. I explained that I was investigating James Alexander and that I had heard something terrible had happened between him and his daughter. I stressed how important it was for Alexander to pay, that he shouldn't benefit politically from her silence. Next thing I knew I was on a plane to Ohio."

"That is pretty cruel," Rob murmured. He could not help getting in the jab after receiving so much abuse from the older man.

"It worked well enough that I didn't have time to be ashamed. It was damn fine work, and I won't make any apologies for it,"

Walden said bluntly, a look of cool resentment creeping into his eyes. "How about you? You ever dig up anything that juicy in your career as a professional journalist?"

Rob held his hands up just above the edge of the table in mock surrender.

"I didn't think so," Walden grumbled. "Anyway, I met with her two days after in her apartment to get a sworn statement. I had called it right. She had forgiven him and was pretty hesitant to clue me in. I told her that if she had considered it all in the past, then she could make that part of her statement too. Then she gave me the goods. She had been sweet on Alexander when they worked together. She hadn't got up the courage to say anything to him though. All the brokers would go out on Fridays to grab drinks. One Friday she decided to tell him. She had sworn to herself that she would do it. She probably had a few too many drinks trying to get up the courage, and she couldn't tell that he was in a bad mood. He left early and she followed him outside to talk to him. He was annoyed that she had followed. Alexander told her that he was going to be leaving the city and putting in his notice soon, that he wanted to be left alone. But she had promised herself."

Walden was staring grimly off into space and nodding slightly as he recounted the story, lost perhaps in Tracy Robinet's moment of desperation.

"She didn't want him to leave without telling him how she felt. He was adamant about getting away. She grabbed his arm. He was frustrated, maybe drunk, but she couldn't remember. He grabbed her wrist to pull her hand away and pushed her back. She stumbled and fell on the sidewalk. She said that he was paralyzed at that point, unsure of whether to take the chance to get away or see if she was alright. She took the chance to struggle up and grab onto the lapels of his jacket before he snapped out of it. She said, 'Please, please, please.' She didn't want to let him go that way. That was when he put his hand on her throat, but only for a second, only long enough to push her back off of him and scare the living daylights out of her. She said that right after he grasped her throat, his hand jumped back like he had touched a hot coal. He got a wild look in his eyes and ran out of there. That was the last time she saw him."

Walden shrugged and resumed chewing on the rib for a moment. He mused and swallowed. "She had sprained her ankle and someone at the bar saw what happened, so word got around to the higher ups at the firm. She said she didn't want to press charges and was sure that it wasn't his intention to hurt her. Alexander left without picking up his things. The firm paid for her to take a medical leave, which she found unnecessary, and that was the end of it until she told me. It wasn't all that terrible all things considered, but presented in the right way, it was pretty damn good. I sent what I had to Collins and pretty soon it was big news. I sat back to watch the fireworks and decided that if James Alexander could survive that scandal, then I would offer my services to him."

"Why?" Rob asked.

"I was tired of working for the man. Honestly the whole Robinet business wore me out. I had toyed with the idea of switching sides before then for some excitement, but I had a nondisclosure agreement with Collins, so it's not like I could have been very useful. I just wanted something fresh."

"So Alexander obviously found out that you were the one who got Robinet to talk."

"It was in the resume I gave him," Walden said triumphantly. His eyes still glittered but had softened a little. "He didn't take it personally. I'm glad. It's been a good ride with Alexander."

"You sound like you think it's over," Rob observed.

"Have you figured out how to follow the path and survive the beast?" Walden asked.

"No."

"Nor have I, and I have spent years considering it." Walden sat and mulled over his last statement for a moment before rising with a grunt and taking up the plate of ribs which were all picked clean. "The governor will see you in the morning. As much as I'm against it, he does as he wishes."

"You're leaving?" Rob asked, a little disappointed. Despite his abrasiveness, Walden was not bad company and, more importantly, a well of potential journalistic material.

"I get up at four in the morning," the older man explained.

"You didn't explain what happened after the Robinet issue," Rob insisted.

"The rest is public record," Walden sighed with a shrug. "I made sure of that." He turned toward the counter to return the plate of ribs and added over his shoulder, "See you around."

CHAPTER

4

After Walden was gone, Rob sat alone at the table and stared with an unfocused gaze across the room into the flames of the nearest hearth. He considered the riddle about the beast and the path for a time, the riddle with no solution. He found it particularly ominous after Walden's story which revealed the depths to which he was willing to stoop. He felt as though he had walked in on the eerie calm before some cataclysm. An unknown evil lurked in the corners of the massive timber building, something only spoken of in whispers behind closed doors.

Rob brought his dish and silverware to the counter and set them in a plastic bin with a stack of others that awaited the staff to come and take them for washing. He returned to his room through the dimming hallways of the lodge. It was much colder there than the dining hall, so he turned on the small heater beneath the window and sat at the little round table. He decided to get reacquainted with the public record following Walden's Robinet scoop. It was easy to find news stories related to the subject from around the time when it first broke.

The first few days after the story dropped, there was massive outrage at James Alexander's actions. Nobody in the papers of record came to his defense, although a few commentators questioned why it was made public in the first place.

One opinion writer for a conservative publication asked, "What is being lost in the firestorm surrounding James Alexander's rough treatment of Miss Robinet is the question of why it matters. I don't mean to say that his behavior was in any way excusable, but why is it important that any of us know about it? Clearly Miss Robinet does not harbor ill-will toward Mr. Alexander. In fact, the empathy of her narrative and the understanding and goodwill extended is Christian charity in the most explicit sense. The question must be asked: if she harbors no resentment, then can the article be seen as anything other than the cynical machinations of politics which seeks to stifle even the sweetest act of forgiveness?"

Confusion reigned in the world of commentary, especially when polling showed that Alexander had not taken much of a hit. One writer even penned a bizarre piece titled, "I Hate Myself for Saying This, but James Alexander and Tracy Robinet Are Perfect Together." That one was widely panned for being a perfect example of internalized misogyny.

Alexander had issued a public apology to Tracy Robinet the day after the story broke. He wrote that his actions had been inexcusable and that he did not deserve her forgiveness. As was customary, it did not take long for the media circus to die down. In all his reading, Rob found no mention of Arthur Walden. He felt strange knowing that he had met the invisible thread which tied the whole series of events together.

Rob wondered whether it was worth bringing Robinet up to the governor. It was old news. On the other hand, enough time had passed that perhaps he was willing to be open to sharing more of his side of the story. He filed it away with some of his other considerations.

After satisfying his curiosity on the Robinet editorials, Rob was suddenly aware of being alone in his room in the dark in this alien place. He was tired and had nothing to occupy his mind. If he sat here much longer, then the malaise would descend. He was not wrong. The silence and suffocating stillness came for him all at once, just as he had suspected it would. He was no longer protected by the constant dull rumble and clatter of the city sounds: the growl of vehicles moving by his apartment; the sudden, garbled eruption of human voice, whether sad or angry or happy or a drunken mixture of them all. Even sirens signaling agony, violence, misery or misfortune would be welcome, anything to stifle the empty loneliness of the silence, which was made all the more terrifying because he was not truly alone. He was trapped in a room with himself, a demonic chameleon that never looked quite the same, a cruel thing of dream-being logic. Each time he was alone with it, the face had changed, although it was still clearly and obviously the shadow of him. There were new tricks, new unexpected deviant projects it had been working on in the background the entire time. As soon as they were alone together in the silence, then the new face would smile surreptitiously and introduce him to the new plan.

The quiet emptiness which had descended was the same kind which visited him when he was young and his parents sat him down on his bed to tell him that they no longer loved each other. Afterward they looked at him as though they expected him to say something. Only smothering, cold silence fell then, just as it did now in the airy and still room of the lodge. He had no answer for them, no thoughts on the matter. He had only felt empty bewilderment at the sudden axiomatic shift in the basic foundation of his world. He could remember the rawness of that silence, as his consciousness traveled down those same neurons of loneliness, abandonment, and confusion at the unjustness of the world, which was of a form so pure that it did not even point to the possibility of justness by its absence.

Now that he was older and alone with the stranger that was himself, the foundation of his world no longer shifted. He had learned to be suspicious of a decent world that made sense and had everything ordered in hierarchies of goodness and badness. If there is no world-lie on which to base expectations, then there would be no axiomatic shift. There was only one axiom, and it was that hypocrisy is the only constant. He had learned that everything was an atomic approximation of an idea, a field of probabilities clustered around a few vague notions of what was real. As one approaches the point at the center of any cluster of ideal-ness, the hypocrisy that imbues everything transports the viewer away to the other magnetic pole and they find themselves approaching from somewhere else entirely. There was only finding the example of hypocrisy. That was the story. That was the world in which the journalist must live. It was what made them suckers for the greater powers. It was this knowledge that made Rob nervous about being here at the mercy of Alexander's people. Perhaps they would show him only the bit of hypocrisy that they wanted him to see.

He peered out the window. Gas lights had come on around the camp and a few ghostly figures moved up and down the paths on occasion. The orange glow of campfires emanated from the direction of the State Corps barracks. Rob wondered what life must be like as a worker for the State Corps. Justine had told him that most people understood that the work was service, that there was no fortune to be made in the business. If this was true and not simply the governor's party line, then what was it that made all these people willing to flock here and work in exchange for a modest living and nothing more? Was it the same thing that made Arthur Walden so certain that he wanted to provide his services to James Alexander?

He had to call his editor. The consideration came to him in a moment of sudden resignation. Rob was a bit surprised she had not called him already. There was no list of definite questions to send to her at this point and there would likely be none. He hoped she was willing to overlook that fact. He had assumed that it was just an unnecessary formality. What he dreaded far more was her reaction to his deviating from the plan and staying at Camp Hope at the governor's behest. Hopefully he could make a case as to why he had gone along with the decision. Margaret Hunter was not the most understanding editor at *The Times*, but she had the sense that everyone working under her was far less intelligent than she was, which actually afforded the bearer of bad news some shelter from too much criticism, provided they had a high tolerance for being patronized. Rob had developed a heavy tolerance over the past two years.

It would be after ten p.m. in the city, but she barely slept. As long as the call came before midnight, she would be awake for certain. Of course that did not mean that she would answer. He made the call. The phone rang twice, and a rising bloom of hope developed in Rob's chest. She answered after the third ring, wilting the sensation abruptly.

"Hello, Robert. How's God's country?" Her tone was gregarious. By the particularly familiar jocularity he could tell that she was a few glasses of wine into her revelry. A bubbling of voices and clattering in the background indicated to him that she was out to dinner with her high-class friends in the news and politics circle. If she was in good spirits, then this may go even better than he had hoped.

"It's ok," he replied. "I made it here alright. I've been told I'll be talking to the governor tomorrow."

"So soon? I will look over your notes as soon as I get home. I will send you my input before I go to bed."

Rob cleared his throat, adjusted his position in the wooden chair and began compulsively doodling on a scrap of notebook paper beside his laptop. "There has been a change in plans." He kept his voice as even and unconcerned as he could manage.

"Jesus Christ, Robert. Why do I not like the sound of this?"

"I'm going for a more involved angle with this story. I think it will pay off."

"More involved," she repeated skeptically. "What does that mean?"

"I'm staying at one of the camps outside Jackson."

"Like a KOA?" she asked, deadpanning. "I didn't realize you brought a tent."

"It's Camp Hope, one of their State Corps depots. The governor is here now. He lives here part-time." He paused, but she said nothing, so he carried on. "I know the policy about accepting gifts and accommodation from subjects of articles, but I think this adds a dimension of involvement to the narrative." He cringed as soon as he uttered the word "involvement." "I've talked to people who work for him here, even his niece and his lawyer from the early days. Believe it or not, he is the same guy who dug up the whole Robinet scandal and he works for Alexander now. The people here have been quite open with me. I may be able to get way more than I could have hoped for with a more clinical approach."

Margaret sighed. "So you're what, Hunter S. Coen now all of a sudden? *The Times* follows the policy of rejecting gifts and favors for a reason. We avoid even the appearance of favoritism. You will have to write a foreword to disclaim all of this."

"I think it's worth it," Rob insisted. "The amount of access I'm getting is huge."

"Sell me, Robert. If I start getting questions about how it's going, then I will need something good to explain this. It was hard enough to get them to send you out on the paper's dime. I hope you know Bruce is expecting good things."

Bruce was the name of the editor-in-chief. Even the brief mention of the name sent a cold tingle down Rob's spine. He cleared his throat and tried to make sense of the rushing jumble of thoughts in his head. "Something is going on here. A few lawyers showed up today, and their business is the one thing nobody will talk about. I've been told that the governor has been in meetings for days now."

"And you think you can get to the bottom of it?" she asked skeptically.

"With this much access and time, I think my chances are pretty good," he replied.

"You say you met his niece?" Margaret asked a little incredulously.

Rob was relieved at her non-sequitur question which changed the subject. "She gave me a tour of the camp," he explained. "I'm telling you; I am a fly on the wall here. They gave me free rein of the place. One of Alexander's guys from back at the beginning even offered to let me look through old campaign recordings. Apparently nobody has ever looked through them before."

His editor made a clicking noise of her tongue against her teeth which indicated that she was considering his words enthusiastically. "Alright, Robert. That actually sounds worthwhile. You may take a beating from some of the sticks in the mud around here, but so long as you promise to look through those tapes, then I will cover for you." She paused for a moment, and the noise of the restaurant came through over the call in the silence. "So you don't have any questions for me to look over?"

Rob took in an inaudible breath through his teeth. "I did some cursory work on the flight over, but they've kept me busy ever since I got here."

"This is why I had asked you to send them before you left," she replied sternly.

"I can send you what I have before I go to bed, but I will have to wing a bit of the interview." The skin on the back of his neck burned.

"Wing?" she asked, unamused. "I'm not sure exactly when you became my gonzo journalist, but don't make this a habit. I have writers who take up my time with their problems, and you have never been one of them."

"This will pay off. I promise," he insisted.

"Alright. I will let you go. Keep me more in the loop. I don't want to have to worry about whether you're joining some kind of religious order and going native on me, and I don't want any more surprises."

"I will," Rob promised.

The call had not gone as badly as he had feared. Rob compiled his notes and added links from some of the articles he had been reading on the Robinet issue and crime and education stats. He typed out a short list of potential questions and sent it in an email to Margaret. By the time he had finished, he was so tired that his head ached behind his eyes. Rob changed into a t-shirt and sweatpants and brushed his teeth before crawling into bed. Sleep did not come. He tumbled and rolled across the mattress for half an hour. He listened to soft music on his phone and stared at the ceiling. None of it did any good. The events of the day passed quickly through his head in jumbled chronological order. Finally he got up, poured himself a glass of water, and decided to walk around the lodge to collects his thoughts.

He took the room key from his nightstand and ventured out into the dim hall with his glass of water in hand. The door to Banks' office was closed. A complete silence had descended on the building and collected in the darkened corners in hallucinatory, morphing anomalies of vision that seemed to shift and slide away in the corner of his eye as he turned his head. Rob stalked the corridors, checking the parallel hallway on the other side of the building. It proved identical to the one where his room was located, complete with a corresponding door at the end. He wondered at whose office was the twin to Banks'. He stepped out onto the upper floor balcony of the entry room where he had met Justine. The doors on the far end beckoned his curiosity. He concluded that they must lead out to the deck above the porch and crossed to the far side, hugging the wall. The cool night air sucked him out onto the raised gallery overlooking the upper areas of the camp.

The thin crescent moon hung over and gave a slight yellow illumination to the darkened scene. He could make out the reflective roofs of the workshops and barns and moved out to the very edge of the balcony to lean against the railing. After setting his glass on the wooden planks, he rested his elbows on the wrought iron and rubbed his eye sockets with the heels of his hands to rid himself of the itching, tired sensation.

A sudden culmination of unexpected stimuli put the hair on the back of his neck on end. A whiff of cigarette smoke drifted beneath his nostrils and soured his tongue as a light rasping noise of something heavy sliding on the planks sounded behind him. He was not alone. Rob did not turn around. He simply waited for a moment in his fog of exhaustion and tried to decide how to react. The decision was made for him, and a smooth voice poured out into the space behind.

"You are not one of the typical denizens of this place," the voice stated methodically and with careful enunciation.

Rob retrieved his glass from the floor of the balcony and took a sip to clear his throat before turning and resting his back against the railing. His unexpected companion sat to the right of the door at a patio table steeped entirely in darkness save for a faint paleness of skin and the slowly roving, red ember of a cigarette.

The voice poured out again. "It can be hard to sleep here. I know. The quiet can be unsettling for us city dwellers."

Rob was no longer surprised by people he had never met knowing who he was. He was too tired and annoyed to give a verbal response so he just nodded.

"There is another chair here," the man's voice offered. "If you want a smoke, then I have plenty."

As he drew nearer to the seated figure, he could make out some features and realized that they were familiar. He was the younger blond of the well-dressed lawyers who had arrived earlier and entered the lodge with Walden. Rob lowered himself into the chair opposite and set the glass of water on the table. The man looked younger than he had first thought and much less imposing with his tie loosened and the top button undone on his dress shirt. On this second examination he determined that they were probably the same age. Perhaps it was the superficial manliness of the other's appearance that had added the impression of age: the square jaw, tailored suit, and clearly well-maintained, muscular frame.

With a flick of his metal lighter the lawyer lit a citronella candle in the center of the table. He then snapped the lighter closed and set it atop a pack of cigarettes and slid the pair over to Rob.

"Thanks," Rob murmured and helped himself. He had quit smoking once he had turned thirty to keep a promise to himself, but he still indulged occasionally in social settings. There had been no such indulgence for a while, and the nicotine hit him like a ton of bricks. "I take it by your comment that you, like everyone around here apparently, know who I am." Rob uttered the statement with less resentment than the words implied. He was too tired to take anything personally anymore.

"You want a nip?" the lawyer asked, lifting a glass bottle of whiskey from beside his chair. "Can't seem to sleep here without it," he added with a slight grimace.

Rob finished the water in his glass and nodded, sliding it across the table. The lawyer tilted the bottle which gave a satisfying sloshing gulp as a generous portion poured out.

"Not sure if it's the quiet or the beds or what," the man mused while setting the bottle back on the boards beside him. "Can't sleep sober whatever it is."

Rob took a sip of the drink. It turned his tongue in on itself and sent mysterious messages to his salivary glands. He let the flavor dissipate entirely before speaking. "And who do I thank for the drink?"

"Tim Steyn." The man reached across to retrieve the cigarettes and craned his neck to light another before adding, "attorney at law."

"How long have you worked for the governor?"

Steyn glowered over at Rob's eyes for a lingering moment. His expression conveyed resentful acknowledgement of an unspoken fact with the ill will somehow expertly extracted from among the other elements. It was a look that said, "I won't blame you for being a bastard and getting right down to business, although I could and probably should."

"Me and another guy have been doing work for the governor for about six months now. Since February. My associate has been on Alexander's projects longer, but that's when we teamed up."

Rob made a mental note of the timing and took another drink of whiskey, relishing the numbing warmth that began to soak into his brain from the back. "So you want to get it over with and just say 'no comment?'" he asked wryly.

Steyn grinned and lifted his own glass to his lips. He answered after the upward spasm of his esophagus subsided. "Let's just imagine you asked and I answered. You seem to have a good grasp on how it would have gone."

"It's that sensitive?" Rob asked.

Steyn shrugged, rested his cigarette against the edge of the ceramic dish holding the candle, and slid back in his chair. He laced his fingers behind his neck so that his elbows stuck out and formed two triangles on either side of his head. "Anyone who said anything would be dealing with Walden, and nobody wants to be in that situation."

"I thought Walden was retired," Rob mused aloud, half-joking.

"Men like Walden don't retire," Steyn sighed. "He's basically Alexander's private investigator now, director of intelligence, spymaster, that kind of thing. Only he doesn't need any orders. He makes his own work. You know the type. I guess he probably considers it a kind of retirement. All the heavy legal lifting gets farmed out to us, and he spends all his time on his little pet projects."

"Pet projects? Like what?"

"You, for one," Steyn chuckled out ominously.

Rob laughed too. With the liquor in him he was becoming

invincible. "Yeah, he seemed to know quite a bit about me. I got the impression he didn't like what he found."

"Walden doesn't like anyone," Steyn replied, laughing again. "Except for the governor. He would die for Alexander if the need arose."

"Why is that?" Rob asked. "Walden struck me as the cynical type. What is different about Governor Alexander?"

"Walden respects strength, endurance, charisma."

"And the governor has all of those?"

Steyn disassembled his relaxed posture and leaned forward. "He better," the lawyer murmured and tipped his glass back for another sip. "For what's coming," he added cryptically before slouching to the side to retrieve the bottle again. He added an inch of liquor to each glass although they were not empty.

"The beast?" Rob asked, keeping things cryptic, hoping for another clue.

"So the old man told you his little riddle," Steyn grunted.

"Yes he did."

The lawyer laughed again, dryly.

"You don't agree with the characterization?" Rob asked.

Steyn shook his head. "It's a little dramatic for my tastes." He paused and stared at the liquid in his glass for a second, entranced. "So what made you want to come see the governor?"

"It's what journalists do," Rob stated bluntly.

"Walden says journalists don't get off their asses anymore. He thinks they are all small-minded cowards. No offense." Steyn was staring directly at Rob now. "Most anyone who wants a statement just calls. You got off your ass. That's probably why you're now one of Walden's projects."

"What does the governor think about journalists?"

"He doesn't."

"I'm supposed to talk to him tomorrow, or so Walden told me."

"The governor?"

Rob nodded.

"I wouldn't count on it," the lawyer said with a shrug.

"I was assured by multiple people that he would speak to me in the morning." A burst of frustration welled up within the journalist. "Has Alexander canceled on people before at the last minute?" He was too tired and careless from the whiskey to hide the acute annoyance in his tone.

Steyn cocked his head to one side. "Don't blame Alexander. He has his hands full. He may forget and you probably shouldn't expect Walden to remind him. You seem like a decent guy, so I just want to prepare you for a bad outcome."

"So you're one of the governor's guys too?" Rob asked bitterly before taking another drink.

"My duty is to the law," Steyn replied cautiously.

"After a few more years of that line you'll be just like Walden." Rob was letting his anger get the better of him, but he could not help it.

"And you'll be writing hit pieces for the folks back home," the lawyer shot back. "The determinist always seeks to escape his own paradigm. Not on my watch."

Rob laughed genuinely. "Walden said basically the same thing about me, that I would try to besmirch the governor whether I wanted to or not."

Steyn blew a geyser of smoke into the air. "There's still time for both of us. I don't even live here. Depending on how long—" He caught himself and gave Rob a grin before continuing in a more careful cadence. "Depending on how long this thing goes on, I could be here for years or just a few more months off and on. I have no strong convictions either way."

"So you just come out here for a while every so often to work for the governor?" Rob asked.

"I work for him all the time," the lawyer explained, reaching forward to rest a hand on the edge of the table. He raised it slightly and let it drop on the lip to punctuate an important word on occasion. "We only come out here when the governor needs a face to face or would prefer we all be in one room. He's a good client, all things considered. We accommodate. Most of the work gets done remotely, though."

Rob took another gulp. His journalistic curiosities were still in fine form even under the fog of exhaustion and whiskey. "This has to be expensive. Is the state paying to keep you guys on retainer?"

Steyn let a short breath out through his nose. "I can't comment on that." His tone was earnest, curt, businesslike, inscrutable.

Rob was not drunk yet, but his brain was floating on a wave of intoxicating fever. "Why did you start working for him?"

"The other lawyer is kind of my mentor in the firm. He's been on this since before I started. He needed the help and I needed an introduction to the business." Steyn downed the rest of his drink and stubbed out his cigarette. "And that's all you get on that subject." He paused and laced his fingers across his chest. "Where are you from anyway? If you don't mind."

"Outside Seattle originally," Rob replied. "You?"

"Des Moines," Steyn answered. Maybe it was all the liquor, but a boyish curiosity seemed to be emerging from him. "You always want to be a journalist?"

"No. I wanted to be a fisherman when I was a kid, but the kind that goes out to the river with a picnic lunch every day. I got this impression that it was a career or something. Then I got older and found out about money. You want to be a lawyer all along?"

"I actually did," Steyn mused pensively. "I used to watch the show Green Acres when I was a kid and I wanted to be like Oliver, a farmer-lawyer in a three-piece suit."

"Not familiar with the show." Rob admitted.

"It's an old one," the lawyer replied. "I was probably more interested in Eva Gabor than anything." He rose from his seat and stretched his arms with a yawn before bending down to retrieve the bottle. "Good to share a drink with someone. Have one for the road." He added some more whiskey to Rob's glass. "I sure hope I'm wrong and you get your meeting tomorrow. It's all work for me, so I have to get some sleep."

Rob took another gulp. It rolled in on him like an angry wave in stormy weather. "Thanks for the drink," he managed.

"No problem," Steyn replied. "You might get an answer to your burning questions sooner than you think," he added with a wink before clattering through the door into the lodge.

Rob sat for a few minutes in the darkness, sipping at the whiskey at intervals. He was not much of a drinker and hoped that the morning would not bring a miserable hangover. He rose and returned to his room a bit unsteadily through the dark corridors of the lodge. Once back in his room, the geometric patterns on the rugs trapped his consciousness for a time and he stood staring at the floor before finally slumping into the chair by the window and waking his laptop. The glow of the screen smeared across the center of his vision against the blackness of the room behind. He finished the whiskey and searched the terms "Tim," "Steyn," and "Lawyer," trying out a few spellings of the last name. He scrolled through a few screens of irrelevant information before coming across what he wanted. Steyn was based out of a firm in Oklahoma City that specialized in finance, banking and governmental law. Rob sat befuddled for a while, the mechanisms in his brain mired in the congealed leavings of liquor.

Finally he slapped down the cover of his laptop and stepped toward the bed. After the first few steps he accelerated uncontrollably as the upper half of his body tilted forward and his legs rushed to keep up. Soon he was leaning forward at forty-five degrees. At the last second, he launched himself forward javelin-like onto the bed to avoid landing facedown on the floor. The bed was much softer than he remembered and it partially enveloped him like a devouring amoeba on impact. He dug and writhed and squirmed blindly to get under the blankets in his half-drunkenness. Rob was too tired and careless at that point to worry what Steyn had said about the possibility that he would be snubbed in the morning.

All he knew at that very moment was that he was late for his flight back to the city. Banks was driving him to the airport in the town car, but the older man's face had changed. The essence of the being sitting beside him in the car was surely Jordan Banks, but the face was unrecognizable. A hollowing sensation of desperation overcame Rob at the prospect of being stuck in Wyoming if he missed the flight. His driver was insisting that they stop somewhere for breakfast.

"We are already late," Rob kept entreating with resigned conviction. He could not stay in this place. He would get out even if he had to hijack a plane. The Jordan Banks with another face laughed in amusement at each protestation. The landscape rushing by outside the car morphed menacingly every few seconds so that it seemed they drove through a kaleidoscope of green jungle, high desert, urban sprawl and then the apocalyptic, smoking ruins of a city after a nuclear blast. It occurred to the journalist that they moved both through time and space so that everywhere at once was both Wyoming and not. The car pulled up to a diner in the middle of a barren field. Rob ran as soon as Banks stopped the car. He left his luggage behind. Nothing would stop him from getting his one ticket out of this place. He somehow instinctively knew the direction of the airport.

After a few moments of running, he came across a forest of massive brambles. They towered above him in a canopy of coiling boughs as he ran. The ground was soft, a dense detritus of a thousand years' slowly, downward drifting debris. A great humming noise grew all around him as he fled further into the thicket. Rob dodged around an especially thick bramble trunk and stumbled over a dome-like mound jutting up from the ground. It caved in to reveal a pale, moist, and pulsating larva the size of a child. He knew what was happening at that moment while recoiling in wordless terror that screamed through his brain in the purest oral tradition of neural doctrine.

The wasps bore down on him from all sides with evil, polymer eyes. Their material seemed that which should not see, but by some wicked miracle of satanic biology they could. The insects swooped and dove at him with clicking mandibles, and he could feel the air of their wings sucking at his skin. Despite knowing that he was likely doomed, his heart rose in his chest at the gratifying roar of airplanes taking off in the distance. He was close to his escape.

Rob broke from the forest into an open field of slate and loose rock which made him lose his footing. A monstrous wasp was on him as soon as he fell, its jaws making a jagged dance into the flesh of his shoulder. He could somehow see the insertion, the evil intent, the skin rent like dough, the viscera oozing out like jelly from a pastry. It was not painful. The venom numbed him so that the violence felt like a robust kneading of his skin and nothing more. An accompanying weakness descended, and the boundaries of his vision darkened and narrowed as he dragged himself over the rocks toward the airport.

Next thing he knew, Walden was standing over him dressed in a doctor's scrubs and shouting orders to a medical staff which bustled around them. Rob was wearing only a gown and lay on his back in a hospital bed. He saw Justine looking at him anxiously yet serenely from the back of the room. At the sight of her, Rob became suddenly aroused and immediately worried that if he got an erection, then Walden would see it. There was no time to do anything about it. Walden leaned over him and peered into his eyes with a look of concern.

"The venom is too concentrated. We have to do a complete blood transfusion." He gripped Rob's shoulder and jabbed it with a needle. "Bring me six bags of type A!"

Fear gripped Rob again. Although unsure of which, he did know at that moment that his blood was not type A. "Wait!" He gasped hoarsely, unable to muster enough strength for more volume. "I can't be given this blood. You'll poison me!"

Walden looked down at him with a furrowed brow and reached up to fasten a surgeon's mask over his mouth. "The patient is delirious. Give him another dose of sedative. If he's too agitated, then he could hurt himself."

Rob became even weaker and his voice fainter as he insisted that they could not give him the blood or he would die.

Walden strapped a cuff to Rob's ankle and fought against the failing resistance to attach the other end to the frame of the bed. "Tie him down!" he declared.

Rob struggled and fought, even as his strength drained out. His head lolled back and he could see the nurses preparing some ancient looking machinery to replace his blood and poison him. Walden finished the left ankle and moved on to the next. Rob thrashed and tugged at his ensnared limb, feeling the pressure of the cuff as he pulled against it. The white illumination of the operating room lights beamed down on him coldly, and a tiny bit of knowing began to expand in the back of his brain. The bit of knowing grew gradually and then exponentially until it enveloped everything and the tide turned so that he realized that he was awake. The cold light still shone down on him and Rob still felt the pressure on his ankle.

The light came from the window across his room. He glanced down at the foot of his bed to see a middle aged man sitting in one of the wooden chairs which had been at the table. In an apparent attempt to wake him, the man gently shook the ankle of Rob's foot that stuck out from the blanket into the cold air of the room. Rob pulled his leg back across the bed in alarm.

"How did you get in here?" he asked in a breathless voice.

The man held his hands up with the palms facing out to indicate that he was no threat. His voice was patient but contained a touch of amusement. "Banks let me in with a spare key." He inclined his head forward and looked at the floor with a wry but also rueful grin. "Banks knocked three times and we tried calling your phone. Consider it a welfare check. You were sleeping like a stone. My availability is somewhat limited today, and I figured you wouldn't want to lose any time to talk."

The realization and recognition struck Rob all at once in an avalanche of horror. Sitting at the foot of his bed was Governor Alexander, who had just a moment before been jostling his leg like a mother to wake him.

PART II

Fleeting Images in a Disembodied Head

CHAPTER

5

Alexander rose and dragged the chair away from the foot of the bed. He moved quickly but delicately. "Sorry for the intrusion. I will meet you downstairs when you are ready," he reassured earnestly, averting his eyes respectfully from Rob's disheveled form. Without another word, the governor left the room and closed the door behind him.

Rob sat frozen on the bed for at least a few minutes and stared blankly at the wood paneling of the door his intruder had just exited. At that moment his brain was incapable of grasping what had transpired. The interaction had occurred so quickly that it seemed to be yet another sequence in his strange dream. It was not. He did not wake up a second time. The ramifications branched out from his consciousness in an infinitely dividing network of probabilities.

He was not hungover, but he felt groggy. His head had the impression that some soft substance had entered and expanded to fill every unused space until a dull, numbing pressure enveloped his brain and filled every fold.

Anger overtook the bewilderment, and he lunged across the mattress to his phone, the author of his downfall, lying unobtrusively on the nightstand. The screen stared back at him blankly, mocking with inscrutable purpose. He held down the power button. The device came on and cycled through a series of colorful splash screens. Somehow between calling his editor and collapsing into bed he had turned off his phone. The details of the evening were hazy. He could think of no reason why he would purposefully do such a thing. The idiocy of his arbitrary misfortune frustrated him even more, and he forcefully threw off the blankets.

The room was colder than anticipated, and Rob gritted his teeth against the chilly wave which puckered the skin on his legs.

All of his suspicions about the governor attempting to manipulate him were thrown into high gear. He dug his nicer shirt and pants from the carry-on bag while grumbling half articulated protestations under his breath. *Alexander watched me while I slept.* The realization arrived with a dreadful finality. *He has gained the ultimate advantage.* Rob turned up the heater below the window and staggered into the bathroom where he began the laborious, scientific undertaking of balancing the fickle and reactionary temperature knobs in the shower. *Alexander must be certain now that my pride is wounded. Surely he thinks that I would not dare venture past the meekest lines of questioning now.*

He stepped into the stream of tepid water, his mind still on fire. *How long was he there at the foot of my bed while I was unconscious and at his mercy? How dare he lay a hand on me without my permission!* He spat at the drain's mocking mouth. *The two of us were alone while I was asleep. I could never have anticipated being at such a disadvantage. How does one overcome such a cataclysm?* He let the spray of water pound on the forehead of his upturned face.

I must be ruthless in my questions, he concluded. *To feel shame is a luxury I no longer have. If there was any weakness in the governor, then I must find it and pull at the thread of hypocrisy until something of significance unravels. Where was that tender spot? Tracy Robinet? Justine? Perhaps there is something related to his brother who died of heroin. Was there something related to his never marrying? What was the fiend on the carousel of Alexander's mind, the monstrosity that he and we all have? The thing that comes around at intervals in the constant rotation of thoughts and causes us to look away from its horrible face before it becomes lost again in the mundane orbit around the supermassive gravity of the ego? I must discover it and take advantage.*

This dogged desire to dig up what is most damaging must be what Walden felt when he pressured Robinet to give her story. I will not be haunted by it as he is. The thought of Walden sent a brief hallucinatory vision through his mind. It was so strong that he almost thought he was still dreaming. Rob had a sudden, neurological impression of Arthur Walden slipping him a tranquilizer via Steyn's whiskey and then sneaking into his room in the dead of night to turn off his phone. The idea was so ludicrous that Rob was not even sure how it had entered his mind. He laughed in the shower for a moment before turning off the water, drying himself, and dressing. He took his recorder, phone, and notebook and a light jacket with him out into the hallway.

Banks' office door was open, and the elderly concierge caught sight of him immediately over a large book he had propped on his desk. He let it drop without marking his place and came out into the corridor. Rob concluded that it was merely a prop to make Banks look occupied until his guest emerged.

"Mr. Coen, I'm very sorry for the intrusion. You were going to miss breakfast, so I called your phone a number of times with no luck. Then the governor asked after you, since he was free, and by then you had missed breakfast for certain. I tried knocking and you didn't answer, so the governor said he would go ahead and check on you." He let out the words in a long stream with his hands clasped and head slightly inclined forward. "I hope we didn't intrude in a way that undermined our attempts at hospitality."

"It's fine. My fault," Rob stated in a tone less reassuring than Banks was looking for. "I'm still on Eastern time, so I couldn't sleep. I ran into one of the lawyer fellows and we shared a drink, so I was out pretty cold."

"Lawyer fellows?" Banks asked with a look of confusion.

"Yeah, he said his name was Steyn."

"Oh, yes, Tim Steyn," Banks remarked with a tone of realization. "I think the governor is waiting for you down in the mess hall. I'm not sure how much time he has for you this morning, but he was eager to get started."

"I won't keep him waiting," Rob assured the older man and turned to navigate the halls down to the bottom floor. If word of this got to Margaret, then he would be on the shit list until the end of his career at the paper.

The lodge was cold and empty. Breakfast had been over for an hour and the staff and workers had all left. Rob descended into the entry room and passed through the double doors onto the gray, stone floor of the dining hall. White light streamed into the massive room from the windows in the angled ceiling high above. The huge space echoed with every scrape of his shoes on the stone. The hearths rested cavernous, dark, and still. He meandered between the tables for a time, focusing his gaze on the ground and trying to quiet his mind. Despite this setback, Margaret and her superiors were expecting great things from him, so there was no balking at the events of the morning. From this point on he did not have the luxury of looking after his own social comfort.

A clattering noise echoed out into the hall from somewhere behind the wide serving counter. He stared in the direction of the sound briefly before realizing that he should investigate. It was most likely caused by Governor Alexander after all, and the sooner he got this interview started the better. Rob slipped through a narrow opening in the counter and around a half-wall which separated the kitchen from the rest of the hall. He stopped in a wide entry and peered at the governor who, entirely unaware of his presence, stood facing away from him in a sea of stainless steel.

James Alexander was very recognizable from all the photos Rob had seen in his research, although he did not look exactly the same. Either he was one of those sorts of people who looked slightly different in person than they do in photographs, due to some morphism of constant motion that cannot be captured in a single frame, or simply because journalists tended to pick a certain kind of photo of him for their articles which bore an expression uncommon in his everyday state of being. Whatever the reason, Rob was struck by the odd sensation that he stared at an unreal version of the governor who weaved back and forth like an anxious horse between an imposing commercial-grade refrigerator and the countertop beside a large, gas range.

Alexander was a little above average height with high and tight styled, salt and pepper hair. His chin and cheeks bore a few days' worth of matching stubble and his features looked more creased and tired than Rob had expected. He was very fit, although thinner in the limbs than one would assume for his body type, as though he had stopped eating consistently of late. He wore a green flannel shirt, tan work pants, and brown hiking boots. He paused in his movements and held the fridge open with one hand while raising the other to the back of his head where it scratched absent-mindedly. He was in the quintessential male posture, transfixed in front of the glowing opening.

Rob decided that it was probably time to make his presence known. As much as it galled him, he opened with an apology. "Governor Alexander, I would like to thank you for your hospitality and apologize for any inconvenience I caused this morning. I suppose I'm still in the wrong time zone," he finished in a tone that indicated he would say more but could not think of anything else to add.

The governor had twisted the top half of his body part way around and listened intently as his guest spoke. Once certain that Rob was finished, he nodded. "And I am sorry, Mr. Coen, for any intrusion into your privacy. I spend much time with the State Corps, and we are not much for boundaries of personal space in the barracks. I understand that it is something to which you are not accustomed." He paused and gave a tired smile. "And the title is unnecessary. Call me James. Steyn told me he kept you up late with his boozing. No hard feelings. Do you like your eggs scrambled?"

The non-sequitur question caught Rob a bit off guard.

"No need for Mr. Coen. Call me Rob. And scrambled is fine. Thank you."

He was coming to the realization that the governor intended to cook breakfast for both of them right then and there. It seemed effortless how in one moment he assured all past debts were forgotten before seamlessly maneuvering himself back into the position of suzerain to those around him. Perhaps Rob was a special case.

"Do you mind if I record us for accuracy and transcription?" Rob asked, feeling awkward at standing impotently in the doorway without a clear idea of what else to do.

Alexander, now crouching in front of the fridge, answered without turning or rising. "Not at all. You can have bacon, yes?" At the question, the governor did turn his head.

"Yes," Rob stated cautiously, not entirely sure of the reason for the question. He had his suspicions.

Alexander had noted the reluctance in the reply. He stated with his rueful smile. "I didn't want to assume either way if you're kosher. Arthur debriefs me whether I ask for it or not. He told me your uncle is a rabbi."

"I'm not religious, only on some holidays and mostly just for the family gatherings."

The governor nodded along and finished compiling his collection of ingredients and kitchen implements onto the counter. A moment of silence passed after Rob finished speaking. Finally Alexander asked, "Did you get along with Justine?" He bent over to start a gas burner after the question was out and hanging between them. He dropped a dollop of butter into a pan. "I trust she represented us well?"

Rob nodded and stepped farther into the room to ensure that

the recorder would capture every word over the sound of the sizzling butter. He leaned against a long rectangular kitchen island a few feet away from the governor, who had turned his back to the stove and stared at him intently. He expected an answer, but the kind he hoped for remained shrouded behind placid, gray eyes.

It was time to be more assertive. Alexander's disarming tactics had worked somewhat effectively up to this point, but Rob's paranoid journalistic tendencies were sharpening gradually as he began to wake more fully. He was determined to parry more when the governor asked questions of his own. "Banks said that you have plans for her, or at least he seemed to think you do."

The steel-colored eyes narrowed, but not in a malicious way. A slightly clouded look came over Alexander's face. "I don't make it a secret that she holds a place of privilege with me. Ultimately, if she wants to get into government, then that's her own choice." He had turned back toward the stove while speaking. "Do you have any issue with onions in the eggs?"

"No."

Alexander began to dice half of a white onion, adeptly rocking the blade back and forth and moving gradually down the pale dome from one side to the other. When he was finished, he tossed the heap into the pan, where it hissed loudly and gave off a rising curtain of steam. He turned and began to crack eggs one by one into a steel mixing bowl, knocking them briskly on the edge with one hand and letting the primordial contents slither out from the empty shrouds. Once satisfied with the number, Alexander hugged the bowl to his abdomen as if he were carrying a child and took up a whisk to beat them all together. His eyes roved over to Rob every so often.

"Are you going to answer my question?" he asked, just as Rob was getting uncomfortable. "About Justine," he qualified.

"She was very professional," Rob replied. It was a placeholder, generic response to buy time for something more substantial. He felt a sudden weakness in his stomach upon realizing that he was squandering this opportunity. Although he did not feel sick from his late night of drinking and was gradually waking more and more, his faculties were still blunted to the point of stagnation. He kicked embryonically through the enveloping retardation of being. "Does she really believe in the state project?" he managed. "She had the sales pitch down, but do you know if she is ambitious about it?”

The whisking paused and then resumed at a more deliberate pace. The governor gave a neutral smile with no feeling behind it, a placeholder of his own. There was no pain or discomfort in the expression, but an apparent effort strove within the workings of his hidden faculties: a steady, faltering buildup of potential energy. Alexander set the bowl on the counter and turned to stir the onions in the pan. They sizzled out in protest. When he replied, his tone was careful and purposeful.

“Justine has never been forced into choosing this place. She volunteered to serve in the Hospitallers of her own volition. She asked to work for my office without any prompting.” He paused and poured the bowl of beaten eggs into the pan with the onions. “Of course none of that answers your question of whether she genuinely believes in the project. Ambition can be more utilitarian than ideological. There is, however, no room for such doubts. I trust her.”

In another pan, Alexander melted more butter and began using a fork to add potato slices from a container. Once he had made a complete layer, he dusted them with a sprinkling of salt and pepper. He moved the eggs to a back burner after pouring shredded cheese on top from another plastic container. He then peeled slices of bacon away from a bulk of meat nestled in a tent of wax paper and placed them in a third skillet which took the place where the eggs had been.

“For the sake of the interview, let’s go back to the beginning,” Rob said, after freeing himself from the mesmerizing display of the cooking process. “You left finance for politics. As far as I can tell, you were doing pretty well for yourself. Why? Why give that up for politics in a state where politics usually can’t make you a big name?”

“I had never really been interested in politics. I just came across the idea while trying to figure out how to change things.” Alexander dug around in a stainless-steel cylinder of utensils on the counter until he found a pair of tongs. As he continued speaking, he used them to turn over the strips of bacon one by one. “The reason I came back and wanted to do anything at all was because of my brother, Anthony’s, death. The timing is no secret if you map it out, and I’m pretty open about it with anybody who asks, which is practically nobody.” He smirked after the last observation. He swapped the tongs for a turner and began flipping the potatoes. The exposed bottom sides showed tantalizing golden blisters. "He overdosed on heroin a number of years back."

"Justine told me," Rob admitted after a beat of silence. "I put two and two together."

The governor nodded. "It was a turbulent time for me. The city wore on me. I made money there and dipped my toes in the river of filth that ran right through its center, but I developed no taste for it. After Anthony died, the iniquity of the place hung over me with a monstrous urgency. I had to get away from it. I traveled around for a little while afterward. I had some money saved up to burn. I saw that the disease was everywhere: poverty, drugs, hopelessness, godlessness. It hung over everything. It was gilded in the city, but everywhere else it was simply ugly. I wanted to do something about it.

"I was certainly not the first person to see this, but I was certain that people needed a spiritual revival, that people were starving for God. That was obvious to me once I noticed it. Man cannot live only on bread, but man can't live without it either. I was torn. I've always been a big reader, and it just so happened that around that time I was reading through Gaddafi's short political treatise, *The Green Book.*"

"You what?" Rob asked, rather surprised but also genuinely unsure that he had heard correctly.

"Muammar Gaddafi's book is derivative of a number of naive, communist ideas of the nineteenth and twentieth centuries. I wouldn't recommend it. I mostly picked it up out of curiosity. He makes the mistake of many others in believing that a direct democracy can create any cohesive body with a singular vector. In this case I mean vector literally, as in velocity in a given direction. The point of a vector is singular. Without a strong leader, the energy of an ideology cannot be unleashed. The moment when Gaddafi did catch my imagination was nearly by accident. He writes that there will be no need for money when a collective has finished." Alexander raised his hands to make air quotes as he recited, "'Transforming society into a fully productive society, and through reaching in production a level where the material needs of the members of society are satisfied.' I took very little from Gaddafi's book save for that passage, which I memorized. It was not even his intent which interested me, but the idea of a society where everyone is directly involved in the unending production of an idea. Each according to his ability, yes, but for what? The progressive advancement of material conditions? As an inspiration for action that doesn't last very long. I had seen the stagnation of the world, which seemed to fall into decay all around me. I wanted to energize it and bring it back to life. People need a reason to live, and most are not bold enough to find it for themselves." Alexander crossed the room to a large diner-style coffee maker. One globe shaped carafe was half full of the dark drink. "I should have offered earlier. You like coffee?"

Rob nodded forcefully.

Alexander opened a cupboard and pulled out two, simple, white-colored, ceramic mugs. "If you take cream, there's some in the fridge."

Rob moved around the island. He found a carton on the bottom shelf and doctored his coffee after Alexander finished pouring. Upon taking the first drink, rejuvenating warmth moved down his extremities in waves of cautious energy.

The governor was back at the food, chopping tomatoes and placing the pieces on top of the mound of scrambled eggs. He turned down the heat under the potatoes and bacon. "It's done. There should be plates and flatware already out in the hall on the counter. I'll bring this out to one of the tables, and we'll just serve ourselves. Bring that pot of coffee with you."

The governor's way of speaking in commands disguised as suggestions was compelling. Rob could see why people obeyed him. The strangeness of the situation was beginning to wear off, and Rob was coming to grips with the possibility that James Alexander, for all his reputation and fiery charisma on the stump, was a simple and gracious person face-to-face. It was a possibility and nothing more. Rob would not let himself be so easily swayed by the outward signs of hospitality. As a journalist it was his purpose to find the hypocrisy. In human stories there are no happy endings, no easy morals with poetic harmony. Hopefully with more time he could uncover the incongruous elements of this presentation-world.

Rob took the coffee out to the dining hall and set it on one of the closest tables before doubling back to retrieve the plates and utensils from the serving counter. Alexander came out of the kitchen with a pan in each hand and towels draped over one arm. The bacon and potatoes had been combined into one pan.

"Do me a favor, Rob, and set two of these out on the table for the pans," Alexander urged, moving his arm to indicate the towels.

Rob took two of the towels and folded them into squares before placing them on the table. Alexander unburdened himself and went back for his cup of coffee and shakers of salt and pepper. After they were both settled, the governor looked around at the contents between them. "My cooking skills are rather rudimentary, so I apologize if anything is bland."

"If it is, then you can read about it later," Rob joked dryly. The comment earned a wry smile from the governor. Rob served himself some of everything and reminded his companion of where they had left off. "So, you were saying that you wanted to change things but hadn't decided on politics?"

Alexander was serving himself at this point and replied as he shoveled potatoes onto his plate with a spoon. "I was a bit hysterical at the time, I'll admit. I was exhilarated to be out of the city, manic even, but that turned into an impatience to do something about the misery I had seen around the country." After transferring the food, the governor shook first the salt and then the pepper shaker vigorously over his eggs and potatoes. He dug in with a knife in one hand and a fork in the other, using them in concert to move and corral the food. Rob was still sitting back and drinking his coffee without touching his utensils. Alexander swallowed his first bite forcefully and his eyes ascended so that he took notice.

"Is everything alright?" he asked.

"Not sure if I'm fully awake," Rob admitted. "Must be the time difference." He took another gulp of coffee and began digging around in the potatoes with his fork. "Not to backtrack too much, but I was curious about one thing concerning your brother if you don't mind."

"No problem at all."

"You mentioned that his death was a catalyst in part for you coming back to Wyoming, but Justine said that she didn't think that you two were close at all."

Alexander nodded and cut in to finish the question. "So you're wondering why it was enough to make such a drastic change in me?"

"Yes," Rob confirmed.

"After he died, then I could never know him more than the little I did. You cannot account the price of losing something you don't know. Honestly, I had been getting sick of the city way of life for a while before then, and Anthony's death made me more acutely aware of the atomizing power of modern life. The allure of success and money stole any chance I had of knowing him. I had chosen not to know him. I was on the brink of leaving, going crazy in the city already when it happened."

Pieces were falling together. *Was it too soon? Should I strike already with a question about Robinet?* Rob considered it while taking his first bite of potatoes. They were a little bland but not bad by any means. He added some salt and pepper while considering the next move. Under all this polite pretense, Rob's pride still stung from his awakening that morning and the violation by physical contact. But would a question about Robinet anger the governor or make him close up? He went for it. "And Tracy Robinet sealed the deal as far as leaving the city?" he asked casually, taking another bite of potatoes.

The governor paused in his eating and looked over at Rob directly in the eyes. His expression was not resentful or begrudging. It was another placeholder, a "Gone Fishing" sign indicating only the indeterminate future return of the occupant. After a few seconds he did return, first showing expressions of wistfulness and then resignation.

"Straight for the juicy heart, then?" he asked.

Rob swallowed his food and qualified the question cautiously, "I'm just trying to understand the chronology. Walden gave me his side of the Robinet business, and it seems that was what made you leave the city for good."

"It's not deception that I did not mention it myself as the major factor. It is more out of the discomfort I have when recalling such things, which is no excuse," Alexander admitted. "Walden is right though, and you were right to catch me." He bit off the end of a piece of bacon and chewed it thoughtfully for a moment, his gray eyes staring unfocused somewhere to the right of Rob's shoulder.

Rob tried his own bacon and was delighted to find that it was the perfect chewy consistency: neither overly burnt, nor limp and underdone. After trying the meat, he moved on to the eggs, which were also very good and required no additional seasoning.

"You know I have visited Tracy Robinet a few times after the whole fiasco in the press?" Alexander asked, still holding his half-eaten bacon aloft between his thumb and forefinger.

Rob paused in his chewing and shook his head. He was just now realizing the scope of what he may uncover. The governor showed no signs of withholding anything. He wanted everything now. The seconds crawled by as though they would never end, and he felt a disorienting dizziness of exhilarating immediacy. *Thank God for the recorder.* His thoughts spun in intersecting microscopic galaxies stared down upon by Werther. He would have to make sense of it all during the autopsy.

Alexander was reminiscing with a slight smile. "The first time I visited her was after my first election victory. She sent me a beautiful handwritten letter apologizing for telling the press about what had happened." He laughed mechanically. "The nation's cultural curators had just spent days skewering me for being the pure manifestation of toxic male abuse of women, and there she was apologizing to me."

"You never told anyone about going to see her?" Rob asked.

Alexander shook his head. "It was my secret to cherish, something to make me smile in solitude. Besides, the election was already over. What would it have gained me besides minor bragging rights and renewed scrutiny from the scribbling, selective moralists? I would not taint such a thing with publicity, not then when it was such a fresh wound. Now it does not matter. It is simply history. Besides, it would have been poetically cruel. I could never do something like that, not when it was so obviously politically expedient." He finished the strip of bacon and took a drink of coffee. "But she said that she wanted to talk to me in person, so I went out to Ohio for part of two days."

Rob said nothing. He ate carefully but furtively, setting his mug and utensils down gingerly so as not to cause any tiny bit of audible disruption.

"She wanted to explain everything from her perspective. I had already heard it all from Walden's point of view at that point, but she clearly felt the need. She was painfully honest about the whole thing and even explained how she had been very attracted to me back when we worked together and how that likely largely contributed to the initial incident and misunderstanding. She was willing to take the entire burden of the whole event. She said that I couldn't be blamed for my actions, since my brother had just died, and she didn't know until after. I told her that such a gracious pardoning was unnecessary. No tragedy could excuse my rashness. We mused at length about how such a big deal had been stirred up about something we both clearly were willing to forgive and forget. She initially completely blamed Walden, which is understandable. He can come across as villainous."

Alexander paused and gestured at Rob with an empty fork. "Walden did tell you all the details, that he was the one who tracked her down and started the whole thing, right?"

"Yes." Rob confirmed.

"Anyway," the governor continued with a wave of his free hand, "she saw him as the evil author of the whole thing. I had to explain to her that he was put onto it by his former employer, the previous governor, and that he would never have done it unless it was his job. He was duty-bound to see it through and done right. Doing it right may have meant cruelty to me and her, but that was not his imperative. She was very hung up on what evil force it was that could compel Walden to exploit her against me when it was not in either of their natures." He cast a knowing glance at Rob for a moment. "I'm sure you have seen it at work in some of your fellow journalists as well, the great invisible force which compels them to violate decency?"

Rob shrugged. "Anyone will do things they know are wrong if they believe they must in order to keep what they have or get what they want in the future."

"Maybe," Governor Alexander replied in a somewhat distant tone. "Or maybe it's all part of one, big chain of cause and effect, energy activating energy on down the line from some distant quasar until, the next thing you know, you're sabotaging the political campaign of some poor sap you've never even met."

"Seems a little melodramatic," Rob jabbed.

The governor smiled while heaping more eggs and bacon onto his plate. He seasoned the eggs while responding, "Perhaps I'm close to Spinoza on this. If everything that is, is within the realm of God, then what's the difference between a quasar and a demonic force except for the name?" He shrugged. "Of course that's about as far as my kinship with Spinoza goes."

"I'm rusty on my philosophy," Rob admitted, figuring it would be better to admit his ignorance right away and avoid embarrassment later when pretending he had some toothless insight.

A look flashed across the governor's face for an instant, and Rob could only catch a glimmer of what it might mean. "Most are," Alexander mused. "Sometimes I think I have more in common with the dead than the living." He chewed a bite of egg for a moment. "The earlier point is that if you trace cause and effect back far enough from Walden to Collins, then it leads to UBI Energy. They wanted Collins in for access to tax breaks and guarantees on land lease proposals. All of that was to maintain their extraction and distribution machine to meet the demand for energy. Sometimes I wonder if you were to measure the amount of energy that went into getting Tracy Robinet to go on the record against me, how much volume that would be in oil or natural gas. I don't see the difference in calling it corporate greed or literally tracing it back to the energy within a great big well of oil. Personify it if you want: gleaming darkly, slithering in on itself underground, and silently plotting its escape for centuries before meeting air and passing energy on into the chain reaction simply because that's what it does. It sets things in motion: vehicles, airplanes, people. It doesn't matter who found it. It uses them and anyone indiscriminately as the means of escape into combustion and transformation. In turn, nobody can deny those who have the energy. In this state there has always been the fear with Collins and those before him that UBI quit us."

"You didn't fear that?" Rob asked.

"Not right away. I was too naive. It wasn't until after the election when I hired Walden on as my legal counsel that I understood how powerful UBI was and how much they influenced politics in the state while Collins was governor. It makes that first win all the more unbelievable now that I know what was stacked against me and how unaware I was. Of course I knew that they were one of the biggest employers in the state and that they generated huge revenue, but I had little time to fathom the implications of such facts. I had spent much of my campaign in the churches and small towns. I had no intention of clashing with UBI after I was elected, primarily because I had not even considered it. So long as their relationship with the state was mutually beneficial, then I had no reason to fight them."

Alexander took a few bites and chewed quickly before swallowing. "It wasn't until after I was elected that Walden gave me an in-depth rundown of what had been going on. UBI had sold Collins a line about needing their taxes kept favorable enough to keep their operations in the state and field their workforce. The threat was not explicit but present: taxes raise, they move out. If that happens, then unemployment spikes and approval tanks, and 'Goodbye, Governor.'"

"So then it would be fine unless you wanted to tax them more. You said that you had no reason to face off with them."

Alexander laughed. "You have to realize how tricky of a situation I was in after getting elected. The state legislature was cautious of me. I was not their kind of political animal, and, as an independent, I did not have any die-hard political allies. I had my own plans, based on my campaign, but the state legislature was interested in one thing: revenue. In this state, the easiest way to get revenue is by selling or leasing state land."

"To UBI," Rob added in a moment of realization.

"Exactly," Alexander confirmed. "UBI was expecting land leases. The way it works is that any private group can petition the state board of land commissioners for a tract to be approved for auction. Collins had been very open to approving whatever he could. UBI was expecting more of the same. I had some of my own ideas for land use, though. I needed land for the Wyoming Project."

"Then why not just use it?"

"Land owned by the state is managed for revenue for schools and other state funds. It would be extremely unpopular with the legislature if I tried using it for anything that didn't add to the ledger books. That's one reason why they were so down on the idea for Mount Calvary. The problem was that I wanted land for the future State Corps camps and settlement for small-time farmers who wanted to move here and get a fresh start. To the legislature, that was just throwing away money. I had to find a way to appease UBI and the other energy companies and keep the legislature happy without selling out everything I stood for in the campaign."

"That's quite the situation to walk into," Rob mused.

Alexander laughed again. "Well, the first, big event of my governorship was the squabble with the state university, but everyone knows all about that. It was a media circus, so I won't bore you with that recollection. The thing about the school was that I knew they had to be completely neutralized. The problem with most reactionaries when they get elected is that they assume a democratic mandate is enough and that the massive infrastructure of the status quo will leave them alone. That's never the case. The agents of the status quo don't care about democracy. If the people vote somebody the status quo doesn't like into power, then they will work tirelessly to either remove or frustrate them. The modern praise of liberalism and democracy is mostly a lie of expediency. Mass media makes it very easy to spread heavily curated ideas and information. Educational institutions catch people young and turn them to the will of established ideologues. I had to get the school under control because it was a tool of that same titanic power. The fact that the administration went after me right away was only proof of that. So I bit the bullet and got it over with."

"You realize that would sound pretty paranoid to a lot of people," Rob replied, trying to avoid making the observation sound too accusatory in tone.

Governor Alexander smiled sadly. "You have to understand. I lived in the world of finance. I knew how these structures operated. I moved their assets around and saw what nonprofits they set up and where they put their money. This world of competing ideologies you see in the media is all a play projected over the real inner workings, which is a cold war of monetary interests. Don't get me wrong, there is real good and evil, there are better forces and worse, but you won't hear about them on the nightly news. I am not paranoid in the least." The last statement was a little colder than what came before. Alexander paused and added, "Forgive me for my defensiveness."

Rob took his last bite and set the fork down with a shrug. "No problem."

"More coffee?" the governor asked, lifting the carafe.

"Yes, please."

Alexander had finished his food as well, and they sat back in their chairs taking occasional sips of coffee.

"So how did you resolve the situation with the legislature and UBI?" Rob coaxed, when it looked like his companion was staring off again with the unfocused look from before. As he awaited a reply, he made a note in his pad about Alexander's reaction to the implication of paranoia. He had taken it personally. Rob wondered if it had anything to do with all the lawyers hanging around the lodge and the secret meetings nobody would discuss. He began exploring avenues of how he might eventually broach the subject without also ruining his chances for other information.

The governor resumed his narrative. "The key was figuring out how to get UBI to invest more in the state without driving them to spiteful retaliations. It was like a hostage situation. They were the ones who asked for a meeting soon after I was sworn in. I had no idea what to expect. Walden said that Collins was a complete sucker for them. They had given him a maximum contribution through their PAC and a speaking fee for talking at some energy summit. Nobody talked about how transactional it all was, but anyone who squinted their eyes to look a little closer could see it right away.

"They sent their VP of operations in the state to meet and feel me out, since they had no idea where I stood on their business. I had said a great deal in the campaign about the evils of money in politics but nothing specific enough to make them hostile out of the gate. Walden told me to make no promises and be as cold as possible, let them stew on it and expect the worst. He said that approach improved my chances of shaking some money out of them for my constituents. Before the meeting, I had to give myself a crash course on gas and oil land leases and UBI's financials over the past few years. I knew in the back of my mind that I was letting Walden run me as the arbiter of his revenge. It was the only time I let it happen. I learned that, while Walden is almost super-humanly knowledgeable and conveniently amoral, his broader pragmatism ends the moment he has decided on an object for destruction. He did the same to me. It explained why he went through with torturing Tracy Robinet despite his well-concealed, inner anguish. He knows everything about the rudder and the wheel, the whole theory of operation of every mechanism in the ship, but I never let him take the helm."

Governor Alexander paused and leaned forward, lacing his fingers loosely over his empty plate. "So the VP wanted to have breakfast, and Walden insisted on being there as well. He said that he had to be present and that I may have to play along with him when I wasn't sure what was being said. We met at this diner that had a meeting room in the back. Lots of business folks in Jackson use it when they want a little privacy. Walden told me he used to do most of his client meetings there. The VP opened with a hard line, saying that UBI expected everything to stay in place: tax rates, land lease fees, and royalties. After making those assumptions clear, Heath, that was his name, said they had been working with Collins to submit for numerous large tracts of land for mineral leases, and that they had been assured they would go through the process with minimal difficulties."

"Was that a problem?" Rob asked.

"Not exactly. It would get the legislature what they wanted, which was revenue. We told Heath that we would get back to him, and that they could submit the proposals if they liked but made no promises. It was after that meeting that I came up with an idea.

If I could tie the Wyoming Plan to future leasing, then the legislature would get what they wanted and UBI and the other energy companies would just give it to me outright."

"How?" Rob was engrossed at this point.

"It was clear that UBI had a plan with those leases, one they had been working on for a while before I got into office. If I could tie land for the Wyoming Plan to future leases, then there would be an incentive for energy companies to help foot the bill, while satisfying the state government as well. My basic idea was this: develop a new kind of lease where a company can submit to lease more than they intended to use, gift a portion to the governor's office of the Wyoming Plan, and receive a discount on their leasing fees for the tract as a whole."

"Would that require a change in the law?" Rob asked.

"Well, yes, but not a change in the state constitution. The State Board of Land Commissioners operates under the governor's discretion. The primary members are me and the secretary of state. The only issues were making sure the state legislature was open to the idea and that we could get UBI to change their pending land tract requests to reflect such a change. If we could get them on board, then it would prove to the legislature that such a leasing system was fiscally responsible and legitimize that Wyoming Plan. At that point it was still just an idea in my head. There was no actual project yet. The state legislature was already skittish about me trying to rule by fiat. The national press gave them plenty of reason. The best way to introduce an actual Wyoming Plan was by coordinating it in a mutually beneficial way with a third party like UBI."

"I thought they were holding you hostage."

"They still were, but I hoped to use them to muscle the state legislature into my corner."

"Were they agreeable?"

"That's where it got difficult," Alexander replied. "We arranged another meeting with Heath and gave him a run-down of the idea and asked if it was something viable. Walden had been telling me all along to keep my expectation low, but I was optimistic. UBI wanted a much better leasing rate than was reasonable. Heath asked why they should do me a favor if it didn't benefit them substantially. My reputation was already so negative in the press that even doing business in the state, let alone making special partnerships, was negative publicity for the company. It wasn't an unexpected development, but it was disappointing. He knew how much weight they had to throw around."

"Were they just giving you a hard line, or was it spite?"

Alexander smiled. "You know, the funny thing is that it was a little of both. After Collins lost the election, they had a chair open for him on the board of UBI, and he took it right away. There is no doubt in my mind that he was responsible and wanted to make me pay for winning the election."

"So what options did you have at that point?"

"I had the Arthur Walden option," Alexander explained slyly. "UBI had Collins working things on their end, someone who knew the ins and outs of Wyoming state policy and finances, but I had someone who knew more than a few of UBI's and Collins' dirty secrets. Once Heath made it clear that they felt no obligation to work with me on my leasing plan, I was pretty distraught. At that point I figured I was utterly powerless to make any change, stuck between the legislature which wanted revenue and UBI which wanted leases and nobody wanting the Wyoming Plan. Walden let me mope around for a few days before sitting me down and explaining that he had a few of his friends from Oklahoma City dig around and find something actionable on Collins and UBI from when he was governor."

Rob raised an eyebrow. "Blackmail?"

"That was my concern as well. I wanted UBI's cooperation, but I also did not want them to turn openly hostile if threatened with legal action. At the same time, if we did find something actionable on them from the Collins years and not act on it in exchange for their cooperation, then that would be extremely unethical. As much as it pained me, I told Arthur to let it rest."

"So then what did you do?"

"I figured it was a loss. I kept working on practical ways to implement the Wyoming Plan while discharging my duties as governor, impotent as they would be at that point. A few weeks later I got word that UBI muscled Collins off the board and that they wanted to meet with me."

"Just like that?"

"Just like that. I have no earthly idea what happened in that time after our second meeting. I'm sure Walden must have put the scare of their lives into them somehow, but I have never asked him, and I never will. The less I know the better."

"And so UBI agreed to the potential new leasing terms?"

"They did, with some minor tweaks here and there. Once I had them on board, I wanted to address the state legislature to make sure they were on board. I would need them to make the Wyoming Plan a viable force in the government. As governor I can make new departments in the executive, but any funding has to come through appropriations. I needed the legislature. So I called for a special session and explained my plan and ideas to them, and it actually went pretty well. That's where the momentum really picked up for what eventually became the State Corps and Mount Calvary."

"All from some unknown workings of Arthur Walden," Rob mused.

Governor Alexander smiled a little sadly in reminiscence. "I didn't have a great handle on Walden at that point. I had no understanding that he was a man of complex and intricate material. There is nothing spiritual or ideological about him. I doubt he believes in the soul. He is a man crafted by the watchmaker god with utterly precise mechanisms that all operate with merciless accuracy. His cunning is very complementary to my own idealistic or romantic tendencies, although he has grown somewhat kinder in my company."

A question had coalesced in the back of Rob's mind. He had stumbled on a loose seam in the smooth grade of Alexander's moral countenance. He waited for the ruminant pause at the end of the recollection before asking, "You are a very religious man. Your government and leadership are unreservedly Christian. Have you made no attempt to save Arthur Walden's soul?"

The governor looked a little surprised for a moment. He leaned forward in his seat and frowned in contemplation. "Are you going to write about this in your article?"

"Not likely, but I wouldn't say so unequivocally. Call it extracurricular curiosity."

Alexander leaned back in his chair, reassured by some unknown inward articulation. The frown was gone, and he smiled almost serenely. "I will speak with you about such things in as detailed a fashion as you please. I trust your judgment and deal with everyone as honestly as I can. There is no use in backing away from difficult or existential topics. Let me finish first with explaining the early days, and then we can talk about the conversion of Arthur Walden. Deal?"

Rob nodded.

"During my address, I explained the new leasing policy and that I had promised my voters during the campaign that the Wyoming Plan would change the direction of the state. I asked them for a modest start to put together a department and exploratory committee. The sum was reasonable. They knew that it would only be the beginning and that I would ask for more money. I had more than a few state senators asking me afterward for assurances that the Department of the Wyoming Plan be profitable, or at least fiscally responsible. They started bogging me down in requirements and demands before agreeing to give me a vote of confidence."

"Pragmatists to the end."

"And I can't blame them," Alexander admitted with a slight shrug. "This state has often walked a fine line, at the mercy of greater powers, having to cling doggedly to the few reliable sources of revenue. That's when I put the idea for the monument on the fast track."

"It seems like that would be the hardest sell of all," Rob interrupted as politely as he could.

"I wasn't overly interested in selling them on the practicality of the Wyoming Plan right away. My ideas for the state required a radical change in perspective for the legislature. I knew that I would have to bully them into seeing things my way, or at least bully them into seeing that the wind was blowing my way. You see, Mount Calvary was very popular in the campaign. I talked about it from the stump all the time. It wasn't so much the explicitly Christian nature of the idea as much as it was the idea of a monument to set the state apart, the idea that they could participate in the next wonder of the world. I had the people behind me. The legislature thought they had all the power to deny me funding, so I started the campaign to break ground on the monument with voluntary donations. It took off not just here but as a national phenomenon. It was more popular than I could have ever guessed. The wave of support didn't solve my problems with the legislature, but it set the tone."

Alexander paused and narrowed his eyes in thought for a moment before recalling Rob's prior question. "Now about your other question on the soul and salvation of Arthur Walden. It seems as much a question about my nature as it is about his nature. The question wonders whether it is hypocritical for me to believe in the salvation of the eternal human soul and the virtue of a Christ-like manner of living while also admiring Walden and using him for his ruthless utilitarian mind, which at times can be rather un-Christian. Does that not entail taking advantage of someone due to the very nature of them not being in a state of grace?"

Rob had not thought through the question to that depth when he had asked, at least not consciously. Now that he heard it out loud, his unrealized fingerprints were all over the structure, right down to the use of the word "hypocrisy." A startling genius hid behind Alexander's sad smiles and disarmingly earnest manner of speaking. Rob kept his face as neutral as possible to provide no indication of how close the governor's characterization of his thinking really was.

Alexander resumed, "The nature of the question displays a level of understanding and cunning that is surprising and admirable. You are admittedly not a religious man, yet you are able to think like one for the purposes of interrogation. *The Times* sent the right guy."

Rob felt a little warmth spreading below his collar. The compliment had been given in such a quick and easy manner, yet it was possibly the nicest thing anyone had ever said to him. Even while steeling himself against the flattery, Rob felt a weakness in the base of his throat and a slight stinging in the corners of his eyes. He silently cursed himself for the softness, for letting his guard down for even an instant.

The governor was speaking again. "My explanation may not be adequate for you, but I do have one. There is something about me which Arthur Walden finds compelling. I don't say this out of pride, but because he has said so himself. Walden does not respond to Christian apologetics. I have tried to speak to him in those terms before, and he is like a stone. He is not moved emotionally by displays of religious fervor. If I can in any way reflect the grace of God and be an example to Arthur Walden, then my hope is that he can discover something of God through our relationship." He gave his sad smile again. "As I said, the explanation may not be adequate for you."

Alexander rose and began collecting the plates and silverware. Rob stood quickly and took up the pans so as not to be waited on again. As they walked toward the kitchen with the items from the table Alexander asked, "Would you like to go for a walk? I walk every morning to clear my head."

"That sounds good," Rob agreed.

They left the dishes in one of the large basin sinks and crossed back through the massive, echoing hall, through the entry and exited out onto the wraparound porch. The air pushed coolly against them, despite the sun being out and the sky wholly bereft of clouds. A few work trucks with State Corps markings rolled by as they stepped down onto the path. Alexander led around the side of the building and past the parking area where the gravel of the walkway ran out.

"There is a trail here which goes up the mountain behind the lodge," the governor explained.

Rob followed onto a well-worn dirt ribbon leading up through some sparse brush and a screen of trees. On the other side, they hit an open incline populated with short prairie grass and occasional tufts of newly grown weeds and flowers. Rob was unaccustomed to the big open sky and felt a bit of vertigo as they walked up the shallow grade into the all-absorbing entity above. The city did not offer such sights. He felt himself thinking of what it must be like to be in space, tethered to a tiny oasis of human machinery and staring out into an unspeakable infinity.

His head was still somewhat submerged in the gelatinous residue of his deep slumber the night before, but a manic energy had at some point entered his skull through the back door from the yard where it had been performing sets of jumping jacks and shadow boxing with the tire swing. Earlier, while he slept, it had trembled secretly in the dark, cool interior of the lodge with the nocturnal anticipation of the child waiting for the first lazy-lidded peek of the sun and subterranean sounds of his father's boots below in the hall. Then it rose and fumbled in the half-light for the materials needed for a day of fishing. Rob smirked. He had only one memory of such a morning with his father and it was a disappointment. Now it was up to him alone to lie in wait for some tug at the end of the line.

Governor Alexander walked ahead on the trail, looking down his shoulder to the left as they rose above the lodge. They could see the buildings of the camp spread out among the collection of pine and spruce trees. The air smelled of miniscule bits of plant sexuality and earth. The birds let out loud shouts of indeterminate purpose.

Rob called ahead to his companion, "So, things have worked out with UBI since you made the deal?"

"With a few minor squabbles, yes," the governor replied with a nod. "We have reached a few significant agreements on land leases with the new method. One of the first packages was used for Mount Calvary. That alone makes it worthwhile in my book."

"Been meaning to ask you about that. Why the monument?"

Alexander glanced back with a slight almost sheepish smile. "It was my intent from the beginning to make this state into a shelter for decent folks who feared God and respected hard work. I wanted to physically anchor that idea in this place. Mount Calvary is the nail sunken in the wall, holding fast a complaint against the world and what it has become. Monuments are more powerful than the materials and men that make them. They inscribe ideas on generations of the hearts that see them. It claims land for a sojourning and invisible power. A monument is a prayer of a whole people."

"But it was your prayer to start with," Rob retorted.

"I didn't impose it by fiat, if that's what you're implying." Alexander's head turned part way around again and the look was sharper this time, although not genuinely wounded. "Much of it was funded by individuals and donors. It had popular support."

Rob smiled wryly. "Democracy at work."

"Democracy is only as good as the people voting. The modern mind does not want to believe that there can be a wicked or unjust people. Our intellectual betters insist that only consumer demand determines what ought to be created or destroyed. The people cannot be wrong, so long as their consumption is necessary for the empire to function."

"And here we are again with the empire. First Justine and then Walden and now you. It runs through you all like a refrain."

Alexander made a muffled noise which could have been a chuckle, but Rob could not tell. "The refrain runs through you as well. We are all born hostages."

"Hostages of what, the federal government?" *Was this really it?* Rob was beginning to get that delirious sour-stomach feeling most commonly felt when he was running up against a deadline and had consumed nothing but large amounts of coffee. The mania was winning, and he was getting grim and careless. *Was the governor simply an amalgamation of collected talk radio bromides? It was disappointing.*

"Not the federal government per se," Alexander corrected. "Although that is part of it. The entity which holds us hostage is more likely similar to that power nestled in the center of that distant quasar."

"Just to clarify, you're not being literal about the quasar?" Rob asked.

"'And the third angel sounded, and there fell a great star from heaven, burning as it were a lamp, and it fell upon the third part of the rivers, and upon the fountains of waters; And the name of the star is called Wormwood: and the third part of the waters became wormwood; and many men died of the waters, because they were made bitter.'" Alexander recited the scripture in a reverent tone. "When it comes to the cosmic, who is to say what is literal and what is not? As far as my specific example, it is metaphorical as far as I know."

"If that's the case, then how do you shelter people from something you can't even describe or identify?" Rob asked, a bit frustrated by all the abstraction.

"'The spirit of the Lord God is upon me; because the Lord hath anointed me to preach good tidings unto the meek; He hath sent me to bind up the brokenhearted, to proclaim liberty to the captives, and the opening of the prison to them that are bound.'" Alexander paused after reciting the words and added, "You can only try."

"You actually think that there is, well, something coming that you need to protect people from?" The journalist was more than a little dumbfounded. "The way you talk about protecting them is, well, it sounds apocalyptic." He avoided using the word "paranoid" again.

"Don't mistake my quoting of Revelation for anything more than illustrating the connectedness of the causal, the cosmic, and the divine. You'll have to look to someone else if you want a dominionist cutout. I don't spend my days making diagrams of the Old Testament and the news headlines." The governor had been looking ahead as they talked. There had been a slight touch of impatience and tiredness in his voice in the atypically terse reply.

"You'll have to forgive me. I'm not well versed in the specifics of competing Christian theologies," Rob admitted. It was true, but also a bit of an olive branch.

"And I should know that," the governor replied. "I should not mistake honest ignorance for malice. Once bitten, twice shy, and when you're bitten a thousand times..." He trailed off.

The world was not kind to Governor James Alexander. The world had its reasons, but Rob had to admit that he could not really understand the level of constant derision and scrutiny the man underwent. Outside of his state and a few sympathetic pockets nearby, he was a pariah, the butt of countless jokes, the scapegoat of a thousand jeering political monologues. He was an alien being, an invading amoeba in the American system which sought to expel him with both active panaceas and involuntary convulsions. Rob did not feel sorry for the governor, but he did understand a little better the circumstances of his present existence. Perhaps he was born a few hundred years too late.

"So you just wanted to attract a certain kind of people and protect them against a world hostile to their way of life?" It was Rob's best shot.

"Essentially yes," Alexander confirmed. "That came to realization through the Wyoming Plan." He stopped and turned toward the camp, which was much more distant now, and looked over it with his hands rested on his hips. "This is why the monument was so essential. We needed a big project to attract people and work and keep the momentum up. I didn't just want to protect the people here, I wanted the state to be a lighthouse to draw in the others around the nation who needed protecting as well."

They walked a little further and came across a large, craggy boulder sunken into the side of the hill. They could see very far now, and Rob spied the gleaming ribbon of the Snake River beyond the road. The grass around them was newly grown in the spring eruption, and the supple deep green flowering plants which rose above it showed the first signs of budding. A few large birds wheeled in an enormous sky so blue that nearest the sun it looked the color of paper. The small of Alexander's back went against the boulder and he pushed his hands into the front pockets of his work pants in an oddly boyish stance.

His way of speaking seemed even more careless and free. "It was then that I came into my own. Walden has always been wise and clever as a serpent when it comes to the machinations of law and the games of interpersonal politics. He was always ready to shed the skin of conviction for a new set of convenient principles." He paused and cocked his head slightly before shaking it. "No, that's not entirely accurate. That is what an idealistic observer thinks. It would be more accurate to say that he has no stated principles apart from success or victory in an endeavor. Either way, he was of little use to me when it came to inspiring the leadership of the state to a common purpose. So, I took it upon myself to organize the first Wyoming State Leadership Convention. It was my way of taking a gradual first step with the Department of the Wyoming Plan."

Rob felt a stifled, strangled feeling at the name of the event. Such things caused a near-incapacitating allergic reaction in him. In his research during the prior days he had read a fair amount about the annual event. Politicians, religious leaders, and people of note all gathered to re-energize the whirling dervish that was the ever-advancing march of the new Wyoming. It was a collective manifestation of all the qualities of the patriarchal, American, white male.

Alexander pulled his hands from his pockets and folded his arms across his chest. "It was an attempt to break through the cynicism and align the whole state with the Wyoming Plan."

"Clearly it worked," Rob observed, propping an elbow against the large stone a few feet away from Alexander's point of contact.

"Not so simple as that," Alexander mused softly while slowly shaking his head. "Plenty of the politicians in the state were good friends with Collins and his retinue. He had influence, even after UBI muscled him out. Who was I to stand up to a system of leadership which had been around for so long before my time? Some of them had been owned by UBI for decades."

"I thought you had a cooperative relationship with UBI."

"They are a many-headed beast," Alexander grunted. "You can

speak to one face which smiles while another bares its teeth behind your back. They are all connected to the same belly, which is hungry as a furnace. The leasing agreement was à la carte. General goodwill is not always a result when politics works with corporate power, nor would one really want it to be. Every interaction is just a single transaction."

"Unless you sell out," Rob qualified.

"Unless that," Alexander agreed with a slight nod. "I worked on the politicians at that first convention though, and I had a strong ally from the campaign: Bill Stevens."

If the cultural elite of the country were allergic to James Alexander, then Bill Stevens was the activating catalyst which made the symptoms unbearable. Stevens was a firebrand preacher who had gained some popularity before the fateful Wyoming governor's race. The difficulty for the intellectual opponents who debated Bill Stevens was that he proved a far more multifaceted character than a common Christian preacher. He did not rely on charisma alone, although it was something he possessed in surplus. The most dangerous thing about Stevens was his broad mastery of intellectual pursuits. The man possessed a PhD in psychology and knew the lingo of the academic elite because he was one of them. He argued for traditional gender roles from the perspective of biology as well as scripture, advocated for sexual chastity from the perspective of evolutionary psychology and genetics, and praised Christian faith not only for its veracity, but also for the societal boons created by religious observance. Then at the end of all those argumentative methods, he would turn against the institutions of psychology and academics themselves, undermining his own previous points simply because he could. He often ended with some statement such as, "I don't need psychology or sociology to prove the efficacy of Christianity. It can stand on its own. But I do like to make them dance for me." His approach had made him one of the most loved and hated men in the country. When James Alexander stepped onto the political scene, Bill Stevens saw his equal, the breath to his flame, one whom he could illuminate and could in turn propel him to greater heights. It was not an exaggeration to say that Alexander would not likely have become governor without the prior rise of Bill Stevens.

Alexander had continued speaking. "I told Bill I would need his considerable talents at the first Leadership Convention. I knew what was necessary and had in mind that line from Gaddafi about the mobilization of a whole people. Such movements are militant by nature, and I had access to the most charismatic and militant man of God I had ever met." Alexander adjusted his back against the boulder. "When I addressed the state legislature that first time, I presented the general points of the Wyoming Plan. It was in its infant stages in my mind. The first Leadership Convention was an opportunity to lay out more specific goals, work to actually convince some people. You see, a wide libertarian streak runs through this state. It always has. Moral authority does not largely appeal to the politicians nor a fair share of the people either. This is why Bill Stevens was my secret weapon for the convention. I hoped he could seal the deal from an intellectually practical standpoint. My other issue was the ambition of the plan. It was bold and required some pretty big leaps of faith to believe that results would follow along with radical policies." The governor turned to Rob and smiled slyly. "On that front, luckily, I had history on my side, but more on that later.

"The Wyoming plan in the first iteration was primarily a recruitment drive directed at those who were disillusioned and needed a community of mutual support. The housing project and State Corps was directed at the homeless and working poor who wanted to make an honest living. The religious component was not merely symbolic. It appealed to those who have been unsatisfied by the immorality of the swiftly changing national ethic. The state does not offer wealth, but it does offer protection from the poisons celebrated by the modern world. The most vehement arguments against me were that people could only be motivated to move to another state for economic opportunity and that religious and cultural revolution could not make up for material self-interest. My hope was that Stevens could generate enough enthusiasm that people would be willing to try."

A stronger breeze whipped through the grass as they rested against the rock for a quiet moment. Rob had lost the initial vertigo caused by the immensity of the yawning sky above him but felt a constant tickling on his head and shoulders as if an immense eye stared down on him. "So, the Stevens speech did the trick?" he asked.

"It generated enthusiasm. It was a real barn burner. He poured his heart and soul and entire being into that one." Alexander leaned his head back so it also rested against the boulder and his face pointed up into the brilliant blue. "I believe it was called

'Momentum, Acceleration and Direction: A Treatise on Moral Life.' If you haven't seen a recording of it on the internet, then you really should." The governor laughed. "It really was something. He explained my goals in ways I could not. It got us promises from a lot of powerful people in the state."

"Forgive me if I find that hard to believe," Rob admitted.

Alexander rolled his head against the rock so that he looked at Rob across its surface. "What do you mean?" His face was still animated by the memories, but his eyes were guarded.

"One speech changed minds?"

"Is that so hard to believe?"

"People don't act against their own self-interest just for words."

The suspicion departed Alexander's eyes and the breeze whipped his head which still lolled against the rock. He looked positively youthful and careless. "There is a point where cynicism becomes idealism," he stated.

"But why would cynicism make them react positively to Stevens' speech?"

"I'm talking about you, not them," the governor clarified with his characteristic sad smile. "You think like Hume." He let the statement hang for a few seconds before resuming. "Believe it or not, the momentum and promises followed through. We funded the Department of the Wyoming Plan. As a direct result the Settlement Project expanded and the State Corps followed a little further on."

The governor straightened from his reclined position, cast one last glance down at Camp Hope, and, after thrusting a shoulder in the direction of the hill to indicate his intent, continued to walk his way up the path.

Rob followed. "I do still find it all hard to believe. I know it's true, but it seems impossible."

"How specifically?"

"That the state, the people here, were so ready to accept an immense change like your plan with no guarantees of success." He paused to get a better handle on his thoughts. "The way I understand the world makes this all sound like convenient fantasy."

The governor turned partway around while walking and looked at Rob for a moment. He took a deep breath before speaking. "You have been taught a vision of the world which ensures the static nature of things and is skeptical of rapid change. It's an unnatural view but pervasive. The world belongs to the titanic financial interests, and all of the prevailing economic assumptions are based on all things being constant. It is essential for the success of those massive entities and their ability to predict the future that stability be the primary attribute of existence. Too big to fail was all about stability, not picking winners. You have been taught that you live in a largely immutable world order, not because it is true, but because it is necessary for the maintenance of the colossal machine that people behave under that assumption. Once you stop believing that lie, then the possibilities expand." Alexander slowed until Rob walked beside him. "How much history of this state do you know?"

"Very little," Rob admitted.

"Most of our history here memorializes an experimental and synthetic place. The existence of towns relied first on the trails and military forts, and then on the Union Pacific. Town leaders would write to the company executives begging to be considered for the location of a switch in the tracks or a repair depot, all to save their tiny patch of civilization from vanishing in weeks or months. Some did disappear in short time. Areas of population exploded and receded based on the rapid ebb and flow of capital wielded by massive corporations. Did you know that Wyoming was the first state to give women the vote?"

Rob nodded subtly. "I had heard that at some point."

"Do you know why?"

"Not really."

"A small part was because the women's suffrage movement was already in motion and some thought it was simply the right thing to do. The bigger draw was that most everyone hoped that the publicity generated by such a bold statement on the issue would bring more women to a state where they were only one in six."

"You're joking," Rob deadpanned.

"No, I'm not. They wrote about it at the time. Sometimes they were a little tongue in cheek about it, but it was no secret that it was an advertisement. Whatever the truest reasons for it deep down, sweeping social changes are nothing new in Wyoming."

"So this new state project, Mount Calvary, the State Corps...they are all a similar advertisement?"

"Wyoming has always been on the way to somewhere else. First it was the trails to Oregon and California, then it was just the scenery along the Transcontinental Railroad. There has always been a strong desire held by those who govern this place to people it. They have always been met with difficulties. Only a few small spots have enough rainfall for farming; most of the large expanses of land can't field large amounts of cattle. For a very long time this place has been a beautiful sepulcher: picturesque natural monuments with some coal and oil, the dead rot and ruin of the last things to live here long term, their bones and the trash heaps of Cambrian consumerism left by the glaciers, which fled too, like everything else. How does one defy ages upon ages of visitation only? Give women the vote? There was no flood of females after that legislation. The only thing that brought anyone was gold, some coal, the railroad, gas, oil and then tourism for the national parks."

Alexander glanced above and ahead of where they walked. The trail led up into a thick forest of spruce and pine which covered the hillside.

"The Wyoming Plan was indeed an attempt to bring people here, and the monument is a source of income which is not controlled by UBI or the federal government."

"And are you satisfied with the results?" Rob asked.

"No," the governor replied. "The state population has more than doubled since I was first elected. Some say we will break two million in another ten years. Comparatively it is a success, but it is never enough."

"Never?"

"No. There is no end, no utopia. There is no heaven on earth. There is no victory, only striving. We do not build fortresses but camps. The militance is in the march. To live here is to embrace the motion. If you lead a movement, you do not simply sit in a citadel unless you wish it all to crumble with the passage of time."

"That seems like a way to avoid speaking definitively about success or failure," Rob observed.

"Call it pragmatism. Call it a complex. Call it embracing the nature of this place. Anything which lived here moved to avoid dying. Even the wind never stops here."

They neared the expanse of trees growing out of the hillside. The aforementioned wind had picked up so that the hearty tufts of mountain grass swayed in waves and whispered chants of cult worship. The trees bowed stiffly in begrudging adherence to convention. Three mule deer watched them from the bottom edge of the mass of pines and spruce, their heads held up to rotate back and forth on thin necks.

We are dancing around it, Rob considered grimly. *Could the governor answer directly what the point of all this mobilization was, even if he wanted? Does he, the very author of it all, only grasp it at times in grazing tangent lines? He says that he wants to bring a certain kind of person here to protect them. From what? The quasar? Where is the hypocrisy laid bare at the molten core?*

They paused where the trail led into the thicket of trees mixed with snarls of fallen branches and rocks which jutted up from the mountain soil. They stood four or five feet away from one another, and Alexander gazed down his shoulder at Rob.

"Keep your eyes open. I should have mentioned before, but there can be mountain lions around these parts, and rattlesnakes. Be careful around piles of rocks and piles of branches. There can sometimes be bears as well, but they tend to be timid."

"You ever have any close calls?" Rob asked.

"I've learned to expect anything and respect the wilderness."

Rob determined that it was time to end the measured queries. It was long past time for caution in the rhetorical realm. He did not want to become a nuisance and swoop repeatedly like a stinging fly, but he must make progress.

"Are you worried about some of the pressure? With the FBI crime stats for example?" he asked.

"The hate crime thing?" Alexander asked in a notably weary voice. "What do you want to know? Whether I take it seriously? If I accept the blame? If I consider it a conspiracy against me by the federal statisticians?" He went silent with one eyebrow raised before turning to continue along the path.

"Any and all of the above."

"All crime is down here," Alexander explained. "However, due to the federal redefinition of a hate crime, the numbers are up everywhere. Since our own crime lowered, these hate-crimes became a much larger share. That's the statistic that is always thrown around, that we have the largest share of hate-crimes in comparison to overall violent crimes. Some fellow with the last name of Morgan wrote about this in your paper with a fair bit of histrionics. He neglected, however, to make clear the mathematical reasoning to our satisfaction."

"So, you reject the characterization entirely."

"The numbers are disingenuous," Alexander stated and let out a heavy breath. "Though I am not denying that there are those here who are hot headed and turn to violence."

"And you had no hand in cultivating an environment for that violence?" Rob was not going to let his explanation stand unchallenged.

"You're specifically referring to attacks on homosexuals?" the governor asked.

"You have stated that you disagree with equality on the record."

"Because I believe it is a sin," Alexander murmured grimly. "I have always maintained this, but I have also always said that it is a greater sin to perform punitive acts of violence or vigilantism in the name of righteousness."

"But your words carry weight. You're partly responsible for the actions of people under you."

"For what, their bodies only and not their souls? Must I give up every precept for the most neutral possible civil peace? I have made clear that such violence will be punished swiftly and that anyone, regardless of their sins, is a son or daughter of God."

"But you must acknowledge," Rob insisted, "that some sins have been punished by people acting in place of God's judgment historically. There is a tradition of violence against some people more than others."

"Which means what?" Alexander asked. "That I should be more concerned with some forms of crime than others?"

"Maybe it means that your beliefs make a difference in what happens? That maybe you could affect the outcomes if you were a little more tolerant."

"This is assuming I am some kind of firebrand on the subject, which I am not. In fact, anything I have said on the subject of sexuality has been drawn out by the media as part of their little games." He gave Rob a pointed glance, a tight-jawed expression which displayed an imperiousness much like Justine's. His tone was not spiteful, however, and it was clear he had not yet lost his patience. "They also call me anti-Semitic, but there are no hate crime statistics to support that accusation."

"Let's be honest," Rob commented with a wry smile, "there are other reasons for those statistics. I'm probably the only Jew in the entire state right now."

Alexander stopped, blinked and then let out a genuine laugh. "That's fair, Rob. Your comedic timing is very good."

Rob had diffused the tension purposefully. He was softening his companion for the next question, one far more personal. Once the governor had resumed walking down the path, the journalist laid it on him. "Any reason why you never got married? It's personal, I know, but it has been chewing at me. I've seen some of your speeches praising the need for strong families as essential to a functioning society." He would find the hypocrisy no matter how uncomfortable it made either of them.

"It is better to marry than to burn with passion," Alexander replied in a muted voice without turning his head. "I am married to this project. One must be married to avoid the sin of sexual intercourse outside of wedlock. Of all the great temptations, this one is not the one I struggle with gravely."

"Are you saying that you aren't attracted to women?" Rob asked, his sinuses burning with the intense self-consciousness he experienced when asking such a dangerous question to someone he barely knew.

Alexander laughed. "You aren't married, are you Coen?"

"No," Rob confirmed. "I knew from a young age that I didn't want to be married or have kids."

"But you still have sex with women despite that?"

"Yes, on occasion." The burning sensation had moved to the back of his neck.

"In this case we are mirrors of one another." Alexander explained. "You pursue women, despite not wanting to bond yourself to one as a constant companion. I would have very much liked the family life for myself, yet I do not allow myself to pursue women." He paused, turned and made eye contact with Rob. "If it is difficult for you to understand, then perhaps scripture can illustrate: 'For I would that all men were even as I myself. But every man hath his proper gift of God, one after this manner, and another after that. I say therefore to the unmarried and widows, it is good for them if they abide even as I.'"

He paused after reciting the verses. "The apostle Paul believed that marriage was a means to avoid sin and was not the calling for all men. There have been many women I have cared for deeply. I have been drawn sexually to some as well, but I have bound myself to another enterprise, a godly mission. I do not think that I could give myself to it fully had I such immense concern for another. To pursue both would be an injustice to either."

"That isn't a post facto justification?" Rob asked.

Alexander smiled. "It's as though they make all of you in a factory," he murmured the words breathily as though under duress. It was an affected tone. He tired of the subject. "Will you ask me next if I want to fuck my mother? Am I a closeted homosexual? Was I sexually abused as a child so that I'm afraid of intimacy? To all of you the world is a fuck." His voice strengthened and he turned back to the winding trail. "There is nothing extraordinary by your estimation, no feats of human will that aren't illusions projected against a sheet, the approximated puppeteer movements of a damaged child, the shadow creatures of sado-sexual aberrations and the polymorphic nature of the reactive animal self. Nobility, morality, it is all a post facto delusion of your Humean, sophomoric sneer at ten thousand years of transcendent imagination. You take the perceived hypocrisy of one man and cast its rope on the neck of the bull of heaven believing you can tear it all down." The governor was speaking to the trees but projecting so that Rob could hear. "Such entry-level psychology has little bearing on my mission." His tone sounded as though he was genuinely let down by the subject matter.

Rob opened his mouth to respond but could not think of anything appropriate. With the mention of hypocrisy, Alexander was getting dangerously close to discovering him. As his last half-formed thoughts died on the doomed venture up to his vocal cords, the governor resumed.

"Rob, have you ever felt the truth bloom within you like the cool, electrical, unfolding blossom of an unknown substance?"

"You mean have I ever felt manic?" Rob asked, feeling rather proud of the riposte.

"Not exactly," Alexander continued, ignoring the jab. "Mania has no object, although the feeling can be similar. What I mean is the sensation that comes with an idea." He went quiet again, clearly waiting for some input.

"When I was younger and more idealistic, perhaps. Not now. It has been a long time since I have felt anything like that."

"So, you are a being of pure reason." Alexander mused aloud. "Shall I call you Charlie Marlowe?"

"I haven't the faintest idea," Rob sighed, at a total loss.

"I have to take a leak," the governor announced. "Let me go ahead a little and find a spot off the trail. I'll be back in a minute or two."

Rob nodded and stood waiting by the trail, which was just a worn and waving line of compacted earth among the detritus of the woods. Alexander moved ahead for a few dozen yards before disappearing into the brush to the left of the path. This part of the forest was denser, and tangles of undergrowth covered the ground in areas. He stood in the stillness and leaned back to stare at the fragmentary spots of pale blue sky which invaded around the edges of the treetops.

A slight muffled crackling noise emanated from the foliage to his right. The trail ran along the spine of a rise in ground, and he peered down the smooth slope to his right into the mass of ferns and shrubs. The moment after hearing the sound, he spied something out of the corner of his eye, a subtle movement beneath the canopy which vanished as soon as he turned, as though it were simply a mote of dust floating lazily in his ocular fluid. Alexander's warning about the possibility of wild animals coalesced in the back of his mind and a hot jolt of panic stampeded from his chest to the tips of his fingers and toes. He had been certain that he had actually seen something and that it was no figment of his imagination. A second crackling noise confirmed that something was indeed moving through the forest below.

Alexander had only been gone a few moments, and there was no indication that he would be back right away, so Rob decided to see if he could identify the source of the noise without endangering himself. He took two steps off the trail down the slope before a dry clump of dirt and packed pine needles gave out under his foot and he pitched forward down the incline, tumbling and rolling uncontrollably through the brush. He had enough presence of mind to tuck his arms in to protect his face and keep them from hitting against something hard in the storm of sudden motion. This meant that he had no way of slowing his downward slide. He decided to wait it out until the end and finally stopped with a sudden jolt, halfway enveloped in a rigid and prickly but fragrant juniper bush. He lay perfectly still, waiting for any sound of the creature which had been moving around before. Bits of dust and fragments of dead plant matter stuck to the sweat on his arms and neck causing an enraging tickling sensation, but he bore it in motionless silence, breathing in and out as slowly and quietly as he could manage. Oddly, despite the tickling sensation, he felt that if he waited there long enough, he might be able to fall asleep in the musty shade of the dense juniper.

He heard nothing for a minute and rose slowly and gradually to a squatting position so that he could see the forest floor around him. As he cautiously brushed the sylvan debris from his neck and forearms, his eyes turned to where he had lost his footing. The trail was probably over one-hundred feet up the incline, which was much steeper than it had appeared from above. The dirt was looser than he had realized, and that no doubt had expedited his cataclysmic fall. His hands slapped instinctively to his pockets. The phone, recorder, and notebook were all still secured in their rightful places. He heaved a sigh of relief and began scanning either direction to see if there was a shallower grade where he could make his way back. Then he heard, in the same direction as before, a rustling sound that whispered out into the air and then stopped abruptly, indicating a purposefulness, as though someone ceased a movement once aware that it had caused a detectable sound.

Rob lowered himself so that he could just barely see around the feathered fingers of the bush. Silence descended again for a few agonizing moments before the sound started once more. It was clearly the noises of someone walking very slowly past Rob's position to the spot where he had slid down the hill not long ago.

Then Governor Alexander's voice echoed down from the trail, a husky, confused and even slightly bemused shout, "Rob? Rob Coen? I left you for two minutes! Have you got yourself lost?"

He considered standing up or calling back, but he did not want to make his presence known to whatever other entity had been moving nearby. Then Rob saw it, the source of the furtive, careful sounds, not twenty feet away from him. Arthur Walden was wearing full hunter's camouflage: tactical pants, a tightly fitted turtleneck shirt and a wool cap pulled down over his bald and domelike head. Even his neck and face were smudged with a dark substance so that he blended in almost perfectly with his surroundings. He wore an earpiece and held some kind of listening device complete with a little dish for capturing sound in a specific direction. It looked almost like some child's toy ray gun clutched in his thick fingers. A hot horror flared up in Rob's stomach. It was a realization for certain, but not some cool, electric blooming of truth. Walden had been following them the entire time and listening to every word.

Alexander was calling out again, "Rob! I didn't take you for the adventurous type. I'm waiting another minute then moving up the trail!"

Rob waited, measuring even his shallow breaths to give nothing away. Through the limbs of the bush, he could see Alexander standing up above on the ridge, spinning slow circles in a befuddled scan of the area. He checked his watch a few times and then continued up the trail and out of sight. Walden began to move parallel to the trail, following Alexander. He was visible for a few minutes as he moved between the trees before he too vanished from sight.

Once assured of their departure, Rob stood upright and resumed his search for an easier way back up to the trail. His mind reeled at the still unbelievable sight of Walden stalking them. The lawyer Steyn had said something about the old man seeing himself as Alexander's secret police, and that observation now seemed much less hyperbolic than Rob had first assumed. What was the purpose of his spying on them? Did the governor know? Was Walden surveilling the journalist or Alexander himself?

Rob backtracked along the bottom of the slope for a few hundred feet before finding a more gradual incline which still required him to clamber and grasp ahold of bushes to struggle up to the top. Each time he took ahold of a woody stalk he made a silent wish that it wasn't some kind of poison oak. He reached the spine of the rise, but it was unfamiliar. It had been so much easier to follow the narrow dirt path when Alexander was walking ahead. He followed the crest, looking down to where he had been after the tumble. Once he caught sight of the familiar juniper bush below, he was able to triangulate the spot where he had been before the fall. After a moment of zigzagging along the hill, he found the subtle signs of traffic, the packed dirt and polished exposed roots which stuck their knuckles up out of the earth. He was very satisfied with his resourcefulness.

Rob followed the path as quickly as he could, thinking once or twice that he heard movement ahead only to burst into a clearing or through some brush and find nothing beyond but more unoccupied trail. Finally, as a brooding weight began to tug down on his abdominal region, he heard the sound of melodic whistling and the rhythmic accompaniment of footsteps. Around the trunk of a large pine tree, Alexander had stopped and turned as Rob arrived and greeted him with a smile.

"I'm impressed. You managed to get yourself lost in record time." His eyes took in the journalist's disheveled appearance. "Did you have a fight with a bear or something?"

Rob felt his face flush. "I fell," he explained simply.

"Oh. Are you alright?"

"A-ok."

"We aren't going much further," the governor explained. "You had better remind me what we were talking about before."

"Not sure," Rob admitted. "I think it had something to do with whether I had felt the energy of knowing something true, and I had said that I didn't put much stock in it."

"Ah, yes," the governor exclaimed. He turned to continue making progress up the trail. "To be honest, I don't remember where I was going with that, probably something about the differences in our perspectives." He paused and made a throaty noise of recognition. "I was excoriating you for your boring accusation that my swearing off women was simply a justification of some sexual deviancy."

Rob sighed. "I don't recall actually saying that, but yes, that was the topic at hand."

"You know it killed me to turn down Tracy Robinet. When I visited her after the election, I had a very strong desire to marry her, especially after all we had been through and the mutual forgiveness and goodwill. I could tell that she had similar sentiments. My very being cried out for the poetry of such an endeavor, but I could not. I had just been elected. I had plans so grandiose that not even I understood them fully. I knew that I would be making enemies. It could not be."

"You regret this?" Rob asked. "Not acting on this feeling?"

"Every day," Alexander said wistfully. "Always. If you have no regret, then you have not lived by a code worth pursuing."

Rob knew that he likely did not have much time left to ask questions. If they were nearing their destination, then they may only have the length of the walk back remaining for conversation. He decided to forge ahead with renewed vigor. "I have been curious about some of the anomalies I've observed since being here."

"Oh? Anomalies?" Alexander asked in a lilting tone of amusement, turning to show a grin.

"Yes," Rob confirmed, seriously. "The lawyers and the meetings. Steyn made it clear to me that there is something big going on, but that I would never hear of it."

The governor chuckled. "And you thought that I would simply tell you about the big mystery?"

"Sometimes you just have to ask."

Alexander stopped and pointed to where the trail branched into a fork. The right side continued on a level trajectory and the left side wound further up the hill. "Up there is a big boulder with a view. I often go up there to pray, which I intend to do now. On the lower path is a clearing with a decent look down on the camp. You are welcome to join me or head on to the clearing, whichever you like. I'll pray for a little while and then we will head back."

"I'll go to the clearing. I don't want to disturb you," Rob responded.

"That's fine. I will see you again in a bit."

The governor branched off onto the higher trail and Rob followed the lower until he came across an open space with a view of the valley through a screen of pines. He found a smooth rock a few feet in diameter where he could sit and watch the small birds flit back and forth between the branches in pursuit of one another. Alexander had not answered the question, of course. What else should he expect? He was reminded of what Walden had said the night before about journalists bashing themselves repeatedly against a wall. He was also reminded of the allegory of the beast and the path, and he wondered where Walden was at that exact moment. Crouching perhaps behind a tree nearby and listening, but for what?

Rob slid down the rock so that his rear rested on the surprisingly soft ground and the firm pressure of the stone nudged his back and neck. Just as when he was under the juniper he felt as though he could fall asleep if he wanted. It had warmed a few degrees since they left the lodge, and the surrounding trees provided enough shelter from the wind that he was quite comfortable. He closed his eyes and took stock of the interview so far. What more did he need? Figuring out anything about the flurry of lawyerly activity was impossible. He had some interesting insights already. The fact that Alexander had considered and resisted the idea of pursuing Robinet romantically was certainly something. He needed to make efficient use of the remaining time.

He let his mind wander and, just as sleep was encroaching on the corners of his consciousness, the sound of Alexander's soles on the ground roused him. Rather than taking the path, he had descended directly from the hill, stepping down the slope gradually and deliberately as though descending stairs. Rob straightened and sat on the rock.

Alexander's face was the serene picture of contentment. He arrived and stopped about twenty feet away with his hands rested on his hips and a bemused smile on his face. "Things are always much clearer after," he stated finally.

"Yeah?" Rob asked, and then added, "good to hear." He tried his best to avoid a patronizing tone.

"In that state of clarity, I have come to a conclusion," the governor explained, as though he had not heard the journalist's generic pleasantry. "I have decided to let you in on the big secret."

An army of cautious insects moved up the back of Rob's neck in formation. Alexander was smiling at him slyly. If true, then what was the meaning of it? Had he overestimated the gravity of the cause behind all that business? Did Alexander believe that God wanted him to do this? Was this madness? Was it a mirage? Had he fallen asleep against the rock and this was some kind of dream? If he questioned it, then would it fade, and merciless realism invade once more onto the scene? He gave voice to the confusion.

"Why?"

The governor's smile straightened, and he raised his eyebrows to wrinkle his forehead in thought. "Because it doesn't really make a difference, and you've shown more tenacity than most journalists who cross my path."

A pat on the head? A treat? This man kills with kindness better than anyone. Rob did his best to mask the seething within his brain with a look of silent reflection, but something must have slipped through.

"You do want to know, yes?"

"Does it matter if it won't make a difference?" Rob asked, skeptically.

"You are very utilitarian for a writer," the governor observed. "They train you all nowadays to be activists and then unleash you on a world much more nuanced than you expect. It makes for rather boring articles and a lack of curiosity. Although you have come further and made more effort than most, you do exhibit many of the typical attributes."

"Alright, spare me the Walden treatment," Rob grunted, surprised at his own boldness. "You're saying indirectly that you don't trust me, which is fine. Only a fool would trust someone after just a few hours of conversation. I do want to hear the secret, though, whether it makes a difference or not."

Alexander laughed. "It will be your big exclusive for a few hours. My office is issuing a press release about it later this afternoon, and then everyone will know."

"If an exclusive drops in the forest..." Rob trailed off in a grim deadpan.

Alexander chuckled at the witticism and gestured toward the path. They began to walk back the way they had come at a leisurely pace. The governor had his hands clasped in front of his chest in an oddly beseeching pose. "The state of Wyoming will issue its own gold-backed currency very soon. That's the announcement that will be made today. The guys from Oklahoma City drafted the proposed legislation along with Walden." Alexander gave Rob a long look out of the corner of his eye.

Was that it? Rob wondered. Now that he had heard it laid out so simply, it seemed like something of no consequence at all. Had he expected some kooky, fanatical plan for revolution? It seemed terribly dull.

"You're disappointed," Alexander observed astutely, still peering at him from the side. "Or at least you're underwhelmed."

"I'm unclear as to what it means," Rob admitted.

"It means more than the act itself. It is a method of grasping some measure of autonomy without rousing the beast."

"So what, you're going to stop using US dollars?" Rob asked.

"No, no," the governor explained in a quick and urgent tone. "That's illegal. We have to accept legal tender for all debts et cetera, and I have no desire to default in that responsibility."

"It's a symbolic gesture?" Rob was still at a loss.

"Somewhat, but it is very practical as well. We spoke earlier about this place being a shelter for decent, godly people. A gold backed internal currency helps protect the citizens here from the outside world. We are not fully at the mercy of the global empire centered in DC."

"Global empire," Rob muttered. "And what? You'll fight off the forces of Babylon?" His neck burned a little and he regretted the sardonic outburst as soon as he finished.

A look of pained surprise pulled back on Alexander's features before a sheepish amusement flooded in. His facial muscles tugged compulsively at the corner of his mouth before responding, a motion Rob had never seen him make before. "You do know how to cut a man," he remarked. "I simply believe that if one stands in the shadow of something heavy and precarious then it is unwise to be idle."

"So then why is it a big secret? Why keep it quiet if it isn't such a big deal?"

"I never said it wasn't a big deal," Alexander corrected. "In fact, it's very dangerous."

"I don't understand." Rob was getting impatient.

"When a massive enterprise shows the initial signs of failure or collapse, those at the top become far more paranoid, reactive, and sensitive to betrayal. When a member of the enterprise shows a vote of no confidence, then they must be punished and brought to heel quickly in order to prevent the spread of designs for self-preservation. If there is even a whiff of every man for himself, then the collapse accelerates uncontrollably. This is how cartels operate and how massive, interdependent financial and government institutions do as well. You see, this currency is not an explicit provocation, but if seen as an act of self-preservation, a vote of no confidence, then it will elicit harsh retaliation."

"What do you think the feds will do?" Rob asked.

"I have some ideas, but I don't know for sure," the governor admitted. "They know everything already. We will know in the days after today's press release."

"Is this the beast and the path that Walden talked about?" Rob asked.

Alexander smiled grimly and nodded. "The only thing you can do is try to lure the beast and hope that on a field of your own choosing it will grow too bold and make some foolish misstep."

"So, you are intentionally provoking them."

"If they do nothing, we will be more than satisfied, trust me. An independent Wyoming dollar is necessary either way."

"As a vote of no confidence?"

"As a vote of self-confidence."

Rob smiled. "These all seem like delicate ways of dancing

around the fact that you are firing the first shot."

"Despite the fact that it should not be an attack by any reasonable estimation," Alexander sighed, "that's certainly how it will be seen."

"And you think this state, this kingdom, will survive?"

"Yes, not that I have the luxury of doubt. If I stopped believing, then I would cease to exist."

"What's the worst they could do? Really?" Rob cajoled.

"Legal retaliation, but Walden would say worse. He'll want me to stay clear of small aircrafts for sure."

Rob laughed. "That seems a bit extreme."

The governor shrugged and cocked his head to one side noncommittally. "Neither you nor I will ever understand the mechanical underpinnings of this world as Walden does: the way it turns, the geometry of events, the chemistry of causation."

"You trust him that much?"

"He understands a dimension of the world that I do not. I must rely on his ability to perceive it for me. It would be foolish to ignore him."

"Do you think he trusts you?" Rob asked the question as naturally as he could manage. He watched Alexander's every slight move to gauge whether he gave any tell that he knew Walden had been following them in the woods and listening.

"He is my most trusted confidant," the governor replied with a furrowed brow. "There would be no need for me to hide anything from him or abuse his trust."

What did it mean? Was it simply ignorance? Was it a veiled admission or entirely innocent? Time was running out. Rob could feel the increasing force of the alpine breeze as the trees thinned and the brooding canopy of the steel blue sky composed more and more of the space above them. A powerful feeling of emptiness poured into Rob's insides as though through a breach in his skin. He felt lonely and disconnected from the world, although Alexander walked alongside him. The beat of his footsteps sounded detached and distant.

"Will we have a chance to talk again?" Rob asked.

"Maybe." Alexander was giving his rueful smile. "The response by the feds determines a great deal. I will have Justine take you to Mount Calvary tomorrow. It has more insight than one thousand hours of conversation. I may have some time the day after, but it depends on what comes up on my agenda."

Rob had the feeling as though he were falling from a great height and that the rope which could save him ran through his fingers. There was not enough time. His brain fumbled for a consequential question.

Finally, he simply blurted out the result of his frustration. "Do you honestly think this can last? As many people have decided to move here, there are at least ten times that many who hate you and resent you and see you as a bigot. It's not only that, but they want to see you fail. They would be genuinely happy if this whole state burned to the ground. I know because I work with some of them. If the feds decide to crack down over this currency, then they will praise the action, salivate over it, crow about how you deserve even worse. You won't find support if things get bad, so what is the point?" Rob was trying to ask something more profound, but he could not find the words. This embarrassed him, and the embarrassment manifested into more frustration. "You say that you're protecting these people, that this is some sort of shelter, but it could also mean that you're just putting them all in a convenient place to be punished at once."

"'Blessed are those who are persecuted for righteousness' sake, for theirs is the kingdom of heaven,'" Alexander stated calmly. "The godless world turns by its laws of mechanism. All must drink the poisoned cup. You speak as though I build a cult of masochism here, but it is I who wish to escape Jonestown, USA." His face was set in stone as he spoke.

Now at last we get to the heart of it, Rob thought, *the fevered maddened core where polarity reverses and we stumble upon the hot nucleus of hypocrisy.*

"Explain yourself," Rob demanded.

"Earlier I told you about the cartel and the vote of no confidence," Alexander declared. He was animated, his gestures more frequent and sweeping. They had reached the open hillside and approached the large boulder where they had paused and spoken before. The air seemed cavernous and electric. "Our own state dollar draws ire as a sign of disbelief in the larger system. The same is true of wickedness. There is an assumption that all partake of the same poison. If we all drink it to the last man, then it is no longer poison. It becomes as breathing air. It is seen as of nature and of God. There can be no dissenters. To live righteously or to strive to live righteously, to look out for one's own soul or to even believe in a soul that can be tarnished, edified, renewed, forgiven, that can endure, that can love with a sort of love that is not merely carnal, to see carnality itself as a failed search for something that is much more real, to accept these things and behave as though they matter becomes a vote of no confidence in the compassionate community of mutually accepted sin. Such righteousness and the striving for it must be stamped out to preserve the balance of the cartel of sin. To seek morality in an immoral world is a provocation. All we can do is endeavor to live righteously, and as I said before, there is victory in the striving."

Rob was taken aback by the words and felt thrown a little off balance by the force and conviction behind them, but he would not let Alexander end with that. "And what of Mount Calvary? What of the camps and mobilization of the State Corps, the brawls with the state university? How is that not an active form of provocation? Is it not enough to live a life of quiet devotion?"

"Much is expected by those given providence. It is not enough to bury the talent and keep it safe. One must always do more in the name of God." The governor sighed. "You must accept that we are very different kinds of people." He paused. Camp Hope was in sight now, nestled in the clusters of trees at the bottom of the hill. "I will try to make time after tomorrow to speak again if we can. Don't hesitate to ask Banks if you need to go anywhere or need any information. Justine will call on you tomorrow morning, but not too early." He accompanied the last few words with a sidelong smile.

Rob felt a slight sting of residual humiliation. "I'll try not to keep her waiting," he promised.

The empty feeling of entropy and collapse returned. The rope was fully through his hands and Rob was in freefall. The opportunity was ending. He suspected that he didn't have enough material. He would have to listen to it all later and find out for certain. They finished the last bit of the path down to the lodge and crossed the wraparound porch where their shoes clunked on the wooden boards. Alexander stopped and turned to him once they were by the door.

It was at that moment, right as the governor looked to be finding some last words to end their conversation, that Rob thought of one final question he could ask. Before Alexander could shut the door on the opportunity, Rob was able to get the words out in some semblance of order.

"I was wondering one last thing. If you aren't afraid of the feds or UBI, then what does keep you up at night?"

Alexander looked a little taken aback by the sudden question as things were winding down. He considered it for a moment and let out a sigh. The slight sound of the exhalation was one more of begrudging amusement than resentment.

"In the French Revolution, the times when they were chopping off heads like crazy, there are a number of anecdotal tales of heads still being alive for a few moments after they had been removed. Some stories relate that the executioner would hold the head up and the eyes or mouth would continue moving for more than a few seconds after decapitation."

Rob nodded along but could tell that his brow was furrowing. He was unsure of where this was going.

Alexander held up a hand to indicate that he was getting to the point. "Sometimes I think about what it must be like in those final moments, to be the disembodied head and see the body for an instant with perfect vision, see the self from outside the self for only a few dying seconds." He shook his head slightly and smiled. "I wonder if, perhaps, my ability to do something with this state and speak to the people, find a common purpose, is merely the fleeting images in a disembodied head. Maybe it is only because our culture has been stricken down, wounded beyond saving, that I can get that brief bit of insight. Then I'll be gone, it will all be gone, and everything will be lifeless and still." He shrugged his shoulders slightly. "That's what keeps me up at night." After a moment of silence between them, he made eye contact with Rob one last time. "It was good to talk to you, Robert."

"Thank you. You as well." Rob replied.

With a firm handshake and a turn on his heels Alexander was gone. Rob stood alone on the porch for a good minute, staring at the floorboards and thinking back on what they had discussed. He checked his phone. Between their meeting in the dining hall and this moment it had been nearly three hours. He needed to call his editor. He needed to review the audio recording of the conversation. He needed a drink.

CHAPTER

8

Rob gritted his teeth under an unexpected wave of anger. If only he had been faster on his feet, more prepared, more determined. If he had the force of will to steer the conversation at some of the critical points, then it could have been better. On top of that, the thought of Walden lurking in the background behind rocks, trees, and bits of foliage was a source of immense frustration. Why? What was he to do such a thing? Rob decided that when he came across the retired lawyer again, then he would ask him about it directly.

The best thing to do at this point was get it over with and call Margaret. After that he could decompress and do the busy work. Rob returned to his room through the empty halls of the lodge and sat down at the wooden table by the window. The blinds were open as he had left them, and he sat in the cascade of sunlight. He made the call and his editor picked up on the third ring.

"Rob, please tell me that I have a reason to celebrate tonight. I'll be getting drinks with some friends visiting from Europe either way, but I would prefer it to be a happy occasion. I'm not good company when drinking morosely."

"Tentatively I would say yes. You should be encouraged."

"You're hedging, Rob." Her tone was a combination of a warning and her typical empty chiding, like a defanged copperhead rattling its tail.

"I just finished talking with Alexander minutes ago. I haven't had time to review the recording. It would be foolish to oversell it so soon."

"How long was the interview?" she asked.

"Between two and three hours," Rob answered, before holding his breath in expectation of her judgment.

"Disappointing, but not unexpected," she remarked briskly. "How was the candor?"

"Informal, personal," Rob assured.

"Rob, you're about as social as a board. You would consider a company mandated training seminar to be a mixer."

"Was that really necessary?" Rob asked, but she was already talking over him.

"Did you get anything good? Anything that will be a surprise?"

"He did give me a bit of information that isn't public yet. Do a quick news search for Governor Alexander and Wyoming and let me know if anything comes up." Rob could hear the clattering noise of her fingers stampeding across the keyboard.

"Nothing recent, aside from local press," he replied.

"He said that there would be a press release later today about the issuing of a gold-backed state currency. If you get a write-up in the next little while, then we can scoop it."

"You're joking. He told you that?" Margaret asked, incredulous. "Let me call our guy at the Treasury on my office phone. Stay on the line," she instructed. "I don't want to go ahead with this and find out we got played."

Rob sat back for a few minutes and listened to the rustling and murmuring noises on her end of the call. He leaned back in the chair and gazed up at the constellation of dark knots spread throughout the timber paneled ceiling, a haphazard collection of animal eyes which stared back unblinkingly. Just as he was about to turn on the speaker phone and deposit the device on the table, Margaret's voice returned.

"Treasury says it isn't bullshit, but he also says he won't go on the record."

"Meaning?" Rob asked.

"Meaning it's true and Treasury has their own plans: big Federal litigation if I had to guess."

"Alexander said they are expecting that sort of reaction," Rob replied.

"Send me the quotes on this, from the governor. I just want exactly what he said. I'll have someone write it up, and we'll push it right away. We have very little time to get this out before the press release."

"Alright. Give me fifteen minutes."

"Five minutes."

"Ten."

"Seven."

"Ok, seven," he relented.

"I'll call if I have any questions. Good work." She hung up after those last words, and he was alone again in his room. There was not enough time to import the audio file from his recorder to the laptop. Rob had to use the buttons on the recorder to jump back and forth until he found the right spot. He had a minute to spare by the time he found the relevant parts and sent off an email.

After Margaret replied that it was satisfactory, he imported the interview to his computer and began the painstaking process of highlighting and bookmarking the topics and notable exchanges. Rob picked up on nuances he had missed during the raw, firsthand experience of the conversation. He hated his voice. Alexander was in control. The anger returned with a slow-burning, acid reflux quality. He put in a few hours of work and decided that a walk might do him some good and clear his head.

Rob turned in his chair and only then noticed something he had not seen before. On the floor directly inside the door to his room was a small, nondescript envelope where someone had clearly slipped it through the crack. He rose, cautiously picked it up and returned to set it on the table in the light of the window. It was cream colored and about five inches wide and four inches tall. It had the appearance of one of those generic envelopes containing an insipid holiday card of some kind. On the front was a single line of strangely perfect block text so straight and even that it looked as though the writer had used a ruler to keep it all on a flawless line. The writing said, "Mr. Journalist Coen."

The dimensionally excellent hand could belong to either a man or a woman. It was impossible to tell. Rob lifted the envelope to his nose. It had no distinctive odor. It was an unaccountable gesture that left him baffled afterward, like a driver dumbstruck after waking up from nodding off behind the wheel. Perhaps he had seen a detective do it on television. This potential development was all such idiotic good luck, but not enough to make him believe in providence. It was enough perhaps for believing the grinning, psychotic episodes of reality such as people being sucked out of airplane windows during random bouts of decompression. He did not believe in miracles, but he did believe in their dark, dreaming cousins which were beautiful and wondrous in their own deranged way: sending winking nonsense in violent hieroglyphics as inexplicably geometric as the writing on the envelope.

He carefully tugged at the inverted triangle on the back of the object, not wanting to tear the paper. The flap was attached at just the very tip and came up with a satisfying and barely audible whisper. Inside was a simple rectangle of cardstock. It was the same neutral hue as the envelope. A few short lines in the same writing ran along the front. There was no writing on the back. He sat down and read it aloud:

I saw you as one drinks cool water darkly darting from a shaded stream. I knew at once that we were made of the same material. Long have I been here, lost and forgotten, untethered, unmoored, and left to wander. Seeing you now, again I have hope and purpose. In every garden pure and unspoiled, there is a hidden source of leeching poison. The stench of death invades the fragrance. Beyond the barracks and the pond goes a short and winding trail. There is the poison. Alas, I cannot show my face or name. Weak runs the vitriol which was once in my veins. I sit and pine like an old woman. Yet I still have my mind. Seek the poison where it boils. Without it your story is incomplete.

Your constant companion,
Nico

Rob sat perplexed at the wooden table. He read it silently again and then a third time. The prose was strangely archaic, child-like, poetic, and absurd. What did the mystery writer mean by thinking he and Rob were made of the same materials? Had he been watching him in secret? Was this Nico person entirely sane? Rob folded the note and placed it into the inner pocket of his jacket. He tore the envelope into tiny pieces and dropped them in the nearby wastebasket.

He considered the strangeness of it all for a few minutes and determined that he had found a destination for that walk. It took some effort to steel himself, risk averse as he was. Rob peered out the window. The breeze still stirred the branches of the trees around the lodge. He donned his light jacket, ensuring that he had his notebook. He decided to leave the recorder, since it was still charging. Rob exited the room, locking the door behind him, and traveled down the halls to the entryway. After stepping down the stairs from the porch, he took a left toward the bunkhouses. A few of the early crews had arrived back recently, but most of the barracks remained dark and empty. He passed beyond the log structures further than Justine had taken him on their brief tour. He was not sure what to expect. Would he trip over a transition seam and stumble into a musty backstage area where he could see all the metal braces and scaffolding which held up the papier-mâché veneer of Alexander's Wyoming? Would he come across bins of unused props and dig through heaps of Banks' reading glasses or racks of Walden's sweaters all just sitting in the dark and waiting for use in some new scene? His mind was veering off into strange abstractions.

Rob saw the pond mentioned in the brief note. It was a rather picturesque, man-made crater a few acres square with a small dock and covered seating area. The gravel path led around the outside. A cloud of small insects pulsated and moved through the shade of a tree which hung over the far edge of the water. Once on the other side, he found a spot where a path branched off into the cover of trees. Rob followed it around a few short bends before stumbling across a cabin resting in a small clearing.

It was a squat building made of naked wood with a tiny lean-to porch propped against the front. A garden of creeping ivy and overflowing wooden planters of flowers and ferns surrounded the small structure. He stopped mid stride to look the place over. Was this the place where there was supposed to be some kind of poison? It fit the location described in the letter perfectly. The place looked old but cared for. He stared at the dark front windows which shone warped reflections at him. A small curl of smoke rose lazily from the metal chimney.

He supposed he should knock if he was going to find out whether this was the place mentioned in the cryptic letter, but his steps faltered on the way to the door. Some part of his subconscious expected an eerie, old hag to burst out from the door at any moment, manifested from some ancient tale of European folklore. No such thing happened, so he moved in and stepped cautiously on the boards of the front porch. They were soft and malleable with age, sinking slightly under his feet. A dark, forest green paint coated the front door and frame.

Rob took in a deep breath and knocked. No noises within followed the announcement. He concluded that it was a timid excuse for a knock and tried again with a little more force. He waited for a response and determined that nobody was home. He had just decided to give up and walk back to the camp when he noticed a rope dangling down against the wall about two feet to the right of the green door. Beside it was a small and simple wooden placard painted with the word "pull." After a moment of pondering, he gave it a tug. Although he expected something to happen, the haphazard clanging of a surprisingly loud bell within the cabin made him jump slightly.

A muffled voice emanated out from the interior, "It's open. It's open. Come on in."

The sudden reversal of events left Rob frozen in place for a moment. After shrugging off the initial surprise, he grasped the handle and let himself in. The interior of the cabin was dim and musty. It smelled of dirt and aged wood. He stood in a small kitchen area which consisted of an old ice box, a wooden table, two old wooden chairs, and a simple, gas range stove complete with a propane tank resting on the ground beside it. The back of the room opened into a seating area with a wide window where the sunlight streamed in. Rob stepped through to find the source of the voice. An old and faded loveseat rested on the left side of the room with a ratty afghan thrown over it and an overstuffed chair facing it on the opposite side. A thick layer of Indian rugs covered the floor. The window was straight ahead, and Rob could see a tin roof structure covering a pile of firewood outside along with some wooden, carved statues of a bear standing on its hind legs and what looked to be rudimentary pietà. He noted a simple lavatory through a doorway to the left by the loveseat, and to the right beyond the big chair was another entry into a tiny compartment with barely enough room for a twin bed and a dresser.

"I thought you were the girl who comes and checks in on me."

Once again, Rob nearly jumped in surprise. The voice emanated from the overstuffed chair, which was turned just enough from the light of the window that he had not noticed an occupant. After a moment, his eyes adjusted to the dim interior and he could see an elderly man sitting in the chair and peering up at him. He wore faded blue-jeans, moccasins, and a gray sweatshirt with a logo on the front that was so cracked and worn with age that it was unidentifiable. The man still had his hair, which was white and combed mostly back with a few odd bits sticking out in different directions. His face was clean-shaven, though weathered and creased. It was thin like the rest of him but not skeletally gaunt like those of some men his age.

"Well, who are you?" he asked in a noncommittal tone. He heaved forward in the chair and took a pipe from a small table along with a package of tobacco. He packed the bowl and traded the tobacco for a small box of matches, striking one and holding it aloft with surprisingly steady hands. He sank his cheeks repeatedly, drawing air to ignite the contents of the pipe.

"I'm Rob Coen," he explained, somewhat entranced by the ritual.

"And how is that spelled? The last name?"

Rob obliged him by spelling it aloud.

"Well, you sure ain't Irish. I can tell by the look of you. My guess would be that your father's side is Jewish and came through Spain."

Rob felt a stinging in his nostrils that was only partly due to the smoke. "That's correct," he confirmed. "And who are you?"

The old man turned his dark eyes up to his visitor and shifted back into the embrace of the chair. He tapped the stem of the pipe against his teeth. "Interesting that you come and call on a man without knowing who he is."

"I was just looking around the camp," Rob stated meekly.

"You're not from around here, are you." The old man stated the question as a conclusion.

"No, I'm not. I'm a journalist. I came here to interview Governor Alexander."

"Jimmy is a fine boy," the old man remarked. "Though I deserve more credit for teaching him everything I know." He paused and took a few more puffs on the pipe before realizing his guest's predicament. "I'm Paul Bartholomew Alexander, Jimmy's uncle."

"The governor's uncle?" Rob asked.

"Yes, his father was my older brother, rest his soul."

Rob had stumbled on quite the opportunity, thanks to the writer of the strange letter. The convenience of it all was very unnerving, however, and he could not help but wonder if he was a pawn in some larger game. When he returned his eyes to the overstuffed chair, the elderly man was staring at him with a furrowed brow.

"You said you're a journalist? Your kind is not friendly to Jimmy and never has been. Forgive me if I find your presence here suspect."

"You wouldn't be the first one," Rob sighed. "I'm just here to write an article. It's nothing more complicated than that."

"You're from back East? One of the big cities?"

Rob nodded.

Paul shook his head. "You urban types never understood. My father used to tell me that back in the times of the Indian trouble the papers back East called us a bunch of greedy speculators because we wanted a strict reservation policy. What did they know about living out here at the edge of the world and trying to scrape together a living? What did they know about the troubles with the Indians? They didn't have to deal with the harshness of it. The newspaper men in the East were fat and soft with their bleeding hearts, and they still are."

"I'm actually in pretty good shape," Rob corrected half-seriously.

Paul Alexander let out a wheeze of a laugh and let the pipe hang unassisted from the corner of his mouth. Smoke crawled in languid tendrils out of his nostrils. "That may be true, but you are against him in the end. You are the natural adversary of men like Jimmy."

"Because I'm a journalist urbanite?" Rob asked a little sardonically.

"Well partly, but more because you're a Jew."

The words came out so quickly and easily that Rob missed the weight of the charge for a few seconds until it slammed into him. His chest tightened suddenly around his vital organs. Never before had such a naked and ugly charge been made against him. He had been criticized for his politics, his writing style, and his attitude, but never something so basically and unchangeably connected to the essence of his corporeal existence. The flippancy of the accusation added an additional dimension of careless malevolence.

"Excuse me?" he asked a little breathlessly. He was so shocked that he had nothing else to say.

Paul held up a hand and removed the pipe from his mouth with the other. "Now don't get me wrong. I'm not saying you can't think for yourself, but there is an undeniable enmity between Jews and the Christian men of Europe. I'm not trying to be overly provocative."

"God forbid," Rob snorted. He had evened out his breathing and recovered a bit from the initial indignation. "What, you mean because of the Second World War?"

Paul shook his head. "A little. That is certainly part of it. The origins are much older than that. It all goes back to the New Testament of scripture and the interplay between the Romans,

Jesus, and the Jews."

Rob was in extremely foreign territory at this point and kicked himself inwardly for not bringing the recorder. He took out his notepad, unconcerned with Paul Alexander's reaction. He was relatively sure that he was about to get a fascinating and ugly insight into theologically justified anti-Semitism. He adjusted himself awkwardly on the loveseat opposite the speaker and crossed his legs but then felt uncomfortable and resumed his former posture.

Old man Alexander gestured and explained with clear excitement and relish. "At the time of Christ, the Jews were under the occupation of the Roman Empire. It was a world power, yes, but it was an undeniably European power with the core of influence and culture positioned above the Mediterranean. The Jews believed that a messianic character emerging at that time would serve as a liberator from the yoke of Roman rule. When Christ came, however, his harshest words were not for the centurions of Rome, but for the Pharisees and Sadducees of the Hebrews themselves. The Jews would not accept Jesus as a messiah because he was seen as not only a traitor to the covenant with God, but also a traitor to the occupied Jewish people. This is illustrated at the time of the Crucifixion when the people of Jerusalem call out for his execution. Pontius Pilate, a man charged with the judicial authority of the European empire of Rome, says that he can find no fault in Jesus. Yet it is the overwhelming demand of the Jews that condemns him to death."

Paul Alexander paused and leaned forward in his seat, extracting a metal tool from the pocket of his jeans with some effort and tamping down the pipe with an additional pinch of tobacco. He drew in on it a few times to ensure that the coal was still burning satisfactorily. After a brief pause and squint of effort, he recalled where he had left off. "Not only that, but after Christ is dead, the veil in the temple is torn in half with great force, signifying the opening of God's covenant to all peoples. In other words, the Christian worldview based on the biblical account indicates that the messiah took the Jewish birthright of Abraham's covenant and gave it over to the very European gentiles who held the Jews in captivity. To the Jew, Jesus was a fascist, or at least was a friend to them. This is why the Jews revile Jesus. He gave salvation to an occupying force. The Christian loves Christ. The Jew mocks him in death. This cannot be reconciled."

"And this somehow colors my feelings toward Governor Alexander?" Rob asked in a tired, tested voice. "I'm not religious. In fact, I'm not even familiar with the scriptural account or that narrative of the Crucifixion."

"It's a collective memory of a people," old man Alexander insisted, as though it were ridiculous to think otherwise. "You don't get rid of that sort of thing by not knowing about it. It lives in you."

"Let me articulate this, so you hear it out loud from me," Rob deadpanned. He jabbed his pen in the air to punctuate each significant phrase. "I have a subconscious desire to sabotage Governor Alexander because Jesus gave the Jewish covenant to the Romans."

"Precisely," the old man confirmed triumphantly, sending a billowing eruption of smoke into the air between them.

"Do you know if the governor prescribes to this same, er, theory of yours?" he asked.

"I don't recall talking about it specifically, but it is theologically sound." He paused and tapped the pipe stem against his bottom teeth a few times. "He's not as strict as I would like. There are ways in which he does not rebuke sin firmly enough. Is that not a sin itself? To see the world working so clearly in the service of Satan and to just watch it carry on?"

"That seems a comparatively minor sin," Rob obliged.

"Perhaps it is," Paul Alexander stated absentmindedly with a faraway look in his eyes.

They sat silently for a time. Rob was getting slightly uncomfortable, so he decided to voice something that had been itching him. "You knew where my family came from. Do you have some kind of encyclopedic knowledge of Jews and their names and where they come from?" he asked.

The old man laughed heartily. "Hardly, though that's part of the whole thing." He nestled himself deeper into the chair. "The Alexanders came from Scotland. We are descended from the kings there. I know this too and many things about where people come from. I spent a good amount of time in Rock Springs when I was younger. There's quite a bit of mineral interest there. I went to look for work during the boom about fifty years ago. There was money to be made for sure. With money came people from all over. It's the story of this place. I worked a little on the coal, but I didn't stay for it. I fell in with the Mormons."

"The Mormons?" Rob was lost.

"Rock Springs has a big Mormon contingent. They were basically the ones who started the place. I got to know a few guys there who decided I wasn't the coal and oil type." He smiled cryptically. "My family had been in the state for a long time. The Alexanders have roots. One of the fellows I got to know pretty well worked for the Genealogical Society of Utah." He could see that Rob was indicating no familiarity with the term. "You see, the Mormons keep a very exact history of their genealogies. It's a rather essential part of their religion. To make a long story short, they wanted me to help by scoping out Wyoming, since I knew the place and the people and history so well. I came for the minerals and I ended up hunting down the family jewels." Paul Alexander let out a loud guffaw.

"So you worked for them?"

"For a bit, yes. I traveled around for a while collecting copies of newspaper clippings and historical records to bring back to Rock Springs. They had a room set up there with a microfilm camera. I would track down old books and copies of newspapers and journals, stuff they couldn't find in the libraries. I put it in the trunk of my car and dropped it off for them to capture and send back to Granite Mountain."

"What's Granite Mountain?" Rob was scribbling furiously and trying to keep up.

"Granite Mountain is their great big vault near Salt Lake City. They have millions and millions of rolls of microfilm documenting genealogies there." He paused and smiled. "I've actually been in there a few times. Darndest thing you ever saw. I was going around the state and digging around all kinds of places. A number of people were quite helpful, willing to loan me old documents so long as I promised to bring them back, and I did." He pointed the stem of his pipe at Rob to ensure that his integrity got in the notes as well. "They liked my work. I wasn't much for formal education, but I had always favored the genealogies in the Bible and found them damned interesting. I have a way with folks too, but I'm sure you've noticed." He gave a wink and took a few more puffs. "That's how I got to know so much about where people came from. I spent years tracing it all and a lot of my spare time too, since I liked it so much. They even asked me along on a few journeys across the country to track down other pieces to the puzzle, but I only did that a few times on account that I'm a homebody for the state. So, to answer your question, yes I know where a lot of Jews come from, but everyone else too."

"How long did you do that work?" Rob asked.

"A number of years. Got a little burnt out on it after a while and then eventually they didn't need me for much anymore. That's the thing about digging up genealogies. It's like prospecting for oil or coal. There's a bottom to it eventually when you hit dirt."

"What did you do then?"

Paul Alexander shrugged. "Then I got other work here and there, did some actual mine work for a bit, and worked in the parks before putting my feet up here."

"So, you spend all your time at Camp Hope?"

"Yes," the old man replied. "What else is out there in the world for me? I cannot endure what I see in the places beyond. It is an affront to God and gives me great pain. The things that people do in plain sight. The drugs and the sex, the race-mixing, the sexualization of children, the killing of children in the womb! Little souls not even yet to taste the world. This is not tolerated merely but celebrated! Yes, I spend my time in Camp Hope and much of that in this cabin. There is nothing for me out there in the wicked world." He paused and went through the ritual of refueling his pipe. He only continued after being assured of the quality of the resulting smoke. "To be perfectly honest, there are times I wish Governor Alexander would just take Francis E. Warren and bring down cleansing fire." He paused and a cool look came over his creased visage. "And you brought it here with you. I can smell it on you, the rotting filth and the stench from the trenches of the Malebolge. You brought it here to drag my nephew in as well, if possible." His voice was thin and strangled from the force of conviction and he drew on the pipe rhythmically in the vitriolic tirade so that he seemed to pump smoke from every part of his head, even his ears. "Zeal be my sin and violent fervor be my temptation. Did not Christ forgive Peter for cutting off the ear of Malchus? And you are of less consequence than he. You're not even a tax collector, not even a man of any convictions. You don't even believe in your own eternal soul. Jimmy is too soft to let you come here. He is not made of the stuff to survive a full onslaught by the prince of this world. He was suckered to let you come here."

Old man Alexander paused for a moment and shook his head sadly. "And it all seemed to happen so quickly. If Jimmy wanted to succeed, he should knock down all the towers."

"Towers?" Rob asked.

"The transmission towers, the data repeaters. The devils who rule the metropolis have much greater power than we do. Think of the work it takes to save a soul, to teach the right way of living, to convince another man to take up the hard life on account of his soul. And yet those devils can just send their poison to the far corners of the world with no effort. He should have knocked down the towers, the inhuman sin generators. That's the true colonization. Our minds infiltrated by the images. You grow up in a small town and go to church with your neighbors, maybe run some cattle, work the oil fields, tend a farm. You only touch the world in distant grazes. They, the big IT, will never approach your life in admiration. Nobody will catch your way of living like a disease. But they do come to you. They come through the clouds of waves, the resonance building to a typhoon, a tidal wave of approaching sin. Your small-town sister becomes a whore who wants to be just like the sluts dancing on the TV screen. Your way of life took sweat and effort and hundreds of years passed down from father to son. It topples and dissolves like a pillar of sand. Their invasion is effortless. When Jimmy was younger, he was right. I shouldn't have set him straight. I shouldn't have stopped him." The old man trailed off and sat quietly breathing out smoke.

"What do you mean by that? Stopped him from what?" Rob coaxed.

The old man's dark eyes darted over, knowing perhaps that he should have been more guarded, that he may have said too much in his agitation. He adjusted his weight in the chair before concluding his prior rant in a calmer manner, leaving the question unanswered.

"Jimmy has accomplished much, but he is not the kind of man who can survive. They will not stop until his precious monument has been leveled into a featureless field and made the foundation for a house of harlots."

An interrupting sound pulsed through the soft, aged timbers of the cabin. Paul Alexander slumped back in his chair and went quiet. The noise had been that of the door opening, and a woman's voice followed.

"Mr. Alexander, I brought you some milk, and I know how you like the cornbread from the meal hall. I'll put the milk in the fridge for you. I forgot if you were getting low on anything else, but I know how you like to cook for yourself and fuss about me prying too much."

The voice roved around the other room and vibrated through the various portions of the wooden wall before pouring directly through the doorway.

"Oh my! I didn't know that you had a visitor."

The woman standing in the doorway was in her early thirties. She had a slim build and straight, light brown hair that went down past her shoulders. She had very white skin and wore a simple dress of hearty, practical material clearly meant for somewhat strenuous domestic work.

Rob raised a hand in a halfhearted wave. "I'm Rob."

"And I'm Sara," she replied. "Are you visiting Camp Hope? I have never seen you before."

"Journalist from out of state," he explained. "Governor Alexander gave me the run of the place." He realized that her arrival offered him an opportunity. "I was actually planning on leaving." He turned to Paul Alexander, who had clearly not lost the vehement energy of his fervent verbal crusade. The old man had sunk deeply into the old chair and peered at him with glittering eyes. He let out a voluminous puff of smoke as Rob addressed him. "It was illuminating talking to you, Mr. Alexander. I can't say I've had a conversation quite like it. I assume this was all on the record?"

"I've talked to a thousand men like you," the old man grumbled. "And you betcha it's on the record."

Rob slapped his knees with his palms and rose to his feet. "Well then, I best be off."

Sara still stood in the doorway, a look of concern etched on her face. It was only then that Rob noted that her eyes were green or hazel, some lighter pigmentation that seemed to match with the cabin's palette. "Let me finish dropping off his things and walk you back to the lodge," she entreated.

"Fine," Rob stated and walked past her as she moved from the doorway. He exited out past the porch and breathed in the fresh air of the clearing. Blood pounded in his head after the discourse with the old man. He wanted to just collapse into bed, although it wasn't even dinner time yet. After a few minutes, Sara emerged from the cabin and walked past him toward the lodge at a steady pace, expecting him to follow, which he did after a moment's hesitation.

"You plan on using his words in an article?" she asked with

one arm folded across her chest and the other propped perpendicularly against it. The raised hand rested against her neck as though guarding it from her companion.

"You seem rather certain he said some things that won't look good in print."

"He has become very bitter and angry in his old age. He doesn't mean a lot of what he says. He's made all sorts of threats to the people who cross him but he's never followed through with any. Sometimes he doesn't even remember what he said the next day."

"Does he have a diagnosed condition of some kind?" Rob asked.

"No," she admitted.

"It's going in the article. I won't apologize for it," the journalist stated firmly.

"I see."

They had reached the pond and began to move around the outside toward the State Corps barracks. There was much more commotion, and it looked like many of the crews had returned for the day. She said nothing more to him until they neared the porch of the lodge and a group of women walked by them. She peeled off after them and said, "I hope you enjoy your time here." The wish contained no feeling whatsoever.

Rob did not feel vindicated or particularly happy. A numbness had taken over about the time Paul Alexander had been discussing the genetic enmity he necessarily possessed toward the governor, that supposed product of some ancient circumstance. Now that he had the ability to take a few steps back from the conversation, he could feel the sickly weight of it all. He hurried back to his room to write down as many more details as he could before they began to fade from his memory.

He worked until the latter end of dinner and ate at a solitary table in the corner of the meal hall. He selected pork tenderloin with rosemary seared red potatoes and a simple salad. He saw no familiar faces the whole time he was eating. The food was decent. He still needed a drink. After leaving the dining room, he went to the upper balcony where he had encountered Steyn the night before, hoping to get a drink or two off him. The space was quiet and empty. Perhaps it was too early, or he was too busy in meetings with Alexander and the other lawyers.

Of course the announcement had been made by now. Rob took out his phone and began browsing the news. He found *The Times* piece scooping the press conference. He was listed as a contributor. How considerate of Margaret. He looked through some reaction pieces that were all rather mocking in their assessment of the decision. It felt very strange to have heard Alexander's reasons for the move firsthand when seeing the final clauses over and over that "Governor Alexander's office could not be reached for comment." It made him a little frustrated on Alexander's behalf. This was not because he felt any particular camaraderie with the man, but due to the fact that the journalists seemed so petty and ignorant. It was perhaps due to his perspective here at the hot core of the unfolding events as they merely passed by inconsequentially in the distant and cold orbit of bitter, blue icy planets. After reading through articles for nearly a half hour he considered it futile to hope the young lawyer would show up with a bottle of whiskey.

He returned to his room. The sky had shifted to a dim orange as the sun stared sideways at him along the edge of the Earth. His quarters were bathed in shadow, save for the horizontal fans of tangerine light running across the walls from the open window. One of the wedges of light cut directly across a face. As Rob identified that it was indeed an unexpected human form inhabiting his room, he grunted out in a stupid and exclamatory tone, "Oh!"

It was Arthur Walden, looking rather inscrutable but detectably stern. He sat on the bed with his legs hanging off the side and his shoulder leaned against the headboard so that he faced the door. His arms were folded on his bulge of a belly. He noted Rob's entry with only a glance.

"What are you doing here?" the journalist asked. He was angry and gave only a small effort at masking it.

The shade of the light on his skin and his stillness made Walden look as though he were made of terracotta. Then the material turned to sand as he moved one hand down to the nightstand beside an odd collection of small, flat objects that Rob could not identify. He took one careful step closer. It was a mosaic of paper scraps, a reconstruction of the envelope that had been slipped under the door earlier.

"What did the note say?" Walden asked firmly. Before Rob could say anything, he followed the question with another. "Any idea who left it for you?"

The violation of his space and privacy was so complete that

Rob did not give an ounce of a damn about Walden's questions. He had no intention of even addressing them.

"I saw you in the forest watching us, listening to us. You're resourceful enough to figure out this mystery for yourself too I'm sure," he taunted, gesturing to the scraps of paper.

Walden's eyes roved over to Rob without any other part of him moving. "I lost track of you after your little tumble, not that it made a difference." He grinned, and then his features turned sober again. "You must realize this is not personal. I simply don't trust you, and this is a very sensitive time for Governor Alexander." He glanced down at the scraps of paper again. "I've known for a while that a thread of sedition runs through here. I will discover the truth in the end." He nodded while staring off at the wall. "I understand you visited the governor's uncle. I trust he was gracious."

"A real charmer."

"You will not let me see the letter?" Walden asked ominously.

"I don't know what you're talking about," Rob replied with faux innocence.

Walden rose and Rob moved aside so that he could exit the room. He expected the older man to say something, but he left without a word. The journalist stood alone in his room and stared at the wash of orange light cutting in through the window, knowing that, despite the strain behind his eyes and bleariness of his pupils, he would probably not sleep a wink.

PART III

The Singing Mountain

Rob had been correct in his initial assessment. He sat awake for hours cutting up and editing the audio files of the interview because he did not feel tired at all. The shock of finding Walden in his room, and the strange conversation that followed, kept him in a perpetual state of restless nervous energy. For the man to go digging through his trash to find the envelope from the anonymous sender was unfathomably invasive. It was clear that there were no rules or standards of propriety when it came to Walden. The man would do anything necessary to pursue his aims. What of the writer of the strange letter? What had Walden called it again, sedition? Clearly there were some factional politics or sabotage at play in the camp. Or was it the whole state? Surely there was dissent. Alexander remained overwhelmingly popular, but could there be some sort of underground force working against him? Was this "Nico" character the face of that element? Rob did some internet searches on the topic and found nothing.

Finally, as the time neared midnight, he stretched out on top of the bedspread. He forced his eyes closed, despite the undercurrent of apprehension, and tried to let his mind wander. Yet it did not drift jellyfish-like in the tranquil, bluish-green and translucent tropical waters of a calm mind. It darted urgently, like a slick-skinned and blind being of the deep, to huddled posts to warm itself beside hot vents releasing acrid, delirious dreaming of the day's most haunting events. Walden stalked him in the woods. Paul Alexander ran an inner-monologue on enmity and the Jews in the back of his brain. Rob opened his eyes and blinked at the ceiling.

There was one other thing he had been intending to do, since sleep seemed entirely out of grasp. Rob took his phone from the bedside table and put on his headphones. After a few moments of browsing, he found a video of Bill Stevens' first speech at the

Wyoming Leadership Convention. He turned to stuff a pillow under his shoulders so that he could sit up comfortably against the headboard.

The footage began with a bubbling murmur of voices and a still shot of an empty wooden podium. The event looked to be held in either an auditorium or large church with dark blue carpeting and wood paneled walls. The angle of the camera was maybe one hundred feet straight ahead of the speaker's lectern and slightly above.

After about half a minute, Stevens appeared near the bottom of the frame in a white button-up shirt. Unlike his ally, Alexander's dark-haired and clean-shaven appearance, he had blond hair, graying on the sides, green eyes under a tawny brow, and a short beard groomed carefully along his jawline. Where the governor was somber and sad, Stevens smiled frequently and widely. He held a clear plastic water bottle in one hand and toyed with the cap while weaving back and forth along the bottom of the frame. He bent out of sight a few times to converse with people in the audience below the stage. Occasionally, a disembodied hand appeared from beneath the shot to clasp his forearm or shake his hand. Stevens looked younger than the more recent photos Rob had seen. He smiled broadly and exuded powerful energy.

After a few minutes of glad-handing, he stepped behind the podium and ensconced the water bottle somewhere inside. He placed his hands on either edge and leaned forward so that he loomed over the audience. "Hello there, everyone." His voice rang out conversational yet clear. It cut out all other sound like a pealing bell. All murmuring tapered off in an instant. "I'm sure none of you know me." He paused for effect and smiled at the ensuing laughter and applause. "I don't live here, although it feels like I do after campaigning so much with your new governor." He gestured and beamed at one specific spot in the room ahead of him where Alexander must have been sitting. "Speaking of which, I would like to thank James Alexander for allowing me to come here and speak to you all today. Honestly I'm surprised he isn't sick to death of hearing me go on and on." More applause and laughter followed.

Stevens' face became more serious and he resumed the looming posture from before. "As I was saying, I don't live here, but I intend to do so for at least part of the year from now on. You see, Alexander winning the governorship was only the first step in a project. I am here today to talk to you all about that project. I am here to talk about momentum, acceleration, and direction. These concepts are most commonly associated with the study of mathematics, physics, and astrophysics, but they are also closely tied to political, social, and cultural movements. When you have all three elements and a proud, strong people, then anything is possible."

Stevens took a breath and raised one hand as though about to hammer some new point home. He made a false start and lowered it before resuming. It was calculated yet played off with flawless nonchalance. "Let me illustrate how easy it is to change the world when you have momentum and direction. Let's take the fast-food industry for example. Those of you familiar with some of my other lectures and speeches know that they are a frequent target of mine. We all know that fast food is bad for us, right?" He waited as smatterings of nervous laughter sounded around the room. His voice resumed loudly and authoritatively, but with a mischievous leading edge. "Oh come on now! We all know our mothers were right! It tastes good, but that doesn't mean it won't kill you!" The second round of laughter was more confident and came from the whole room. "Besides, we know that less processed foods are healthier, that the kitchen is the soul of the home, that the fast-food companies don't pay their workers a damn, they create massive waste, they advance the factory farming interests which in turn fuels the chemical companies who can make a weed dance a jig before thanking you for the pleasure of killing it."

He spoke in rhythmic waves: each clause building on the last to form a powerful swell of invigorating oratory. "Then we find out that all these things make people sick and unhealthy. We all know that fast food is not good for us and our world. We all know that quick and easy satisfaction is not good for our souls." The room was very quiet. Stevens paused and turned one way and then the other to survey the audience before adding in a near-whisper, "We know. Deep down, we all know."

He straightened and waited a few more beats before returning to his former robust tone. "It makes us impatient, erodes our sense of value and hard work. But you know what it would take to bring the fast-food industries down to their knees? If everyone made their meals in their homes for a month, then the whole industry would collapse into bankruptcy." He gave a defiant look to those directly ahead of him. "If we lived like responsible, functioning families for a few weeks, an entire conglomerate worth billions of dollars would dissolve just like that." He snapped his fingers near the microphone and the sound cracked cleanly through the hall like a gunshot.

When he continued, his voice was low and hypnotic, his cadence deliberate. Rob was getting drawn in, despite his natural resistance toward the speaker. "How easy is that? We know it's bad for us, bad for our bodies, for our culture. Those big signs that stick up all down the highways and interstates are the tombstones of family farms, local diners, and small-town grocery stores; they are the garish monuments celebrating disease and sloth and carelessness." He paused and took a deep breath. "And if we just put in a little effort, then it could be gone in just a few short weeks." He leaned one palm on the lectern and turned to glance coolly at one side of the crowd.

"That is the power that is possible when people are on the same page. The problem is that it's not as easy as it should be. These types of institutions, and I'm talking about the big conglomerates, have made it easier for our lives to fall apart. They have become the safety net of the broken individual. When there is no society of large, responsible, and intact families involved in the local community, these industries are the life support of the lone, dying body. And how can we expect the patient to turn on what seems to be the only source of survival?"

Stevens returned his hands to either side of the podium. The jocular crowd-pleasing was all gone, ripped out like the oxygen through a breach in an aircraft fuselage at ten thousand feet. "Momentum, acceleration, and direction," he stated with finality. "This state has the first one of those essential elements, coming off the election of your new governor. James Alexander also provides the last of the elements: direction. But what of acceleration? True acceleration—ethical, moral, rejuvenating acceleration—comes from sweat and effort. It can only come through our collective rejection of the easy in favor of the right. For years, the most cynical sociologists and philosophers have claimed that people only act in their own immediate self-interest. This state, bound for a greater purpose, is an opportunity to prove them wrong. This is not merely a political movement, but a cultural and spiritual one."

Stevens paused and smiled, twisting in his looming pose with arms still planted to look at every part of the audience. "Having spent so much time with your new governor, I have gotten to know the history of your state quite well. It is a long history of big promises made by men who lacked the tenacity and moral character to see them through. There were the land promoters promising millions of acres of the best farmland, then came the reclamation speculators who said they could irrigate it into the most productive soil in the country, then the ore speculators." He flung his hand up to emphasize each point. "Then the gold bubble burst, and the copper bubble burst, the land lay arid and dry, massive irrigation projects, aside from oil, stalled and then disappeared, every one of the empty miracle mirages that promised some hidden treasure just over the horizon came to very little for a very long time. Each one of these promises brought the sort of people who wanted fast money along with all the other vices their kind enjoyed. The whole history of Wyoming is that it has not been peopled. The men who led this state strove by various means to bring in others to work the land and develop the resources, create infrastructure and civilize the wilderness. Governor Alexander's plan represents the latest effort, but it is the only one that can succeed where others have failed."

There was some applause, and he paused until it ended. "I have spent most of my time the last few years traveling around the country and speaking to the people. I discovered in that time that there is a great hunger in this nation for a sense of purpose and belonging. Simply punching a clock and consuming mass-produced products and entertainment is not enough. The people, especially the young, want to be part of something that has meaning. This is the most perfect time for a project such as James Alexander's. The cynics would claim that we do not have enough resources or draw, but those are the idle claims of the merchants of mediocrity."

Stevens was starting to build to something. He spoke with complete authority and perfect enunciation. He added no dramatic turns or superfluous theatrics that could suddenly draw the listener out of the moment. He gestured simply with one hand pulled repeatedly toward his chest, as though beckoning all who heard to follow him to another place. "We have an opportunity for a new Wyoming, an energized Wyoming, one which attracts the disheartened but strong, the upright who have been abandoned in their uprightness, the disillusioned faithful, those who have sat in pained silence as immoral, worldly powers devour everything around them, the ones who fear that there will be no answer to their prayers. A thick darkness covers their faces. They look to the east, and they do not see God; they look west; they look north and south. I have an idea for a new turn of phrase when it comes to this state. It is simply this: 'Wyoming, come home.'" The crowd exploded into a sudden roar, and Stevens shouted right over the top of the rolling wave, "If they are to the south of us, then let them look north! If they are to our east, then let them look west! If they are north, then let them look south! Let them look home! Let them look to Wyoming, the new center of the world!"

It took minutes for the applause to stop. Rob could see the domed shapes of heads bobbing along the bottom of the shot. Stevens was getting a standing ovation. Once calm had resumed, he took a deep breath and smiled. "Polling data shows that a significant portion of Americans believe that the country has lost its moral center. Let them look here. This state produces agriculture and energy, but the most valuable cultivation we must be known for is the human soul. If this is our aim, then who can stand against us? This state must be the center of a new revival, a rejuvenation of a country whose heart is weary and whose hands are stained with filth and blood and grime." Stevens reached down to pick up a small slip of paper. "Let me relay to you what a visitor said about this state some many years ago. There may be some hyperbole in here, but it illustrates a hope in our potential."

He began reading, "'Then tell me oh, ye prophets, what will it be like, when the first half of this new century is history? What sort of people will then inhabit this oasis in the Great American Desert? I will tell you. Women so surpassing fair that all the world pays homage. Men of vigorous strength, with an unheard-of power for effective action, capable of solving the deepest riddles of the ages. Giants, physically, intellectually, and morally. Made so by their natural environment. Made so by an omnipotent, omniscient, omnipresent force. Made so by the spirit of these rugged mountains, by the voiceless influence of these matchless plains, by the intoxication of this high, dry, perfect atmosphere.'" He paused after the reading and the audience broke once more into enthusiastic applause.

"With momentum, acceleration, and direction this state can do anything. We must first draw in those who are of like mind with us. This will require sacrifice, but the reward is far more valuable. There are powerful forces in this world that do not want such a project to succeed. They fear a resolute and upright people who are not swayed by the baubles and trinkets of the consumeristic life that they hope to impose on all peoples. They want us all to feel disconnected and alone. They want us to believe that only their goods and services can provide that fleeting sense of belonging. It is in defiance to this blasphemy that we must find courage. Marketing has become so powerful and pervasive that it is no longer about appealing to different types of people. The entertainment marketing complex has taken upon itself to instruct people how they should live. They must be accepting of all iniquities, since tolerance of all sin is openness to all ways of living, and, in turn, this is openness to all manners and means of consumption. In the death of true culture, they can make their own weak imitation, one that only serves to advance and protect their own interests. I don't want to live in such a way. Do you?"

It was at that point that Rob fell asleep on the bedspread with his headphones still on. He awoke suddenly in the dark hours of the morning with the headphones down around his neck and his phone discarded next to his thigh. He did not finish Stevens' address. He sat up in the darkness and considered it and the lingering apprehension at what was possible.

According to his phone it was a little after four o'clock. He rose in the shadowy stillness of the room and changed into his athletic shorts and took off his button-up shirt. He crawled under the blankets before falling asleep. He woke again at a little after five thirty and was no longer tired, despite sleeping only four hours in total. Rob turned to the window and watched the glowing, ghostly emanations of the approaching sun send silver light through the drapes. He heard the steady, soft sound of footsteps in the hallway and rose to listen at the door. After Walden's ambush the prior evening he was taking no more chances with being caught unaware. The muffled impacts passed by, and he could hear the door to Banks' office opening. Despite being in shorts and a white undershirt, he decided to investigate.

When Rob stepped into the hall, Banks was standing in his office with his back to the open doorway and his hands on his hips. He turned once he heard the noise and smiled.

"Up early this morning, Mr. Coen."

Rob shrugged and moved over to lean his shoulder on the doorway to the office. "I didn't sleep very much last night. I've had a lot on my mind."

"Yeah?" the older man asked, looking suddenly apprehensive, as though someone were about to hand him something fragile which he did not trust himself to hold.

"Nothing personal or existential," Rob reassured him. "But I have come across a number of strange things in the last day."

"Strange?" Banks was still wary.

"I had a good conversation with the governor. That was fine. But I had an odd run-in with Walden."

At that statement, Banks gave a hint of a knowing smile and leaned back against his desk. "Walden is not one for making people, well, comfortable," he admitted.

"Does the governor just let him do anything he wants?" Rob asked, trying to keep his frustration in check.

"I'm going to guess he did something typically invasive," Banks mused.

"Does the governor know what kinds of liberties he takes?"

Banks folded his arms and sighed. "You have to realize that I go back to the times before Arthur Walden was an element. I knew Alexander when he was much younger. Walden was not part of the campaign or any of that. I know my place, so I never said that I had any reservations about the man, but he is not like the governor. He does not hold the same values."

"You didn't want him around?" Rob asked.

Banks' eyes darted over very quickly and then turned down to his shoes. "Not in such stark terms. I am not like him. We get along, but do not see eye to eye. When I first heard that he would be working for Alexander, I asked the governor if he trusted him. That is as close as I have ever come to voicing any dislike. I am a simple person. I have known it my whole life. Trust and honesty are straightforward to me. I drove for Alexander. I simply go from starting point A to destination B. For this reason, I do not presume to give Alexander advice and I cannot dislike Walden. To do so would presume beyond my capacity."

They were both quiet for a moment before Rob responded, "You know that isn't true. You know that you find Walden to be unsavory in his methods. You just won't let yourself say it because it might unravel this little world."

Banks held up a hand, an oddly assertive move from him. "I apologize if Walden did anything intrusive, but my own personal apprehensions are unimportant. Walden is a man of the world. Such people are necessary."

"That's more or less what Alexander said." Rob paused and took in a silent breath. "Have you ever heard of anyone who goes by the pseudonym Nico?"

Banks raised an eyebrow. "Yes. How did you hear that name?"

Rob felt a sudden exhilarating burst of energy, as though he had just solved a vexing puzzle of some kind. "I heard it in passing. Someone mentioning the name. The context was curious. I wanted to find out more."

"Well that's strange," Banks remarked. "Nobody has heard anything from whomever that is in a few years. Back near the beginning of the governor's first term, someone published a number of editorials under that name. He or she was bent on deconstructing the governor systematically. They came out in the *Casper Star-Tribune*, the widest circulating newspaper in the state. If I recall, the first one compared Alexander to Nels H. Smith, one of the more unpopular former governors of the state, who only served one term. You see, Smith did the same thing as Alexander. He also stacked the university board to oust a sitting college president, albeit a far more popular one with many friends. It was clear from the editorials that this Nico character knew the state very well and had likely lived here most of their life. The articles went on for about a year, maybe, before they stopped."

"Just stopped?" Rob asked. "Out of nowhere?"

"As far as I know," Banks said with a shrug. "I know Walden was on the warpath for a while. He had his own secret investigation going on until the editor of the *Tribune* called up and asked Alexander to call him off, which he did. As far as I know, Walden never tracked down the true source of the editorials. There was a lot of suspicion at the time that it was the former president of the college trying to get some revenge, but Walden claimed that he knew it wasn't him." The concierge furrowed his brow and steepled his fingers. "That's why it is so curious that you would hear someone talking about it. That name hasn't really cropped up since the editorials stopped years ago."

"There was no indication as to why this person had such a problem with Alexander?"

Banks shrugged. "Well, it was a lot of the typical complaint. This character was clearly a liberal of the modern kind, giving dire warnings of authoritarianism and damage to human rights. Those things don't really play well around here, so it was all a bit futile. Some people liked the vocal opposition, but not very many."

"Do you know where I could find a copy of the editorials?" Rob asked. "All this mysteriousness has me pretty intrigued."

"That I don't know," Banks admitted. "I don't know if they were ever posted online or if they're still up. If not, then you could get ahold of someone at the *Tribune* and see if they could send them to you."

"Good idea."

"So, did you like the governor?" Banks asked after letting a brief silence justify his change in topic.

"He is both exactly like and nothing like they say he is," Rob mused. "He is more intelligent than they give him credit for, and he is more invested in his ideology than they could possibly imagine. There is a sense in the rest of the country that he is on some level a pragmatist, and I don't mean that in the sense that he can get reasonable things done. They think that on some level he cannot possibly believe the things that he says, and that this is all an intricate ruse to get the desired result. While I disagree with him on almost everything, I can't disbelieve his earnest desire to bring it all about. So, in that way, I do like him. It's a strange paradox, I guess. Maybe in the same way that he can bring himself to trust a man like Walden."

"Perhaps," Banks murmured. The older man stared at the floor for a moment before rousing himself. "So, you are going to Mount Calvary this morning?"

"As I understand it, yes."

"It has been too long since I have been there. I do hope you can get outside your journalistic skepticism enough to enjoy it."

Rob laughed. "That is probably not going to happen," he admitted. "And I can't promise that I'll try."

Banks smiled knowingly and simply said, "I suppose so."

"I won't bother you anymore," Rob assured him and gave a nod of acknowledgement before turning back into the hall and entering his room.

"Anytime," Banks replied as he departed.

Rob showered and left the lodge to walk the camp. The meal hall did not open to serve breakfast for a little while yet. The air was cool, and a steady breeze wound between the buildings. There was movement in the bunkhouses and a semi-circle of workmen stood in the middle of them sending up coils of cigarette smoke. A gradually building hum sounded as Rob walked by the silent workshops and stables. The noise grew from a distant buzz to a roar. After a minute, he could see the source of the sound. A low flying helicopter approached the camp from the south. It slowed and lowered as it neared. He moved toward the hovering object as it came down in the lower area of the camp between his location and the river. The helicopter bore similar coloring to the State Corps trucks he had seen frequently over the past day. He watched it descend out of sight before winding the paths for a bit and then returning to the lodge.

The first rush had arrived in the meal hall, and he had to wait a few minutes before receiving a stack of hotcakes, scrambled eggs, and ham. If anything on this trip had exceeded expectations, it was the food. Rob poured himself some coffee from a great big, heated drum with a spout at the bottom and found a solitary table at the corner of the room. He took a few cautious sips while perusing the archives of the *Casper Star-Tribune* website on his phone. He could not find the Nico editorials, so he sent an email to the editor in hopes that he could get a PDF. He took a few bites of egg and stared into space, wondering why this Nico character would re-emerge years later and how he would know to reach out. *How was he or she even aware that I'm here or which room is mine?* he wondered.

Rob was interrupted in his musing by a gallant looking young man who strode right up to the table and set a heaping plate down with a resounding clatter. He was blond and quintessentially handsome with a square jaw and broad shoulders. His features were young, and he was clean-shaven. He wore a brown bomber jacket with leather gloves sticking out of the front pocket. He sat down and looked at Rob with piercing blue eyes before remarking, "Glad I waited for the pancakes here. Say what you will about camp life, but the food sure doesn't disappoint. Something about it is just absolutely supreme."

Rob nodded, not quite sure how to react to the sudden disturbance.

"You're the journalist, right?" the young man asked after swallowing a heaping forkful. "I'm Daniel Marshall."

"Yeah, I'm the journalist. Rob Coen," Rob replied hesitantly.

Daniel smiled and pushed a metallic yellow lock of hair back from his forehead. "I'm your ride to Mount Calvary." He stated it as though the information should elicit delight on the part of his new acquaintance. "I'm going to fly you over in the helicopter."

"So that was you coming in earlier?" Rob asked, a little more interested.

The pilot nodded enthusiastically.

Rob took a bite of ham, chewed it methodically and swallowed. "No offense intended, but you seem a little young for a pilot."

The young man shrugged. "I've been flying since I was sixteen. I had a couple hundred hours in before I even got my driver's license. I fly the governor around all the time." He paused to devour some ham. "When Justine shows up, we can split whenever you're ready." Daniel leaned in a little across the table and cast a few glances over his shoulders before continuing in a conspiratorial tone. "You have met Justine, right?"

"Yes," Rob confirmed before taking a gulp of coffee. "What do you think of her?"

"I mean, she's nice and all, but it's kind of scary being around her, since her uncle is the governor." He shrugged. "Maybe it's because we are around the same age. It just makes me nervous that I might say something stupid that will make it back to him."

"I thought you said that you flew the governor all the time," Rob observed in a more mocking tone than he had intended.

"That's totally different," Daniel insisted. "How do you do, sir? Good day for flying, sir. Watch your head, sir. Not with Justine. She's a nice girl. You can let your guard down. Different story." He held his palms out as though warning something away.

"Are you afraid of the governor?" Rob asked.

"No," the pilot replied. "It's hard to describe I guess."

"So what? You're attracted to her?" the journalist asked with a smirk.

Daniel's face got a little red. "That's not it either," he insisted before taking a few more bites and changing the subject. "Is this your first time in the state?"

"It is."

"It must be kind of strange. I grew up here, so everything is normal to me, but I can't imagine what it must be like to come from some big city and see this place for the first time."

"It is certainly unique," Rob conceded. "Tell me a little about yourself," he added, mostly just wanting to enjoy his meal without having to add anything to the conversation.

"I grew up in Cheyenne. My dad works at the airport there. That's how I got into flying at a young age. I joined the Corps after high school, since I didn't really want to go to college. They have programs where you can learn things anyway, so I don't think I missed out. They need pilots for a lot of different projects, so it worked out pretty well."

"You like the corps?" Rob asked between bites.

"I do," Daniel replied with an emphatic nod. "If you're a specialist then you get a decent stipend and you feel like you're actually accomplishing something. I mean, there are slackers in the Corps like in any group, but it works out pretty well."

"Have you ever been out of the state?" Rob asked.

Daniel laughed. "As a pilot I would have eventually even by accident. I've been all over the Western states and the Midwest. I don't really like it back East though. It's too humid. Something about it doesn't agree with me."

At that moment Rob glanced over his companion's shoulder and spied Justine approaching from across the hall. She wore a pleated navy skirt that went just past her knees, a white blouse, and a caramel-colored blazer, and she carried some sort of notebook or folder. Her appearance was strangely collegiate in a stereotypical way. The attire gave her such a different appearance from the work clothes he had seen her in before that it took him a moment to recognize her. Daniel noticed that Rob was looking at something of interest and turned to look over his shoulder.

"Hey Justine," he called out and then turned back around to take another bite of food with a look of slight bewilderment on his face.

She reached the table and sat at an equal distance to each of them on Rob's right. She inclined her head to one and then the other before setting the binder down in front of her.

"You going to eat anything?" Rob asked.

"No, I already ate," she said, eyeing Daniel's plate with a slight grimace. "Besides, they don't really concern themselves too much with nutrition here."

"Worried that you'll put on a few pounds if you fall in love with the pancakes?" Rob teased. He was emboldened by all he had endured the previous day at the hands of Walden and the acid-tongued Paul Alexander.

Daniel shot Rob a nervous look, as though he expected to receive retribution by proxy.

"And so what if I am?" Justine asked coolly. "Are we ready to go as soon as you two are finished?"

Daniel nodded while swallowing. "Yeah, the helicopter should be ready to go right about now."

She turned to Rob. "You?"

He patted the chest of his jacket. "I'm just bringing my notebook, so I can go whenever."

The pilot looked at Rob and then Justine before shrugging. "No rush though. I have the helicopter all day, unless you're in a hurry."

"The monument will be less crowded if we get there earlier," Justine explained.

Daniel rose. "Let me get a few more pancakes and coffee and then I'll be good."

Rob had finished eating and sat back to finish his cup of coffee. "Those pancakes were filling as hell. I don't know how that guy can eat any more."

She ignored his attempt at levity. "How did the interview go with my uncle? It was good?"

"For him or me?" Rob asked wryly.

"For him," she clarified with her imperious look.

"I think it went well for both of us," he mused. "He's an intelligent man and very good with words. He gave me some interesting history and insight into the first few years he was in office. To be honest it all sounds pretty unbelievable, and I told him that. He said it was a problem with my perspective."

"He said that you've been taught to believe that the world cannot be changed," she added.

"Yes," he confirmed with a nod. "Do you believe that?"

She looked over at him. "It makes sense, just like inertia. Objects at rest tend to stay at rest."

"And for an object to be in motion, it needs acceleration, momentum, and direction." He said with a smirk.

"You do your homework," she admitted. "I'll give you that."

"I was always good at homework," Rob murmured, thinking back briefly to being alone in his room in the evening and reading ahead in his textbooks under the light of his desk lamp, reading on into the future to know more than his classmates. They knew things only as one knows a gift—that it is presented with no story—just as they knew their families which came to them out of a void of unacknowledged but accepted being. And he knew sometimes his mother and less often his father and that they had unknown each other as one rejects the accident of being in favor of the void. Alone he surpassed them on into the future.

He shook himself from the cold memory. "How well do you

know the pilot?" he asked.

"I met Daniel a few years ago when I volunteered with the Hospitallers," she recounted in a disinterested tone.

Rob could not tell if it was calculated or genuine. Perhaps it was instead simply faraway, a tone which meandered outside with the cool breeze under the moon and in a youthful embrace of faltering sexual approach, the secret, stumbling, pantomime approximation played out with hushed and hypoxic determination as everyone else slept. Maybe it was the tone that seeks to forget such things while remembering them, to put a pin in the unknowing for a future time. Most likely it was none of these and Rob had been unexpectedly cast into one of his compulsively analytic moods, trapped by the coiling thought strangulations.

"I actually don't know him very well," she added. "He's nice enough, and my uncle likes him."

"I think he's a little scared of you," Rob murmured with a grin. He typically would not play the trickster, but he was among younger people, which always made him feel a bit more careless and frivolous.

Justine raised a cool eyebrow. "Some people could take a lesson from that."

Daniel returned with his additional food, and they made small talk as he finished. Rob asked them about the Wyoming dollar. Daniel was bullish and idealistic on the development. He thought that it was important to set the tone that the state would not be pushed around by the federal government. Justine was more calculated in her responses. She agreed that it was necessary but added that the reactions of the federal government would be important in determining how viable it was in the long run.

"We have a good deal of federal infrastructure here, between the military bases and national parks. In the long run they have almost unlimited heft to leverage against us."

They returned their plates and passed through the bustling hall of echoing voices out into the entry. Rob took note of the Latin words of iron above the door and realized that he had forgotten to ask Alexander about them. He turned to Justine as they walked out onto the porch.

"What do the words above the door mean?"

"They translate to 'Now always we are free.'"

"In what way?"

"The phrase is above all the entryways to the lodges around the state. They are meant to be seen while exiting. It has to do with the notion that the state is bound to a singular purpose, that even as you exit the lodge into the outside, there still remains the purpose."

"That seems a little ironic." Rob observed.

"It's honest."

"That's what I don't get," he replied. "That way of thinking seems so alien to a place that is known for the big skies and independence of the self-made man."

"Why does the man make himself?" she asked.

Rob shrugged. They were winding the gravel paths toward where the helicopter had landed. Daniel was a few paces ahead. "The man makes himself because he wants power I guess, which is just freedom over circumstances."

"Then we agree," she retorted slyly. "Man strives to be like God. Man seeks dominion because he is made in God's image."

"That's not what I said."

"Either God is real, and man seeks to be like Him, or God is a retroactively implanted mirage of the deep subconscious and man seeks to be that idea. Does the existence or non-existence of God change the nature of the striving?"

"Only in name," Rob argued.

"And that is where we disagree," she concluded.

After a few more minutes of walking, they reached a leveled-out area beyond the buildings of the camp. The helicopter sat waiting in the middle of a concrete pad near a large, metal building with open sliding doors at the front. Daniel hastened and turned to the opening to converse with a man in mechanic's coveralls. Justine and Rob waited by the helicopter. After a minute, the pilot looked over and said, "You guys can get in."

Justine opened the rear door where four seats were positioned, two side by side facing another two. She climbed into the craft first and Rob clambered awkwardly into the seat facing her. She opened the binder and leafed through some papers absentmindedly.

"Mount Calvary can be overwhelming and tedious for those uninitiated in Christian theology. It not only attracts tourists, but also those devoted to the deepest and most intertwined machinations of scriptural metaphor and prophecy."

"Meaning that it's somewhat self-fulfilling," Rob mused.

"You're pretty clever for a journalist," she replied with a withering smile. He could not tell if it was earnest or not.

Daniel was running through pre-flight checks, flipping through pages on a clipboard, and entering the cockpit occasionally to check on one instrument or another before leaving only to enter again. After another minute of activity, he settled into the pilot's seat and gingerly placed a headset over his ears. He twisted around in the seat.

"This baby is a Bell 407. We should make good time to the monument. It's going to get pretty loud here in a minute, so I'll let you guys get your headsets on."

Rob and Justine took the hint.

"Everything coming in clear?" he asked, once they had put them on.

Justine gave him a thumbs up. Rob nodded.

Daniel reached down to his left to twist the throttle and power up the engine. The rotor whined and began to turn slowly before gradually spinning up to a throbbing roar. As the pilot adjusted the pedals and hand controls, the craft gradually lifted until the skids hovered a few feet above the ground. Then in a swift motion he swept them up higher and higher and pitched the nose so that they swooped forward in an exhilarating leap. Once they had reached a cruising altitude, Daniel's voice came through their headsets, "We'll be in the air a little over an hour. It should be a pretty smooth ride. There isn't too much wind coming down off the Wyomings."

Rob peered down at the rocky mountainsides and the toothpick model pine and spruce trees. It was remarkable how one could be suddenly wrenched into a very fantastical sense of reality with a nearly instantaneous change of perspective. He had always marveled at the human ability to adapt to circumstances which were impossibly absurd to man in his natural state. The extreme, compounding capital of modern reality was still not enough to unravel the human ability to adapt. Or maybe it was, and, while the advancement of technology had been rapid, the collapse of the human being occurred in slow motion. Of course, that would imply that Alexander was right.

They cut through the air with the occasional lilting stutter and nothing more. Much of the time passed in silence broken at times by Daniel narrating the landscape and pointing out landmarks as they passed by. Rob had no frame of reference, and the names of the sights faded from him soon after they had faded from view. Daniel named all the peaks of the Wyomings as they traveled along them in a southerly parallel. Wyoming and Coffin peaks only stood out because they were the tallest. The rest passed by in a somber procession of patient indictment. Justine said nothing and haunted her facing seat as the customary unknown quantity she represented.

After the mountains leveled out, Daniel pointed to something directly ahead and below. Rob unbuckled and turned to lean between the two cockpit seats and get a better look.

"Up ahead is Lake Viva Naughton. I go ice fishing there in the winter. It freezes over pretty good when it gets cold. As you can see, things flatten out here. It means we're close. Up way beyond there is Fort Bridger, but that's past where we're going. Before long you'll be able to see Evanston. It's the biggest town in the area. It's actually grown quite a bit since the monument opened."

As they neared the lake, the land had turned to plains which were broken occasionally by smooth hills and folds. Then Rob saw the town of Evanston as the helicopter began to slow and lower.

"You'll want to buckle in for the landing."

After a few minutes they had slowed to a hover a few hundred feet above the ground. They began to lower down with a light swaying, as though the craft hung dangling from a thread.

"Where are we landing?" Rob asked.

"At the monument," Daniel explained. "There is a small hangar and landing strip here."

"I didn't see it, the monument that is."

Daniel twisted around to smile at Rob. "Here you go."

The tail of the helicopter swung around as they gradually descended, and the hill came into view outside Rob's window. The monument was larger and less synthetic looking than he had expected. He was not entirely sure what he had really anticipated. He had seen a few photos online, but they were all from the ground. Mount Calvary was not symmetrical or dome-like. The mountain was formed roughly, with boulders jutting out of the dirt all over and a light scattering of desert shrubs giving it a very genuine appearance. It would have been very much at home somewhere in the Middle East. Some kind of reflective structure covered the very top of the monument, and he could make out the twin spiral paths running around the sides. A few large buildings rested at the bottom along with a large parking area nearly halfway populated with vehicles.

"Looks like we got here early enough that it isn't too busy," Daniel remarked. He turned around again to acknowledge Justine. "Good thinking."

They came down lightly on a cement pad a few hundred yards away from the parking lot and structures, stirring up billowing waves of dust. A herd of goats milled about on the far side of the landing strip away from the monument. They frolicked at the noise and sudden activity.

"What's with the goats?" Rob asked.

"The Benedictine monks look after them," Justine explained. "They use them for milk, meat, and cheese for celebration meals around Christmas and Easter."

"Really adds to the rustic charm," Rob commented under his

breath. He paused and turned back to her. "Benedictines? I was under the impression that the Catholic Church had no opinions on whether Mount Calvary was a site with any religious significance."

"And yet, the governor extended an open invitation which some have accepted. You can ask Brother Manuel yourself."

The whine of the engine decreased, and the blades slowed after they had touched down. Daniel clambered out of the cockpit and motioned that they could get out as well. The air was warm outside, and a slight breeze stirred the floating veils of dust. The pilot moved off to talk to another Corpsman who approached the landing pad. Another man about Rob's age neared from the direction of the monument. He was dark haired but significantly balding. He wore a simple black robe and walked deliberately with his hands clasped behind his back. Rob looked quizzically at Justine.

"That is José Manuel. As I was saying before, he is with the Benedictines who stay here. One could say he is the unofficial liaison between my uncle and the Catholic Church."

"Interesting," Rob murmured.

"When one has many enemies, they must make friends in unconventional ways."

When the monk was close enough to be heard over the noise of the helicopter, he inclined his head first to Justine and then Rob before extending a hand. "I am José Manuel."

Rob shook his hand. "Rob Coen. I was just telling Justine that I was a little surprised to find a Catholic presence here."

Manuel smiled. "Because there is something that seems so distinctly American and Protestant about Governor Alexander's projects?" He had a notable Spanish accent of the European variety.

"I'm not sure I would use those exact words, but that describes it pretty well." Rob replied.

"It is good to see you again," the monk said to Justine, turning so that he faced her directly. "How is your uncle?"

"He is doing well, but many things are happening very quickly now. If you could pray for him, it would be appreciated."

"I do always," Manuel assured her before returning his attention to the journalist and indicating the path he had traveled to the landing area with an outstretched hand. He resumed talking as they began following it back from where he had approached.

"You would not be wrong in questioning our presence here. But you must realize that there is something about him which appeals also to the Catholic mind. Yes, he may not be a member of the Holy Roman Church, but he is clearly devoted to the cause of Christ in this world and is a righteous leader. He does not contend to rule by divine right, but he does bear some resemblance to the Christian kings of Europe."

Justine laughed. "José, when you talk like this, I can never tell if you're joking."

The monk flushed a little but smiled. "I get carried away at times perhaps, but do not let potential exaggeration take from the point."

He turned to Rob with steepled fingers held at chest level. "To address the politics of our presence here: it is far less complicated than you might imagine. When Mount Calvary neared completion, Alexander made an open invitation for Churches to establish embassies of a sort here at the monument. It was a very intelligent idea, as it caused a clamor of escalating competing attempts to commit the greatest sign of faith. Churches were motivated to encourage their members to visit after making the investment. It drew in representatives from all the Protestant sects. After a while it became clear that the Catholic Church had no intention of making a similar move. I felt moved to offer myself as a presence here. To my surprise, a number of my Benedictine brothers fell in with me and showed an interest in coming along."

He paused and pondered the asphalt-paved path ahead of them. "At the risk of sounding rather juvenile, I had become transfixed with James Alexander. I came across a number of his addresses from his political campaign. I was so mesmerized by his manner of speaking and his advocation for a life of religious fervor and devotion to God. It was that secret admiration that drove me to ask the authorities in the Benedictine Confederation for their blessing to establish a presence here. I had already been interested in starting a community in Wyoming. The state was largely unchurched before Alexander, especially by the Roman Catholic Church. Before I tried to convince my superiors that it was a wise choice to put a presence here at the monument, I put together a presentation with videos of speeches by both Alexander and Bill Stevens." He laughed and turned to smile at his companions. "Can you imagine it? A group of monks, some old enough to be my grandfather, all waiting with Christ-like patience as I set up an old television to show them what I had put together."

"That's quite the image," Rob assented.

"Yes, it was," Manuel chuckled. "Well, the reaction was mixed. Many were preoccupied with Alexander's status as a Protestant and others were uncomfortable with his 'authoritarian leanings,' as they called it. Many of the younger monks agreed with me, that Alexander presented much too significant an opportunity, and that ignoring his invitation would be a mistake. I did not know that my modest idea would cause a stir, but it did. There was a good deal of worry that it was not our place to give what would look to be a tacit blessing to an enterprise which the Church had not addressed. Another criticism maintained that Alexander's reactionary project could end in disaster and that our presence at the center of his workings could cause unneeded criticism of the order. You see, our order is rather independent by community, but the abbot is the last word on who comes and goes. I needed his permission, but I also wanted his blessing. And this alone was not enough. I wanted the blessing of the confederation."

"Sounds like a tall order," Rob interjected.

"It was. I was respectful but replied to my superiors' concerns. I argued that a presence was needed at the monument, since it was the best place to display by example the beautified life of both our order and mother Church. I also explained that, while Alexander may not be Catholic, that he was clearly an upright man who sought to serve God. If God can work through the wicked, then he can work with even greater wonders through a man who is upright. Additionally, our order is devoted to living a life of Christian reflection and devotion to God. Alexander himself expressed a desire for the people of the state to be bound up to one purpose, and that God was central to that mission. What better place could I want to be? I added that I truly believed that God was calling me here, and that a community at the monument would be blessed and successful. That last part was perhaps a bit unfair."

"Unfair?" Rob asked.

"It is not a logical or theological argument," Manuel admitted. "It is an appeal to emotion, a non-falsifiable non-argument."

"And you regret using it?"

"I regret nothing which led me here," Manuel replied. "I only wish in retrospect that I had been more intellectually exhaustive in my argument."

"Well it must have worked," Rob observed.

"There was some back and forth, but ultimately my abbot was willing to let me and a few others come here as a satellite community. We have limited authority over ourselves and still answer to our parent leadership. Occasionally the abbot visits here. He seems pleased with my work and the arrangement. We have a small prayer chapel, simple quarters, and a farm. It is hard work and fulfilling. I meet many people who come here to visit the monument. It is a good life."

"Are you our tour guide for my visit here?" Rob asked with a smirk.

Manuel laughed. "When I heard that a journalist from *The Times* was coming here, I wanted to be present for the occasion. The desire, I hope, does not come from self-importance. I want to help represent the monument in the best way possible. Treat me as a resource for theological questions. Miss Justine is our guide."

Rob considered what the monk had said. "Would you be in trouble with your abbot if I included you in my article?" he asked.

Manuel let a shadow of anxiety ripple over his features briefly. "I would prefer if you did not, but it is up to you. It is not the place of the Benedictine to seek influence on the world. We are called to look to Christ and focus on silence, diligence, and contemplation."

"I understand," Rob assured him. "As far as your being a source of information, assume that I know absolutely nothing about the monument or Christian symbology. That's probably your best bet. I'll just try to soak it all in."

Justine took over at that point. "Well, we should start at the visitor's center." She pulled a pass attached to a lanyard out of her binder and gave it to Rob. "We can skip all the lines and go wherever you want with this. It doesn't look like we'll have much need though."

They reached the front of the visitor's center, a large timber building with a green metal roof, and entered through large glass doors. A number of park workers in uniforms milled around the polished concrete floor of the expansive lobby. An older woman took notice of Justine and came over to intercept her. Rob and Manuel went through into a large hallway of displays and placards of historical information.

"I noticed you have a slight accent," Rob stated after they meandered between the exhibits for a minute.

"Yes," the monk replied. "My family is from Spain. When I was still in school, things were getting very hard in the country. My parents were worried about the future there, so they sent me to live with my aunt and uncle here in America. It was here that I joined the Benedictines."

"Do you like it here? In America?"

"It is strange that everything is so young. I miss old buildings and the length of history in Spain. Also, there are fewer Christians in Europe, but they are more devout. Or so it seems. Many here in America claim to believe in God but they are not Christians."

"You believe Governor Alexander is a Christian?"

"In the strictest sense of the laws of my Church, it is hard to say, but in my own understanding of God and His love, I believe that Alexander is one of His favorite sons." The monk smiled to himself and then asked, "You have met the governor?"

"Yes, I interviewed him for a few hours yesterday. We got along fine. What about you? Do you speak to him often?"

"At least a few times a year when he comes to the monument," Manuel explained. "He says that he likes to get the Catholic perspective from time to time, which, believe me, is a nerve-wracking proposition."

Justine had finished her conversation and moved past them further into the hallway. She spun a slow circle and indicated the displays all around. "This section basically gives information on the planning and funding of the monument. The short version is that it was Alexander's idea, and the state legislature passed a bill as part of the Wyoming Plan package to break ground after the private crowd-funding drives took off. Governor Alexander asked Jeremiah Robertson, an American mountaineer, writer, and photographer, to lead the design committee, despite his having no prior engineering or managerial experience. The choice raised some eyebrows, but Robertson was good at deferring to those who had more knowledge on the finer points. Bill Stevens went on a nationwide funding tour, and within a few months the first phase was funded and construction began, and so on," she concluded. "If you want to know more, then feel free to peruse or ask."

"How many years did it take to finish the monument?" Rob asked, glancing over at a photograph of Jeremiah Robertson.

"The monument is not really finished," Justine explained. "It is always being expanded. A rather extensive garden was added to the southwest side last year. Mount Calvary itself took about two and half years to complete."

"That's pretty fast."

"A number of large donors gifted support in the form of labor and excavation crews. One oil speculator from Texas had his guys move a significant portion of the dirt and boulders gratis."

"How many visitors come here per year?"

"The numbers have steadily increased. We get draw from Yellowstone and other national parks. Last year was the highest traffic yet at about two million. Some church organizations set up large annual visits for thousands of parishioners."

"That's a pretty good haul," Rob admitted. "Doesn't it seem a bit, well, hypocritical to monetize a monument that is intended to be spiritual?"

"Access to the monument, gardens, and visitor's center are all free," she explained. "There is a fee for parking and guided tours, but we offer a shuttle to Evanston residents for free. Some locals come and use the paths every day."

"What should I expect?" Rob asked.

"There is a scale model of the monument over here." Justine beckoned them down the hallway toward a large circular room. A glass dome rested over an expansive round table in the center of the space. A pool of yellow light illuminated a painstakingly detailed replica of the mountain and visitor's center. Justine pointed to the structures at the bottom. "We are here. The path up the monument is to the right of the visitor's center. It spirals up to the top, marked by Stations of the Cross."

"What is that structure?" Rob asked, indicating a dome-like covering that sat on top of the mountain.

"That is the place of the crucifix." She paused, realizing the statement raised more questions than it answered. "I'm not even going to try to explain it. You will just have to see it for yourself."

"How do you even go about building a mountain?" Rob puzzled aloud.

Justine turned to one side of the room and crossed to a collection of photographs and boxes of text on the wall. "This explains the process. There was already a natural hill at this site. Most of the dirt and rock which was added came from construction and State Corps projects. The topsoil came from the desert portions of the state east of here to better mimic the arid setting of the original Golgotha."

Rob glanced over the photos of the monument at its various stages of development. One image showed it in a strange, stepped spiral so that trucks and equipment could drive up and down the corkscrew sides. In one picture a group of workmen stood at the yawning mouth of a cave opening.

"What's this?" he asked, pointing at the photo. "Is there some kind of chamber inside the monument?"

"Yes, that's where the choir goes," Justine stated.

Rob gave her a look of surprise. "Let me guess, I should just see it for myself."

She bobbed her head to one side and then the other. "That would probably be easier than trying to explain every mechanism."

Rob spun around to survey the room. Manuel was leaning over the scale model peering at some detail which had taken his notice.

"Is there anything else I should know, or should we just head up?"

"We should probably head up," Justine urged. "José's knowledge of the site is categorical, so if you think of anything later on, then I'm sure he will be able to answer any questions." She beckoned to the monk, who stirred from his perusal of the tiny shrubs atop the model mountain and raised his eyebrows in anticipation. "We're heading up."

Manuel nodded and led the way down the hall and back out through the entry. A guided tour of Asian tourists had convened outside, and the three maneuvered around them to the base of the trail. The monk indicated an informational sign at the marker for the beginning of the ascent.

"This explains that the path is not easy. It is two miles uphill along the fourteen Stations of the Cross. Each one is displayed by an illuminated painted mural within a sheltered rock alcove."

"Two miles uphill sounds pretty arduous," the journalist observed. "How do the sick or elderly make it?"

"'Straight is the gate and narrow is the way, which leadeth to life, and few are those who find it,'" Manuel remarked. "The monument has wheelchairs and volunteers to help those who need it if their families cannot. There are no shortcuts. The path is the same for everyone."

"Seems a bit harsh."

"Faith is harsh. Life is harsh." The monk looked down at his feet and clasped his hands behind his back again as they began to walk up the path. "Have you heard Bill Stevens' speech called 'The Quality of Mercy: Compassion and the Gas Chamber?'"

A tickling numbness crawled over Rob's skin, and he suddenly felt very hot on the inside. "No," he replied simply.

"It addresses your wonderings about difficulty and mercy."

"I'm not very acquainted with Stevens' body of work," Rob admitted. "Besides, I'm still not sure you've explained adequately why a Benedictine monk is so interested in a Protestant philosopher."

The monk paused in his walking and indicated the first mural to their left. A mound of sandy colored boulders sheltered a smooth, painted stone face which was protected by glass and illuminated by lights. A man in purple robes pointed to a haloed Christ. An evil looking crowd loitered behind him. The style was more Byzantine than modern. The pigments used were intense and the gold portions shone in the light.

"This is the first station," Manuel explained. "Pontius Pilate condemns Christ to death at the demand of the crowd."

Rob leaned in to get a closer look at the painting. Some of the lines were so fine that they seemed rendered by a single hair. He pointed to a tombstone shaped rock jutting up in the background.

"Is that what I think it is?"

Manuel smiled. "Yes, Devil's Tower. In all the murals there is imagery of Wyoming."

They resumed walking in silence for a time before the monk meekly resumed their prior conversation. "You said that you were not exactly satisfied with my explanations as to why a monk would show such interest in the causes of men such as James Alexander and Bill Stevens. It would be a lie to claim that I have fully fathomed it myself or made peace with it. I am very drawn to them, to the energy and power of their convictions, to the vigor with which they condemn sin. I wish on some level that I could find such zeal within my own Church, but it seems that the highest virtues of ours now are tolerance and forgiveness. I am not denying that these are values to be cherished, but a large part of me wishes that the Roman Church would have its own Bill Stevens. I am uncertain if this is a good or a bad feeling. Part of me believes that I am young and foolish, yet another says that I am right, and it is precisely why I am here."

"So, you're conflicted," Rob mused.

The monk's brow furrowed, and his mouth worked back and forth for a moment before he responded. "Perhaps. I would never leave my Church, that is not even a consideration, but I cannot deny the stirring I feel in my soul sometimes when Alexander or

Stevens speaks." His hands were in front now, tumbling one over the other in a constant concentric rotation, like the forward lumbering mechanism of some piece of industrial equipment. He moved as though he must in order to churn out the words with kinetic energy. "If you don't mind the longer version, then I have often explained it to myself in the same terms as my attraction to the Benedictine order. You see, we have a dedication to authority. Part of our vows is to accept stability. This ties into our dedication to an abbey as a permanent place of quiet religious life. The world all around us is a blur. Capital and people move at blinding rates just to find that next most efficient production of whatever modern caprice has decided needs producing. To accept stability is to reject that caprice. Stevens talks about this often, and it is monastic in a sense."

"Governor Alexander told me that motion sustains his cause," Rob interjected.

"But stability is not a rejection of motion," Manuel insisted. "Sometimes crops must be rotated to maintain stability or herds of goats moved to allow for the lands to recover. We must move within the framework of limitations set by our moral boundaries. What must be certain, however, is that those boundaries do not shift to accommodate motion for its own sake."

"You see a monastic element in the State Corps?" Rob asked. "You see a self-imposed boundary at the borders of this state? Stevens and Alexander represent a moral hierarchy?"

The monk squinted at the path in front of them as they walked. "I believe that is where the attraction stems from, yes."

Manuel turned and Rob could see that they had reached the second station.

"Jesus accepts his cross," the monk explained.

The painting was of the same style as the first. Christ knelt beneath the descending burden of the cross, which was lowered by two Roman soldiers.

"Where is the Wyoming connection in this one?" Rob asked.

"The Roman soldier with the moustache and his face turned toward us is rendered in the likeness of Frank Canton. He was a gunman who was a sheriff in the state for a number of years in the nineteenth century. He was also involved with the Johnson County War."

"Why him?" Rob asked.

"From my understanding he was a character of moral

ambiguity. He was often a gun for hire and hid his real name for years. Later on, he became a member of the Oklahoma National Guard. He is looked on with a measure of contempt mixed with admiration. Such is the same for a soldier under orders at the Crucifixion. He is ambiguous in his cruelty."

"That's pretty deep," Rob admitted.

"A great deal of thought went into the symbolism here at the monument." The monk explained. "Some of it is very intricate, almost medieval even in the scholastic sense." He paused. "Forgive me if this is too personal, but are you a religious man?"

They continued walking up the path, Justine lagging a little behind.

"Comfortably agnostic."

"Do you ever feel as though you wish that you were religious?" Manuel asked.

"I don't really think about it. My family was not religious when I was growing up, so it was never really much of a consideration for me. No offense, but you are the anomaly in American society. Most people aren't religious at all, and even those who say they are would view a monk as some kind of extreme case."

Manuel laughed. "Yes, I know that. Honestly sometimes I forget about the larger world and its concerns. Sometimes I go weeks without even thinking about it. I am grateful for such a life."

"Ignorance is bliss."

"But is it ignorance?" the monk asked, not offended but adamant. "The word has a negative connotation. Is it ignorance to not know of that which does not concern you? Or is that simply being in a state which is more authentic to the actuality of being?"

"I make my living telling people about things that don't really concern them, so I'm probably not the best person to ask about that," Rob replied with a smirk. "Maybe that's a cynical thing for a journalist to say, but it wouldn't be the first time since I've been here that the term was used to describe me."

"Maybe so," Manuel assented. "And maybe the idea of cynicism has been misappropriated as of late."

Rob decided to get in his own barbed question. "I know you said that you would never leave your Church, but by being here aren't you implicitly disagreeing with their neutrality on the monument?"

"I doubt the abbot would have let us come here if it was a significant concern." The monk explained. "I trust his judgment and I would have accepted if he had said no."

Rob admitted that it was a good point. He slowed so that Justine caught up to them a little. "What about you?" he asked. "You know a lot about this place, but what do you really think about it?"

Justine moved up so that she was between them and a few steps back. "My uncle used to bring me here when I was a kid and it was under construction," she replied. "I'm the generation that came of age with the new Wyoming. Quite a few older people thought it was pretentious. They weren't entirely opposed to the monument, but it was not in keeping with the rugged simplicity of the state. They were pragmatists in the best sense. But I think it's just as important as a natural wonder."

"Really?" Rob asked. Justine remained a puzzle. He could never determine if she was telling him exactly what he did not want to hear just to spite his skepticism. Was it an exaggeration for the sake of constructing the bulwark of state mythos to oppose his cultural invasion?

"Natural wonders are God speaking to us, and human monuments are our reply. It is an odd mix of rivalry and respect."

"Here is the third station," Manuel interrupted. "In this mural Christ falls for the first time."

Rob turned his attention and joined the monk. In the painting, Christ had fallen. His foot was bloodied. One hand steadied the cross on His shoulder and the other reached up to grasp onto a twisted piece of metal to pull Him up. Splotches of blood trailed back to another twisted piece of metal which had tripped Him. Upon closer inspection, Rob could see that the two pieces of metal were connected, obscured slightly in the middle by a snarl of timbers and sooty debris. The same bent beam which had cast Him down served as his aid in rising. Another Roman soldier stooped in the background, pulling planks from the wreckage where he sorted them into piles of timber and iron spikes. A second man fashioned more crosses from the materials.

"Reveal the mystery to me," Rob deadpanned.

Manuel chuckled. "This is the first of three falls of Christ. The nature of stumbling under the cross is conflicted. His destination is death, but it is also salvation for humanity. His pain is immediate. His destination is inevitable. His progress has paused. What is the meaning of falling on a death march? Is it solace? Is it misfortune? Perhaps it is both."

"I did notice that the same beam that made him stumble was raising him from the ground."

"An astute observation. It is a piece of railroad track. The first stumble parallels the dominance of the railway and the power of the Union Pacific in the state's early history. The railroads brought faster access, the ability to bring in workers and equipment and ship out raw materials, but the company had massive power and was given large swaths of land. It provided some opportunity but forced much of the state and the young territorial government to live at its mercy. There is significant thematic relation to a passage from First Peter: 'Wherefore also it is contained in the scripture, behold, I lay in Zion a chief corner stone, elect, precious: and he that believeth on him shall not be confounded. Unto you therefore which believe he is precious: but unto them which be disobedient, the stone which the builders disallowed, the same is made the head of the corner, and a stone of stumbling, and a rock of offense, even to them which stumble at the word, being disobedient: whereunto also they were appointed. But ye are a chosen generation, a royal priesthood, an holy nation, a peculiar people; that ye should shew forth the praises of him who hath called you out of darkness into his marvelous light; which in time past were not a people, but are now the people of God: which had not obtained mercy, but now have obtained mercy.'"

"You're going to have to explain that one to me," Rob admitted.

"It merely draws a symbolic parallel between Christ's stumbling on the same object which raises Him, the state's existence by powers both adversarial and beneficial, and the combined difficulties and mission for us to live by His laws which provide grace, set against the perils of choosing wickedness."

Rob turned to Justine. "You weren't exaggerating about this place being an endless inward spiral of theology."

She raised an eyebrow. "It has layers. It can satisfy every level of curiosity sufficiently."

"All the symbolism and detail, Jeremiah Robertson isn't responsible for all that is he?" Rob asked.

"He had a team dedicated to the artistry and design," Justine explained. "Some local artists he knew from his photography days, a Wyoming historian, Bill Stevens, they all dreamed up the details. I even heard that they consulted a semiotician and theologian somewhere in Europe, but I'm not sure if that was anything more than a rumor."

"I'll admit this is a bit more impressive than I expected," Rob stated. "Not that I thought the monument would be insignificant. I'm not sure if I was preparing myself for Sunday school pleasantries or what."

"I am glad you are not disappointed," Manuel replied with a smile and a slight incline of his head.

Justine scrutinized the monk and then the journalist with a much less accommodating glance. "Yes, God forbid our humble superstitions bore you."

Rob sighed audibly.

They resumed the walk up the hill, passing by a group of dark-skinned visitors. Manuel explained that they were African Seventh Day Adventists who made up a surprising number of the patrons.

"The different denominations and sects all get along here?" Rob asked.

"There is a mutual understanding that nobody steps on each other's toes," the monk asserted.

"No petty squabbles?"

"There are complaints sometimes about one group or another taking liberties or expecting preferential treatment. The balance is imperfect, but it has remained so far relatively intact."

They paused after a time for the fourth station. This one depicted Christ meeting his mother. Behind the figures, the land rose steeply and suddenly into a wall of reddish bluffs. They were alien in their color and scale. Manuel explained that the landscape was taken from the Bighorn Basin. They did not linger at the mural for very long.

They spoke occasionally while walking to the next stop. Justine explained some of the finer economic points of the monument and the nearby city of Evanston. She described how water reclamation projects had contributed significant portions of the dirt for the monument.

The fifth station depicted Simon of Cyrene carrying the cross. The monk explained that his features were an amalgamation of many of the great men in Wyoming's history.

"His eyes are those of Governor Moonlight, his mouth belongs to Governor Hathaway, his nose belongs to Governor Herschler and so on."

"That seems a bit self-important, doesn't it?" Rob asked. "That the touchstones of Wyoming leadership are carrying the cross?"

"Not exactly," the monk explained. "In scripture it is not clear whether Simon of Cyrene is a willing participant in the carrying of the cross. Many theorize that he was merely an able man caught in the right place at the wrong time when Christ was too beaten and weary to go on. The most frequent interpretation of the symbology in this mural is not that the leaders of the state actively carried on the burdens of the Savior, but that they, whether willingly and knowingly or not, contributed to the development of a place that would at some point become invested in the advancement of Christ's kingdom. The use of their features pays tribute to their accomplishments. The intentionality is ambiguous."

"Clever," Rob mused. He took a closer look at Simon's face. The features had been taken from so many sources that the entire creation looked oddly severe and bloodless, almost too human in a manufactured way. He could find no way to express exactly what feeling the resulting appearance evoked.

A slight wind began to blow, and they picked up the pace to get to the sheltered side of the monument. Rob looked up to the summit where he could see a cloud of dust blowing over the reflective dome. Its dark glass obscured everything underneath. Rob felt for a moment as if he were looking at structures on Mars. They reached the sixth station. It was in a hollow nestled under some rocks.

"This station is the most controversial, oddly enough." Manuel explained as they neared. "The mural depicts Veronica wiping Christ's face with a cloth."

A young woman stooped before Jesus and held a rectangular blue cloth with a red border up to his sweating brow.

"What's so controversial?" Rob asked.

"Two things," The monk answered. "Firstly, the story of Veronica is most closely associated with the Catholic and Orthodox Churches. The story does not make an appearance in the Gospels. As you can imagine, this does not sit well with the Evangelical sola scriptura types. Not to say that they are strongly against it, but many view it with not only skepticism, but mild derision as well."

"Layman's terms," Rob grunted, feeling a little annoyed at his own ignorance.

"The story of Veronica was not fully elaborated until around the thirteenth century. It is based on apocryphal writings. Many Protestants have very iconoclastic tendencies, which extend to the additional medieval Church writings. As it is not alluded to in the Gospel, many don't accept its significance."

"The Catholics in the Middle Ages were avid fan fiction writers," Justine retorted with a grin.

The monk raised his hand in measured argumentation. It was not an aggressive motion, but it contained some conviction. "Now, Miss Justine, I know you're trying to provoke me. You must not put it in such crass terms. Keep in mind, they lived closer in time to the age of Christ's time on earth and much of the very old documentation has been lost to us. The destruction of the library in Alexandria in the third century removed untold historical records."

"You're arguing from the basis of potentialities?" she asked.

"I'm just glad I'm not the only one getting rough treatment," Rob murmured.

Manuel chuckled and took a short breath to center himself. "Sourcing and Church history issues aside, the other controversy is over the nature of the cloth itself. The coloration and design are meant to mimic that of the Wyoming flag. As you can see, it is missing the Bison and the state seal. Historically, the veil of Veronica is said to be the cloth she used to wipe the brow of Christ. Miraculously, it bore an image of his face impressed upon it. Many who were not so convinced by Alexander's zealous tendencies, saw this flag symbology as an allusion that the state seal be replaced with the face of Jesus: a usurpation of state history by explicit religiosity. It did not help that many have taken to using their own Wyoming flag with the state seal replaced with the image of Mount Calvary with the three crosses sitting in the heart of the Bison."

"I can understand the indignation," Rob commented. "I imagine Nico had a thing or two to say about that." He was curious if the name would get a reaction.

Justine turned to him with a look of deep suspicion. "What do you know about that?"

"Banks told me about the editorials this morning. This Veronica flag business just seemed to me like the kind of thing that character would use as ammunition," he hazarded cautiously.

"The Nico editorials were all written before Mount Calvary was completed," she explained.

"Speaking of which, do you know where I could get a copy of those?" Rob asked.

"Ask Walden," she replied. "He had marked up copies of them on his wall for months."

Ask Walden. The chances of that happening were extremely low.

They moved on from the station at a much more leisurely pace, now that the breeze had slowed, and the warmth of the sun anointed their shoulders. They forgot about the Nico discussion, and Justine pointed out the newly added gardens as they walked. From their height, the area was a patchwork geometric jigsaw puzzle of gemstone colors, a mosaic of vibrant pigments that reminded Rob of the rugs on the floor of his room back in the lodge.

The seventh station showed Christ's second fall. Water flowed from a rock on one side of the painting and soaked the ground where His foot had slipped, smearing the mud. He had fallen against a rock, bracing His fall. On top of the slab rested a small animal skull and a shattered jug. A sweating Roman soldier heaved up on His shoulder above, trying to bring Him to His feet.

"This one is striking," Rob noted. "What does the second fall represent?"

"The second fall is reclamation," the monk replied. "This mural uses imagery of water and drought. Irrigation troubles brought endless misery to the state. Much like the first fall, it is a combined blessing and curse. Water is precious here. It was promised over the years that new projects would make tens of thousands more acres of fertile land. Often it was false advertising in an attempt to draw in more settlers."

"And the Roman soldier trying to raise Him up?"

"That represents federal efforts in reclamation projects. Like much symbology here the federal government is associated with the Roman Empire. They had vast resources at their disposal but different aims. Often federal projects ended up not benefitting Wyoming as much as neighboring states. The Roman soldier does not hate Christ yet leads him to his destruction. Even his acts of mercy are part of the death process."

"I ran into this same theme when I interviewed Alexander, the scapegoating of the federal government." Rob interjected.

"Scapegoat? Perhaps, in simplistic terms," Manuel replied.

"It's more complicated than that," Justine cut in. "Do you see where Jesus' foot slips in the mud? It represents the excesses and irresponsibility of irrigators. When there was successful water diversion or storage, oftentimes people overused it and caused saturation, damaging the land, flooding it and making it unusable. The dual images of overuse and desertification capture the multiple pitfalls and responsibilities. To call it 'scapegoating' ignores the complexity of the whole image."

Justine was as defensive as ever. Rob had noticed that she seemed much more professional and impersonal than two days prior. He did not know what to make of it and missed the faltering and awkward interaction of the day he had arrived. It did not matter either way in the end.

They continued the ascent, coming across a fountain with potable water where people drank and filled bottles. Manuel waited for his turn to take a drink, and Rob stood on the outer edge of the path to look over the visitor's center and the parking lot. Quite a few more vehicles had arrived at this point, and he could see a steady stream of buses nearing and departing.

Justine read his mind. "Many churches have retreats or hostels in Evanston. They coordinate trips for their people and then bus them in. It probably accounts for half of the visitors to the monument each year."

"Does that bring in much income?" he asked.

"Most of the funding of operations comes from voluntary donations, so the more people who visit, the more contributions to the monument."

As they waited for the monk, Rob heard a sound drifting on the wind at intervals. It was very faint, and at first, he thought that he had imagined it. After the third or fourth occurrence, he was certain that it was not merely an artifact of his own faculties. It was a cooing sound and very distant. He turned to Justine.

"What is that sound?"

"That is the choir inside the mountain. They will be faint until we reach the top, where the acoustics are ideal."

"What exactly happens at the top? Some kind of show?"

"Yes. Some kind of show."

Manuel got his drink of water and they followed the path up to the next station. The music of the voices coiled out from invisible crevices in the sides of the monument, giving the rest of the walk up a haunted quality.

They reached the eighth station. In the mural Christ stood bleeding before a group of desperate-looking women who all had hollow cheeks and hungry eyes. Although his shoulders were hunched in agony, Christ gestured out with one arm and spoke to them. The women's faces were etched with deep sadness, and they held in their slack arms indeterminate objects. Rob leaned in to get a better look as Justine explained from behind.

"At this station, Jesus speaks to the women of Jerusalem."

There was something particularly disturbing about the mural which Rob could not place. Perhaps it was the vacant look in the women's eyes or that one of the objects in one woman's arms glowed ominously.

"What does it mean?" he asked apprehensively.

Manuel quoted scripture from memory: "'And there followed him a great company of people, and of women, which also bewailed and lamented him. But Jesus turning unto them said, "Daughters of Jerusalem, weep not for me, but weep for yourselves, and for your children. For, behold, the days are coming, in which they shall say, 'Blessed are the barren, and the wombs that never bare, and the paps which never gave suck.' Then shall they begin to say to the mountains, 'Fall on us'; and to the hills, 'Cover us.' For if they do these things in a green tree, what shall be done in the dry?"'"

The words invoked a creeping coldness which crawled up Rob's limbs. "What are they holding in their arms?" he asked. "It looks like a few of them have stones of some kind and vessels of fluid."

Justine moved forward so that she stood between him and the mural, but slightly to the side so as not to obstruct his view. "Wyoming has always relied heavily on mining and energy extraction for income. More often than not, historically, the raw materials were sent out of the state by pipeline or by rail. So long as there was minimal refining or industrial facilities here in the state, then the fear always remained that we were selling our future for pennies on the dollar. This is why the fight over severance tax took up much of the state legislature's focus for so long. It came from the fear that, once non-renewable resources were removed, then the state would have no future, nothing to leave our descendants. What the women hold in their arms is the pride of the state's wealth but also its burden. There will come a time when this state is barren of all things which once gave it economic value, at least those things which can be taken and moved. It has been the night terror of every politician here that the plains and mountains will be an empty wasteland of depleted strip mines and empty oil wells and nothing more." She pointed to the objects in the women's arms one by one: "Iron, coal, trona, crude oil, uranium, natural gas."

"This is unexpectedly sobering," Rob noted.

She turned to him as the three of them resumed the ascent. "What did you expect? Untempered jingoism?"

"You have to admit, some of the 'Wyoming forever' and 'Wyoming, come home' slogan business doesn't give the impression of a whole lot of introspection," he replied.

"Everything has its time," Manuel interjected from the side. He had resumed his bent posture with his hands clasped in the small of his back.

"So long as you learn from your mistaken impressions," Justine commented. "Although I'm not expecting your article to praise the level of our symbolic insight."

"It will be fair," he insisted.

"What about you, José?" she asked. "Do you think Mr. Coen's article will be fair?"

The monk cleared his throat uncomfortably. "I am certain Mr. Coen will be truthful in his recounting of his time here."

"I always forget that you're charity-bound to assume the best of people, even when common sense dictates the opposite," she retorted.

Manuel blushed slightly but smiled. He knew that she was using him against the journalist but was too good natured to say it.

Justine continued, "It's a good thing you fellows spend so much time in solitude fasting and praying or you might get the opportunity to be somebody's fool."

"I am Christ's fool already," he murmured.

"The same thing happened the day before yesterday," Rob observed. "We got along alright until you decided I was up to no good."

She sighed. "Is it really so cruel of me to begrudge him for what he is, José?"

"The apostle Paul, before becoming one of the preeminent men of the Church, was a virulent persecutor of Christians," the monk replied.

She made a dissenting humming sound through her nostrils. "I understand the comparison, but at best Mr. Coen is a nuisance."

"No, no," the monk insisted with energized insistence. "I am not speaking in terms of extremes or degrees. I am merely referring to the mystery of God's purposes and the limitations of our ability to judge the quality or nature of others."

"He's a journalist. You know how vicious they can be."

Manuel's hands were in front of him now, weaving around each other. "One must be gracious. Even if you perceive one as an adversary, behaving in only an adversarial manner becomes a self-fulfilling omen. Treat those who oppose you with respect and you may heap up coals on their head."

"Ok, what the fuck?" Rob broke in, frustrated at being picked apart as if he wasn't even there. He noted the subtle stiffening of his companions at his use of such profanity.

"Heaping coals only sounds threatening," the monk explained with a smile. "The cultural context gives the statement a much different meaning."

"That's not it," Rob grunted. "I mean, I'm right here. It's like a damn inquisition."

The Benedictine gave a stunned look, no doubt nonplussed at the choice of words before breaking out into a hearty laugh. "I'm sorry, Mr. Coen. Of course. It was rude of me. Justine is right, I spend most of my time alone."

"Well, at least you have an excuse." Rob gave Justine a wounded glance.

She sighed again and replied in a singsong voice of mock apology. "It was rude of me, though I'll admit that was partly my intent." After a reflective pause her tone became more conciliatory. "I will try to have a more optimistic view of your intentions. To be fair you have been a decent and agreeable guest here so far. Even if you are a journalist," she added.

Rob wondered if he deserved the contrition. He doubted it. Maybe he would surprise even himself and the article would present Alexander's Wyoming in a more positive light. Then he was reminded of the interactions with Walden and Paul Alexander the day prior. It was not likely.

They moved on through the music, which seemed to hang in pockets as though trapped by some strange barometric phenomenon. The sound would surround them at one moment and then fade into the fringes of suspect hallucination or drop off so abruptly that it could be forgotten entirely. He could not decide if it added to the mystical quality of the ascent up the monument or merely made the whole experience even more unbelievable. The possibility of this whole construction being here and existing by the merits of a few million people's superstitions was almost too much to fathom at times. Of course Alexander would tell him that such cynicism was a form of superstition as well.

"And here we are at the ninth station." Manuel broke Rob out of his somewhat scrambled musing. "Here is depicted Christ falling a third time."

"He's kneeling in oil."

"Yes," the monk confirmed with a smile. "Anything else?"

"In the background I can see a broken pipeline spilling crude and some small structures at the edge of the pool, miniscule, like sandcastles being dissolved."

"That's the capitol building in Cheyenne," Justine explained.

Rob felt a jab of annoyance, like a small child had poked his back from behind in an infantile prank. "You know, the symbolism is interesting and all, but doesn't it all seem a bit self-aggrandizing? Of course the state symbology makes you all a party to the death of Jesus, I get that, but isn't that also a form of collective egoism? I'm not trying to be rude. Like I said before, I'm no expert in theology, but doesn't this whole fusion of the state and the Crucifixion border on surreptitious idolatry?"

Manuel did not shrug or admit the possibility this time. His features became very serious following the suggestion. "Does a little oil, the shape of a mountain's slope or the features of a character take from Christ's suffering? If they gave Christ the face of James Alexander, then it would be blasphemy, but I do not think that is the case."

"But isn't it tiresome? Tortured?" Rob insisted. "The obvious attempt at self-mythologizing? It suspends the ability to maintain serious reflection. It begs scrutiny. It's humility on parade." He took a deep breath, realizing that he might have gone too far. "I'm not trying to be a total asshole. I can't help but have that doubt in the back of my mind eating at me this whole time."

"You miraculously develop ideals at the most convenient times," Justine mused.

The monk gave a sad look, not defeated or hurt, but signifying that he realized a hope of some kind had been extinguished.

Rob sensed a swelling undercurrent of contempt at their simplicity and predictability. These people and their parables and shallow allegory were all covered in a thin glaze of moral superiority. They may have exceeded his expectations, but the bar had been set pretty low. He let his head clear for a moment so as not to let the unexpected indignation get the better of him.

"I meant no offense," he assured.

"And it would be wrong of us to assume that you share our same response to such imagery," Manuel replied. "My only answer would be that the kingdom of God is everywhere. To suggest that it is in this place is not to say that it only belongs to us. Let's continue to the summit." He said that last bit with a tone of well concealed resignation. "Not much further is the tenth station and then things become a little more abstract as we approach the Crucifixion."

As they walked, the hum of the singing was much louder, so that Rob thought at moments that he could feel a buzzing in the ground when his feet made contact. The curves of the trail became sharper and more frequent as the mountain became smaller near the top. The number of large, jutting boulders increased so that they moved at times in shadow with looming shapes blocking the view of what lay below.

Rob leaned over to the monk when it became clear that he intended to say no more without prompting. "I didn't mean to say by my criticism that I don't want any more explanation of the symbology. That was not my intent."

Manuel smiled pensively. "You should not feel bad for speaking your mind. There is not much else to say from this point."

They passed between two large stones. One of them stuck from the outer edge of the path. On the inner facing side was the tenth station mural. The paint rendered Christ in colors of sharp contrast. His tunic was torn from His back by disembodied arms emerging from the dim beyond of the background. His skin was a ghostly pale color with deep red gouts of blood spattered on His shoulders and a speckling across His forehead. His eyes were bottomless pits, and a look of abject horror contorted His features. He seemed to be staring in a specific direction with one arm half raised to indicate the source of the violence.

Rob was struck by the realism of the features, the genuinely youthful energy of the fear. It was idealized in its lack of idealism about the subject. He turned to follow the gaze. Christ seemed to be indicating the path continuing up the mountain.

Manuel nodded and the three of them continued along the path. The spiral up to the top was carefully crafted. The trail ran along a rock face covered in a continuous mural. The music was still muffled but constant. It no longer fell off at the enveloping borders of aural bubbles or faded suddenly into obscurity.

Unlike the Stations of the Cross, this mural did not seem to follow a readily discernible narrative of symbolic progression. Gone was the well-known advance of Christ through a progression of mistreatments and abuses. It seemed to be a series of unnerving motifs. Near the start, the sun, a golden half circle emerging from the top, was rent by a crack in the side. A silver pipeline, much like that in the ninth station, led across a field near the bottom. After running a ways along the lower edge, the line was severed. A huge locust rested in a ruined field, surrounded by a thousand of its tiny compatriots. Its abdomen swelled monstrously. A farmer plowing a field had turned to look behind him, and a small child sat in the path of his horses. Starving cattle wandered in a snowy landscape around a heap of bones. Further on, a cluster of smooth, white cones rose from the prairie, belching smoke all around them. One of them had been torn open to show honeycomb which was empty and skeletal in appearance. A native scalped a soldier on a hill above an army detachment burning a collection of longhouses. A woman was hanged. Men in masks pulled the entrails out of dead sheep at the edge of a pile of hundreds more. Men stooped in dim mine shafts, illuminated slightly by the distant glow of an explosion that flung bodies and limbs in every direction. The figures soon stretched out to where a huge, cyclone whirlwind swallowed it all up before the mural became entirely black. As the spiral path constricted even more, the wall simply contained white block letters repeating, "Vanity, vanity, vanity." It gave the impression of an insistent fatal error code on a computer screen. Rob did not get the same tongue in cheek self-affirmation feeling as he had from the stations. Instead he felt cold, tired and alone, despite walking beside two others.

Around one last sharp corner they reached a tall set of wooden double doors with a cluster of tourists waiting outside. Rob leaned over to Justine.

"What's this all about?" he asked.

"They let people up to the summit in groups. The Crucifixion runs on a cycle. We have to wait for the last one to end."

The mood was sober among those around them. A few people murmured to each other in hushed tones, and a reverent energy hung over the people. The monk stood a few paces away with his head lowered and hands clasped at his waist. He appeared to be either praying or resting his eyes. Justine looked quietly anxious for some reason.

After a few minutes passed, a graying man in a park uniform emerged from one door and looked over the group of people waiting outside. He seemed to be getting an approximate count in his head. After a moment of scrutinizing he nodded to himself.

"You can all come in," He beckoned with one arm and pushed the door outward, holding it open.

The cluster of people pushed through the opening. The movement was not enthusiastic, but it was anticipatory. They gave off the energy of animals before a storm. A group that had come up from behind while they waited swept Rob along in their forward motion. As he moved with the flow, he could see Justine a few yards back. Manuel had disappeared somewhere in the sudden activity.

On the other side of the door was a slight final rise up roughly hewn stone steps. High slabs of rock on either side funneled the walkway up under the glass canopy he had seen on the scale model in the visitor's center. Nothing could have prepared him for being underneath it. The glass was tinted so that the entire sky appeared darkened. For all Rob could tell, it had become suddenly overcast and neared dusk. He could make out a rippling, morphing motion on the glass. It gave the impression that brooding clouds hung overhead. Rob had a difficult time shaking the illusion. His faculties continually tried to convince him that the time and weather had indeed changed. He spun a slow circle searching for the sun but could not find it.

Once Rob turned his focus forward, he could see three white crosses. He could not get a good look as the canopy darkened more and more, but as best he could tell, there was some kind of nearly translucent membrane hovering around each one, a slightly clouded and hazy transparency. He turned around again and could see the man in the park uniform at the door waiting for a few stragglers to come in from the path. After checking his watch and taking one last look, he closed the door.

The sound of thunder shook the ground, and a bloom of bloody orange color emerged at the bottom edge of the dome to indicate a sunset. With the morphing of the sky came the sound of the choir. It surrounded them as though the music was a floating element within the air's very chemistry. He could see no speakers. It had no tinny manufactured quality. The acoustics were such that the singers could not be seen, but the sound rushed over the summit like an engulfing wave.

"Were you there when they crucified my Lord?

"Were you there when they crucified my Lord?"

It was a familiar gospel tune, though sung with more formality and intricate harmony layered more complexly than he had heard before.

"Sometimes it causes me to

"Tremble

"Tremble

"Tremble."

A subtle movement brought his attention back to the fore. The membrane around the crosses had come alive, and their once blank features showed three men hanging from them in visceral detail. What was creating the images? Some kind of high-fidelity projector? Rob glanced around to see if he could solve the riddle. He saw a few points of light above and behind that could be the source. Whatever it was did the trick quite well. The men on the crosses look unnervingly real and writhed as blood oozed down to the ground.

Confusion fell upon the scene. Loud voices shouted back and forth in another language. Rob could not tell if it was part of the display or people really were shouting in the crowd. A group of older women from one of the tour groups fell weeping at the foot of Christ's Cross where He struggled to pull Himself up against the downward weight of His own dying form.

Rob stepped closer to get a better look at the details. He realized that he could smell the sharp odors of blood and sweat. He could also detect a burning smell, but fragrant. Along the ground, at either side of the open area where the visitors all stood, rested censers with nearly indiscernible coils of smoke rolling out across the ground. An agonized cry cut through the other noise with such clarity that he jumped a little despite himself.

"Were you there when they nailed Him to the tree?

"Were you there when they nailed Him to the tree?"

Rob suddenly felt extremely uncomfortable, hot, and claustrophobic. He was embarrassed for the women who had fallen in front of the Cross. He wanted to tell them to stand up and compose themselves. He was ill at ease with the whole scene. The noise and melodrama were oppressive in its brashness. The constant realization that none of it was real gave him a tortured feeling of a child too old to watch an animatronic song and dance show with the pneumatic pistons and pivoting joints a little too obvious to his skeptical faculties.

A slight breeze moved the dust at their feet. He was not sure if it was a true artifact of the weather or another part of the show. He just wanted it to be over and stood with a pained grimace etched on his face. The absurdity of it all gave him the strange feeling that he should laugh, but he forced it down, hoping his face did not make too much of a jeering smile. In spite of all the ridiculousness, he did not want to cause offense. It would be the worst time to do such a thing.

"Sometimes it causes me to

"Tremble

"Tremble

"Tremble."

He looked over at the people around him. Some watched quietly. Some wiped at their eyes. Others simply looked overwhelmed. Finally, his eyes reached Justine. She was looking at him with a mixture of sadness and what might be disappointment. They both recoiled from the brief moment of eye contact so quickly that he could not make a judgment. Had he made his disapproval obvious? Had he been sneering despite his efforts?

Rob found a quiet corner of his mind where his consciousness could curl up and cover its ears to drown out the onslaught of perplexing stimuli. The peals of thunder and swelling tide of the choir heaved against the membrane of his psychic shelter. None of it could affect him. All one had to do was endure and remain untouched.

Truly survival was the mark of strength. He had understood this from a young age. No matter how much his parents fought or pulled at him in their own direction, so long as he withheld his love from either of them in any observable way, then neither of them could claim victory. So long as neither of them had an observable effect on him, then he could become his own being, a cool amorphous being, an intangible approximation. People like James Alexander would always be their own undoing. They showed their hands right away. Living by a strict ideological code allowed them only two outcomes: to be nailed to it eventually, or become a hypocrite if they did survive in the end. It was a defeat either way.

He allowed himself to look directly at the figure of Christ. He was naked except for a wrapped undergarment. The fidelity of every detail, from the streaks of dirt to the thorns on His crown, looked extremely clear and precise. His movements were so strangely lifelike, and the quality of whatever rendered Him was technically rather impressive. Was it simply a projection or some kind of hologram? If he had been alone and not surrounded by other people, he might have approached to put his hand on the form to see if it was only flat light or some kind of multi-dimensional image.

The first song was ending, and a new and unfamiliar one was taken up by the choir in the mountain. Unlike the gospel style of the first, this one was more gothic. It built in solemnity and volume over time. The figure of Christ was looking upward into the sky and repeating something in another language. The swirling breeze, which Rob was now sure had been manufactured, increased and seemed to coil from multiple directions. It added to the sensory confusion. The boulders stacked up around the summit began to shake and split. He did not wonder at the mechanism which caused it. To wonder would require him to lower the psychic shield, which now required all his concentration to maintain. The singing built to a crescendo. The glass covering darkened more and more. A single warm light cast a glow on the center of the three crosses. With one last spasm, Christ's head drooped down toward the bloody chest.

Silence fell on the group of people. Daylight eked onto the rocks in a large ring around the bottom edge of the canopy. Nobody seemed certain of what to do. Was it over? Rob let out a slow and cautious breath of relief.

Just as he was about to turn toward Justine, the canopy darkened to pure black. A bright flash of light raced upward from the crosses and exploded onto the canopy above them. A loud shout of agony mixed with defiance, pain, and victorious exhilaration sounded deafeningly all around. The ceiling canopy came to life with a field of stars. They seemed now to stand somewhere in the deepest reaches of outer space. The depth and distance of the stars felt very real. Rob had to keep blinking and adjusting his view at intervals to overcome the power of the illusion and convince himself that he was merely staring at a screen or projection or some combination of the two.

The voice of the choir had diminished from its earlier bombast to a soothing coo. The stars on the canopy drifted slowly, indicating motion, searching. It was all dangerously calming.

After a minute of the celestial journey, a deep voice rang out. It was a man's voice. The timbre was almost conversational but solemn. The screen's viewpoint moved more deliberately, smoothly curving around nebulae with vast clouds of iridescent color, fields of asteroids, a dark and sleeping planet covered entirely in glassy water and the cataclysmic swallowing of a galaxy into a quasar.

All the while the voice spoke: "How have you helped him who is without power? How have you saved the arm that has no strength? How have you counseled one who has no wisdom? And how have you declared sound advice to many? To whom have you uttered words? And whose spirit came from you? The dead tremble, those under the waters and those inhabiting them. Sheol is naked before Him, and destruction has no covering. He stretches out the north over empty space; He hangs the earth on nothing. He binds up the water in His thick clouds, yet the clouds are not broken under it. He covers the face of his throne, and spreads His cloud over it. He drew a circular horizon on the face of the waters, at the boundary of light and darkness. The pillars of heaven tremble, and are astonished at his rebuke. He stirs up the sea with His power, and by His understanding He breaks up the storm. By His Spirit he adorned the heavens; His hand pierced the fleeing serpent. Indeed these are the mere edges of His ways, and how small a whisper we hear of Him! But the thunder of His power who can understand?'"

As the voice quieted, the field of view slowed before a dim, floating field of ice in the most distant reaches of the cosmos. Massive chunks of clouded, frozen material rolled by. The slowly rotating monoliths heaved into one another at times. Smaller fragmenting shards of ice spun in expanding fans out through the emptiness. Beyond the tumult shone a pale golden glow of light, much like a morning beam of sunrise through a frosty windowpane.

The choir had transitioned seamlessly into "Ave Maria," which they let out in rich and reverent tones. The source of the warm light came into view on the canopy: an amber-colored kaleidoscope corridor made up of angels stretched out into the distance. They slowly swirled around one another and boiled up and rolled over in syrupy motion. The image was nearly identical to the one in Gustave Doré's *Paradiso, Canto 34*, and the frame of view moved slowly down the spiraling cylinder to the blinding point of light at the end. They passed by ice in the process of melting, and the resulting floating blobs of water, before reaching a thick veil of steam and billowing clouds. The movement slowed even more and broke through to a brilliant and gleaming throne.

Rob glanced around at the others. They all leaned back to stare up at the images. The glowing light poured down on them. Every single other visitor of the monument stared up. They had lost all awareness of anything outside what was shown on the canopy.

The deep voice from before spoke again: "I see the heavens opened and the Son of Man standing at the right hand of God."

The same Christ as before, the image which had hung on the Cross, stood by the throne. The heavenly seat gleamed brilliantly under a mist, which refracted a rainbow of shifting lights and colors. Christ wore richly decorated robes and a golden crown. He gave a sad smile and reached out to the viewers with a still wounded hand. Blood radiated out from the gouge in tiny droplets that hovered in the weightlessness. The drops caught the light and sent out deep red beams from within.

Jesus' lips did not move. The same voice as before resumed one final time, and the view moved to focus on His face and beckoning, earnest eyes: "I am the resurrection and the life. He who believes in me, though he may die, he shall live. And whoever lives and believes in me shall never die."

With the final ringing words, the images on the canopy quickly faded and it turned back to glass so that the blue sky and sun hung above and everything before that moment seemed to have been a strange dream. The visitors all around blinked in the sudden natural light. Some had been crying and dabbed at their eyes. Others embraced and clung to each other. A few blinked in bewilderment at everything around them.

The man who had let them in the doors to the summit stepped in front of the group and addressed them: "The way down is here. Take your time if you need." He waved an arm to indicate a walkway down at the left of the three crosses. Rob spun a slow circle to get his bearings and saw the monk approaching him from near the door they had entered.

"What now?" he asked.

"Now we go down."

The three of them waited until the last of the other visitors had gone before stepping to the opening. It looked to be the mouth of a cave dug into the rock of the mountain's summit. They went down. The walls of the descending cavern twisted clockwise in a wide spiral. The sound of singing was building once more. The tune was familiar: "Amazing Grace." After a few moments of walking with only a lamp every few yards to illuminate their way, the inner wall of the twisting cavern opened up to show the inside chamber of the monument's upper reaches. The choir stood on a tiered platform under a massive glowing chandelier. Despite his cynicism, Rob found the sight rather breathtaking. A railing ran along the circular shelf of stone so that those moving downward could lean out and look at the golden glow of the crystalline light and the members of the choir all in white and singing the hymn. It reminded him of reading *The Journey to the Center of the Earth* as a child and imagining fantastical, primordial anomalies nestled deep underneath the ground.

"Striking, isn't it?" Manuel asked.

"Yes." Rob considered for a moment. "Are they in here all day? The choir? How is that practical? There must be around fifty of them."

The monk leaned against the railing and looked outward at the glowing scene as he replied, and light poured over his smiling face. "They are not here all day. They come and go in shifts. Some are volunteers. Others work here all year. It seems somewhat laborious to insist on live voices. But one could expect no less from such an enterprise. I do know that the designers were insistent that there be a choir for the monument."

"Why?"

"I believe there was an understanding that it must require human efforts. The designers did not want it to be automated and run on its own for everything. Besides, in scripture it is written: 'Let the word of Christ dwell in you richly in all wisdom, teaching and admonishing one another in psalms and hymns and spiritual songs, singing with grace in your hearts to the Lord.' It is not merely pageantry. This choir is also a gift to God from the people."

The shelf of stone ran in a downward spiral along the inside edge of the chamber for a full circle. They followed it slowly. Near the exit, they could hear the choir begin the first hymn of the Crucifixion cycle again. They exited out into blinding sunlight partway down the mountain.

"Are there any more stations?" Rob asked.

"The final four are condensed into the display at the top and within the summit. Christ is nailed to the cross, dies, is taken down and put in the tomb. That completes the fourteen."

"It was more, uh, involved than I thought it would be," he admitted.

"It is not without controversy." Manuel explained. "There are many who do not approve of the display and find it distasteful or too modern."

"A gimmick?"

"Yes, in a word."

What about you?" Rob asked.

The monk paused and thought for a long while, his mouth working and eyes squinting.

"Let me guess, you're conflicted?" Rob laughed.

"Yes," Manuel admitted. "That is not to say that I don't think it is very impressive or that I find it expressly disrespectful. I only wonder at the implications. I find myself discouraged by the modern desire for sensory participation in religious experiences. I believe virtually every heresy has come from either the demand for that sensory experience or a need to reconcile the precepts of theology with the individual experience. This is not to say that I find the display at the summit heretical or even ridiculous. In fact, I find it very moving and beautiful. There is a confusion between ritual, sacrament, and allegory that makes me apprehensive is all. Forgive me if I find it difficult to express myself. I am still unsure what exactly I believe about it."

"What about you?" Rob asked, turning to address Justine, who was walking a few paces behind.

"I never tire of it," she stated. "Sometimes when I'm elsewhere doing schoolwork or just walking, I think to myself that right here Christ is being crucified again. It is a never-ending cycle. People need a reminder, and sometimes a visceral one, of the things that last. Do I think there is some kind of mystical magic to it? No. Do I get weak in the knees or cry when I see it? No. But when the sun comes up in the morning, it's good to know that here the cycle turns with the same regularity. It's why the mountain's path is a spiraling loop. It ends where it began. The bottom of the descent goes by the gardens."

"By the gardens? What's the significance?" He asked after realizing she was not going to explain further.

"Before Jesus was taken to be crucified, he went to pray in the garden. It ends where it begins."

"But that seems more Eastern than anything, the cycle that is," Rob mused.

"There is motion within motion," she replied. "You are definitively born and die with finality, but still you rise in the morning and go to sleep every day. Every new generation discovers God in their time. For them there will be the repeating Crucifixion here at the mountain."

"I think I understand." Rob fished in his pocket for his notebook and jotted down some of her words and details about the monument that he did not want to forget. After ensuring that he would not lose anything essential, he turned to the monk. "So, there are no stations on the way down?"

"Not of the sort on the way up. There are murals depicting the Resurrection and the early Church. It is less regimented though. They are vignettes of various forms. For example, these two bronze figures beside the path represent the two men on the road to Emmaus. Two disciples of Jesus met him after the Crucifixion. He walked with them in disguise and later ate with them. Their recognition comes when they break bread, an allusion to the sacrament of the Eucharist."

They neared the figures: two men in movement beside the path with somber looks on their faces, frozen in the gesticulation of conversation. They wore what looked to be mid-century clothing: slacks and button-down shirts.

"They look somewhat modern," Rob observed.

"They are men out of time," Manuel explained. "And this is the moment before Christ has joined them. They are in a moment of expectation which is unknown even to them. They live as we do, in a world of doubt, yet on the brink of union with Christ. As Justine said before, every generation discovers God in their own time."

They worked their way down the monument, Manuel fastidiously maintaining his informal role of guide and interpreter of symbology. They walked by a painted mural depicting the Pentecost; another displayed the conversion of Saint Paul. The monk listed the names of the martyrs while indicating their renderings: the stoning of Stephen, the crucifixion of Peter, John the Revelator in exile. After a time, the path evened out and they moved along a short stone wall and hedge marking the outer boundary of the gardens.

"Would you like to walk through and take a look around?" Justine asked.

Rob nodded, and they diverted to the right. Under an arbor of vines, a large wrought iron gate stood open. The path inside turned to brick and branched out in right angles to other subsequent walkways. Beds of plants bordered the path on both sides. The monk moved ahead and led them down the avenues in a labyrinthian route that seemed to make sense only to him. Justine explained that Manuel spent much of his free time either working in the gardens or reading and reflecting there. The animation in his movements made his investment obvious. He would stop and stoop to indicate a bed of plants and then lean down to place a finger beneath a petal or leaf and gently raise it while explaining every detail.

"Many of the plants here are native to the state. These shrub-like trees with the delicate petals are dogwood. You can see them all over the garden. In this bed is blue flax. Over here you can see a small, white flower. It is known as a woodland star."

They passed through the center, where a circular area contained a large fountain. A number of people read or talked quietly in small groups of two or three. The whole place was picturesque and very peaceful, and Rob much preferred it to the bizarre tumult at the summit. The monk was distracted at some point and wandered off by himself. Rob got turned around in a maze of hedges and realized that he was alone. After a minute of walking aimlessly, he realized that the paths were not even a maze, but merely three circles contained within one another in descending size with an opening at either end. He escaped after the realization and spilled out into a clearing with a mound of grass and a large voluminous tree. It reminded him of an immense brain, with the multitudes of splitting branches forming neural pathways and constituting its amoebic form. It was very quiet and no one else was around. A circle of curved stone benches rested around the border of the grassy rise where the tree rested.

12

"It's a plains cottonwood. It was here before the garden, but they moved it so that it could be in just the right spot."

Rob jumped slightly at the unexpected voice. Justine had followed him through the hedges.

"It's very picturesque," he observed.

A long silence passed between them. Finally, she continued. "I am sorry for being unfair to you. It's not right of me, especially when I'm representing my uncle as well. He was the one who agreed to host you and talk with you."

"Any idea why?" Rob asked, turning to scrutinize her.

One of her arms hung straight down and she held the other up to rest her hand on the opposite shoulder. She looked tired, not defeated or demoralized, but tired. She lifted her shoulders in a shrug. "I honestly don't know. Part of me thinks he wants mixed news. With the whole frenzy that's bound to come with the Wyoming dollar, I think he wants something else out there too, and not even necessarily positive, just something else."

"I called him, not the other way around," Rob replied.

"All I mean is maybe he would have said no unless this other business was in the works. Maybe, when you called his office and asked for an interview, he realized it would be a good way to muddy the waters or relieve some pressure on that other front."

"I think you probably overestimate my influence in the media sphere. I'm not exactly H. L. Mencken."

She let an amused breath out through her nose, jostling her head back slightly with the sound. "What's it like anyway being a journalist in the city?"

"Not glamorous. Everything they say about journalists drinking too much, having too high an opinion of themselves and too low an opinion of other people is all true. That's not to say there aren't decent writers and honest people, but they never make it much of anywhere in the business. Like anything else related to politics and media, it all comes down to who you know and how well you get along with them."

"I'm a little surprised," she mused. "That you're so honest about it. How do you reconcile that? With being honest and trying to move up in that world?"

"You don't. You forget about it or don't think about it. You have to live in the ambiguity of it all and hope that, at some point every once in a while, you can reorient yourself for long enough to say something real about something that matters, whether you believe in it or not."

"That sounds a lot like going along to get along."

"It is." Rob confirmed. "And you just hope that, in the process of going and getting, that you don't become so much a fixture of the enduring mechanism that you can't find a damaged piece every once in a while that could use some attention."

"Survival first and truth second?" she asked with a raised brow.

"That's how it has to be. Survival is truth," he replied.

She mulled it over for a few seconds. "So, what do you think about everything? The state, the monument, my uncle. Everything."

"I think it's insane," he stated bluntly. "I can respect his ability to accomplish what he has, but I can't make any sense of the why. Once you get too far into the realm of formulating what you can touch and see on behalf of things that you can't, then you lose me. I don't know how so many people follow him." He held up a hand to indicate a qualification. "No, I get that he is charismatic and that the cultural trends have worked in his favor and all that, but I don't understand how so many people are willing to change the way they live for the sake of a man's ideas, no matter how lofty. It's not putting on the team colors or singing the fight song over the weekend. We are talking about a big cultural shift here."

"No part of you at all finds any of it inspiring?"

"I can respect the dedication, sure, but the devotion, the willingness to be a part of something so radical, I have a hard time understanding it."

"You think it's radical?"

"Well, yeah," he deadpanned. "You don't?"

"The world writ large became radical by degrees in its own way. A lot of people look at the governor's movement as a correction to a hundred years of a steady march of radicalization."

"Ok, so reactionary for today is normal for the nineteenth century? What is the standard then? Mid-twentieth century? The Middle Ages? What is the perfect balance that modern culture has diverted from so much? Throughout all of time everything is in constant fluctuation. Clinging to a snapshot of culture is just as unnatural as you see modernity to be."

"It's not a snapshot," she insisted. "It's a way of living that is most common with the massive majority of human history. Hard work, respect for the divine, connection to the land, investment in physical community. Those are all things that everyone is losing and have never been lost before. Are you really going to deny that?"

"Then what is the fix? An artificial approximation of the conditions that existed when mankind was healthier in your estimation? How is that any less synthetic than living your entire life in a virtual reality machine?"

She made a frustrated sound in her throat. "Because it isn't virtual! Do you honestly believe that eschewing the lifestyle of the common denominator of society is somehow unreal? What is *your* measure of reality then, since you seem to be the arbiter of such things? You said it yourself, that you go along to get along. You abstract the world to escape its consequences. In my mind that makes you one of the most unqualified people to talk with any authority about what should or ought to be. You have abrogated your ability to speak on the subject."

"Hey, you asked for my opinion on this place and everything. If you don't like it, then just revoke my ability to have one, I guess. You will make an excellent future Governor Alexander."

"Just because everyone has an opinion doesn't mean they're all good ones."

"How predictably authoritarian," he snorted and then paused to calm himself. "Look, I didn't want to have an argument, alright? I was hoping you would just take what I said clinically, ok?"

She visibly made an effort to calm herself as well, taking a deep breath. "You have to understand why I'm defensive. Not that many people are even willing to consider that we aren't all crazy. It gets to you after a while."

"I can understand that," he admitted. "I haven't exactly been the peerless high and mighty judge here. I've had my own difficulties since arriving."

She shot him a suspicious look. "What does that mean?"

"Walden," he stated simply.

She laughed. "He's playing with you like a cat with a mouse, isn't he? That's not surprising at all."

"I'm glad you find it so amusing," he grumbled. "That man is a psychopath."

"He doesn't have a violent bone in his body," she insisted. "He's trying to throw you off psychologically. It's what he does with everyone he thinks could hurt my uncle in any way."

"Consider my fears assuaged."

"Hey, this is your job. I'm not going to try to stop him. May the better man win."

"You know, you're kind of sadistic," Rob observed. "You're not as bad as he is, but you have your own methods. Don't think I haven't noticed."

She gave him a look of very genuine confusion. "Have you ever considered that you're just a paranoid sort of person?"

"Oh, I am," he confirmed, "but just enough to be more observant than most people."

Just as she was about to put together a reply, which judging by her expression would have been quite scathing, Manuel emerged from the hedges with a blissful look on his face.

"Ah, there you are. I stepped away back to my brothers for midday prayers. I was able to find you because I could hear your voices. I hope there wasn't an argument."

"Not really," Justine assured him. "Just a heated discussion."

The monk gave each of them a surprisingly mischievous look. "Alright." The single word was full of observation about what he really knew of the situation. He then turned to Rob. "I forgot to ask you what you thought of the display at the summit. I don't expect you to view it through the same lens obviously."

Justine was giving Rob a defiant expression, perhaps daring him to be as blunt with Manuel as he had with her.

"Technically, it was very impressive. It far exceeded anything I could even imagine. As far as the experience itself, it was a bit overwhelming. Honestly I would have a difficult time trying to describe how I felt during the whole experience."

It was an honest answer, and as far as he was willing to go. There was no point in delving into any of the details of how uncomfortable it had been. The monk's courtesy toward him did not deserve such naked criticism.

They walked the garden for a little longer before Manuel asked if they wanted to have lunch at the Benedictine's small abbey. Rob and Justine agreed, and they picked up Daniel at the visitor's center, where he was loitering around the entrance looking bored.

The place where the Benedictines lived was a small collection of three timber buildings and a barn. Each was simple, rectangular and unrefined. One was the chapel where they prayed, another was the bunkhouse with their simple sleeping quarters, and the third and largest contained a dining area with a large kitchen and work area. The metal sided barn out back provided space for the goats during the cold months. A large yard surrounded the structure and contained a garden and covered space for chopping and storing firewood.

Three other monks lived there with Manuel. They were all American and rather young. Manuel was likely the oldest. When the visitors entered, they were in the kitchen preparing a meal. They introduced themselves one by one as Samuel, Henry, and Mitchell. Rob was not sure what exactly one asks a monk in his home setting when it came to small talk, so he stood back and observed.

Henry, a tall and sandy-haired young man in his mid-twenties, was the most talkative aside from Manuel. He explained a little about life at the monument, their hours of prayer, and the sort of work they did. The others labored quietly. Samuel, a short and stocky young man, brought them glasses of water.

"We eat very simply. I hope it is to your liking," Henry relayed at one point.

"Honestly a boiled shoe would be delicious to me right now. I'm famished," Daniel commented, and then added, "No offense."

The monks smiled pleasantly. "None taken," Henry assured. "I hope you like goat."

"I thought you fellows didn't eat meat," Daniel replied.

"We only eat it three days a week," Manuel explained, "and in small quantities. Most often we have poultry or fish as a protein, but our abbot has found that caring for and using animals is beneficial to a healthy diet and work routines. We catch many of our own fish at the lake."

After a prayer, Henry served the simple meal of dark bread, cooked goat meat, and greens from the garden. It was not a culinary masterpiece by any stretch, but Rob was grateful. The food was fresh and hearty. The monks ate in silence, as was their custom, and the visitors respected their time of reflection. Rob imagined that during the bitterly cold Wyoming winters this place was harder living than most could endure.

After they had finished, the monks returned to the kitchen to clean up and Manuel explained that he had shirked his duties for long enough. He walked them back down the dirt path leading from the small abbey to the visitor's center. "Let me give a prayer of blessing before you go." They stopped, and he stood in front of them with his head slightly bowed and hands clasped. "May God and His excellent servant Saint Benedict help you to walk in grace and protect you from wickedness, and may you be blessed in your journeys from here. Amen."

"Thank you," Justine said earnestly with a smile.

"Thank you for your hospitality," Rob added.

"And for the prayer," Daniel tacked onto the end.

With one final wave they went their separate ways: the monk back to his brothers and the three visitors back to the monument. The number of people traversing the paths and moving up and down the mountain had increased significantly.

"What now?" Rob asked. "Was there anything else here that you guys wanted to show me?"

"The helicopter's all fueled up. We can go anywhere," Daniel replied with a grin. "Hell, I could show you some pretty good stunt flying on the way back up."

"That's not happening," Justine stated sternly. She checked the time on her phone. "We should probably head back."

They returned down the pathway to the landing area. The mountain loomed over their shoulders. Once they reached the helicopter, Daniel repeated his earlier routine of pre-flight checks as Rob and Justine settled into the back.

"José Manuel is an interesting man," Rob mused aloud.

"He is uncommonly decent," Justine replied.

The helicopter came to life again. The engine and rotors slid up a scale of mechanical tones with increasing intensity. Daniel was less talkative on the return trip. Justine was placid and silent and rolled gazes to various fixed points within the cabin and outside. Rob was pensive and content to sit quietly as the throbbing machinery provided a bed of white noise for his fitful daydreams. He stared disinterestedly at the passing plains below.

As time passed with nothing said, Rob began to feel a little cold and distant from the idea of other human beings, even more so than usual. All he had seen at the monument convinced him that there are distinct groups of people who are irreconcilably different. He had very little in common with those transfixed by the symbolism in the stations along the ascent. He had nothing in common with those who had been weeping on the summit at the electric Jesus display. It had meant nothing to him, or if not nothing, then it was slightly unnerving: a childhood fear not yet remembered with a smile and a shake of the head. Standing up there on the summit, he had been four feet tall again and peering goose-fleshed into the yawning, dark windows of an abandoned house at the edge of the neighborhood. Perhaps that was merely his own closest association with nothingness as a concrete idea. *Nothing as a concrete idea,* he chuckled to himself.

Possibly this is what Nico had meant when he or she had written that they thought the two of them were made of the same materials. Had Nico felt the same crawling nothingness with enveloping strength as the state which was home changed all around? Had Nico gone to the monument and felt the same heat of embarrassment for everyone gathered around?

Rob watched the peaks of the Wyomings go by in reverse order and thought of the choir in the mountain and what Justine had said about the importance of someone always being present for the endless cycle of Crucifixion. He was still uncertain if it was all just pseudo-philosophical posturing disguising the simplistic, hard-wired, neurological desire to believe. When reduced to such mechanisms, was any belief more legitimate than another, regardless of the argument's complexity or epistemological intricacy? Was he abstracting himself from the world to escape its consequences?

All such thinking only made him feel colder, so he sat in silence still and considered only stupid and pointless subjects for the rest of the flight.

They touched down at Camp Hope a little after three p.m. to a flurry of activity. Banks was pacing near the landing area. They could first see him from the air as a distant dot moving in tight ellipses. As the helicopter powered down and they clambered out, he stopped and stood in a sagging posture.

"What is it?" Justine called out to him once it was quiet enough to be heard.

He walked over to them while wringing his hands anxiously. "Department of the Treasury lawyers are supposed to be here by the end of the day to talk to the governor."

"They're suing the state," Justine concluded bluntly.

"Could be," Banks sighed. "It is not unexpected, but now that things are in motion, I'm in agony. I'm going to get an ulcer from this."

"Where is my uncle?" Justine asked.

"In the conference room with Walden and the lawyers from Oklahoma City."

She marched past him toward the lodge, leaving Rob and Banks standing awkwardly a few paces apart.

Daniel approached in a leisurely manner once the helicopter had calmed. "What's she running off for?"

"The feds are coming to talk about the Wyoming dollar," Banks explained.

Daniel gave a youthful smirk and pulled a pack of cigarettes from the inside pocket of his bomber jacket. He offered it to both of them. Banks shook his head, and Rob accepted.

"Smoke 'em if you got 'em," the pilot remarked. "Those federal boys will be running back out of here with their tails between their legs as soon as they get a licking from Alexander and Walden."

Banks shook his head and shrugged his shoulders, seemingly uncertain of what nervous conviction he was trying to convey. He left after a minute of kicking at the dirt while the other two smoked.

"You really believe that?" Rob asked after a minute.

"I do," Daniel replied. "I'm only about as religious as one has to be to get along here, but I certainly do believe in the power of the right man and the necessity of his victory over those of lesser natures, bureaucrats being a primary example. It is by right natural order that Alexander will win this thing."

"It's an interesting theory," Rob replied.

They finished smoking in silence before shaking hands and going their separate ways. Rob returned to his room in the lodge and caught up on the news, resting on the bed and scrolling through lists of headlines and social media timelines on his phone. *The Times* message group was all abuzz about the Wyoming news and asking him if he had anything from the inside. He sent a few messages to dampen their curiosity. After a few hours of such activity and some light work on the interview audio, he took his notebook and went out through the halls to the balcony overlooking the front of the lodge. He wanted to sit and collect his thoughts for a bit while there was still some daylight.

It turned out that there was not much to collect, and he ended up drawing a sketch of the monument with a cutaway of the hollow inside. When not drawing he stared out over the metal roofs of the camp buildings and noted each movement of the State Corps workers who came and went. Just as he was deciding to return to his room and prepare for dinner, he noted an increase in motion below. Two black SUVs meandered their way up the road from the highway. As they approached, the workers and cattlemen going about their business paused and cast sidelong and suspicious glances at the vehicles. Everyone seemed to be at least subconsciously aware of what was unfolding.

Rob could hear footsteps below on the porch and rose to step to the railing and peer over the side. Arthur Walden's bald head bobbed along as he stepped down the stairs and onto the edge of the asphalt drive. Seen from above, the older man's body expanded outward strangely with each breath, his belly forming a clear protrusion surrounding the front of his shiny head. In one sudden and swift motion, the skin on the cranium reared backward and shoulders slumped as the eyes rolled back to look directly up at Rob.

"Your friends are coming," Walden stated after a brief instant of searching and then recognition. "I thought I heard somebody up there."

"It seems a bit of extra effort for them to come here in person." Rob observed.

"Tentatively it's a good sign. If they did not believe we could present a real problem, then they would just send a letter or hold a press conference in DC. If it was shock and awe, then they would want it more public. This likely means they don't want to look like bumbling fools on national television, at least not yet."

"I have questions about Nico," Rob stated, not bothering to segue. The hour was growing late on his time there. There was no sense in being subtle anymore. He had to be assertive and push away any reservations. He had a red-eye flight back to the city the next night.

"Depending on how this goes, we may have time to talk about that, but who knows?" Walden evaded, his head bobbing toward one shoulder and then the other. "Although I doubt it."

The black SUVs were rounding the last curve in the road. Walden squared his shoulders and began deliberately walking to the spot where they were most likely to stop. Once stationary, the back door of the foremost vehicle opened and a man in a suit stepped out. The old lawyer said something to him gruffly and reached out a hand for a loveless shake. Rob watched for a minute as two similarly dressed men emerged from the second vehicle and they all stood to talk. After some gesturing and nodding, all four of them turned to walk toward the lodge. A younger man stepped out of the front SUV a moment later with a briefcase in either hand. Once he was gone as well, there was no further activity.

Rob slipped in the door above the entry as quietly as he could and managed to hear a little hushed conversation as they moved below into the halls of the lower floor. The older of the suited arrivals was saying that he wanted to wait to talk to the governor directly and Walden was assuring him that Alexander had all the time in the world to listen.

Rob returned to his room, washed his face, and went down to the hall for dinner. He ate roast chicken and a simple garden salad, sitting at the edge of the room by one of the crackling hearths. Banks had let him in on the secret of requesting an after-dinner cappuccino, which he did with satisfying results. He sat back and sipped and observed, pulling his lips back against his teeth with each bitter introduction of caffeine, knowing once again that sleep would not come easily. He sat and thought until the dinner crowd ebbed to a trickle of tired laborers, some still dirty and desperate to catch the last moment of the meal window. He returned his dishes and went back to the upper halls of the lodge.

When he neared his room, Rob could see that Banks was closing up his office for the day: organizing stacks of paper on the desk, filing away pages in the drawers, and returning pencils to a cup on the corner. When he heard the soft sounds of Rob's approach, he became animated.

"With all the commotion I forgot to ask you what you thought of the monument." Banks moved into the doorway and leaned one shoulder against the frame. The older man looked to have calmed since his earlier despair.

"It was something else," Rob stated cryptically. It was more of a deflection than anything. He was too burned out on sustained willful suspension of disbelief.

Banks folded his arms and raised his brows slightly. It was perhaps as close as he could come to outright rejecting the reply.

"I'm not playing coy," Rob insisted haltingly. "There was a lot to take in, and I think any subtle layers of significance are lost on someone like me. In purely spatial terms, however, the monument is undeniably impressive."

Banks nodded with a satisfied smile before smoothing his features and then finally jerking into a spasm of realization. He turned back into his office and dug through the drawers for a moment before returning with a manila envelope.

"I found them."

"Found what?" Rob asked, genuinely confused.

"The Nico editorials. These are paper copies of all of them." He smiled again at Rob's clear loss of basic social functions. "It was easy actually. Both Walden and Alexander had digital copies they had requested from *The Star-Ledger* a while back. All I had to do was print them out." He held out the envelope.

"That's very thoughtful," Rob managed, taking the packet and sticking it under his arm. "I'll make good use of it." He realized that sounded strange and added, "It will be helpful for context."

Banks shrugged. "Personally, I never read more than the first few. Not very engaging reading, in my opinion."

The stroke of good luck was animating Rob, and the caffeine was taking effect. "Are you busy tomorrow?" he asked.

"Not really, but who knows with all the activity around here today."

"If the offer still stands, then I think I'll take you up on looking through those campaign videos."

"Well, even if I'm not here, if the door is open, then help yourself," Banks offered.

"You seem in better spirits now," Rob remarked, "after we talked earlier."

"When I saw Alexander and the Treasury guys meet for the first few moments and the way they held themselves and interacted, it put me much more at ease." The older man waved a hand as if to dismiss a flight of fancy. "It may be shallow of me, but after that moment I felt better. I think we will be alright."

Rob held up the envelope. "Thank you again. I'm going to tear into these."

"No problem; you have a good night," Banks urged and turned to finish his end of the day routines.

Rob unlocked his room and surveyed the dim corners. He had left a lamp on by the window. Ever since he had come in to find Walden sitting on the bed the day prior, he was no longer taking any chances with potential ambushes. He passed over the obscured garden's geometry of the rugs to the bed, where he heaved his body and squirmed over to reach the lamp. He opened the envelope and a stack of pages spilled out onto the comforter. They were arranged chronologically. The first editorial was dated a few days before the election, and it was titled "An Appeal to Fellow Americans of Wyoming."

PART IV

A Stillborn Lie

CHAPTER

13

The first editorial began with a brief overview of the history of infrastructure in the state of Wyoming, recounting all the difficulties of reaching a point where a decent economy could emerge. Nico reminded readers that isolation from the nation's markets had kept Wyoming oil prices low and warded off capital and investment. The resulting desperation made the citizens of the territory vulnerable to those who would come in and make bold promises of wealth or other utopias. One particular passage read:

> *Patience, industriousness and time made our modern state, with all its modest blessings, possible. The last thing we need is to turn back to isolation or stubborn illusions of self-sufficiency. This is not to say that we are not a strong or capable people, but to mistake this for absolute autonomy and shut the door on opportunities for cooperation would be an error that could very well cause us to recreate the same climate for malaise which troubled us so much less than a century ago.*

It was all very reasonable and measured, but it lacked the flair and bombast of Alexander or Stevens. Rob could see immediately why Nico's articles had not roused any sort of popular electoral resistance to the new politics that had entered the state. The first editorial was a long one. The second half pivoted to an analysis of the people's reaction to the start of the Second World War. Nico recounted the high percentages of Wyoming volunteers and enlisted men when compared to the other states and their enviable level of competence and readiness when put up against other regions.

Wyoming is perhaps one of the most American states when defining such things by the measures of patriotism, sacrifice, and other classic definitions of American virtue. Wyoming punches like a state twice its size. We have reaped many benefits from this. Although many make the argument that we received more in federal aid than we contribute, this is not wholly the case. In the fifty-five years following the Oil and Gas Leasing act of 1920, Wyoming put nearly one hundred-million dollars more into the reclamation fund than was spent on projects in our state. This is not to say that one side is wrong or right to argue that something is owed, or someone is short changed, but that there is nuance and give and take. We cannot cast aside opportunity for the sake of ideology masquerading as state pride.

What was clear from the opinion pieces was that Nico had certainly done the research and truly wanted what was best for the state in the long run. In the face of a charismatic movement none of it would be overly convincing, but it was a good try. Rob flipped through to a later article that seemed to address the ousting of the college president. It was titled, "Shades of Mao from Alexander." The piece recounted governor Nels Smith's successful packing of the university board of trustees to oust the popular Arthur G. Crane. Nico then wrote:

Although Alexander's strong-arming is only as unsophisti-cated and crude as Smith's, it is even more dangerous in that he does not try to hide his intent. Clearly his brand of politics will not allow for dissenting voices, even those typically protected by the respect given to academic pursuits. Alexander seeks a revolution which cannot endure intellectual criticism. If we allow him to accomplish this silencing of voices without consequences, then likely nothing will be beyond his grasp.

It was clear that, as Alexander's reign in Wyoming continued, Nico became more and more agitated and concerned. By the last editorial there were allusions to an attempt to uncover his identity:

Not even the peaceful criticism allowed by my anonymity can be allowed. On all counts I have wished to be wrong, but I do

> *not see my political opinions lasting much longer in this venue.*

Rob glanced at the clock on the bedside table. It was nearly eleven p.m. and he was feeling tired enough to sleep. He changed into his athletic shorts and undershirt before washing his face and brushing his teeth. The editorials went in a neat stack on the wooden table by the window. He would give them a closer look in the morning. After he crawled into bed, images of Mount Calvary and the bizarre show on the summit crawled back into his mind and began dancing on the periphery of his attempts at sleep. He could hear unfamiliar gospel songs and hymns that meandered into odd combinations of verses and choruses never put on a page.

Rob spasmed at the sound of deliberate knocking. He opened his eyes in the darkness and rolled over to face the door where a little bit of warm light pooled under from the hallway. He was unaware whether he had imagined the sound while on the verge of sleep. He often thought he heard noises while drifting off. He held his breath and waited. He hoped earnestly that it had been a confabulated creation of his mind under the auspices of shallow REM sleep. He gripped a knot of blankets in his hands and entreated all of reality that it had been nothing. A second round of knocking followed.

He fumbled feebly at the bedspread until he was free to sit up on the edge of the mattress. The red letters on the clock read after midnight. He made no noise and continued to watch the bottom of the door where two darkened areas morphed and shifted to indicate the feet of some intruder.

A deep voice leaked through the cracks between the door and the frame. "I'll huff and I'll puff, Coen. I know you're in there."

Rob's organs squirmed against one another. It was the voice of Arthur Walden. Silence followed the initial warning, and the two shadows moved off to the side and out of sight. Rob had nearly breathed a sigh of relief when they returned and passed by to the other side. Clearly the man was pacing outside and had no intention of leaving.

"You're a journalist, for God's sake. You can sleep when you're back in the city. Besides, I have a bottle of whiskey to share. You won't say no to a nightcap, will you?"

Rob let out a sigh and crossed the room to the door. He opened it about six inches and peered out into the hallway. Walden had stopped pacing and was leaning against the opposite wall. His arms were folded atop his belly and, true to his word, he gripped an amber colored bottle of whiskey in one hand.

"What do you want?" Rob asked impatiently.

Walden smiled. "A truce, a summit, a drink."

"I'm guessing you want to come in?" he asked. Then he remembered the stack of Nico editorials on the table and was not sure what sort of a reaction they would garner, so he suggested: "Why don't we go down to the meal hall?"

Walden's eyes narrowed in suspicion and then clouded briefly as he considered the suggestion. Then he smiled wolfishly. "Yes, the meal hall. We can raid the kitchen."

Rob turned to retrieve the room key from his pants, joined the other man in the hall, and locked the door behind him. They headed downstairs, Rob a little behind as Walden hummed an unfamiliar tune in the back of his throat. They pushed through the large doors into the massive, dark hall, and Walden fumbled at the wall for a moment before finding the light switch and illuminating about a quarter of the chandeliers.

"Let's keep it dim," the older man remarked. "No use in drawing any attention or waking anyone up." His voice echoed in the far reaches of the dim and cavernous room.

Rob followed as he crossed the room to one of the great hearths and stooped to grab a poker and dig around in some remaining embers. Walden made a triumphant noise.

"Still some life here. Let me get this going. You check the kitchen for some soda water and something salty. Pretzels or nuts. I'm not picky." He paused and grunted while grabbing a narrow piece of kindling wood from the side of the stone hearth. "And get a pitcher of water too."

Rob begrudgingly agreed and meandered between the tables across the echoing expanse toward the counter. He slipped around and entered the black space beyond, stopping short to let his eyes adjust. After some counter edges and door frames began to creep into view from the saturating dark, he could see some switches on the wall. With a little trial and error, the room was light enough to begin the search.

As far as he could tell, the refrigerator's contents were all meat and dairy. The cupboards beneath the stainless-steel counters contained assortments of pots, pans, and utensils that all stared out at him from stacks made with military precision. The cabinets above held coffee mugs, plates, and glassware. Finally, after making a few lazy circles around the room, he noticed a row of tall doors on the far side of the room. He pulled open the closest set to reveal a walk-in pantry. A small row of lights came on, beckoned by the sudden motion. Rob stepped in, his eyes roving over row upon row of flour, oats, shortening, molasses, sugar, oil, jars of preserves, canned goods, nuts, bread, and everything else one could imagine. He took some pretzels and peanuts in the shell and put them on the counter before entering into the next pantry where he found drums of coffee, stacks of bottled water, and the soda water Walden had requested. He retrieved a pitcher on his way out.

He returned to Walden, who had revived the fire and was sitting at the nearest table listening to the dancing flame pop and crackle as the orange light made a shifting veil across his face.

The old lawyer turned at the sounds of Rob nearing. "Oh-ho! Not bad, Coen, not bad at all!"

"I still need to get glasses." Rob explained, depositing his armload and making the return trip. Once everything was situated, they settled in. Walden poured some whiskey into each glass and added some soda water to his own. Rob shook his head when offered. Walden rested his glass on the round top of his belly and returned his gaze to the fire.

Rob took a few sips of his drink and gazed around at the dim hall uncomfortably before breaking the silence. "So, what is this all about?" he asked.

Walden snorted. "Don't you have questions?"

"Yes. Do you have any intention to actually answer them?"

"There's only one way to find out," Walden answered after a gulp.

"Ok," Rob murmured, making sure his tone showed that he was unconvinced. "How did things go with the feds?"

"Ha!" Walden heaved out forcefully, causing his glass to leap upward and the surface of his drink to swirl and lap against the sides of his glass. He kept his face directed toward the fire while speaking. "Those fucking pricks." His voice was low and gruff but not angry. He took another drink. "You know they think that everything belongs to them. It's really quite remarkable and sounds like a cliché I'm sure, but it's true. Not like some movie scene where they say it outright. It's the way they talk, the assumptions made in the language they use."

"They're suing?" Rob asked.

Walden nodded. "Damn right they are. Those arrogant bastards want to take us down a few notches. The thing is they aren't even vengeful about it in their demeanor. That's the worst of it. Like a bunch of damn doctors scrubbing in to do surgery on a diseased organ. We are ready for them though. Me and my friends from Oklahoma City have been preparing for this for a long time."

"You think you can win?" Rob asked, cursing himself internally for not having the foresight to bring his recorder or notepad from his room.

"Oh, most certainly," Walden replied. He turned and set his glass on the table before starting in on the peanuts. He crushed the brittle shells between his thick forefingers and let the shrapnel and debris fall onto the table as he spoke. "You see, we have some precedent on our side, *Briscoe v. The Bank of the Commonwealth of Kentucky*. We had that in mind from the beginning when starting the Wyoming Project."

Rob interrupted, his desperation at the information flowing by with no way to record it too much to bear. "Do you mind if I get something to write this down?"

Walden leaned over the table and stretched an arm toward the entry. "In the desk out there in the atrium you should find a legal pad and some pens. Knock yourself out."

"Thank you," Rob replied, and hurried out to retrieve them. As soon as he was back in earshot, Walden continued his explanation. Rob returned to his chair and began scrawling down notes.

"You see, Article One of the US Constitution forbids emitting bills of credit, which is where they intend to get us."

"That seems pretty straightforward to me," Rob interjected, buying himself some time to jot down a few details before they faded from his short-term memory.

"They wish," Walden spat out derisively. "*Briscoe v. Kentucky* establishes that a state issuing bonds through an independent bank, so that it is not issuing on its own credit alone, escapes violating the language of Article One. In fact, that state won the case on those grounds." Peanut shells crackled in an odd harmony with the flames in the hearth. Walden was humming on all cylinders, perfectly in his element. "The Bank of Wyoming is a private institution held by the citizens of the state. Wyoming dollars are backed by gold and issued by that bank. Their value is determined by the price of gold and a complex formula of state economic health. Based on the victory of Kentucky in their own case, we actually have the advantage. If we can deliver a very public stinging rebuke to a federal attempt to stall the Wyoming Plan, then our momentum can only increase."

"Formula? What are you talking about?"

"I'm not as much into finance as Alexander," Walden admitted. "All I know is that gold has its weaknesses and vulnerabilities. For that reason, it is not the sole determiner of the Wyoming dollar's value. Combining it with some measure of the state's success is a way to keep people motivated. That's all the detail I know."

"What angle do you think the feds will try?" Rob asked, grabbing a handful of pretzels.

Walden grunted and shifted in his seat. "Well, if I were to try to put myself in the shoes of a federal prosecutor, then I would probably use Alexander's own words against him. They will likely try to establish that his rhetoric makes a convincing case that he is trying to subvert the spirit of the law. Article One, Section 10 was written to curb the power of the states to operate as independent authorities and interfere with the aims of other states or the nation as a whole. The feds will probably cite Alexander's own admissions that he wants the state to undertake its own project et cetera and claim that he is, by establishing a state currency, doing exactly that."

"And would they be right?" Rob asked.

"Do you honestly think I'm stupid enough to answer that any other way than 'no'?" Walden asked with a mocking tone.

Rob took another gulp of whiskey. "I suppose that's fair." He made a few more notes. "So why does it matter so much?" he asked. "Alexander was telling me that it's just as much an important symbolic move as anything else, but I'm not sure I believe that."

"It's quarantine," Walden mused bluntly. "Insulation."

"Go on," Rob coaxed.

The lawyer shrugged. "It's simple. A small number of financial entities run the entire world. This isn't conspiracy talk, it's a basic fact. You know where the big banks and credit card companies get a big chunk of their money?"

"No idea."

"Transactions. Every time you swipe a card with their name on it, they get a cut. More swipes mean more money. The economy lives and dies by growth and spending." He paused. "Do you know what velocity of money is?"

"No."

"Velocity of money is the amount of times a unit of currency is used within a given time period. If lots of people are buying and selling, then it means that the velocity is higher. There is a fair bit of argument as to whether it matters to a healthy economy or not, but what does matter is velocity of non-physical money. You won't find a whole lot of it in textbooks, but it matters. Credit is based on the promise to compensate at a future time for goods and services rendered now. Spending the same dollar bill ten times or one hundred times in a week doesn't matter very much, but ten credit transactions in one week is very different from one hundred. This is because it creates interest. When you pay the bank back, they end up with a bigger cut in their hands, which they in turn loan out, increasing the money supply. This causes inflation. The result of all this is that the banks get money when you swipe your card, the banks get money when you pay off your card, and the dollars you have are now worth less. The velocity of non-physical money is basically a measure of how much richer the financial institutions are getting compared to the general population. Because of this, the US economy is a long-term, barely controlled inflation spiral."

Rob did not know enough about finance to tell if Walden was right, so he moved on. "Ok, so how is the Wyoming dollar quarantine?"

"World financial turbulence can be hedged against by isolating oneself from the effects of the larger markets bleeding in. The Wyoming dollar offers a refuge from a banking crisis, which is inevitable in the debt-based economy. Value these days comes from promises backed by power."

"So, you're shorting the federal government," Rob ventured.

Walden grimaced. "Not at all. That's a terrible simile. The idea is to hedge against US and world market instability. Gold is not a great short-term inflation hedge, but long-term it endures. The Bank of Wyoming has a relatively high ceiling reserve requirement. What that means is if the US market crashes or becomes extremely volatile, then we are offered more protection. Since the Wyoming dollar also derives value from the economic health of the state, all we have to do is endure, have the will and resourcefulness to stand up for ourselves in a crisis, and we can come out even stronger than those around us."

"But in the event of a global financial crisis, won't your economy be devastated as well?"

"Like I said." Walden explained. "I don't know the full details of the whole value formula, but it's tied to the Wyoming Plan. Financial success is only part of it. Besides, in the event of a crash, people can get their money out of the bank here where otherwise they wouldn't be able to do so." Walden cleared his throat and took another sip. "The goal is to wean people off credit at the hands of the multinationals. Which is more desirable, that they purchase goods and services with plastic that sends a cut of every transaction to some massive conglomerate, or that they save money in the Bank of Wyoming and keep our long-term value more stable?"

"Honestly I don't know enough about this kind of thing to tell if you're all crazy or geniuses," Rob admitted. "You do know that it sounds pretty nutty though, right? Like the kind of thing you see on a fringe website that wants you to buy water filters or boxes of silver dollars."

Walden sighed and rubbed his chin. "I may not be a religious man like the governor or pretend to see the world as he sees it, the long arc of things I guess you could say. I'm not paranoid about the direction of the world or coming cataclysms." He paused and added, "Not to say that Alexander is really. But even I, blind as I am to some things, can see that there is an exceeding darkness in this world." Walden mused this while staring over Rob's shoulder with an uncharacteristic gravity. "And it's not created by the absence of a good God who would otherwise dispel it. It is man-made, a thoughtless, accidental, maddened darkness too pure for our cogent faculties to fully grasp. It is created by a disingenuous misanthropy."

"I'm lost," Rob managed.

"Let's say for example, that a visionary technologist designs a program to better organize humans' productive capacities by assigning tasks. Ostensibly he does this because human beings are not good enough to order themselves efficiently. Yet, his supposed artificial intelligence is inherently human in its design and implementation. It's Oedipal, even the escape. The disease is inherent in the biology. He only doesn't realize that he's fucking his own mother because he's got the blinders on. There is no escaping. There is trying I suppose." Walden shifted in his seat and leaned back to prop an elbow on the edge of the table. "Just like the Wyoming dollar and the gold hedge and all that. It's a good try, but you cannot escape from the human disease that seeks to control and manage and infect. Adoption, infiltration, retrofitting, remodeling, standards and practices, generally accepted accounting principles, interchangeable parts, economies of scale..." he trailed off.

"So what is the darkness then?" Rob asked, befuddled.

"The darkness is what drives men to calculate deadweight loss, to calculate for what was not and should have been in the perfect machine. There is no name for it really, but it tabulates things like opportunity cost. It writes its laws on spreadsheets and memos. You are seeing something rare, Coen, so you better appreciate it. I live in this darkness. I breathe it and drink it willingly. You are seeing Arthur Walden with his head above water for an instant. Appreciate it, because next thing you know, I'll be out of sight and something under the surface will be brushing against your leg."

A chill ran down Rob's spine, and he sat still with the pen held about an inch above the legal pad. Walden was silently staring at him while leaned back in the chair, his glittering eyes catching a little light from the fire.

Rob pushed through the uneasiness. "I asked Alexander why he keeps you around, since you aren't exactly the savory and moral type one would expect to be at the right hand of someone like him. He said that he hopes that you would learn something of God from him by example."

The lawyer seemed to move very slightly. It was not a flinch, at least not in any sense that most would notice. It was a nearly invisible shift in energy perhaps. Maybe Rob was imagining it, wishing to believe that his response could have any effect, that he could faze the indomitable character seated across from him.

"Alexander had better hope that's not the case." Walden replied with a smirk. "I can be his sin-eater, his talisman of protection, but not if I get religion. Not that there is any concern on that front."

"And you do not diminish him by association?" Rob asked.

"So long as I can calculate the opportunity cost for him and make the necessary adjustments behind the scenes, then Alexander is free to act as he desires."

"So, Alexander would never be where he is without you?"

Walden laughed. "And you say that you aren't a federal agent? A saboteur? It's textbook counter-intelligence: divide and undermine."

"You're giving me too much credit," Rob answered grudgingly, taking another drink of his whiskey.

"Do you think I'm just paranoid?" Walden asked. "Do you think that this is just a bit that I do in order to keep you on edge?"

"Paranoid? Maybe. I mean, you did eavesdrop on my interview with the governor."

"Well you had Banks fetch those editorials, right?" Walden insisted. "Am I just supposed to pretend that you aren't snooping around outside the typical bounds of a visit and interview?"

Rob felt some heat developing under his collar. "Speaking of paranoia, Banks told me that you were running a full inquiry into the author, and you had to get begged off by the editor at the *Tribune*."

The lawyer rose forcefully from his seat. Rob spasmed backward as well, unsure of what the other man intended to do. After a moment it was clear that he was merely crossing to the hearth to add another log and stoke the coals with the iron poker. Rob let out a slow and silent breath.

Walden spoke after a time while still hunched over the fire. "Well, you read some of the editorials by now I imagine. What do you think?"

"I don't know. They were well thought out and researched, probably not very convincing though. They lacked a certain persuasive punch, I guess."

"Correct," the lawyer replied and straightened to return to his seat. He opened the bottle of whiskey and added to both of their glasses before leaning over to crack some more peanut shells. "Banks knows very little about what happened. He's not exactly in the loop, and he is somewhat of a squeamish character, not unlike yourself."

"Hey," Rob protested weakly.

"Don't deny it, you practically fell out of the chair when I got up to tend to the fire. It's just who you are."

The heat had spread to Rob's face, and he could feel his ears burning as though they crackled along with the fire.

After adding some soda water to his drink and taking a healthy swig, Walden steamed ahead. "The truth is that I knew very well who this character writing the editorials was from pretty early."

"Wait, really?" Rob asked, rather taken aback.

"Why do you think the editorials stopped?" the lawyer asked.

"I don't know. I hadn't really thought about it." Rob took a sip of his own drink. "So what's the truth?"

"Pass me that legal pad and pen," Walden demanded. "Just tear off the pages you're using and send it my way." He gestured with an insistent beckoning arm.

Rob complied, and Walden began scrawling down lines of text and making sweeping lines at intervals. He was fully engrossed for nearly a minute before the journalist ventured to ask what he was doing.

"I'm writing up a quick non-disclosure agreement for you to sign."

"What?" Rob asked incredulously, even laughing a little. The warm and numbing sensation of the alcohol had made an appearance at the base of the back of his head.

"There are things I don't want you writing about in your little article," Walden explained. "I don't mind relaying the story so long as it stays between us. Plus I wouldn't mind going after you legally someday, and this opens up that possibility." He paused and glanced up with the evil smile he showed on occasion. "I'm only halfway serious about that last bit, but don't let that give you the impression that I wouldn't do it."

"You don't trust me?" Rob asked with a smirk.

"You have proven yourself to be as slippery as any other journalist." The pen made a series of rasping noises across the paper and the thick-fingered hand moved mechanically to dot some I's and cross some T's. Finally, Walden slid the notepad over.

Rob scanned the page, making note of any significant details. The other man's handwriting was a very legible longhand with a sharp tilt to it, the sort he had not seen for a long time.

"This pertains to anything involving the Nico issue and anything that stems from it?"

Walden nodded.

"What is this about me being legally liable for any damages you incur as a result of my disclosing any of the covered information?"

The lawyer gave him an ominous look before tossing a few pretzels into his mouth and crunching away on them. His moustache made its strange inchworm motions with each movement of his jaw.

"You signed your own non-disclosure and you want me on the hook for that too," Rob observed with a revelatory tone.

"At the bottom," Walden explained without confirming, "you will find a line needing your signature and the date and another for your printed name. It needs to be legible. Also, please initial near the top where there is a very small line asking for confirmation that you are of sound mind and are capable of understanding the legal gravity of the document."

Rob held the pen about an inch above the sheet of paper and thought it over. Whether sworn to secrecy or not, getting more information could never be a bad thing. Of course, knowing more about Walden and being bound legally could always result in some kind of disaster down the road. He took another sip of whiskey and shrugged before signing, dating, and initialing.

As soon as the pen came off the page, Walden drew the sheet back across the table and took out his phone to snap a picture.

"You are of sound mind and you agree not to disclose anything we discuss relating to the editorials, their writer, and any related information?"

"Yes," the journalist agreed, hesitantly.

Walden reached inside his shirt and fiddled with something.

"What are you doing?" Rob asked, perplexed.

"I record everything," Walden answered as though it was a perfectly normal thing to say. "But obviously I won't be recording anything that comes after. The photo and your spoken admission should be enough of a corroboration."

"In case I what? Steal the nondisclosure and burn it?" Rob asked.

"In case of anything. It would be foolish not to take precautions."

The lawyer paused and then leaned back in the chair and folded his arms. His eyes roved back so that they seemed to look toward the ceiling or as far back as possible into the mass of neurons collected beneath his bald dome of a head.

"The story began here in Wyoming, during the winter, and years before I had ever met James Alexander. I had finished with some litigation for one of the big lodges up in Jackson Hole. They gave me a room to use as an office for the duration, and things went well enough that I got them to let me stay for the winter. I'm not much for skiing or any of that, but I like the alpine life, the snow, going out for quick jaunts into the blizzard, maybe doing some hunting. I was set for a bit financially and ready to put my heels up for a month or so. Usually I would sit in the dining area in the morning and read the papers, drink some coffee, and watch the people come in and out: the young college girls in their ludicrous snow outfits with the fake fur and the nylon and polyester. That damned sound like nothing else in the world, the whisking thin screech when people walk around in that material is utterly absurd."

Rob let his rear slide forward in the seat and folded his arms. Walden took note of his slouch immediately and his eyes narrowed and locked on with weapons-grade precision.

"What, am I boring you already? If you want the short version, then we can just forget it."

Rob shook his head. "Take your time. Just getting comfortable."

"I had not been wasting too much time before I ran into another guy who was not like the others. I don't want to mention his name, but you could figure it out pretty easily. He was a former navy officer. I'll call him Charles for the sake of convenience. Charles was a little younger than me and also had a taste for the alpine winter life. He had come to Jackson for a few days before going on to Aspen. He was going to one of those bullshit conferences where a bunch of ex-this brass and ex-that state department assholes get together and publicly jerk each other off about the big long-running joke of world affairs and foreign policy."

"I'm familiar with that sort of event," Rob interjected.

Walden gave a sly grin. "Yes, well, I did not like the kind of person Charles represented, but those kinds of people often operate as portals to worlds of opportunity. We took a liking to one another because we read the same kind of newspapers in the morning, although I doubt for the same reasons. We both enjoyed ice fishing and went on a couple of outings together. That's when we first got to talking about things of gravity. Nothing quite like being stuck in a shack in freezing weather for hours with boredom setting in to open up some avenues of conversation. On one of those days, Charles told me that he had been naval intelligence and that he worked in the private sector now. You see, a lot of those guys will get jobs with firms that their intel groups invest in. It's all a big money carousel in that circle. Sometimes it's not clear if you're working for an information technology company or the government, especially when you plan on selling anything you make to the military and half of what you make is based on military research anyway."

They both leaned forward to take drinks from their glasses. After a glance over at the fire, Walden rose and approached to add some more wood. He grasped the poker and re-arranged some bits of burning material before returning.

"The thing is that Charles had rivals. They all do. CIA and NSA and naval intelligence are always in a sort of proxy war over funding and partnerships with business. He was under the impression that some of his former associates were going to try to nail him for using classified military technology in his latest private venture. He claimed to me that, while there were some similarities, he had done nothing wrong. After a few days of fishing and drinking late into the evening at the lodge, he decided to hire me temporarily to do some digging and filled me in on some of the details. He was working for an internet marketing company that was trying to create profiling software that could take in the information offered by people on social media and output language or methods of reasoning that would appeal to them. Now, we aren't talking about a flash pop-up ad that they will like. People are pretty tired of banner ads based on previous search history and that kind of thing. This is more like an entire pitch for a product that appeals to someone's worldview and language. Now, the government has been working on this kind of thing for quite some time. They developed a Cuban social media app in order to draw in users and eventually try to influence them politically to affect the regime there, for example."

"I heard about that," Rob confirmed with a nod.

"That's a pretty rudimentary example of what they were eventually going for. According to Charles, and I don't know if this information is classified, but there was a project called ICON that naval intelligence was cooking up for quite some time. It stands for Intelligently Counteracting Outlier Narratives. Basically, that word salad says that they were trying to create a program that could generate authentic-sounding counter-narratives to spontaneous or destabilizing political movements. Charles said that some of his concepts for marketing were similar, but he used none of the actual technology in his own venture."

"Wait, so the goal of ICON was to suppress populism?"

"In so few words, yes. When you think of typical counter-propaganda methods, they usually involve inserting an agent of a sort into a group to temper a message or push back from within. When you recognize someone who is one of your own counter-signaling a message, then there can be de-escalation or reversal. Maybe even infighting just causes a group to collapse because of disagreement. In the age of social media, the goal of ICON, as I understand it, was to make sock puppet entities online that were autonomous to an extent. They would do their own research, embed in groups and take on the common language of the milieu. Charles told me that there were a number of very influential anonymous characters on social media sites that had thousands of followers and were a complete invention. His goal was to use similar methods in marketing. Why pay an influencer on social media to market a product, when you can spend much less and pay for a company to add their product surreptitiously into otherwise resilient internet subcultures?"

"And it was effective?"

"From what he told me, it was very effective. He even said that there were some test programs involved with controversial political groups that would intentionally break the terms of service of social media sites and get banned only to create alternate accounts as though a real person was coming back to the platform under a similar moniker. What this did was create the image that controversial characters were getting screwed over by the powers that be and thus increase the solidarity of the group. Introduce a product into that climate and next thing you know, you have ostensible internet socialists all using the same consumer items out of some kind of solidarity, despite it being entirely against the group's stated ideology. The concept of community, and a threatened one especially, increased product adoption to previously unheard-of levels. And there is an added bonus: the mainstream social media user's squeamish draw toward controversial content would make aesthetics and cultures involving target products break out into insane virality. The former in group bemoans the uptake by "posers," but the marketer rolls in the money even more."

"Was ICON itself ever used effectively?"

"That I don't know," Walden mused. "Charles did imply that there had been setbacks with the original program, that sometimes sock puppet accounts left to their own devices and their own semi-autonomous research would sometimes veer extremist themselves over time, and attempts to correct them broke the believability. Whether stuck in a spiral of increasing extremism or forced into contradiction by the corrective hand of an intervening technician, either resulted in an unnatural voice which led to other social media users identifying them as interlopers. I did my own research about it, the effect on subcultures, and I think there are at least a few mass shooting events that can be tied to project ICON."

"You're joking." Rob interjected in disbelief.

"As is often the case, you can never draw a clear line from one point to another, but you can get a decent pattern of data that points in a certain direction."

Suddenly something clicked in the back of Rob's mind with such instantaneous clarity that he sat bolt upright in his chair. "You believe that the Nico editorials were a result of project ICON."

Walden smiled. "Of course, I did. That's getting a little ahead. You see, Charles and his little project and what he had told me about naval intelligence was not at the top of my mind when I first began trying to track down the author. My first suspicion was also a closed avenue."

"Who?" Rob was very curious.

Walden took another sip and gave a victorious smile. He was clearly relishing his role as keeper of fascinating secrets. "It was obvious to me that George Collins was the most likely culprit. After he lost the governorship to Alexander, he took up a position in the energy company UBI and did his best to stymie our early efforts."

"Alexander told me," Rob explained, grabbing a few pretzels. "He also told me that you somehow got him to back off. Any chance you want to tell me what you had on him? Me being under a nondisclosure and all?" He tried to look as disinterested as possible while chewing on the pretzels and scanning over his notes on the legal pad.

"There is no chance," Walden replied bluntly. His face had gone hard, and the edges of his jaws and brows seemed almost sharper, as though his flesh had transformed into a more geological material than before. "There are some things that you never repeat, words that contain too much power. If they are set loose, then they may wreak havoc and never stop."

"Alright then," Rob relented. "I'm not surprised, I'll admit."

"When I want to surprise you, then I will," Walden replied gruffly. "Anyway, obviously Collins was a no go. I knew that approaching the paper directly would be counterproductive as well, so I went to the next best person: Jeffrey Collins."

"A relation, I take it?" Rob had just finished another sip of whiskey and knew the question was idiotic, but he did not really care.

"Obviously a relation, yes. He is George Collins' brother. He's a historian who teaches at the university. Lucky for me, Jeffrey is not a political man. Even more lucky for me, he's a schmoozer, a real socialite intellectual type. He fancies himself above his brother's squabbles, so it was pretty easy to get his help. Jeffrey knows a good deal about the state. He wrote a few books about Wyoming history and politics. Most importantly, he knows all the other writers and how they write. I showed up at his office with copies of the first few editorials and a bottle of Bordeaux."

"I'm sure that helped," Rob interjected with a scoff.

"It sure did. Jeffrey Collins is terrible with money. Gifts go a long way. I did my research on him before the first meeting. It was easy enough. The damn fool keeps a blog with all his tastes, preferences, and interests laid out for the taking. Obviously, the wine was a hit. I didn't pick his very favorite because that would have been obvious. I went back more than a year in his blog archives and found one that he had praised moderately. I told him that I had heard through the grapevine that he liked Bordeaux. I think he appreciated the pun even more than the wine. From that point on we were best friends."

Rob had realized pretty early on that Arthur Walden was some very rare brand of sociopath, but he was still surprised at times when listening to the man talk. What was it Alexander had said about him being made by the watchmaker god? The comment was proving more and more accurate as time went on.

The lawyer was forging ahead. "He knew a little about who I was, and that didn't prove to be a liability. He fancied me some kind of character. Clearly, I was the villain of his brother's existence, and I tried to not let that go to my head. Anyway, he had read the Nico editorials already. As far as he knew, his brother was no direct tie to them. Jeffrey explained that the nuance was a bit too subtle and intelligent for his brother. George would not think to use a writer to subvert and persuade. His methods were much more direct and nakedly political. Luckily, I had got his interest though. I may mock Jeffrey Collins for his professorial vanities, but he is a true academic."

"I'm a little shocked to hear that from you," Rob observed. "I would think that you have nothing but disdain for academics."

"Is that a hint of surprise I hear in your tone?" Walden asked with an unexpectedly jovial smile.

They shared a small laugh as Walden added some more liquor to the glasses. He rose again to tend to the fire. His stooped, hulking form blocking the flames made the air around Rob a few degrees cooler. Rob had the sudden and distinct impression that he was a planetary body suspended in the dark reaches of space and Walden had passed in front of the warm light of the sun and eclipsed him. He was going to have to slow down in his drinking.

Walden returned to his seat and began crushing some more peanut shells between his forefingers. "I admired Jeffrey Collins somewhat because he exceeded my expectations. I knew that he was neutral when it came to his brother's world of politics and rivalries. I did not expect him to throw himself so diligently into solving the riddle of the editorials. We met up a few times in the interim to have dinner or a drink. He would tell me that he was making progress, but honestly, I suspected that he was stringing me along. Could you blame me, really? The man had champagne taste, and I was picking up the majority of the tabs. Finally, after a few months, and just when I was nearly at the point of cutting him off, Jeffrey invited me to his office at the university. I knew it had to be something, since it wasn't a dinner and drinks call. He laid it all out for me. He had cross-referenced language from the editorials with authors and commentators in recent Wyoming history. He had even used a database query program that the university has for identifying authors of unsigned work. He had narrowed it down to one strong possibility. The language and references and scope of knowledge pointed to one writer: Andrew T. Laren."

"I haven't heard of him," Rob murmured.

"I doubt you would. He's only well-known in Wyoming, since his focus is on state history. He had taught at the university for a number of years, but it was before Jeff Collins' time. Nobody had really kept up with him after he left his teaching post, but that wasn't the main difficulty." Walden smiled ruefully and took another drink. "The biggest problem was that he had been dead for two years."

Rob furrowed his brow. "So that meant he couldn't have written any of the editorials."

"Precisely. I asked Jeff Collins if there were any other

possibilities. He told me that the second most similar writer to the language and style was not even worth checking. Laren was the only possibility. So I thanked him for his help and was left on my own with an even bigger mystery."

"Somebody else was mimicking Laren's style?" Rob questioned aloud.

"That was my first thought too, that somebody at the *Tribune* was writing the editorials and using Laren's old material to mask their own writing style. So that's when I started sniffing around their operation. My first step was to walk into their offices and talk directly to their opinion editor. The paper was a smaller operation. I figured some low-level intimidation might be enough to get me some information. The editor was a cynical guy about my age. I think he's still there. His name is Norman Grant, or something like that. Anyway, I walked in, sat down, told him I was one of Alexander's lawyers and asked him how I could get in touch with this Nico fellow writing the editorials."

Walden took another sip and pursed his lips, perhaps feeling some residual annoyance from the memory. "I had read up on him. Grant was not a fan of Alexander. He was no alarmist, but he had made his reservations plain during the campaign. He's one of those typical, red-state liberals who gets by with being very practical, appealing to the free-thinking spirit of the people and common-sense politics. He doesn't believe in it. None of them do. It's a hedge to make folks falter for a moment and think that maybe they should listen and be reasonable. It's a stalling tactic when they worry that something they don't like may have momentum. It's basic survival mechanism as an ethos. It makes them tough nuts to crack."

"So, intimidation didn't work," Rob observed.

Walden chuckled. "No, no it didn't. He told me that he would never under any circumstances reveal the identity of the writer and said that he sadly was not surprised to see such thuggish tactics already coming from James Alexander. I made it clear to him that I was there entirely on my own initiative. I told him that if I'm doing my job right, then Alexander's problems go away without him even having to take the trouble. I was laying it on a little thick, but I wanted to put a scare into him."

"Why? Sadism?" Rob asked with a smirk.

Walden twisted his mouth and made a rough sound in his throat. "Hardly. I wanted to find out how he was communicating with the writer. In order to do that, I needed to get him concerned enough to reach out. If he felt he needed to caution this Nico character, then maybe I could catch him sending some kind of message."

"By what, tapping his phone?" Rob suggested sardonically.

"No, by bugging his office. That's why I wanted to walk in there in the first place."

Rob stopped with his glass half raised to his lips. He stared at Walden. The older man had sunk back into his chair with a look of menacing coolness on his features.

"You're serious?" Rob asked.

"Of course I'm serious. Why do you think I had you sign a nondisclosure agreement? Do you think I get off on that kind of thing?"

"That is, well, not to mention illegal, that is so unethical. I don't know where to begin." The liquor had given Rob the carelessness needed to voice his disturbance. "I mean, you're a lawyer. You didn't feel bad stooping to criminal methods just to try to figure out who wrote some editorials?"

"There are three types of people who go into law," Walden declared with a coolly determined expression. As he continued speaking, his eyes flicked over to Rob's face at intervals as though by necessity, a slide mechanism rolling back at the end of each thought in order to stamp out new lines of explanation. "The most pernicious of them are the idealists who believe that the law ought to be preserved and guarded by an almost priestly class of scholars. These sorts usually go into law because they're really interested in politics or social justice, whatever that means. They tend to exalt the law with a traitorous veneration. Because they respect its power, they seek to transform it. The law is like their father. They respect its authority and experience but resent its old-fashioned restraint and inconvenient bigotries. They see the law as a power which contains the world of men, and they seek to place the confines securely around themselves and everyone else. Those are the most contemptible people who study and practice the law.

"The second kind of people who get into law are the most common. It's a lucrative field. They have no strong ideals really about what the law means in a metaphysical sense or how it forms and shapes the world of men. They don't love the law just as an electrician doesn't love copper wiring. They understand it and use it. They simply apply it in a way that saves their clients' money or helps them avoid legal headaches.

"Then there is the third kind of person who studies the law. This sort of lawyer is like the first and second in some ways. He possesses an ideological view of law, but not because he reveres it. Like the second kind of person, he uses it for his profit too at times. His purpose for knowing the law is primarily so that he knows how to move in the world. Unlike the first sort of legal scholar, he does not seek to set boundaries to contain himself and his adversaries. He dwells outside and around the world of law. His kingdom is whatever he wishes it to be. He knows the law as the wilderness traveler knows the nature of a serpent. He learns its behaviors, the effect of its venom, the pattern of its skin. I strive to be this third sort of person. I do not owe the law any allegiance, nor do I stand in awe of its complexity and dimensions. I do, however, like to know the sound it makes when it's about to bite me."

Rob scrunched up his eyes and furrowed his brow for a moment after the lawyer finished speaking. "That's all very eloquent, but you have practiced law as a trade, right? I'm not sure your relationship with the law is as cool and calculated as you make it sound."

"I've worked it as a trade at times, yes," Walden asserted with a nod. "But all of my most interesting projects have fallen more accurately under the wide umbrella of what could be called 'consulting.'" He gave a wolfish grin.

"What about Alexander?" Rob asked. "He puts up with it? Your views on the law? I find it hard to believe that he knows you do not respect or revere the law and has no issue."

Walden raised an eyebrow and tilted his head to one side slightly. "It's funny. I'm not sure that you understand him at all. It was Alexander who told me one of the profoundest things about the law, something I'm not sure I still yet understand. I had not been working for him for very long, and in a meeting, one of his other people was telling him that a certain political move could result in legal trouble. Alexander responded by asking what the law is."

The lawyer's eyes rolled over. "Do you know what the law is, Mr. Journalist?"

Rob shrugged. "Agreed upon principles," he tossed out half-heartedly.

"'The law is words.' That's what Alexander said. He said the law is words, and, while all laws are made up of words, not all words are laws. He said that in the beginning was the Word and thus also was the law, but the Word is greater than the law. And then later on, the Word became flesh and dwelt in the world, and the law was within the Word, but the word was not only law. He ended by saying again, simply: 'The Word is greater than the law, because the Word contains the law.'"

Rob took a gulp of his drink. "Sounds like a bunch of semantics to me." All this talk about law and power and things being greater than the law was reminding him of something he could not quite place.

"Perhaps it is," Walden replied. "But it spoke to me and the way I had approached the law. It was the closest I ever came to believing in Alexander as more than just a leader."

"Forgot where this was going." Rob ran his fingers through his hair in frustration. He was feeling sullen about the stagnating conversation and that none of it mattered, since he had signed the nondisclosure.

"You were asking how I could, as a lawyer, purposefully breach the law by bugging a journalist's office. And that was my explanation."

"Right," Rob replied with a nod.

Walden cleared his throat and settled back into his chair. "I'm not sure what happened to the microphone I planted on Grant's desk, but it only transmitted for a few days. Out of those two days, there was only one possible relevant thing I picked up about the editorials. Grant made a phone call to someone to tell them that I was snooping around. He said that he was pretty sure that I didn't know anything and that all he knew himself was the email contact from the guy at Pneuma who had helped set it up."

"What is Pneuma?" Rob asked.

"It's exactly what you would expect," Walden explained in a tired voice. "It was some extremely nebulous non-profit organization focused on 'pro-democracy' and 'free society' messaging for big corporations that wanted to give back to the world. It didn't seem like much, but it was my only lead."

"Do you have any theories about what happened to your bug in the office?" Rob asked. "Before you get too far ahead?"

"I don't know," Walden said with a frown. His voice meandered the words out and he sounded uncharacteristically unsure of himself. "It could have been a faulty microphone, or it was knocked off the underside of the desk by accident. Of course it could have been picked up in a bug sweep." His light brown, tiger's eye pupils jerked over to stare directly at Rob's face.

"But why would a small newspaper be sweeping for bugs?"

"Exactly," the old lawyer agreed with the open-ended question. "But that wasn't my concern at the time. Things started to click when I began my research on Pneuma. You see, I knew one of the advisors on the board. It was my old ice fishing buddy Charles from years back. That was when I remembered what he told me about project ICON and began to wonder if there was a connection."

"You checked out Pneuma?" Rob was engrossed at this point.

"There wasn't much to check out. It was a shell. The address in New York was one tiny office. I never saw it open. It was just a sign on a door as far as I could tell. The whole operation was a ghost. Somewhere in the middle of it all, that writer Andrew Laren fit in. I went back to the *Tribune* and started working the small fish. After a few weeks of nothing useful, they got suspicious and the editor-in-chief called Alexander. He pulled me off it. I lost my chance."

Walden's brow had slid down low over his eyes and his lips were pulled tight over his front teeth. They would have been bared angrily if the skin was not covering them.

"You think Pneuma was a cover for ICON?" Rob asked.

"I think it was one of the many masks it wore in public."

"And you think Laren worked for them in some capacity?"

"The only surviving relative at that point was his daughter. She said he had moved out of the state after he retired from the university, and they lost contact. She never heard from him until the call explaining that he was dead. Heart attack in California someplace."

"Then you weren't entirely honest when you said that you knew who was writing the editorials," Rob chided with a grin.

"I know who was involved. I have guesses about the whole process, but I don't like to talk about my speculations."

"For legal reasons?"

"That, and I wonder if I've gone crazy when I speculate too much. If I step outside myself and look at what I'm thinking, then it looks completely insane."

"What, that it's all part of a secret government program?"

"No," Walden ventured grimly. "About Andrew Laren himself. Sometimes I think that maybe they don't let you die anymore if they don't want you to."

Rob took another drink. "They?"

"Exactly."

Rob heaved an exhausted sigh and finished his glass of whiskey. Walden seemed to have trailed off and lost himself. Rob checked the time. It was late and he was tired. "I think I'm going to go back to bed." He paused. "Do you think there is any chance I can talk to Alexander again tomorrow?"

"I doubt it," Walden stated, rousing slightly from his dark turn. "He's extremely busy with the Treasury Department business."

"Well, thank you for the drink."

"You are very welcome, Coen."

Rob picked up his sheets of notes, stood a little unsteadily and shuffled through the dim meal hall to the entry of the lodge. He cast one last glance back to Walden, a black boulder of a silhouette which stared into the flames with one elbow propped on the table and his glass held aloft. It was entirely possible Walden was lying about the entire thing, that there was no project ICON, that it was all a ruse to discourage Rob from looking too closely at anything.

He clambered up the steps and went down the hall toward his room, his right shoulder grazing the wall all the way down. He fumbled with the key and dropped it once before getting the door open. Directly inside another note lay on the floor. Rob turned to look each way down the hall before stooping to pick it up and then enter his room. He turned on the lamp and then collapsed into bed. This time it was a sheet of paper that read:

Miscellaneous Four: Thirty-Seven Minutes. Do not forsake the archival materials. They hold the key. If you doubt my intentions, then let me give you a sign that I speak the truth. If you look to the sky a little after seven p.m., you will see a light moving from the southeast to the northwest. Let this be an assurance that I have the best intentions for you and for the people of this state. To know is to hold and to hold is to care for.

Your friend,
Nico.

Rob stared at the words for a few minutes, too tired and intoxicated to make much sense of them. He set it on the table along with his notes from the conversation with Walden, turned off the light, and rolled over to go to sleep.

In the morning he was very groggy and rolled out from under the blankets into the light of the room before stumbling to the small bathroom to take a boiling shower. All the strangeness with Walden from the night before lurked in the back of his mind. As the water poured down his head and back and down his limbs and fingers, he suddenly remembered what he had been trying to think of the night before when Walden was talking about the law and the Word being greater than the law.

Not long after Alexander won the governorship of Wyoming, a scandal broke out in the world of journalism. Perhaps scandal was too strong a word. It was an uncomfortable series of events that resulted in a significant bit of infighting between the columns within the battalions of commentary. Someone broke ranks and publicly defected from what were the acceptable lines of thinking. The man in question was Ron Franks. He was one of those kept, ostensible traditionalists who endured a long humiliation of his own ideology in order to be printed in a paper accepted by the wider journalistic society. Rob never understood how those types could live with themselves. They ate the scraps of the socially liberal, religiously neutral, commercially friendly table, while somehow perceiving to have reactionary bona fides of some kind. It came across to most as ineffectual complaining, the muffled protestations of a man bound and gagged in the cupboard as conversation made its way around the dining room.

Ron Franks was viewed by most as a pathetic character, the cowed pet of the media establishment who preached civic peace at the most fervent peaks of cultural conflict. The left shrugged and gave him patronizing tomcat smiles typically reserved for plump field mice. The reactionary right openly scorned him. Rob wondered what gene of shamelessness was needed for survival in such circumstances: to live at the pleasure of your enemies in spite of your ostensible allies. For Ron Franks to fall from the constellation of opinion journalism luminaries was no great loss. He was after all, little more than a toothless, taxidermied trophy set above the mantle as an amusing conversation piece. The problem was the way that he fell out: biting every hand which had fed him all those years in the urban, progressive core. He went very quickly from being a joke to being the most hated man in journalism with one article titled "The Last Laborer in the Vineyard." The piece opened with an apology:

Despite being a conservative and a Christian, I have been critical and at times even hostile to the goals and methods of James Alexander during his campaign for the governorship of Wyoming. This was earnest criticism, born from my belief that America is most importantly a neutral space where ideas, ideologies, and political movements can compete for influence without fear of institutional abuse suppressing the spread of competing ideas and ethics. It has taken me a long time to acknowledge that this view is naive, that things have already gotten to the point where I have no good faith rivals on the other side of the political divide. This leaves me alone in the middle, trying to play referee, criticizing equally my political allies and opponents for not upholding the ideal of institutional neutrality in favor of short-term victories. I believed, mistakenly, that so long as there was a free market and open square for public discourse and debate, the best ideas would win out in the end. I was wrong. We do not have a free market. There is no good faith maintenance of neutral institutions.

Following James Alexander's victory in Wyoming, a democratic mandate given by the will of the people living in that state, I have heard my colleagues and even friends in the world of politics, business, media, and entertainment openly live out fantasies of political, economic, and, at times, revoltingly literal war upon the state of Wyoming. Massive corporations have suggested that they will no longer do business in the state. Members of congress have suggested methods of sanction. I was wrong to side against Alexander. I beg the forgiveness of those I accused of exaggeration, extremism or doomsday prophecy. The founders enshrined interstate commerce protections to prevent conflict between members of the union, but they did not expect massive corporations to become as large and powerful as small states, to be unaccountable to the national ethic.

Sex sells, vanity sells, sloth sells, pride sells, violence sells, sin sells. An upright people is the enemy of a corporation. Big business and financial powers will make war on the democratic mandate of an upright people who will narrow their consumer base. I was wrong, I was so very wrong.

The nakedly honest candor and the unfettered willingness to admit false conscience proved exceedingly jarring to Ron Frank's journalist colleagues. This sort of sudden shift made everyone else very nervous. They were even more nervous after reading the following bit:

I have long made the constitutionalist and legalistic arguments that moderate policy precedent, neutrality of culture, and checks and balances matter more than anything. James Alexander's willingness to shatter norms and civility long held in the public square caused me to balk. But no longer. It has taken time and prayer for me to recognize that Alexander approaches civics and civic morality from a supra-legal, mythic perspective. He is driven by the heroic politics of the Puritan founders of America, not the cautious liberality of the Virginian landholders.

What good are volumes and tomes of constitutional law and checks and balances, when the men and women supposedly executing and protecting these laws are morally bankrupt? When history reaches the end of civilization's small arc, and the decent men are few, they must slip off the bonds of legalistic thinking in order to preserve their own and their people's righteousness. I believed too much in the libertarian dream, that diametrically opposed ideologies could exist side by side in friendly competition and that this friendly struggle was the end to history. This is not so. One will always gain the upper hand and seize upon the machinations of justice. Then we are all at their mercy, unless mercy is not a virtue found in their code. What is left for a man such as myself? One who long saw himself as the keeper of civility and this as the greatest good? There is only one option: Find the truth, which is not the conditional laws of a fickle people, seize upon it, and survive.

Ron Franks was not only voluntarily ending his career in the polite circles of political commentary, he was going on a reputation ending suicide dive. His editors let him do it. They knew it would create massive buzz. They were right. It generated the intense buzzing of a thousand angry hornets armed with stinging pens and looking for retribution. It was the closing exhortation of the article which caused the most fury:

As of today, I resign my position as an opinion writer for this publication. I resign my position as straddler and advocate of the neutral framework of American civic society for its own sake. I resign my position as chief necrophiliac and necromancer, futilely romancing the great moderate consensus, falling upon the safety of indifference, which is no longer safe at all.

The people selling you insurance have an interest in your personal beliefs. The company making your soft drinks or selling you groceries would like to talk to you about sexual ethics. Your credit card company may have some concerns about your political stances. The conflict is already over. It grieves me that I did not see until it was too late.

Like the last laborer in the vineyard, I have contributed little, but expect to reap the rewards of those who labored early and long. I even at times worked against them. For that I am ashamed. Although the hour is late, I will do what I can. I resign from this publication. I resign from this city. I resign from this culture. I will be moving my family to Wyoming and I urge all decent Christians to do the same. This is a war of ideas, but it is also an existential struggle to survive. Words are not enough anymore. We must all have faith to leap, to flee, to escape this culture that seeks to destroy us. We may all still be destroyed, but at least we will be crushed together and side by side with looks of resolute determination on our faces.

I entreat all of you to come with me to Wyoming: Baptists from the South, Presbyterians from New England. Pentecostals from Appalachia, Catholics and Lutherans from the Midwest. Our differences are not too great to keep us from common cause. There are men and women from every corner of the Christian faith who have smelled the hot spark of danger. To all of you I say: Come with me. We can only survive together.

The paper had not predicted that they would receive even more fury than the author himself. For a day or so, Ron Franks was dragged through the mud and vivisected on the opinion pages of every other publication. He was criticized for weakness of mind, for giving in to the extremists to his right, for allowing himself to revel in the foolish exhilaration of autarky. He did not respond publicly to any of it, and once the commentariat finished savaging the lifeless corpse of his reputation, they turned on the editors who had allowed him to voice himself publicly. Titles ranged from: "A Paper of Record Just Published Fascist Propaganda" to "The Case for Protecting the Public from Dangerous Ideas."

One veteran newsman stepped out of retirement to write the following:

Perhaps his editors told themselves that the attention would be worth it. Maybe they felt that Franks deserved one final platform to voice his reasons for resignation. If the former, then they have chosen self-interest over civic duty. If the latter, then the editors have proven themselves unfit and their judgment deeply flawed. If they have any self-respect, then they should resign. Whatever their reasons, they have published what amounts to a fascist propaganda poster, a rallying cry for the most reactionary and subversive elements in this nation, the ideology that does not deserve an advocate, even if he is merely a dim star falling swiftly from the sky. Ron Franks may be little more than a dupe for James Alexander's insurgent brand of extremism, but his editors have proven themselves to be accomplices.

Some of Franks' colleagues resigned. A boycott ensued. All in all, the storm took a few months to blow over, which is an eternity in the world of news and current events. Attention flared up again one last time a little later on. Franks posted a video to one of his social media accounts of meeting Bill Stevens in Cheyenne and shaking his hand. Stevens pulled him in for an embrace and said, "Welcome home." Within twenty-four hours, his social media accounts were deleted. Nobody was certain if he had done it himself. Nobody really seemed to care. After that moment, Ron Franks disappeared from public life.

What Alexander seemed most capable of doing with men like Franks and Walden was convincing them that the world's current hierarchies were held in place by an immoral or undeserving usurpation, that the accepted mainstream political values merely needed to be disbelieved. Justine had mentioned similar ideas. It was a strange kind of autocratic populism. He wondered if it could outlive Alexander. *Could he keep the militant motion alive long enough? Surely not. It had never been done before.*

Rob dried off, dressed, and took up the newest note from Nico. He read through the cryptic message again and folded it into the pocket of his jeans. He checked his email and messages before heading down to breakfast. He was not very hungry and ate sparingly: oatmeal, coffee, and some scrambled eggs. He did not see anyone he knew and concluded that most of those in close orbit around the governor were shut in some back conference room or office in damage control mode over the visit from the Treasury lawyers the day prior.

After returning his dishes to the counter, he returned to the upper halls of the lodge and went past his own room to Banks' office. The door was cracked open slightly, so he pushed his way in. The room smelled like some kind of freshly cut wood. A handwritten note on the desk read, "Busy most of the day. Help yourself to the television and the discs. Please make sure they are all returned."

Rob opened the folding doors and rolled the television stand out so that it was angled toward the desk. He sat in Banks' chair to sort through the plastic bin of DVD boxes on the shelf below the screen and glanced around the room to get a look at what it must be like to be Jordan Banks on an average day. A wooden duck figurine rested on the left corner of the desk by a cup of pens and pencils. A photograph of what must have been his relatives hung by the door. The chair was very comfortable.

Rob decided to start with some of the earliest dated discs he found, all related to the first gubernatorial campaign. He sat back with the television remote and meandered through the footage. He was quickly absorbed by the atmosphere and energy of the speeches and events, which passed by in strange, oasis-type scenes of a specific time and place. He was watching the unfolding of Governor Alexander, the idea.

Words and collections of words emerged and coalesced in the foreground of the footage and then stood out in proud formation. Their first appearance was often carried on faltering steps with uncomfortable cadence, the arrhythmic footfalls of the forays into experimental phraseology. Then they became mainstays, bread and butter box-checking to bring out a cheer of recognition, the kind of cheer given with a smile both inward and outward, the one that exalts in the joy of ritual as well as the surreptitious pride of being in on the joke and surrounded by others also in on the joke all while nobody mentions it out loud. To speak of it would break the magic.

Rob sped up the video at points to find subtle movements that indicated items of interest. He watched Alexander lurch back and forth in the unnatural animatronics of acceleration and let out rapid voiceless streams of words. The movement on the screen trivialized him, made him seem like a child's wind-up toy on the fritz. Maybe this was how a theoretical god saw human beings: laughable, try-hard children taking themselves so very seriously as he tried with all his divine might not to shoot his morning coffee out his nose at their very appearance. Maybe mankind was some practical joke. Someone in the control room said "Hey, George, check this out," and flipped a switch, and everyone thought it was so fucking hilarious that they let it run. True or not, it did make Rob feel a little better when he had the remote, and a little more in control over what this version of James Alexander did.

Many of the speeches took place in churches, community centers, or grange halls. Sometimes everyone stood outdoors. Rob slowed down enough times to get a good feeling for the common issues: the oil business, federal land, reclamation, drugs, the need for strong communities, the insidious creep of frivolous technology. One of Alexander's philosophical turns, particularly with the more religious crowds, was the seeming contradictions in morality, ideology, and politics. He often addressed it in a conversational manner, pacing close to the crowd and conversing directly with the audience.

"The New Testament and politics are a tricky mixture. Anybody know why?"

Sometimes people knew why, although that was rare. More often suggestions were shouted out, and occasionally Alexander would wade out into the audience to hear the explanation up close before relaying it to the rest of the onlookers and getting their reaction. On the rare chance that anyone had a close enough answer, Alexander would smile broadly and ask, "You interested in working for a political campaign?" If nobody was even close, he would scan back and forth for a moment with his hands on his hips before addressing it himself.

"Politics, particularly American politics, and the New Testament is a tricky mix because, in its origin and early foundation, Christianity was a persecuted faith. Christ himself is a persecuted figure throughout his short adult life. America from its founding was a nation of Christians, yet the New Testament, including the Epistles and Acts of the Apostles, were all written under the auspices of an overbearing, secular, and even anti-Christian power." He let that soak in for a moment before continuing. "Then we come to the difficulty of how does one render to Caesar in what is ostensibly 'one nation under God'? Caesar and God are separate entities because historically they were much more distinct. You see, in the Old Testament and in Europe during the past nearly one thousand years it was simple. You were part of a nation that could be chosen by God or that followed a distinct Church. You followed your ruler because he ruled by God's divine authority. In the New Testament you have the covenant moving from a singular temporal authority to a voluntary church body. Caesar will do as he will and God's people will do as they will, all while complying with Caesar as best they can. So, what if Caesar says that he is invoking Christ in his authoritative acts as temporal ruler outside the Church? How much must the meek Church balk at this idea? What fear ought to shake the man who claims to govern in the name of God." He straightened his back and pronounced in a very official sounding voice, "Apply to me and you will have all that you need: Caesar, God, all is encompassed within." Then he paused to let the words take full effect. "It's pretty easy to see why not many good Christians go into politics."

Typically, Alexander then brought it around to the heart of the issue at hand. "It is a bit of a sticky situation. There is no New Covenant blueprint for Christian leaders in temporal power. While I am a Christian, and it strongly informs my ideas of moral leadership, it is not my goal that you should render only to me. It is not my prerogative to lead a singular Church as well as a state. Remember that the meek will inherit the earth and, hell, you all know by now that I am not meek." The line generated laughter every time and often a smattering of applause.

"It is, however, my goal as leader of the state to make it damned easy to live here and be a member of the Church, to be a citizen without violating your conscience. I want to make it easy for churches to serve their communities."

Rob sped up the playback to the end, finding only more similar speeches without anything noteworthy. He picked his way through the stacks of plastic cases again and found another that looked interesting. The label read, "Alexander and Stevens Post Election." He swapped it out for the one in the DVD player.

The footage seemed to depict an interview of some kind. The questioner was somewhere off camera, which captured a slightly younger looking Bill Stevens and Governor Alexander sitting a few feet apart at a large, wooden table. They each had a glass of water set in front of them on paper napkins. After a moment of glancing around and inaudible murmuring back and forth, the interviewer's voice sounded. It was an older man's tone: thin but clear.

"First, I would like to thank the two of you for agreeing to speak to me, agreeing to indulge my whims, I suppose. As I explained before, this conversation is primarily for the historical record and my own curiosity."

"Feel free to use it for anything you like. My man Banks is recording." Alexander explained, gesturing off to the side where presumably Banks was standing by and watching.

The older man's voice let out a chuckle. "I believe my filmmaking days are behind me, but I probably will request a copy for my own collection." After a brief pause, the disembodied voice shifted gears. "Now if you both are comfortable, then I would like to get started."

The two men at the table glanced at one another and nodded, shifting slightly in their seats. Alexander grasped his glass of water and took a quick sip.

The questioner's voice returned. "So, Mr. Alexander. You won the governorship. Congratulations." The governor nodded and gave a modest smile. Bill Stevens laughed.

"Your campaign generated nationwide conversation. Why? What exactly is the appeal of your movement? Why is it so controversial? And how did you win with the entire national media against you? I don't mean this to be a barrage, since all the questions are connected. I would just like for you to address the idea of you: the appeal and attraction of adversarial powers."

Alexander cleared his throat. When he spoke, his voice was measured and calm. He often gestured with a flat hand held out perpendicular to the table's surface bringing it down lightly before moving it and doing it again in a smooth repeated chopping motion.

"I owe nearly all of it to Bill and to the media itself. The national media being against me actually improved my chances, since the media is so intensely unpopular. As I said initially, though, Mr. Stevens is almost exclusively responsible."

"Do you agree, Mr. Stevens?" the interviewer asked.

Bill Stevens laughed. "I don't know about that."

Alexander clarified, "Let me put it this way: if you want to know how I won, then you have to go back to the beginning of the story, and that's Bill Stevens."

"You want the short or the long version?" Stevens asked.

"Whichever is the best version," the interviewer replied.

"If anyone wants my full story, it's all over the place," Stevens explained. "I came to Wyoming after I had already been traveling around further east touring the states and giving talks. I had been focusing early in places like Iowa and Indiana."

"Was it clear what you wanted at that point?" the interviewer cut in.

"Revival. Renewal," Stevens stated seriously. "I was blind-driven nearly faster than I could think at that point. It was clear that people wanted someone like me to tell them that we all needed to shape up. I had early success. There was desire for a traditionalist renewal, a return to uncompromising faith. Then after the early momentum, I ran up against Wyoming."

"And what is different about Wyoming?"

"The history of the state does not lend itself to evangelism. They lived with years and years of scam artists making promises while enduring continual hardship. It results in a kind of earthy cynicism, an earned cynicism. Intellectual cynicism is one thing, but practical cynicism is like trying to drag a twice bitten mule through a swarm of horseflies."

"How do you overcome that cynicism?"

"That's pretty difficult," Stevens admitted. "You don't want to work too hard to tailor a message which is supposed to be universal. Fundamentally I don't believe in doing that. I think a system of ideas should be as unified as possible. What I do believe is possible is a multi-directional approach with an emphasis on role."

"What does that mean?" the interviewer asked.

"It means that, while the kingdom of heaven is universal in presence and nature, it possesses dimensions like an earthly kingdom—spiritual dimensions." He held up a hand as though expecting an objection. "This is not to say that it is flawed or limited by human frailties, or even reliant on them. What I mean is that, as humans with limitations, we must each approach it from our own position of weakness. The difficulty with Wyoming folks by and large is that they tend to see religion as somewhat weak. If you aren't strong or resilient, this place, with its bitter winters, wide open spaces, sparse amenities and deserts, can end you pretty quickly or force you out. Appealing to the limitations of the individual and the need for God as a sense of safety or shelter does not resonate very strongly with people who deal with harsh elements and circumstances anyway."

"So how did you approach making a revival here?"

"The kingdom of heaven hungers after all people," Stevens explained. "It desires everyone: the weak and the strong, the stern and the playful, the diligent and the whimsical. I inverted the theme of preservation at the mercy of God's kingdom. To whom much is given, much is required." He stared unblinkingly at the interviewer.

"I'm not sure I understand," the voice admitted.

"The kingdom of God is manifest on this earth in the form of the Church, which needs the strong as well as the weak. The people of Wyoming are strong, self-reliant, and adventurous where others may be physically weak or timid with child-like faith. The Church, which is the manifestation of God's kingdom on earth, requires their strength to persevere."

"So, you used flattery."

"Not at all. I spoke to their role in the multi-dimensional approach to the kingdom. They have their own weaknesses and vices."

"And it was successful?"

"Over time there was momentum. Eventually, yes, it worked out pretty well."

"And you capitalized on that success, Mr. Alexander?" the interviewer asked.

The governor came alive and leaned forward in his chair.

"Somewhat. It wasn't that I wanted to use Bill's revival to piggyback a political movement. When I came back from New York, he had not really picked up too much steam here. I was more a product of him than trying to use his momentum in some Machiavellian way."

Rob, while intrigued, knew that there was not enough time to watch all the footage without being more selective. He sped through to the end of the DVD and then turned to dig through the other discs. He read the labels stuck to each case, trying to be more discriminating this time. He found one labeled "Miscellaneous Two" and felt a sudden jolt of recognition. He pulled the mysterious note left in his room the night before from his pocket and unfolded it. "Miscellaneous Four: Thirty-Seven Minutes." There was no doubt that it was referring to one of Banks' DVDs. Thirty-seven minutes must be the time code for some relevant information. Rob returned the slip of paper to his pocket and flipped a few more discs off the stack until he found the one in question. His hands fumbled with anticipation as he removed the DVD from the case and swapped it with the one in the player. The remote trembled as he worked the buttons to find the right spot. He took a deep breath and pressed play.

Alexander was standing slightly off to the side of the camera's view in an unfamiliar room. The surroundings were odd: anachronistic wood-paneled walls, indistinguishable framed lines of text hung on the wall in a few places. The lighting was warm but not dim. It appeared to be the basement of a church or recreation center. The governor was conversing quietly with someone off the screen to the left. Occasionally a figure in the foreground would move in front of the camera for a brief moment, causing odd eclipses to the unaccountable vision. After a moment, Alexander addressed the room.

"My man Banks is out getting some coffee. We have some time for general discussion, but while I am here with all you men of God, I wanted to say something. I want to make a confession to you all, especially since I have come here as a potential ally to your causes."

It was clear that Alexander did not know that the camera was recording. Banks must have forgotten to turn it off before leaving to run some errands. James Alexander continued, visibly apprehensive, atypically nervous.

"When I came back to this state from New York City, I was a

lost person. I was in a very dark place. I was extremely angry. This was not an anger that smoldered on occasions, but a constant and relentless, white-hot rage. I fell in with my uncle Paul when I returned." Alexander smiled. "I'm sure some of you know Paul. He is not a bad man. In fact, he is a very upright man with extremely strong convictions. He does, however, have a way of fanning the flames. For an angry, young man, being exposed to him every day was like pouring gasoline on a fire. I was fresh from the metropolis and that thick concentration of money. It's like some kind of chemical in its purest form that can leach into your body just by touching your bare skin. The arrogance of the place drove me crazy, the idea that they are the keepers of some world culture.

"I was also disillusioned with politics. My brother's death had made it all the more intense. There are entire towns, whole regions of the United States overrun with drugs, poverty, and despair. The multinational corporations moved the jobs overseas, and they sent along just enough assets to avoid taxes—that or they just struck deals with politicians to avoid them. More money was spent in Iraq and Afghanistan or some other godforsaken place than in helping any state here in America. They want all the courageous types dying off in some cursed sandbox halfway across the world instead of sitting here at home reading legislation and watching where the money goes. The joke of it is that it isn't even money, really. It's all just promissory notes written on the credit of a giant boot-heel on the world's neck.

"I fell into despair just thinking about it. I honestly wanted to die. In New York I was already drinking pretty heavily to cope with the lifestyle of the big city. It only got worse once I came back. I was in a deep downward spiral. I went out and bought a few guns."

A murmuring resounded in the room, a quiet sound of surprise and slight confusion and alarm. Alexander held up a hand and gave a rueful smile.

"I already had a revolver that had been my father's, but I bought a few rifles, too, and a decent bit of ammunition. I found a website that sold military surplus equipment and tactical equipment, and I bought a vest and a few other items."

A voice cut in through Alexander's narration. From the tone and cadence, it sounded to be an older man. "James, are you sure you want to tell us this? What is the meaning of this?"

James Alexander had frozen in place and stared at the source of the sound with piercing eyes, but after a moment they softened, and he gave a self-conscious grin. He began speaking again but in a calmer tone. "Elliott, I can understand your concerns, but I want to relay this for two reasons. The first reason is that my goal for this state is not to be a government in the transactional, bureaucratic sense. I do not believe that we live in a time and place where the bureaucratic professionalism of liberal state governance is either preferable or good. I called all of the prominent Christian leaders of Wyoming together because I want us to be a people."

He paused and gave a bashful dip of his head. "You see there is a state and then there is a people. A state is simply a managerial hierarchy. A people share something more. They all approach one thing together, in a wide line holding hands and walking over an open field toward the face of God. Maybe that's a bit romantic. I've been accused of that sort of thinking before. A people have to trust each other. A people can accomplish great things because they know the others will pick them up when things turn bad."

Alexander straightened, overcoming his brief moment of awkwardness. "The second reason is that we are all Christian men. To be Christian is to be in communion with one another. You see, a secret is a stillborn lie, especially when it's an evil secret. Confession is the only way to mend the wounding of our own souls. I am confessing to you all now, not to implicate you or diminish myself, but to complete myself. I have no desire to be seen as some sort of untarnished figurehead. I do not want your blessing as men of God while keeping a hideous secret. What sort of blessing is that? Perhaps I am more like Esau."

He smiled and the room resounded with a murmur of knowing laughter.

"Now I'll finish the story." He glanced around the room and nodded. "I was full of anger, hate, blind and foolish as it was. I told my uncle Paul that I believed in God and that I knew what I was planning to do was wrong, that it was the very depths of evil, and that I would certainly go to hell for it. I told him that I was planning to drive to Washington D.C. to kill as many congressmen and senators as I could."

The room was dead silent. Rob could hear some kind of background hum in the recording. He still had not recognized what exactly he was hearing and the implications of it all, since he was so engrossed in Alexander's delivery.

"I can see you all are pretty shocked and disappointed in me, but I'm going to finish because this is a confession, after all." He took a breath and swallowed. "I told my uncle that I knew I would go to hell but that I wanted God's people to be secure in their innocence. I believed that the satanic swallowing up of the godless empire that is our nation was inevitable. I was convinced that I had to do my part in bringing it down. I wanted to save decent people here at home without them having to bloody their own hands. I thought that I had to damn myself on their behalf or nobody would do anything and it would be too late."

Alexander paused and scratched his jaw pensively for a moment. "My uncle Paul slapped me across the face and did not hold back. I saw splotches of light and color, he hit me so hard."

A nervous laugh was audible in one corner of the room. Alexander took in a sharp breath when he resumed speaking, and his voice caught in his throat. He was clearly emotional.

"My uncle told me that God loved me. He said that the slap in the face was the same I was doing to Christ by saying that He wasn't enough. Paul said that what I intended to do was a wretched imitation of a sacrifice, that it was pure and simple blasphemy. He took me in his arms and told me that he missed my brother too, and that we all go a little crazy sometimes."

Alexander looked at the ground for an uncomfortably long time. Rob was not sure if he was trying to hide his emotions or recollect some evasive details.

"His embrace, such a sign of affection, was not customary for my uncle. It was maybe even more shocking than the slap on the face. It was that more than anything that brought me around. That night he drove me out to stay with one of his old friends, another very devout man who raised sheep and had a ranch out in the sticks. I cleaned up from drinking there and got my head right again." He took another breath and surveyed the room. "We all say that we want our leaders to be honest with us. The most honest fact is that we really probably don't. The truth is ugly. That is a shameful and ugly story. But it is part of me, and I must be forthright."

Alexander rested his back against the wood-paneled wall looking tired.

"You have never since then had any violent inclinations?" a voice asked.

Alexander shook his head. "All of us have wicked thoughts, but I knew very quickly after that there was no good or any godliness in what I had intended to do. When I think back on it now, it is as if it were another person. We have all been young once and angry at the world. Few of us would pass muster if judged by our most desperate and weakened moments."

Another voice cut in, "I must ask you, Mr. Alexander, have you changed too much since then? I don't think that would be particularly desirable either."

Some quiet laughter bubbled around the room.

"I can assure you that I have the same enemies," Alexander replied with a sad smile. "I still want to see them defeated and I am still willing to die for what I believe. None of those convictions have changed."

Rob came alive, all at once aware of his surroundings and context. The gravity of what he had just seen struck him with full force. The insanity of it all rushed over him. The chances that Banks had accidentally recorded such an explosive confession and that some unseen hand had directed him on how to find it were too infinitesimally obscure to comprehend. He could not take the disc with him. His trembling hands fumbled with the remote. He rewound back to the beginning of the confession and took out his phone to record. Afterward he played it back to ensure that it was all audible and clearly visible. With frantic energy, he stacked the discs back in the bin and returned the television to the nook.

He returned to his room. It was early afternoon. He did not know what to do with himself and paced back and forth for a few minutes. What would he do with the video? How was this part of the article? It would have to come at the end. He would have to telegraph, though. No way the editors would let something so explosive hide out in a long form expose without top billing. What really was Nico? How did they know about the disc? None of it made any sense, or it made a terrible sort of sense that he had to ignore. He was the author of this project and nobody else.

He had to call his editor and let her know that this thing was about to go into high gear. Margaret answered after the second ring.

"How is my problem child?" she asked.

"I'm your golden boy," Rob retorted.

"And what do you mean by that?"

"I've got the story of the year."

"What happened since the last time we talked? You sound pretty certain of that." Her voice was the anxious, stamping horse's cadence of anticipation.

"And since when do I oversell?" Rob asked.

"Never," she admitted. "What do you have?"

"I have a video clip of Governor Alexander recalling a psychological break he had before going into politics."

"How good are we talking?"

"We are talking Unabomber. We are talking about Timothy McVeigh."

"Jesus Christ. When do you fly back?"

"Tonight."

"This changes the approach," she observed. "I'll need to think about this. Call me as soon as you get back in the city."

"This is *my* article," Rob insisted, not liking her ruminating tone. "If you bring in anyone else, then I want the final say."

"Of course." She assured him.

"Ok. I'll call."

Rob collapsed onto the bed. He would not let them take this away from him in the name of expanding the scope. He knew how the editors could operate sometimes. If a junior writer struck gold, oftentimes the more experienced journalists would get assigned in order to ensure it was handled correctly. Pretty soon your name was only one of three or four at the top. He did not intend to let that happen if it could be avoided.

After a few minutes of staring at the ceiling and letting the adrenaline wear off, he went to the table by the window and transferred the video to his laptop before uploading a copy to his online drive. He was not going to take any chances with this. After a moment of centering himself, he realized that he needed to find out how he would get to the airport. He had watched the footage in Banks' office all through the afternoon. Dinner was in about an hour, and not too long after, he would need a ride to catch his flight. He decided on going downstairs to see if he could find Banks or anyone who knew where Banks was.

When he stepped into the hallway, he could see that Banks' office was exactly how he had left it. There was no sign that the man had returned. Rob moved down the corridors to the entry atrium. He was about to descend to the first floor when he noticed a figure standing out on the balcony. It was the young lawyer, Tim Steyn, pacing and smoking. Rob decided to bum a smoke and see if he knew anything.

The young lawyer turned anxiously at the sound of the door when Rob stepped out onto the wooden planks.

"You're still here?" Steyn asked with a look of surprise. "Wait. How many days has it been since we shared that drink?"

His features were tired, the sunken areas around his eyes were dark, and his clothes looked a little disheveled. His shirtsleeves were rolled up and his jacket was nowhere to be seen. He stood with a straight back, one arm down at an angle by his side holding a cigarette and the other close to his chest, cradling a paper cup of coffee which let off wisps of steam. He took a gulp of the drink after finishing the question.

"Two nights ago. I leave this evening. You mind if I bum a cigarette?"

Steyn shrugged a shoulder toward the table where his pack and a lighter both rested.

"You sleep since I last saw you?" Rob asked after the flick of flame and the first puff of smoke.

"A little," the lawyer admitted in a low grumble. "Bottom of the totem pole gets you stuck with all the busy work, and there is a lot of it. We were prepared for this outcome for a while, but the feds have so much more personnel and resources. They are pretty bullish. It's moved the timetable up."

"When I talked to Walden about it, he sounded reasonably confident," Rob observed.

Steyn scoffed and gave an exaggerated smile. Given his appearance, it came off a bit manic. "Of course, Arthur Walden has high hopes. He's not doing any of the hard work. He gets to hear the synopsis of twelve hours of research and nod approvingly." He made an exasperated sound in his throat. "What do I care? He's retired anyway."

"You disagree with his assessment?" Rob asked.

"No, no," Steyn clarified. "We have a decent shot. If anything gets us, then it's lack of resources. Inability to follow up on all their potential lines of attack. From what I hear we may be getting some reinforcements though."

"Yeah?"

"Word is that a big fan of Alexander is offering support. A big fish who stays in deep water and out of sight is going to lend some resources. I hear he is going to pay for Emory Rosenbaum and his cadre to come in on our side of this thing. You heard of him?"

"Can't say that I have," Rob admitted, although the name did sound familiar.

"He's a real heavy hitter," Steyn explained. "He likes a

challenge and being that David to some Goliath. He was in the news a few years back for a class action against one of the big insurance companies."

Rob shook his head. Rosenbaum. What he would give to see the look on Paul Alexander's face when he heard that the forever rival of European Christendom was being brought in to salvage the kingdom. It was all like damn clockwork. He did not even realize that he gave an outward sign of reaction until he noticed Steyn giving a look of bemused curiosity.

"What's so funny?"

"Everything is just so ridiculous," Rob observed.

"What, you mean absurd?" Steyn asked.

"Not exactly," Rob explained. He took a drag on the cigarette while thinking. "Absurd would imply that there is no rhyme or reason or correlation. A joke may be moronic and ridiculous, but it has component parts that point to one another. I guess what I'm trying to say is that sometimes it's so obvious how much things correlate, yet people just go along with the stream of correlation without thinking about it. Then they talk in high-minded ideology like none of it is even there."

"Is that what you learned while staying here?" Steyn asked after another gulp of coffee.

"Maybe."

"So, what did you learn? I mean I guess I could read about it eventually anyway." The young lawyer chuckled.

Rob laughed. "Honestly, I don't think I learned anything, at least in the realm of ideas. I got information, though, and I guess that's what matters." He paused. "You should probably keep your relationship with this place as transactional as possible."

"Why? You know something I don't?"

Rob shook his head. "I don't know anything everyone doesn't already know."

"Well, that's the good thing about being one of the lawyers," Steyn sighed while stubbing out his cigarette and collecting the pack and lighter. "Win or lose, you bill for the hours either way." He twisted his freed arm to look at his watch. "I should probably get back in there." He set the coffee down so he could reach for a handshake. "It was nice meeting you, Mr. Coen. Good luck with your article."

He turned to go inside, but Rob remembered himself and stopped him with a question. "Before you go, do you have any idea where I can find Banks?"

Steyn paused halfway in the door. "I think he took Justine back to town. He should be back for dinner."

"Thanks."

The lawyer departed and left Rob standing alone with the last portion of his cigarette and a feeling of disappointment. He would have liked to talk to Justine one last time. It felt as though something was unfinished. He paced the boards of the deck and finished smoking.

He passed the hour before dinner catching up on the news and transcribing his notes from the conversation with Walden into his working document for the article. When he went down to the meal hall, Banks was by the counter conversing with the staff. Rob crossed the large room and stood a few feet behind him, waiting for a moment. After a minute, the older man turned to survey the room and caught sight of the familiar face.

"Ah, Mr. Coen. I was just going to find you in a bit. I'm having some meals put together for Alexander and the legal team. What time do you need to get to the airport?"

"My flight leaves at nine p.m., so I should be there by eight."

Banks squinted at his watch. "Alright, so meet me out front of the lodge at seven-thirty. That should give you two hours to eat and get your things together. Don't worry. I'm never late."

"Thanks for the hospitality," Rob replied earnestly, and for a very brief moment, while looking at the older man's smiling face, he felt a twinge of regret. It was the odd kind of regret for something that has not happened yet but will most certainly happen. It was the inverted, sinister regret that is more focused inward than outward. It was the kind that says, "I will not change what I will do, and yet I know it will hurt you."

"No trouble at all," Banks replied brightly.

The staff brought a tray of dishes and heaped containers of food: mashed potatoes, piles of steamed greens, a stack of grilled chicken legs and breasts and thighs. Banks took it and, with one last nod of acknowledgement, turned to head back out through the hall.

Rob acquired his own plate of food and ate near where he and Walden had sat the night before. Much like at breakfast, he did not feel very hungry, although the food was good. He picked at the chicken and stirred the potatoes absentmindedly. After about twenty minutes he returned to his room and began packing away his things.

There was no additional mysterious note, although he had not expected one and did not even think about the possibility until checking his pockets and feeling the rough caress of the folded paper. He packed his toiletries in their small zip-up bag, stored his laptop in its case, and folded his clothes. He gave the room a once-over and then a twice-over. He stared at the strange, geometric patterns on the overlapping rugs. He felt as though he was forgetting something. He checked his flight itinerary once and then again. He again felt as though he was forgetting something and wondered if the feeling was stronger this time because he really was. He wondered if it was possible to even know if one had forgotten something or if the entire sensation was some neurological sabotage.

Finally, he sat down and wrote a note by hand thanking Banks, Alexander, and everyone for looking to his needs while he stayed in the lodge. He thanked the pilot and Justine as well and made sure to leave out Walden but also wondered if that was giving the man too much credit by omission. He finished and left the slip of paper on the table.

He stepped out onto the big wraparound porch of the lodge a bit early. The air was cold, and the sun was nearly hidden behind the mountains. The clear sky was a rich, purple color, and he could already see the stars. That was when he remembered the mysterious bit in the note left in his room the night before. He dropped his carry-on bag onto the porch with a careless thud and dug in the pocket of his jeans. He could barely make out the writing in the dim light: "If you look at the sky a little after seven p.m...."

He checked his phone again. It was three minutes after seven. He glanced down at the note again: "...you will see a light moving from the southeast to the northwest." Which way was north? They had flown south to the monument, and that was to the left, so north would be to the right. Southeast was over his left shoulder behind the lodge. He looked up at the rich purple of the darkening sky and backed down the steps and onto the drive to see over the roof of the lodge. He waited for a minute. He must be too late. The time had not been definite. What was the point of the light in the sky? That it would prove what exactly? That this Nico entity was trustworthy? That it had knowledge? He had already found the video disc. Some kind of cosmic sign was a bit grandiose at this point.

Just as he was about to return to the porch and retrieve his bag, he noticed a small pinpoint of light emerge from behind the lodge's roof. It looked like a star, a tiny speck of white or blue that fluidly carved a straight line across the sky. It was so inobtrusive that anyone not looking for it would never see it, or at least think nothing of it. What did it mean and how did the writer of the letters know? He watched it move slowly and deliberately along until, after a few minutes, it disappeared behind the mountains. He stood baffled and somewhat unnerved until a wash of yellow light carved across his lower half.

Banks had pulled up in the town car a little way off. Rob roused himself from the moment of confusion and returned to the porch to grab his bag. When he approached the car, Banks dutifully stepped around to take the bag and put it in the trunk. They settled into the front seats.

"What were you looking at?" the older man asked, as he shifted out of park and they meandered down the drive to the highway.

"I don't know," Rob admitted. "Have you ever noticed any odd lights in the sky?"

The older man scoffed and glanced over from the driver's seat to see if his passenger was putting him on. After a moment he seemed assured that Rob was being serious. "No, I can't say that I have. What, did you see something?"

"I don't know."

A moment of awkward silence passed. "And so, it ends as it began," Banks finally observed wistfully as he pulled out onto the highway. "I hope you enjoyed your stay here. I'm sure it was more eventful than you expected with the Treasury folks showing up and all."

"That was actually a stroke of good luck for me," Rob explained. "No offense. It all makes for good material. Thanks again for letting me look through all that old footage," he added. "There was some interesting stuff in there."

Banks nodded. "I really should end up making a film out of it all. Such a shame to just leave it all collecting dust. It is one of those stories the world ought to know from the inside. I feel that it is important. I don't think I could put it together myself, but I would like to find someone who can do it justice."

"You might. You could probably get some producers interested if you reached out. Nobody in Hollywood likes Alexander, but some of them certainly have morbid fascination. You might want to go through it all and take out everything you wouldn't want them to have first." Rob added. "So, you can keep some editorial control over what people see."

Banks nodded. "Probably not a bad idea." He paused and mulled something over for a moment. "Is that what brought you out here? Morbid fascination?"

Rob chuckled. "Honestly? A mistake brought me out here, a total accident of time and place."

"Really?" Banks asked, glancing over from the road for an instant with an incredulous look.

"Apparently I am destined to live by happenstance. Better to fall into the winner's circle than never get there at all."

"I suppose," the driver replied pensively. "Though it feels better to earn something."

"Nothing is earned, I don't think." Rob stated. He was feeling careless and powerful. He would be free of this place soon. He longed for the city more than he had realized up until that very moment. Each turning of the wheels brought him closer. "Everything is the gift of something we barely understand. Maybe it is an intelligent entity, maybe it isn't."

Banks went silent for a while and thought it over. He seemed about to speak a few times before adjusting his head and thinking some more. Finally, he replied: "I honestly think both things can be true."

They passed the rest of the drive with occasional observations and replies. It was nearly dark before too long, and the mountains stood imposingly over everything like shadowy monuments to a race of giants. Soon they were among the lights of the city. They drove through to the heart and then turned north.

"How long before you finish your article?" Banks asked.

"Honestly I don't know," Rob explained. "There's going to be some politics involved in getting it done. Could be a week or two, or months. It will be out of my hands. Chances are they will want it sooner with all this litigation news."

"What a world," Banks sighed.

They arrived at the small airport and pulled up to the loading area where a timber overhang and golden lights greeted them. The driver got out to retrieve Rob's bags. They shook hands.

"I left a note on the table in my room." Rob explained.

"That reminds me. Damn, I almost forgot." Banks fished a

folded piece of paper out of his jacket pocket. "That would have been bad if it slipped my mind. Justine wanted me to give you this note. She had to go back this morning and didn't have time to track you down."

A strange mixture of surprise, embarrassment, and excitement washed over Rob, and he could feel his skin flush. He took the paper and slipped it into his laptop bag.

"That was thoughtful of her. Thank you."

"No problem. You have a good trip back."

"Thanks."

The car pulled away and Rob went inside to get checked in. He emptied his pockets and took off his shoes. He removed his laptop and put it in a separate bin. He placed his bags on the rollers. He lifted his arms. He was scanned. He regrouped and wandered to his gate. Rob decided for some reason that he would not read Justine's note until he was on the plane and off the ground, until he was on his way out probably never to return. He could not account for why, but it seemed the best course of action.

The plane was small, and the boarding went quickly. Before long they roared down the runway and lurched upward into steep ascent. He could feel the acceleration viscerally, that he was hurtling purposefully back, spit out to whence he came. It was an oddly reassuring feeling. Finally, after the craft leveled out, he reached up to turn on the reading light and fished the note out from his laptop bag. Justine's writing was a very legible cursive:

Rob, I am sorry not to say goodbye to you face-to-face. I had to go back to get on with my schoolwork and other obligations. I apologize if I was overly confrontational while showing you around. I have been told that I have strong convictions and not much restraint in keeping them to myself. I only hope that you took something from being here and talking to my uncle. I hope that you gained some tiny bit of insight and perspective at Mount Calvary. Perhaps it is hoping too much, but that is my earnest wish. You may not understand us, but please do not hate us. Despite what my less friendly moments may have indicated, I do not hate you.

Best,
Justine

The seat belt light came on again, although it had just turned off a few moments before. The pilot's voice came on overhead: "If you could please remain seated, we have just turned the seatbelt light on. There will be a bit of turbulence. Thank you."

Rob was not sure what he had expected from the letter. The sentiments expressed by Justine were futile. The content was predictable. Maybe it was the unrealized dream of some subconscious sentiment that would now remain entirely stillborn. The note irked him unaccountably. She understood nothing. He was expected to have learned from them, their way of living, the monument, but they had learned nothing from him. None of them did. They had their Mount Calvary and little insular world and chose to see nothing else. It was so utterly pre-ordained in its limitations. There was no moving any of them from whatever it was that held them to one outcome. He almost pitied them. Almost. None of it mattered in the end. Soon he would be in the city and putting everything into this scorcher of an article, and they would be living out their devoted little lives like clockwork figurines, unaware of the danger. Unaware that they were sleepwalking into what was always going to be. Rob was not so delusional to see himself as an instrument of divine judgment. Perhaps he was an instrument of a paradoxical judgment that falls together from the chaotic leavings of the universe's basic functions, the bits of fractions left behind, the ones carried over and forgotten. He could not help but smile and chuckle as he folded the note and slipped it back into his laptop bag. He sat back in the seat and laughed quietly, at the ridiculousness of it all. These people and what they did not know. The plane trembled from the first bout of rough air, and he simply sat back and smiled.

www.ingramcontent.com/pod-product-compliance
Lightning Source LLC
Chambersburg PA
CBHW060706190726
48289CB00002B/565